"I want to thank you again. If there's any way I can make it up to you..."

J___ _____ _____ ____ __oby to fight bac_ ___ ___ _____ ____ ___ ter collecting ___ _____ __ ___ throat, she sto__

"___ ___ ___ ____ ___ said, "before my young hoodlum knocks over one of the stores."

Wyatt remained standing as he watched Gabby leave the restaurant. Her stride was unconsciously seductive, causing several men to turn their heads as she went by. Only then did Wyatt sit back down at the table. To his surprise, for the first time since starting to come here for Sunday brunch some five years ago, he felt completely alone in a sea of people...

By Robert Barclay

IF WISHES WERE HORSES

Forthcoming
MORE THAN WORDS CAN SAY

IF
WISHES
WERE
HORSES

ROBERT BARCLAY

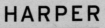

HARPER

An Imprint of HarperCollins*Publishers*

This is a work of fiction. The characters, incidents, and dialogue are drawn from the author's imagination and are not to be construed as real. Any resemblance to actual events or persons, living or dead, is entirely coincidental.

HARPER

An Imprint of HarperCollins*Publishers*
10 East 53rd Street
New York, New York 10022-5299

Copyright © 2011 by Robert Newcomb
Excerpt from *More Than Words Can Say* copyright © 2012 by Robert Newcomb
ISBN 978-0-06-204668-0

First Harper mass market printing: October 2011
First William Morrow hardcover printing: March 2011

HarperCollins® and Harper® are registered trademarks of Harper-Collins Publishers.

Printed in the United States of America

Visit Harper paperbacks on the World Wide Web at
www.harpercollins.com

10 9 8 7 6 5 4 3 2 1

This one's for Michael.

You are missed…

Mankind has often enforced a savage dominance over the horse, and for that he should apologize. These magnificent beasts toiled mightily over the centuries to help us tame the wilds, plow and harvest our fields, transport our possessions, even die in our wars; and sometimes under the cruelest of masters. I am proud to say that I never participated in their abject slavery. Even so, I humbly request forgiveness from every horse that has crossed my path, for they are truly God's noblest creatures.

~ANONYMOUS

IF
WISHES
WERE
HORSES

PROLOGUE

THE NEWS ARRIVED suddenly, its only warning the ringing telephone as it fought to be heard above the happy sounds of Wyatt Blaine's birthday party. He would later wish that the tragedy had been preceded by some dark omen, designed to alert him of its coming. But no such warning arrived, so there was nothing to cushion the blow. As Wyatt's brother, Morgan, put down the telephone receiver, his face turned ashen.

There has been a car crash, Morgan said. Wyatt's wife, Krista, and his son, Danny, were seriously injured. The other driver was drunk, and also badly hurt. In a split second, Wyatt's world collapsed. As he turned to look at the many friends who had gathered in his living room, their gaiety melted away.

Today Wyatt was thirty-five years young, one of the partiers had happily announced. But as Wyatt stared blankly at his guests, the terrible news wandered through the room like some dark predator no one wished to acknowledge, for fear that it might touch his or her life, too.

Someone discreetly turned off the music; another caring soul took Wyatt by one arm and guided him toward a chair. Then the phone rang again.

Morgan reluctantly left Wyatt's side to answer it. This time, however, its insistent ring attracted dread rather than curiosity.

Suddenly nothing looked familiar to Wyatt. Not one stick of furniture did he recognize. The many photographs that Krista had lovingly taken were foreign to him, as were the strangers who had gathered about him for some reason he could no longer recall. He found himself desperately hoping that Krista and Danny would happily return through the front door, bearing the extra ice cream they had gone to buy on the spur of the moment.

Ice cream, his stunned mind thought. *Something as foolish as ice cream . . .*

As Wyatt stared dumbly around the living room, everything looked bizarrely wrong. The huge birthday cake laden with candles and the dozens of colorfully wrapped gifts suddenly seemed embarrassing and irreverent. His guests were dressed casually, their colorful party attire at direct odds with the deep shock registering on their faces. The inappropriateness of the scene was startling.

Morgan again placed the telephone receiver onto its cradle then came to sit by Wyatt's side. Filled with shock, Wyatt's aging father joined them. Morgan's wife, Sissy, stood beside Wyatt, her hands quivering and salty tears streaming down her cheeks. Her two young children huddled near her, seeking protection from a calamity beyond their comprehension. Morgan gripped his brother's shaking hands.

"Krista and Danny were rushed to Community Memorial," Morgan said softly. "They each died on the way. I'm so sorry . . ."

When finally Wyatt spoke, his voice sounded frail. "I have to see them," were the words he uttered. "You must take me . . ."

But as he tried to rise, the room spun and everything darkened. It was then when he first realized that a private part of him was forever lost.

∞

HER NAME WAS Gabrielle Powers. As she ran down the hospital corridor, her body shook with terror. Her nine-year-old son, Trevor, could barely keep hold of her hand as he tried to keep pace with his desperate mother.

When Gabrielle skidded to a stop before the emergency room reception desk, the nurse saw a terrified look in her eyes. Sadly, in this place such expressions were all too common.

"Jason Powers!" Gabrielle shouted. "I was told that he was in a car crash, and that he was brought here! Where is he?"

As precious seconds mounted, the nurse, with agonizing slowness, consulted some sort of chart.

"Where is he?" Gabrielle literally screamed.

"He's in the ICU," the nurse finally said. "His injuries were severe."

"Which way is the ICU?" Gabrielle demanded.

"Are you immediate family?" the nurse asked.

"I'm his wife!" Gabrielle shouted. *"Now where is the ICU?"*

The nurse pointed down one hallway. "It's that way," she said, "but—"

Before the nurse could finish her sentence, Gabrielle and Trevor were gone. Their hearts pounding, they ran down the hall.

It wasn't only for herself that Gabrielle raced, but also for her son. The police had told her that Jason's condition was desperate, and that he might not live to reach the hospital. If Jason were to die, and there was any chance that she and Trevor could say their good-byes before that happened, she must do her best to make it so.

They soon found themselves standing before a pair of glass doors, behind which lay Jason. His face was smashed and bloodied to such an extent that they could barely recognize him. Tubes snaked from his arms and nostrils; a machine monitoring his vital signs displayed numbers and lines that Gabrielle could not comprehend. Irregular beeping noises filtered from the room, their sharp tones supplying a slim lifeline of hope.

But just as Gabrielle was about to force her way inside, the beeping noises became a single, telltale tone. The paddles were used several times; the doctors pumped their hands up and down on Jason's bare chest.

When Gabrielle saw one of the doctors finally stand back from the body and consult the clock on the wall, she knew.

Still not understanding completely, Trevor exploded into tears. Stunned almost beyond comprehension, Gabrielle suddenly felt faint, and she wobbled toward a nearby bench.

When Trevor joined her, she held him in her arms.

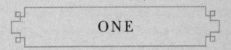

ONE

Boca Raton, Five Years Later

GABRIELLE POWERS SAT in her usual place at church, listening as one of the acolytes finished reading the Lord's Prayer, and then the Bible passage that would provide the basis for today's sermon. Born in Fort Lauderdale, she had been raised in the Episcopalian faith by her two loving parents. Her father, Everett, was a retired schoolteacher; her mother, Justine, had been a registered nurse.

Gabrielle watched Reverend Jacobson approach the pulpit and adjust the microphone to his liking. A large man with a thick shock of white hair, he was a recent throat cancer survivor. Although he still tired easily, his appearance remained as commanding as his voice had once been.

"As you know, I always start my sermons with a humorous anecdote that helps to illustrate the message for the day," he began, his voice rough, not wanting to cooperate.

"And so I'll tell you about a retiring minister," Jacobson continued. "It seems that a mother decided to take her young son to church for the first time. Hoping to induce reverence in the lad, she chose seats in the front row. Because she hadn't attended church for some time, she didn't know that they had come on an eventful day. This was to be the minister's farewell sermon. He had therefore resolved to make it full of hellfire and brimstone, ensuring that it would never be forgotten." Pausing for a moment, the reverend allowed a dramatic silence to hang in the air.

"As the minister ranted, the boy became startled and his mother soon regretted seating them so near the pulpit," Jacobson added. "After the service, the reverend saw that the young lad had wandered down one of the church hallways. His hands clasped respectfully before him, the boy was looking at the many portraits hanging on the wall. As the reverend approached, the boy pointed to the portraits then stared up at him with God-fearing eyes.

"'Who are those people?' the boy asked.

"The reverend smiled. 'They're all members of this church who died in the service,' he answered.

"'Oh . . . ,' the boy replied timidly. 'Was that the nine o'clock service, or the eleven o'clock one?'"

The congregation enjoyed the joke, and their laughter lasted for some time. As she waited for her fellow worshippers to quiet, Gabrielle took a moment to admire the church that she so loved.

St. Andrew's Episcopal was a beautiful place, its majesty

impressive without being ostentatious. Like most churches, the sanctuary was its greatest attribute. A white marble altar stood on top of an octagonal podium near the far wall, its surrounding floor laden with red velvet pillows on which parishioners could kneel and take Holy Communion. The massive rear wall was crafted entirely of stained glass portraying a rather modern interpretation of the crucifixion that fostered lively debate. More stained-glass panels lay in the sidewalls at regular intervals, allowing the Florida sunlight streaming through them to grant a majestic feel to the room.

Twenty minutes later, the reverend finished his sermon. On leaving the pulpit and walking toward the altar, he prepared himself for the next part of the service.

Jacobson raised his hands. "Anyone wanting to celebrate a birthday, an anniversary, or other special day, please come forward and take the blessings," he said.

Gabrielle watched as about one dozen souls left their seats and approached the altar. She then looked to the last pew on the opposite side of the sanctuary, just as she had done on so many Sundays over the past five years.

Will this be the day? she wondered. *Will he stay, or will he leave like he has always done before?*

A man stood from the last row. He was tall and lean, his dark hair showing a hint of gray at the temples. As if on cue, he handed some cash to one of the ushers then departed the church.

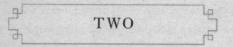

TWO

THIRTY MINUTES LATER, the service was finished. After attending the coffee hour that always followed, the dutiful reverend was even more tired. Then he sighed as he remembered what his oncologist had said. *You will tire easily for some time yet, but with the good Lord's help, you'll eventually regain your strength.*

The walk to his private office took him through open gardens at the rear of the church, and then along a familiar stone path that ended at his office door. Bright sunlight streamed down onto the small patio there, and the water in the stone fountain burbled happily. Then someone caught Jacobson's eye.

A wrought-iron bench stood alongside the wall near Jacobson's office door. Sitting on the bench sat the same man Jacobson had watched leave the service. Jacobson took a seat beside him. At first neither man spoke, both of them content to watch the fountain and to listen to the warbling birds.

"I was sorry to see you leave again, Wyatt," Jacobson finally said. "Someday you'll find the strength to take the blessings. But for now, I'm just thankful that you're here every Sunday."

"You know why I can't take the blessings, James," Wyatt replied. "Anyway, it's your sermons that matter most to me. I can do quite well without all the other trappings."

Wyatt smiled. "Besides," he added, "you should be thankful that my father doesn't come to church anymore. These days we never know what he'll say, and it could be blasphemous as hell."

Knowing Wyatt's father as he did, Jacobson smiled. "So why are you here?"

Wyatt hesitated, as if not knowing how to start. "I've decided to reinstate the New Beginnings Program," he finally said. "It's been five years since we stopped. I want Krista's dream to live again. Plus, this time it's going to be free of charge."

Jacobson was thrilled, and his broad smile said as much. Turning, he grabbed Wyatt's shoulders and gave him a good-natured jostling.

"That's wonderful!" he added enthusiastically. "I can already think of several parents who might want to enroll their teens. We'll need the usual release forms, of course. I'll see if I can find them."

Jacobson stole a few moments to count his blessings. He could hardly contain his glee. The reverend also hoped this was a sign that Wyatt might finally be getting past the deaths of Krista and Danny.

Jacobson knew the horrors of that tragedy well, for he had counseled Wyatt after the tragic car crash, and he had performed the burial services. A hard Florida thunderstorm had arrived that afternoon, the heavy raindrops matching the tears shed by the more than four hundred mourners who had come to pay their last respects. Closing his eyes for a moment, Jacobson silently thanked the Lord for Wyatt's unexpected gift.

"When will you start?" he asked.

"As soon as there are enough teens enrolled to make it worthwhile," Wyatt answered. "That's about thirty, give or take. Would you post a notice in next Sunday's church bulletin and make an announcement from the pulpit? I'll work on the schools."

"I suppose that, like before, these sessions will be on the weekends?" Jacobson asked.

When Wyatt didn't reply, Jacobson guessed that there was more news to come. Knowing Wyatt as he did, he decided to wait rather than ask. When Wyatt turned again to look at his friend and pastor, his expression was resolute.

"No," he answered simply. "They'll be three afternoons a week, provided we have enough takers."

"But some days you work so late . . . ," Jacobson said.

"Not anymore," Wyatt answered. "Last week I left the firm."

Jacobson was stunned. "Does your father know?" he asked.

Wyatt smiled sadly. "I've told him," he answered. "But these days, we can't be sure of anything that he really *knows*. Sometimes his clarity's as fickle as the wind."

"Why did you quit?" Jacobson asked. "This is a big surprise."

Wyatt crossed one long leg over the other and leaned his head back against the wall. "You know that I was never happy practicing law," he answered. "Besides, Morgan and the other partners will still be there, working their tails off. Blaine and Blaine won't vanish just because I'm gone. And as a partner, I'll still be paid my weekly salary. It's what Krista would have wanted."

Jacobson understood, and he nodded his approval. He had known the Blaine family for many years. They had long been among St. Andrew's strongest financial and spiritual supporters.

Of the two Blaine brothers, Wyatt was clearly the handsomest, and by all accounts the most enigmatic. Named by their rather eccentric father after the fabled Earp bothers, Wyatt and Morgan had grown up on the Flying B, the Blaine family horse ranch. Because Wyatt was as comfortable in ranch clothes as he was in a tailored suit, Jacobson had often wondered which lifestyle Wyatt preferred. If the reverend were a betting man, he would put his money on the former. But just now, Jacobson thought Wyatt looked every bit the polished Boca lawyer and highly eligible widower that most people took him for.

Standing just over six feet tall, Wyatt was lean and agile. His impeccable dark blue suit matched his penetrating eyes. The Rolex surrounding his left wrist was solid gold, as was the wedding ring that he had steadfastly refused to remove since Krista's sudden death. When he'd turned forty years of age last summer, Wyatt had joked about the subtle gray appearing at his dark temples.

But as the reverend looked closer, Wyatt did not look like someone who spent most of his time indoors. His skin was tan and crow's-feet etched the corners of his eyes, courtesy of his many days beneath the harsh Florida sun. His strong hands looked like they belonged to some manual laborer rather than to an accomplished counselor-at-law.

"I wish you well in this project," Jacobson said. "If there's anything else I can do, just let me know."

When Wyatt stood, the reverend followed suit. Wyatt took Jacobson's hand into his and shook it firmly.

"Thanks, James," Wyatt said. "Please just start spreading the word." For the first time today, Wyatt's piratical smile surfaced. "That's what you were put on this earth for, right? To spread the word?"

Jacobson smiled back. "That's the rumor," he answered.

"Good-bye, then," Wyatt said.

"Good-bye, my son," Jacobson said. "And thank you."

While Wyatt walked away, Jacobson sat back down on the stone bench to fully absorb his friend's unexpected news. *This is truly a gift*, he thought. His mind automatically assembled a list of parents who might wish to enroll their teenagers in Wyatt's revived program.

Then he suddenly thought of Gabby and Trevor, and he caught his breath.

THREE

ALTHOUGH HE WAS seventy-seven, Ramsey Blaine, or "Ram," as he was known to his friends and family, was still a resolute man, as strong as an old oak tree and nearly as gnarled. And much the same as an oak tree, his roots ran deep. Tall and lean like his son Wyatt, he possessed a gruff kind of charm that had served him well both on the family ranch and in the courtroom. Despite his diagnosis of Alzheimer's disease, Ram remained the family patriarch, a position neither of his sons was eager to assume.

It was early evening in Florida, and the sun was setting behind the distant horizon of the Flying B Ranch. Ram's two golden retrievers, Butch and Sundance, lounged lazily near his feet. By now most of the hired hands had gone home, leaving only Ram and two others behind. Ram smiled at that thought, for "Aunt Lou" and "Big John" Beauregard meant far more to him than the other hired hands. The Cajun couple were in their late sixties, and for more than forty years they had lived and worked on the ranch like part of the family.

Aunt Lou had virtually raised Wyatt and Morgan after the untimely death of their mother from cancer. Her husband, Big John, served as the Flying B foreman. Under Ram's and Big John's care, over the prior four decades the Flying B had been transformed from a sprawling citrus concern into one of the finest American quarter horse ranches in the country. Ram had put Aunt Lou and Big John's son Peter through college and law school, and Peter had become a respected partner at Blaine & Blaine, LLC.

Today was Ram's favorite day of the week, in no small part because Aunt Lou always cooked her wonderful fried chicken. Sunday dinner was a tradition at the Flying B, and as Ram waited for Wyatt to come home and for Morgan and his family to arrive from Boca, he could smell Aunt Lou's marvelous handiwork wafting from the kitchen. Sunday dinner was always at seven o'clock sharp, and any family member not attending needed a damned good excuse.

Rocking back and forth in a white chair on the shaded porch of the magnificent house, Ram lit a cigarette. He then looked across the huge front lawn and toward the old family graveyard that lay near the main barn. The little cemetery's manicured grounds and mildewed headstones were surrounded by a black wrought-iron fence that was nearly as old as the cemetery itself. Many generations of Blaines had been laid to rest there. Among them was Ram's late wife, Phoebe, mother to Wyatt and Morgan. Alongside her lay Krista and Danny.

Ram was grateful that he could pay his respects this way, for it was far more appealing than visiting some crowded public cemetery. Moreover, personally keeping the grave sites well tended helped to soften his grief. Late in the day, he would sometimes sit on the porch and whisper softly to Phoebe, telling her the latest family news while the crickets chirped and he nursed his nightly bourbon.

Although he had been diagnosed with Alzheimer's two years before, Ram's lucid days still outnumbered their darker counterparts. His medication helped, but he hated the idea of having to rely on it. Oddly enough, the forgetting came easily. The difficult part came when he learned that he had lost a day, or part of one. If Ram could not recall the entire preceding day, he insisted on being told about it. Because Wyatt found it too painful, it was usually Aunt Lou who obliged him.

How strange, he thought, as he propped his boots on top of the porch rail and took another sip of the smoky bourbon. *To be afflicted with a disease that is most painful only when it's in remission.*

As he stared out at the small graveyard, for the thousandth time he took care to recall his family history. Since learning of his shattering diagnosis, doing so had become important to him. He treasured each instance that he still could, for it meant that he was spending another moment in clarity rather than confusion.

Ram snorted out a laugh as he also remembered his father, Jacob Blaine. During the roaring twenties Jacob had been one of the south's most notorious moonshiners, and no small share of the family's enduring wealth had been derived from Jacob's dubious occupation. Because his father was frequently arrested, Ram had taken an interest in the law and become an attorney. Fifty-some years ago, it was Ram who'd founded the Blaine law firm in the quickly growing burg of Boca Raton.

Since his earliest days, Ram loved anything that smacked of the Old West. After his father's death, he reinstated the Flying B's horse-breeding program, thereby returning the ranch to its original purpose. Ram recognized that his was a rare combination of professions. And like Wyatt, he had never truly decided which he loved most. His other son, Morgan, had always preferred the firm.

Just then Ram saw Wyatt's Jaguar convertible turn off the highway in the distance and onto the long, paved road that led to the main house. Smiling slyly, he nudged Butch and Sundance awake.

"Look, boys!" he shouted. "Wyatt's home! Go get 'im!"

At once the dogs leaped from the porch and tore off down the road to meet Wyatt's car. As Wyatt watched them come, he shook his head. This was a scenario that had been repeated many times before, always at Ram's bidding. The dogs loved Wyatt. Aunt Lou brazenly claimed that they cared more for him than they did for Ram—an opinion with which Ram stubbornly took issue. From behind the wheel of his car, Wyatt could only surrender to the inevitable.

As soon as Wyatt's car slowed, Butch and Sundance started barking and jumping on the driver's door in their eagerness to see him. The dogs' claws had scratched the car door so many times that Wyatt had simply given up having it repainted. Wyatt's "scratchy Jag," as the family called it, looked terrible, but Wyatt had become resigned to it.

Ram put his boots back on top of the rail then swallowed another generous slug of bourbon as he watched Wyatt walk up the stone steps and onto the broad porch.

"Dinner's almost ready," he said. "Go get changed, then come have a drink with me. And bring the bottle back with you."

After answering his father with an affectionate touch on one shoulder, Wyatt entered the house. The Blaine residence was a magnificent place, and Wyatt had lived there nearly all his life.

A series of massive white columns graced the front of the redbrick mansion. All around it lay sprawling, manicured lawns and rolling flower beds. A marble fountain set into the center of the circular drive playfully sprayed water into the air, and waxy-leafed magnolia trees lined either side of the paved road leading in from the highway that lay some three hundred feet to the east. All told, the mansion was three stories high, with more than fifty rooms. As Wyatt strode across the foyer's checkerboard floor and headed for the huge curved staircase, he smelled chicken frying. On reaching the second floor, he turned down one of many red-carpeted hallways adorned with Old West paintings and Remington bronzes, then headed toward his private rooms.

Swinging the door open, he strode inside and tossed his suit coat onto the huge four-poster bed. He then walked to the leaded-glass balcony doors and opened them wide to admire the view from the front of the house. Because it was February, the air-conditioning wasn't needed. He quickly changed into a pair of worn jeans, a denim shirt, and his most comfortable boots. Sunday dinner was mandatory at the Flying B, but it was never dressy.

He returned downstairs and entered the game room. Complete with a billiards table, a poker table, and a full-length bar, it was Wyatt's favorite room in the house. Behind the bar, he poured some bourbon into a leaded highball glass and took an appreciative sip. Then he grabbed the bottle and made his way toward the kitchen. As he neared, he could hear Aunt Lou singing to herself, a sure sign that she was pleased with the way her dinner was progressing.

When Aunt Lou cooked she always did so manically, like she was at war with the food. And like any cook worth her salt, she considered the kitchen her own special province. On occasion she had been known to banish even the abrasive Ram.

Like everything else about the Flying B, the kitchen was impressive. There were triple stainless-steel ovens, long granite countertops, and three Sub-Zero refrigerators with accompanying freezers. Copper pots and pans hung from the ceiling and walls. Aging southern hams and maple bacon clung to meat hooks in one corner, and ripening chilies, peppers, and garlic cloves hung in another. French doors lay open in the far wall, revealing the side yard with its stone terraces, gaslight torches, and kidney-shaped swimming pool.

As was usual for a Sunday, the three uniformed house girls and all the ranch hands besides Aunt Lou and Big John had gone home early, leaving Lou alone to create dinner. Wyatt knew that this was another reason Ram liked Sundays best. With most of the help gone, it was easier for him to hold court with his family.

"Hey, Aunt Lou," Wyatt said. He walked into the kitchen, glass and bottle in hand.

After putting down her meat cleaver, Aunt Lou turned and

gave Wyatt a look of mock ferociousness. She was a wide, commanding woman, her gray hair collected at the back of her head in a severe bun. She and her husband had been born and raised in New Orleans. Many of her old-time recipes were from there, and her cooking was extraordinary. Aunt Lou was worth her considerable weight in gold, and everyone at the Flying B knew it.

"Hey, yourself," she answered back, while wiping her fingers on her apron. "It's high time that you got home! I swear, your father must've asked about you ten times! He acts like I should somehow know your every movement, for God's sake. Where *have* you been, anyway?"

"I had things to do," Wyatt answered. "For one, I met with Reverend Jacobson. He was happy to hear about Krista's revived program."

Aunt Lou's demeanor quickly mellowed. In her own way, she had loved Krista and Danny as much as anyone else. Walking closer, she gave Wyatt a kiss on one cheek.

"They would be proud of you, Mr. Wyatt," she said. "I just know it."

"I hope so," he answered quietly.

Ever since Wyatt's and Morgan's births, Aunt Lou and Big John had called them "Mr.," the same way they always respectfully addressed Ram. Despite repeated attempts by the brothers to get them to drop the habit and join the twenty-first century, the couple steadfastly refused. Wyatt had become resigned to it long ago, although it still embarrassed him slightly.

Wyatt walked to one of the cupboards and opened it. Taking out a glass, he poured two fingers of bourbon for Aunt Lou.

She gave him a wide smile as he handed it to her. Aunt Lou liked her bourbon, but true to her stern work ethic, she drank only on weekends.

"Here's to Krista and Danny," Wyatt said reverently.

"You bet," Aunt Lou answered.

After gently clinking her glass against his and taking a welcome sip, Aunt Lou turned back toward the countertop. She again brought her meat cleaver down, expertly splitting another chicken for her special brand of basting and frying.

Rolling his glass between his palms, Wyatt leaned back against the counter. After thinking for a time, he stared at Aunt Lou's broad back.

"How was he today?" he asked. "He seems okay, but that doesn't mean much sometimes."

Aunt Lou turned back around. "Today was a good day, Mr. Wyatt. Old Mr. Ram didn't miss a trick. Come tomorrow, I won't be needin' to tell him about it."

"Good," Wyatt said. "I'll take all these normal days that I can get. I'm going to see how he's doing. Besides, he asked me to bring the bottle."

"That don't surprise me none," Aunt Lou answered. "Besides, I don't need no men messing up my kitchen, anyway."

Wyatt sneaked up behind her and pecked her cheek.

"Out!" she shouted, again waving the small cleaver in the air.

On leaving the kitchen, Wyatt sauntered back through the grand foyer. He stepped onto the porch and pulled a rocking chair up alongside his father's.

"Took you long enough," Ram said.

"I had a talk with Aunt Lou," Wyatt answered. "Dinner will be ready soon. Where are Morgan and Sissy?"

Ram snorted out a laugh. "He's always late. I swear, sometimes that man can't get out of his own way."

Wyatt smiled at that because he agreed with Ram about his brother. Morgan was a brilliant attorney, and a good husband and father. He was also a bit obsessive-compulsive, especially when it came to lawyering. That was just as well, for Morgan had never been much of a rancher.

Just then they saw Morgan's Mercedes pull off the highway and start up the drive toward the house. After giving Wyatt a sly grin, Ram nudged the dogs with one boot.

At once Butch and Sundance left the porch to go running toward Morgan's car. Although he had taken no hand in it, Wyatt winced at the ensuing carnage. As Morgan, Sissy, and their two children exited the Mercedes, the look on Morgan's face said it all. Morgan was heavier than Wyatt, his brown hair thinning at the temples.

"Jesus Christ, Dad!" Morgan shouted as he clambered up the steps. "That car's brand new! Can't you control those damn mutts of yours?"

"They love you, that's all," Ram answered innocently. "Besides, turning them loose like that was Wyatt's idea."

Wyatt was about to protest, but Morgan raised a hand. "Don't worry, little brother," he said. "I'm lawyer enough to know a lie when I hear it. Besides, I need a drink." Without further ado, he stomped into the house.

Sissy next ascended the steps, followed by Jack and Esther,

ages ten and twelve. Sissy was a pretty blonde, with long hair and an attractive figure. Leaning down, she gave Wyatt a peck on the cheek.

"Hey, hot stuff," she said.

"Hey, Sissy," he answered.

Sissy put her hands on her hips and gave Ram a ferocious glare that all three of them knew wasn't real. "Hello, old man," she said. "Does this little stunt of yours mean that it's going to be one of those nights?"

"I dunno what you're talking about," Ram answered. "All I want is a nice, quiet drink, and then dinner with my family. When in hell did everybody's vehicles become my problem?"

"Uh-huh," Sissy answered. She looked over at Jack and Esther. "Come on, kids. Let's go inside and see Aunt Lou."

Ram and Wyatt drank in silence for a while as the sun set in earnest, the evening dew gathered, and the night creatures started to sing. This was Wyatt's favorite time of day at the ranch. The hard, physical work was usually finished, and the first bourbon of the night was settling comfortably into his bones. For all he cared, everyone could just leave him out here while they feasted on fried chicken and shared the latest Boca gossip.

It was Ram who finally broke the silence. Lifting his long legs from the rail, he set his boots on the porch floor and leaned forward in his chair. When he next gazed at Wyatt, there was a softer look in his eyes. He patted Wyatt on one knee.

"Let's go inside, son," he said. "Krista and Danny will be here soon, and then we can start."

Wyatt closed his eyes for a moment. *And there it is,* he realized.

Part of my father has abandoned him again, leaving us to wonder when—if ever—it will return.

Doing his best to smile, Wyatt looked back at his father. "You go ahead, Dad," he answered softly. "I'll wait here for Krista and Danny."

"Good boy," Ram said. His gait a bit slower than usual, Ram walked into the house.

Wyatt took another sip of bourbon as he stared at the family cemetery. Aunt Lou had been wrong. Come tomorrow, she would have to describe this evening to Ram after all.

FOUR

REVEREND JACOBSON SAT behind his office desk at St. Andrew's, trying his best to control his nervousness. There was no doubt that the butterflies in his stomach were the result of his own scheming. Sighing, he silently asked the Lord for strength as he fought back his seemingly never-ending need for a cigarette.

Gabrielle Powers, or "Gabby," as she was known to friends and family, sat in a guest chair before Jacobson's desk. At thirty-five she remained a very attractive woman. Her long, dark hair was styled like something from the forties, parted on one side and waving to her shoulders. Arching brows rested above her large hazel eyes, and her chin held just a hint of a cleft. Her figure was still excellent, due in no small part to her lifelong love of swimming. Although her clothes and shoes were not expensive, they were stylish and chosen with care.

Even though Jacobson had invited her here today, she, too, was ill at ease. She knew that Wyatt Blaine was scheduled to arrive soon, supposedly to discuss the final details of his revived program with the reverend. Wyatt knew Gabrielle only by sight, and he was unaware that she would be there. As she looked at the reverend, her face revealed her nervousness about tricking Wyatt in this way.

Two weeks had passed since Wyatt had told Jacobson of his plans. As Wyatt requested, Jacobson made several announcements from the pulpit regarding the revived horse-therapy program. In the meantime, Wyatt visited the local schools. There he handed out fliers, and patiently conducted question-and-answer sessions with scores of teachers, students, and parents.

The response had been excellent, and thirty-four teens had enrolled. Wyatt had called Jacobson to say that the number was adequate, and that the program would start one week from next Monday. Wyatt also added that Ram wanted this program to happen, come hell or high water. Moreover, Ram demanded that Jacobson put in a good word with the Lord, to ensure that neither of those inconveniences occurred. Despite his nervousness, Jacobson smiled.

But hell has little to do with this, he thought.

Then again, he couldn't be sure of Wyatt's reaction to Gabby, and this might become a hellish meeting after all. He was taking a chance, and Wyatt might be as likely to storm out and never set foot in St. Andrew's again as to agree with Jacobson's jarring request.

Perhaps worse, he might alienate the entire Blaine family.

Jacobson knew that losing the support of the Blaines would be
a harsh blow to St. Andrew's. He also realized that Gabby had
much to lose should Wyatt decline. She and Jacobson would succeed today, or they would fail miserably, for with Wyatt Blaine
there would be no middle ground.

And therein lies the rub, Jacobson thought.

As when Krista ran the program, Jacobson was involved not
only because he could use his pulpit to inform parents about it, but
also because he had counseled some of his parishioners about their
difficult teenagers, and knew their problems intimately. He also
knew that Gabby and Trevor would be a special case, and so he
had decided to ask Gabby to meet him here, at his office.

Leaning forward, Jacobson placed his palms flat on the desk.
"Don't worry, my dear," he said. "Wyatt's a reasonable man. I
think we can convince him."

Trying to quell her nervousness, Gabby reached down and
smoothed out her skirt. She was willing to endure this meeting for
Trevor's sake, but even if Wyatt agreed, she wondered if Trevor
would participate. Trevor had revered his late father, and he had
always been an obedient child. But since he'd become a teen, Trev-
or's behavior had been a growing problem.

"I hope so," she said.

"Don't be discouraged," Jacobson answered. "I've known
Wyatt for a long time. But if this is to work, we have to give him
the benefit of the doubt."

Jacobson sighed and sat back in his chair. *Blessed are the peace-
makers,* he thought. *We'll soon see about that.*

Despite her concerns, Gabby was forced to agree with the

reverend. Jacobson and St. Andrew's had been a great source of strength for her since the death of her husband. Jason had been hard on her sometimes, and he had surely possessed his unfair share of faults. Even so, his unexpected death had hit her hard, and Trevor harder.

Like most people in Boca, Gabby knew of the Blaine family. She was also aware that, like herself, Wyatt was a member of St. Andrew's. Although they had never spoken, she knew him by sight. She had also noticed that he always left the services early.

"Can you tell me something?" Gabby asked. "Why does Mr. Blaine always leave the service during the blessings?"

Jacobson sighed. "If I tell you, you've got to keep it just between us. If Wyatt knew, he'd skin me alive. It's not some great secret, Gabby. Rather, it's because Wyatt mustn't learn that you heard it from me. I'm already risking enough ill will just by asking you here today."

"I promise," she answered.

Jacobson stared down at the desktop for a time before answering.

"The reason is simple," he said. "Krista and Danny died on Wyatt's thirty-fifth birthday. They were hosting a party for him, and their house was full of well-wishers. Krista and Danny were killed when they went out to buy some extra ice cream, of all things. His brother, Morgan, took the phone call from the police then informed Wyatt in front of all the guests. Morgan has never forgiven himself for not ushering Wyatt into another room to tell him. But in his defense, Morgan was in shock and not thinking straight either. Because his family died on his birthday and because the blessings are in part about the celebration of such days, Wyatt finds it impossible to stay."

"My God," Gabby breathed. "I never knew that."

"Not many people do," Jacobson said. "Wyatt has dated a few women since, but nothing meaningful ever developed. For a while I believed that reviving Krista's program would help him to heal and to get on with his life. But lately I worry more and more that Wyatt might be doing it for the wrong reasons."

"I don't understand," Gabby said.

"Wyatt says that this is what Krista would have wanted," Jacobson said, "and that's certainly true. The New Beginnings Program was her baby, through and through. Make no mistake— he wants to help troubled teens, just as Krista did. But I worry that this is his way of living in the past rather than embracing the future. He even took a sabbatical from his family law firm so that he could personally manage the project. I understand that he's looking for closure, but I fear that his decision might only further insulate him from the world. I also suspect that providing the program free of charge is his way of ensuring that enough teens will enroll. The last thing he wants is to see Krista's dream fail on his watch."

As Jacobson waited for Wyatt to arrive, he regarded Gabby from the other side of his desk. He liked Gabby and Trevor very much. He had never been able to say the same, however, of Gabby's late husband.

From the start, Gabby's marriage had been troubled. She had realized that Jason was more than a social drinker, but only after their marriage did she learn how bad his habit truly was. When

Trevor was born, Gabby stopped teaching and the financial pressures mounted. Because he could no longer count on Gabby's income, Jason worked even harder. But he also started drinking more to cope with all the newfound stress.

The final straw came without warning. Late one night, Jason stumbled through the doorway of their home, blind drunk and enraged over a lucrative real estate deal that had gone bad that afternoon. He slammed his fist into Gabby's face, knocking her to the floor. For several moments she simply lay there, dazed and unbelieving.

The ensuing divorce process was heart wrenching and expensive. Gabby's parents did their best to help her and Trevor financially, but they were not well off. Just as the divorce was to become final, Jason died. And he took two innocent people with him.

Jason's death benefits helped for a time, but Gabby soon realized that she would have to return to work. And so she decided to accept another position teaching history. After a time she also started coaching the girls' swim team. The town house she rented in Boca for herself and Trevor was pricy, but lovely.

With Jason gone, Trevor became her entire world. She tried to be a good disciplinarian, and most of the time she succeeded. But sometimes, when real sternness was called for, she remembered how much Trevor mourned his late father, and she couldn't bring herself to enforce the tough love that her son so badly needed.

Trevor was fourteen now, and although he had yet to embroil himself in serious trouble, Gabby could see it coming. But as a single parent, she was unable to afford counseling for him. Then, to her surprise, Jacobson called her at home, asking her to come and discuss the New Beginnings Program. Only after her arrival at the church did she learn that it was Wyatt Blaine's program, and that he was also attending this meeting.

At first Gabby wanted to be angry with Jacobson for not telling her everything. But as she sat waiting, her anger morphed into a kind of nervous hopefulness. Not only would she be talking to Wyatt for the first time, but to a certain degree he would be passing judgment on her and her son.

Although she loved Trevor and enjoyed her job, Gabby remained lonely. The few dates she had gone on since Jason's death had been disappointing, to say the least.

One man who took her to dinner ended up talking about himself the entire night. After she refused to sleep with another, he tersely announced that he was married, anyway. Marriage suited Gabby, but it seemed that the possibility of finding a good man to share her life was becoming more of a dream than a reality. She had made a mistake once, and she couldn't help but worry about her ability to make the right choices in men.

She was a modern woman, but at the same time she could be stubbornly old-fashioned about certain things, and finding romantic love was one of them. She would rather remain lonely than surrender her deepest hopes and dreams to some matchmaking service to synthetically produce a chapter in her life that she believed should unfold naturally. For her, such artificial measures took the magic out of the experience and reduced it to a mere business deal. She wanted the fairy tale, that much was true. But she was just stubborn and traditional enough to want it without the contrivances, or not at all.

"What was she like?" she asked Jacobson.

"Who?" he asked in return.

"Wyatt's late wife. What was she like?"

After rummaging through one of his desk drawers, Jacobson produced a framed photograph. He handed it to Gabby. "That's Krista in the back row, third from the right."

Gabby looked at the photo. It had been shot outdoors and at night. Ten people were included, and everyone was dressed in formal attire. The woman to whom Jacobson had referred was tall and pretty. She had a bright smile and wayward, dirty blond hair. Wyatt stood beside her. On the other side of Wyatt stood a boy with brown hair, his grin wide and toothy. Aside from Wyatt, the reverend was the only other person she recognized.

"Krista was pretty," Gabby said. "And I see that you're in the photo, too. Where was this picture taken?"

"That was six years ago, at the Flying B annual ball," Jacobson answered. "The Blaines hold the ball each year largely as a way to reinforce their many business relationships. While Krista's program was in effect, all the New Beginnings teens and their parents were invited, too. I suppose that's how it will be this year as well. Aunt Lou—she's the Flying B's cook, chief, and bottle washer—always caters enough food and booze to feed an army. Wyatt and Morgan's father is named Ram, and he's a real piece of work! He started the tradition some forty years ago. Out of respect, the only exception was the year Danny and Krista died. The ball is always held on the last Saturday of May. That's not far away, now that I think of it."

"You still haven't told me about Krista," Gabby said.

Jacobson sighed and laced his fingers. "She was everything to Wyatt. They met at school, while she was finishing her PhD in psychology. After she and Danny passed, Wyatt sold the house and moved back to the ranch. He's lived there ever since."

"And so he went home," Gabby answered.

Jacobson nodded.

"And Mr. Blaine's equine-therapy program?" Gabby asked. "I still don't know much about it, save that you believe in it. To tell you the truth, horses have always scared me. Would Trevor be in good hands there?"

"The best," Jacobson answered. "The staff consists of psychologists and specially selected ranch hands. The goal is to help troubled teens with a combination of group psychotherapy and equestrianism. The theory is that if they're given an animal to bond with and care for, the teens find that their psychotherapy takes on added meaning. Although there are various forms of equine therapy, Krista's New Beginnings Program was of her own devising."

"I see," Gabby said. "It sounds wonderful."

Jacobson nodded. "Krista and her team helped many teens while her program was in place. I can only hope that the results will be the same this time as well."

"I'm sure that's true," Gabby said. "But Trevor's deteriorating behavior scares me to death. In all honesty, if this doesn't work, I don't know what will end up happening to him."

Just then an insistent knock came on the office door. "Come in," Jacobson said.

Stella Branch opened the door and walked into the office.

She was a black, matronly woman in her midfifties who was well known as Jacobson's secretary and also his strong right arm. Often he would have been lost had it not been for her superb organizational skills. Stella was also Jacobson's sounding board for his newly minted sermons. Unless a new sermon got an enthusiastic thumbs-up from Stella, it went straight into the shredder.

"Mr. Blaine is here," she said. "He's waiting outside."

Jacobson nodded. "Are you ready?" he asked Gabby. "Let me do most of the talking. This was my idea, after all. I'll make sure Wyatt understands that, whichever way it goes."

"I'm as ready as I'll ever be," Gabby answered.

"Okay," Jacobson replied. He looked back at Stella. "You can let him in."

Moments later, Wyatt entered. At first, he saw only Gabby's back. As he neared her chair, he smiled at Jacobson.

"I thought we were meeting alone, James," Wyatt said. "May I ask who I have the pleasure of—"

Just then Wyatt's and Gabby's eyes locked. Shock quickly overtook Wyatt's face. His angry gaze darted toward Jacobson.

"Is this some kind of sick joke?" he demanded.

"Please sit down, Wyatt," Jacobson answered calmly. "If you'll give me a chance, I'll explain."

"Explain *what*?" Wyatt demanded. "What the hell is she doing here?"

"Sit down, Wyatt," Jacobson asked again. "Please hear us out. Then if you still want to storm out of here, you can. But you need to hear what we have to say."

"I can't imagine why," Wyatt growled.

After a period of tense silence, Wyatt finally took the chair next to Gabby's.

"This was my idea, not hers," Jacobson began. "Gabby has a fourteen-year-old son named Trevor. Trevor's having a difficult time adjusting since the death of his father, and he's headed for trouble. Gabby and I believe he would do well in your program. Rather than simply enroll him, she has come to ask for your blessing first."

"Do you really expect me to do her a favor?" Wyatt asked harshly.

"As a matter of fact, I do," Jacobson pressed.

"Her husband took everything from me!" Wyatt shot back.

"I'm not asking this for myself," Gabby said quietly. "I'm asking for my son. He needs help, and I can't afford proper treatment for him. Without it, I'm afraid he'll grow up to be like his father. He's getting into fights at school, and his grades are slipping badly. He's rudderless, and I can't keep him on course. Please, Mr. Blaine, let some good arise from what happened between our families."

For several long moments, Wyatt stared at Gabby like she had lost her mind. The only other time he had been this close to her was when she had attended the combined funeral. Because of the grave injuries, both caskets had been closed.

As the service ended, Gabby had joined the line of departing mourners. She tried to take Wyatt's hand, but he refused it. Deciding to say nothing, she left the church without telling him how sorry she was. It was a mistake that she had long regretted. But if she accomplished nothing else from this meeting, she could do so now she decided.

"I'm sorry for what Jason did to your family," she offered. "He badly hurt Trevor and me as well. If I could take it all back, I would. And if I could pay you in return for this favor, I would do that, too. But I can't. Please don't punish my son for his father's mistake."

While Wyatt sat thinking, no one spoke. As the silence deepened, Gabby took a closer look at the man sitting across from her. His face seemed more tanned and creased than she remembered, but she pushed her observation aside.

Wyatt finally turned and glared at Jacobson. "Goddamnit, I'd bet the entire Flying B that this was your doing! Did that tender plea truly come from her, or did you coach her?"

"It was hers, I assure you," Jacobson answered. "And heartfelt, I would add. I hope that you can agree to this, Wyatt. But whatever you decide, we'll respect it. Even so, I know what you're thinking."

Wyatt scowled. "And just what would that be, other than that I'd like to kick your smug ass from here to the Flying B and back again?"

"You believe that by granting Gabrielle's request, you will somehow be betraying your memories of Krista and Danny," Jacobson answered calmly. "But did Krista ever deny *any* teen?"

Wyatt shook his head. "For a supposedly pious man, you can sure hit below the belt."

As tense seconds ticked by, Jacobson glanced narrowly at Gabby, warning her not to speak.

"All right," Wyatt finally answered. "Trevor's in. But he'd better keep his nose clean or he's out. You understand?"

Although Gabby could hardly contain her joy, she realized that Wyatt wouldn't appreciate a happy outburst. But she did relax enough to give him a smile.

"Thank you, Mr. Blaine," she said. "I don't know how I'll ever repay you."

"For one thing, drop the 'Mr.' part," Wyatt answered gruffly. "I get enough of that at the ranch! Just call me Wyatt. And go buy your son a Stetson and a pair of cowboy boots. They're mandatory. The good and manipulative reverend here can tell you where to get them."

Wyatt stood and gave Jacobson another harsh glare. Placing his fists on top of the desk, he leaned menacingly toward his pastor.

"And as for you," he said, "well, let's just say that you're not fully forgiven."

"No doubt," Jacobson answered. "But remember this: 'For if ye forgive men their trespasses, your heavenly Father will forgive you.' Matthew, chapter six, verse twelve."

"Sure," Wyatt answered dryly. "Now if there are no more mountains that need moving, I'll be on my way."

"No," Jacobson said. "Our work here is done."

"Thank you . . . Wyatt," Gabby said, using his Christian name for the first name.

After giving Gabby a cursory nod, Wyatt strode from the office and firmly shut the door.

On his way back to his car, Wyatt remained stunned and angered by what had just happened. He knew full well why Jacobson had included the Powers woman in the meeting. Those big, pleading eyes of hers had made it nearly impossible to say no, and the good reverend had been counting on it.

God only knows what her boy is like, Wyatt thought. All of the other teens entering the New Beginnings Program had been interviewed for their suitability, but not Trevor Powers. *Jesus, this is crazy . . . And what sort of flies in the ointment will this boy and his mother become, once they're out at the ranch?*

When Wyatt reached his car, he stared back at St. Andrew's, wondering what Jacobson and Gabrielle were talking about now. Were they celebrating their victory? *I sure as hell hadn't planned on this,* he thought. He angrily unlocked his Jaguar and got in.

As he turned the key and the Jag's V-8 engine roared to life, Wyatt scowled and shook his head. "Son of a bitch . . . ," he said aloud.

After that, his ride home was a quiet one.

FIVE

G ABBY COULDN'T HELP but hope that Trevor might benefit from the program, if only he would agree to take part in it. Despite her optimism, she knew that convincing him might be impossible. But she also realized that if a miracle like gaining Wyatt Blaine's permission could happen, then perhaps fate might grant her another one and Trevor would agree to try.

Gabby soon came to a realization. Despite their vast differences, Trevor and Wyatt had much in common. Neither one had truly healed from the shared tragedy that still colored their lives. Furthermore, Wyatt and Trevor each needed someone to blame, if for no reason other than to try to make sense of their overwhelming loss. Wyatt had every right to blame Jason—but not her, or Trevor. But Trevor wrongly blamed Krista Blaine, and by association, the entire Blaine family.

From the day of the accident, Trevor had refused to believe that his father had been at fault. The nine-year-old had angrily decided that the crash had been caused by "that rich Blaine woman" rather than his father. Jason had been everything to Trevor, and he could do no wrong in his son's adoring eyes. Despite Gabby's many heartfelt attempts to convince Trevor of the real story, he would have none of it.

More than anything else, it was Trevor's rejection of the truth that kept him and Gabby apart. She desperately wanted to bridge the gap between them, but Trevor even refused to read the newspaper clippings or the official police report that she had saved. Nothing, it seemed, could correct Trevor's warped version of the tale.

At one thirty the following afternoon, Gabby was deep in a discussion of the Punic Wars before a class of uninterested tenth-graders when a knock came on the classroom door. Leaving her blackboard, she went to see who it was.

Jacob Glassman stood in the hallway. Jacob, a fellow teacher nearing retirement, knew the politics of Jefferson High School better than anyone else. A bent-over man with a balding head and a hangdog face, he had often counseled Gabby as she wrestled with Trevor's deteriorating behavior.

"Jacob?" she asked. "What is it?"

Jacob motioned that she should shut the door behind her. After she did, he gave her an apologetic look.

"It's about Trevor," he whispered stealthily, although the hallway was empty. "He's landed himself in the principal's office again. Another fight, I'm afraid."

Gabby closed her eyes. "Was anyone hurt?"

"The Richardson boy," Jacob answered, "though not badly, I hear. Trevor gave him a bloody nose. It might have been much worse had the fight not been broken up."

Gabby opened her eyes. "Can you cover for me?"

"Sure," Jacob answered. "But may I give you some advice before you go?"

"I'll take all that I can get."

"You've got to get Trevor under control, Gabby," Jacob said. "This is his third dustup lately, and rumor has it that Principal Marshall wants to expel him. He's fed up with your boy. You know as well as I that he can't give special treatment to teachers' kids."

"Yes," Gabby answered.

Jacob gave her a consoling look. "Then you'd better get going while there might still be a chance to intervene."

"Thank you."

She started down the hall toward the principal's office, her heel strikes echoing loudly in the school hallways, causing her to feel even more pressured and alone. On reaching her destination, she opened the glass-paneled door and walked inside.

Principal Marshall's outer office was unimpressive. A couple of glass-block windows, a ceiling fan, and a closed door leading to his inner office dominated the room. Marshall's personal assistant, Celia Ward, sat at her computer, her ubiquitous reading glasses' strings gently swinging to and fro with the speedy rhythm of her typing.

A kindly, red-haired woman in her late forties, Celia had

befriended Gabby soon after she was hired. The two women quickly became best friends. Looking up from her work, Celia gave Gabby a compassionate glance then motioned toward the other side of the room.

Trevor sat in a chair alongside the far wall. When he saw his mother he remained emotionless, as if he couldn't care less about his troubles. As Gabby approached him, she realized that despite the bad situation Trevor had created, it was his brooding, uncaring attitude that concerned her most. Stopping before his chair, she looked down at her son.

Trevor was taller and stronger than most boys his age, attributes Gabby believed contributed to his aggressive nature. He was a good-looking young man who had inherited his build and his facial features from his late father. Because he insisted that backpacks were for sissies, his schoolbooks lay on the floor beside his chair, bound together with an old leather belt that had once belonged to his father. Although he was very bright and had once been near the top of his class, his grades had been slipping for some time. He slouched lazily, as if it was some kind of personal trademark.

Trevor clearly stood apart from the herd, and that was how he liked it. Unlike other teens his age, he didn't try to emulate contemporary celebrities or famous athletes. His personal hero was James Dean, and he could easily recite dialogue from each of his late idol's three films. The red Windbreaker that rarely left his person looked like it had come straight out of the movie *Rebel Without a Cause.* So, too, did his white T-shirt, his worn blue jeans with their rolled-up cuffs, and his black penny loafers.

In a world where other boys his age coveted baggy pants, baseball caps, and MP3 players, Trevor couldn't care less about such "stupid junk," as he called it. Driven by his own vision of what was cool, he even insisted that his dark hair be cut greaser-style, like Dean's had been.

Gabby tolerated Trevor's appearance because, as odd as it might seem, she considered it a step up from the truly slovenly look that many teenage boys cultivated these days. Trevor's style ostracized him from most of the boys, but some of the girls found him darkly alluring, providing yet another temptation that worried her.

Aside from being fatherless, there was another factor adding to Trevor's growing rebelliousness. Gabby's daily presence at school gave Trevor the feeling that he was being constantly watched, and he resented it. Although Gabby had wisely arranged things so that Trevor didn't attend any of her classes, they always rode to and from school together and often crossed paths in the halls.

Whenever he saw his mother at school, Trevor looked away. It hurt Gabby, but she understood. She had to admit that if the roles were reversed, she wouldn't like it any more than Trevor did. For a time she considered enrolling him in a different school. But his behavior had deteriorated so much that she needed to be near him, and today's fracas proved it. Ironically, her presence at Jefferson High was fast adding to the distance between them.

"'Live fast, die young, and leave a good-looking corpse,'" Trevor often said, quoting James Dean's famous phrase. Its sad symbolism was not lost on Gabby, who understood that Trevor was referring as much to his late father's car crash as he was to the similar one that took James Dean's life. As she looked down at him, his brooding expression remained unchanged.

"Tell me," she demanded.

Trevor scowled. "What's to tell? Richardson started in on me again, so I pasted him."

"Why?" Gabby asked.

"He had it coming!" Trevor answered grudgingly. "Christ, do I have to explain everything I do?"

"When you land in the principal's office, yes!" Gabby snapped back. "And stop swearing! I've a good mind to—"

"Ms. Powers?" a male voice called out. "Could you join me? Please leave Trevor there for now."

After nodding at Roy Marshall, Gabby looked back at Trevor. "Stay here until I call for you," she whispered. "I have to go and see if I can keep you from getting expelled!" In response, Trevor only shrugged.

Leaving Trevor behind, Gabby followed Marshall into his office. She had been summoned to this room several times before, and always for the same reason. Principal Marshall's office was well appointed. An open window behind his desk allowed a fresh Florida breeze to come flowing in, carrying with it the sporadic sounds of the girls' tennis team. As Marshall took a seat behind his desk, Gabby sat down in one of the chairs directly opposite.

Roy Marshall was a no-nonsense man in his fifties, with graying hair and a thick middle. His short-sleeved shirt, skinny black tie, and horn-rimmed glasses made him seem outdated. But his methods of running a high school were decidedly modern, and he was known for being a straight shooter.

"I'm sorry to tell you this, Gabrielle," he said grimly, "but I have no choice other than to expel Trevor. I know how hard it's been on both of you since Jason died, but this kind of thing just can't go on. Tim Richardson wasn't badly hurt, thank God. Tim's a bully, but this time Trevor swung first. I've informed Tim's parents, and they've agreed, for the good of the school, not to take legal action. But given the number of fights Trevor has been involved in, it's a damned miracle that we haven't been sued. Surely you can understand that I must take action now, before someone is badly hurt and we're dragged into court by less-forgiving parents. Trevor has a short fuse, and it's getting shorter by the day. Sorry, but there it is."

Gabby took a deep breath. If there was to be a last chance for Trevor, her plea must come from the heart.

"I know, Roy," she said, "and I understand your need to protect the school. But if I enrolled Trevor in an approved counseling program right away, would you give him another chance?"

Marshall sighed. "I don't know . . . I like you, Gabrielle. And believe it or not, I like Trevor, too. Who wouldn't be intrigued by a kid who imitates James Dean? It certainly beats the hell out of some of the other things I see in this place! But Trevor's explosive temper concerns me greatly. If he doesn't get help, one day he'll seriously injure someone. Even the school counselor couldn't make any headway with him. Listen, I think that you're a helluva good teacher. Everybody here does. But we've had this conversation before. You can't afford to put Trevor into outside therapy, and that's that."

"Suppose that as of yesterday, I could," Gabby said.

Marshall's eyebrows lifted. "What's changed?" he asked. For the first time since starting the conversation, he smiled. "Did you win the Florida lottery or something?"

"Sort of," she answered. "Yesterday I enrolled Trevor in Wyatt Blaine's New Beginnings Program. As I'm sure you know, it's free."

Marshall looked surprised. "You did?" he asked. "I know Wyatt. But given your tangled histories, he might send Trevor packing."

"I met with Wyatt personally, and he gave me his blessing."

Marshall sat back in his chair. "Jesus, Gabby, how'd you pull that one off? I'm acquainted with Wyatt's program, and it's a good one. Several other students from this school have also enrolled."

"Let's just say that I had some divine intervention."

"Have you told Trevor?" Marshall asked.

"Not yet."

"It won't go down well with him, you know," Marshall said.

"I know," she answered. "But I have to try. So, will you give Trevor another chance?"

Marshall scowled. "Fine," he answered. "Just don't make me sorry."

"Will you help me tell Trevor?" she asked. "This will need a man's touch. We'll tell him the truth—either he enters the horse-therapy program or he's expelled."

Marshall sat back in his chair, thinking. "There might be a way to convince Trevor by playing up to his James Dean image after all," he said.

"How so?" Gabby asked.

"You leave that to me. Let's get this over with. I've got a school to run."

When Gabby returned with Trevor, his sullenness and signature slouch remained brazenly evident. In an attempt to steel his resolve, he had flipped up the collar of his red Windbreaker, James Dean style. After he and Gabby took seats in the two chairs across from Marshall's desk, Gabby gave Trevor a quick kick in the shins, prompting him to sit up straight.

Leaning forward, Marshall laced his fingers together. "I'm sure you know why you're here, young man."

"Yeah," Trevor answered. "It's because I clocked that idiot Tim Richardson."

"Do you have anything else to say about it?" Marshall asked.

"Only that I'd do it again," Trevor answered obstinately. "Twice, if I thought I could get away with it."

"Uh-huh," Marshall answered. "Well, your mother and I have some news for you."

"I know—I'm being expelled. Suits me fine."

"No," Marshall answered, "but you came close this time. I'm letting you off, provided you do something for me in return."

"What?" Trevor asked skeptically.

"You know that horse-therapy program that everybody's been talking about? I'm sure that you've seen the fliers being passed around school. Well, you just joined it. You start next Monday."

Trevor suddenly looked as if he had been slapped across the face, and he bolted upright in his chair. "I'd rather be expelled!" he shouted. "That program is for losers—everybody knows that! And I'm no loser!"

"I see," Marshall answered. "Then how come you're the only kid sitting in my office?"

This time Trevor had no response. Hoping for a miraculous reprieve, he looked at his mother. His expression had softened, telling Gabby that she and Marshall might be getting somewhere after all. This wasn't quite a good cop/bad cop routine, but it was close. Sensing Trevor's discomfort, Marshall decided to turn up the heat.

"There's another reason you're going to do this, young man," he said. "If you don't, your mother will be out of work. Not because I would fire her—she's too good a teacher. Instead, she'd have to quit."

"Why . . . ?" Trevor asked.

"That's simple," Marshall answered. "How long do you think that she could walk these halls after her only child was expelled?"

Realizing that Marshall was bluffing, Gabby chimed in. "He's right, Trevor. I'd have no choice but to leave. And if you think things are hard for us now . . ."

"But I . . . can't," Trevor said. "That Blaine woman killed my father!"

"You can, and you will," Gabby said sternly. "It's the only way left. As a matter of fact, tonight we're buying a Stetson and a pair of cowboy boots for you. They're required."

"No way!" Trevor shouted. "I'll never wear cowboy clothes!"

"Why not?" Marshall answered. "James Dean did. I'm sure you've seen the movie *Giant,* right?"

"Yeah, but he wore that stuff only cause he was acting!" Trevor countered.

"That's not true," Marshall answered. "If memory serves, Dean liked Western clothes, and he wore them a lot before he died. He also took up roping, even when he didn't need to. He did more than just act, brood, and race Porsches, you know."

Marshall leaned closer, his gaze hardened. "So what's it going to be? Are you in or out?"

For several long moments, silence hung in the air. "All right," Trevor said grudgingly. "I'll try. But it's going to be really lame. Therapy . . . cowboys . . . Jesus . . ."

SIX

"W HERE YOU HEADED, Mr. Wyatt?" Big John Beauregard asked. "Off to do a little hunting, are ya?"

Before answering, Wyatt slung a Western-style saddle onto the bay mare's back. Next he hoisted up the saddle bags and tied them on. After cinching the saddle, he reached for a bridle hanging on the near wall.

"What tipped you off?" he asked.

Big John pointed across the wide concrete corridor that bisected the huge horse barn. The morning sun shone through its many skylights, bringing the promise of a beautiful day. Horse stalls built from dark hardwoods lined either side of the long divide. Nearby, Wyatt's bolt-action rifle with a telescopic sight lay inside a tooled leather scabbard.

Big John grinned knowingly. "Cause that's your gator gun,"

he answered. "And when I see that gun, I always know."

Wyatt smiled, his first since meeting with Gabrielle Powers and James Jacobson two days ago. His decision to allow Trevor into the therapy program still weighed on him, and he wanted to get away for a while to sort through his feelings. But little went unnoticed at the Flying B, and it seemed that his plan had been found out. Living at the ranch was sometimes like existing in a fishbowl—especially where his inquisitive father was concerned.

"I'm going out to my lake cabin," Wyatt answered as he removed the mare's halter.

He then pushed the bridle bit against the bay mare's uniform teeth and gently slid it home. After mouthing it for a few moments, the mare snorted and pawed the concrete floor with one shod hoof.

"I have some thinking to do," Wyatt added, "and I do it best out there. If I see a gator or two, so be it."

After lifting the top of the bridle over the mare's ears, he grabbed the loose straps and buckled them together under her jaw.

Big John smiled. "When you get that look on your face, you rarely come back empty-handed. Two of the hands said they saw a couple of the nasty bastards sunning themselves on the southeastern lakeshore yesterday, but they missed 'em. Must be they told you, too. Good thing they're in season just now, cause God knows we don't need those sons a bitches skulking around. Besides, I could do with a new pair of gator-hide boots."

"And I could use a change of scenery," Wyatt answered. "So you've got a deal."

After retrieving his gun, Wyatt strode back to the horse. He slid the rifle and scabbard beneath the right-hand stirrup then tied them off. Without a need for the stirrup, he easily swung himself up into the saddle.

"Will you be gone overnight?" Big John asked. "You know Mr. Ram. If me or Lou don't have the answer, he'll cuss us out good."

Wyatt shook his head. "Can't say. But I have my cell phone with me. If I decide to stay, I'll call."

Wyatt suddenly realized what he had just said, and he scowled. *Jesus . . .* , he thought. *A cowboy with a cell phone.* Somewhere up in Wild West heaven, his famous namesake was surely laughing at him.

Before leaving, Wyatt looked appreciatively at Big John. Like everyone in his family, he loved the man. "B.J.," as he was sometimes called, had been a fixture at the Flying B since before Wyatt and Morgan were born. Standing nearly six feet, five inches tall, Big John was a barrel-chested giant. His curly gray hair was slowly vanishing and an old gray Stetson sat on his head, its rakish angle matching his perpetually lopsided smile.

Big John's casual appearance and poor grammar were deceptive, for he served not only as the Flying B foreman but also as the ranch veterinarian. Recently married and seeking work, Big John and Aunt Lou had shown up on the doorstep of the Flying B more than forty years ago. Seeing promise in the couple, Ram had assigned the running of the house to Lou, and had eventually paid for John's college education and subsequent DVM.

Wyatt smiled. "I'll see what I can do about getting a gator for you. But if I do, you're going to have to take one of the Jeeps out there and drag the bastard back yourself!"

Big John laughed; Wyatt tipped his hat. Eager to go, Wyatt wheeled his mare around and started to ride out of the barn. No sooner had his mare trotted a few paces than Ram sauntered into view, blocking Wyatt's way. Ram reached out and grasped the horse's bridle, making it clear that Wyatt wouldn't be leaving until the old patriarch had said his piece.

"Where are you headed?" Ram asked.

Wyatt leaned a forearm down on his saddle horn. "Two gators were seen out along the southeastern lakeshore. I thought I'd go look for them."

"Are you sure you're not hunting more than gators?" Ram asked.

"What else would it be?"

Ram's eyes quickly acquired the same penetrating gaze that his many legal opponents had dreaded seeing in the courtroom. "Peace of mind, maybe?" he asked in return.

"I just hung up with Reverend Jacobson," Ram continued. "He told me all about your meeting with the Powers woman. He knew that you left upset, and he wanted to see how you were doing. He's surprised that you haven't gone back and given him a good tongue lashing for sticking his pious nose into your personal business. He was also surprised that you hadn't told me about it. But don't blame him for spilling the beans, son. You know how persuasive I am. That's just the lawyer in me, I guess."

Ram looked at Big John. "Give us a moment, okay?"

After Big John departed, Ram walked to a pile of straw bales stacked against one wall and sat down among them. Wyatt tied his mare's reins to a metal ring on the wall and then joined his father.

Wyatt didn't know how this talk would go, but one thing was certain. For better or for worse, the decision to allow Trevor into the program had been his to make and he wouldn't tolerate any guff over it. He had given his word, and he would keep it.

Ram finally looked into Wyatt's eyes. "I'm proud of you, son," he said. "You did the right thing. Then again, I'm halfway surprised that you didn't tell Jacobson to go to hell for setting you up like that."

"Don't think that I didn't want to!"

Ram laughed and slapped one knee. "That Jacobson's the real deal! Don't feel guilty about his getting the upper hand on you! More than once he's conned me into doing things in the name of the Lord—especially when money was concerned. After all, it's easy to shower morality down on others when you supposedly stand on a higher moral plane. I imagine that he used the shame angle on you, right?"

Wyatt nodded. "They both did. Gabrielle's no slouch at that either."

"Jacobson says she's a real looker."

Wyatt shrugged his shoulders. "I didn't notice."

"Bullshit," Ram answered. "From what he told me, a man would have to be dead not to notice her."

"Then I guess that part of me *is* dead," Wyatt answered.

"We need to talk," Ram said simply.

"About what?"

"About you," Ram answered. After thinking for a time, he turned and looked at his son.

"Lately you've been moping around here like the world is about to end," he said. "And after talking to Jacobson, I know why. Like I said, you made the honorable decision about the Powers boy. What happened wasn't his fault, after all. But I don't want him and his mother to cause you even greater pain. So tell me— when the program starts three days from now, are you going to buck up? Or are you going to continue sulking around the ranch like some gelding that's just lost his family jewels?"

Ram's bluntness hit Wyatt hard. Ram had always had a way of getting straight to the heart of things where his boys were concerned. Wyatt and Morgan knew that his unvarnished brand of parenting was caused by the untimely death of their mother. The boys could have used a bit more tenderness as they grew into manhood, but Wyatt believed that his father had done the best he could.

"I've never told you how to run your life," Ram said, "although it must seem like it. Maybe that's because you live out here with me, and Morg doesn't. But you're my son, and I only want what's best for you. It's high time that you got on with your life. I'd literally give a million bucks if you'd take up with some good woman and see what happens! Your heart is dying a slow death, Wyatt, and it seems that everyone knows it but you. No horse-therapy program in the world is going to change that. Just promise me that you won't get so bound up in Krista's revived program that you become a recluse out here. The Flying B is your home, and you're right to love it. But you mustn't let this ranch become some kind of self-imposed prison."

Ram's words stung Wyatt again, largely because they were true. But Krista's memory still lingered everywhere for him, touching his life every moment of every day. He had loved her so deeply that it seemed she would come breezing through the big-house doors at any moment, her unruly blond hair tousled and her bright smile lighting up the room like only hers could. And then she and Danny were taken away so suddenly, so cruelly . . .

Wyatt shoved his feelings aside, then he stood and untied the mare's reins from the wall ring. He looked down at his father.

"Is there anything else?" he asked.

Ram unfolded his old legs and stood up. "Nope. You know what you're doing with the gators. Just come home safe."

"I will," Wyatt answered.

"You want the dogs to tag along?"

Wyatt shook his head. "This trip is about being alone," he answered quietly.

Ram nodded. "So be it. They'd probably scare the gators off before you could get a proper shot, anyway."

Wyatt threw himself up into the saddle again then wheeled the mare around. After leaving the barn, he steered the horse toward a dirt road heading northwest, and he spurred her into a light canter. As Wyatt's form grew smaller in the morning sun-light, Big John returned to Ram's side.

"Is everything all right, Mr. Ram?" he asked.

"Can't say, B.J.," Ram answered as his son disappeared from view. "Where Wyatt's concerned, you never know."

SEVEN

LATER THAT AFTERNOON, Wyatt arrived at the edge of a pristine lake. Shifting his weight in his saddle, he looked down from the little knoll on which his mare stood. He could have used one of the Flying B's Jeeps to bring him here, but he loved coming on horseback. Besides, the sound of the Jeep would have scared off any alligators lounging on the lake shore.

Measuring about one mile across, the lake was in the shape of a lopsided circle. It lay about ten miles from the big house, and had been a godsend to past generations of Blaines who had worked the ranch as a citrus concern. Fed by underground springs, the deep lake was unusually cool for Florida and provided good fishing.

To keep out trespassers, Ram had bordered the entire ranch with a barbed-wire fence. Ram insisted that the fence always be in good repair, keeping many Flying B hands continually busy.

Today the hands traveled the perimeter with four-wheel-drive Jeeps rather than on horseback. Even so, "riding fence" was only a slightly more agreeable job than it had been some 150 years ago, when the ranch was founded. Wyatt had worked many hours riding fence as a young man, and he knew firsthand how exhausting the task could be.

Because of their high monetary value, the Flying B horses roamed in far more luxurious settings. Whitewashed, split-rail paddocks hemmed in many acres of pasture lying near the main barn. The paddocks had cost Ram a small fortune, but they had been needed. It was there that the horses roamed safely, rather than across the scruffy tracts of land that Wyatt now rode. Despite this area's lonely nature, Wyatt liked it here. Ten years ago he'd built the small lakeshore cabin that stood about half a mile away. But should the Blaines ever decide to again pasture their horses here, it was necessary that these lands be as free from predators as possible—especially alligators.

Few Floridians had much compassion for alligators. During the past few decades, the alligator ranks had in fact swelled to the point that there was now at least one for every nine of the state's human beings. Worse, alligator attacks on humans were increasing. And given that an alligator could run upward of thirty miles an hour across open ground, children were particularly vulnerable.

In Florida it was legal to hunt adult alligators on private land, provided the landowner held a state permit. The permit-approval process was a complicated and arduous one, and by mutual agreement it had fallen to Morgan to make sure that all the needed paperwork for the Flying B was properly filed each year. From

September through March, adult alligators greater than nine feet could be taken by firearms during daylight hours. So that state officials could best monitor the results, an alligator harvest report had to be submitted by the permittee within twenty-four hours of the kill.

Wyatt slipped his rifle from its scabbard. He then loaded it and set the safety. After taking the reins into his left hand, he rested the gunstock on his right thigh and pointed the muzzle skyward.

Wyatt had chosen to search this part of the lakeshore for two reasons. It held a sandy stretch of bank where alligators sometimes warmed themselves in the sun, and it wasn't far from his cabin. He gently spurred his mare. Guiding her northeast, around the rim of the little knoll surrounding the lake, he surveyed the sandy bank.

He had ridden along the lake bank for another half hour or so when his mare danced nervously. Trying to calm her down, he patted her neck and spoke to her softly. Wyatt raised his gun and looked into the telescopic sight to survey the distant shore. At first he saw nothing, but as he checked farther afield he found two alligators on the sandy bank.

The dark, leathery predators lay stock-still, basking in the sunshine. Wyatt was an excellent marksman, but they were too distant to shoot offhand. Looking around, he saw what he needed then steered his mare down the far side of the knoll. After sliding to the ground, he tied the reins to a nearby tree.

Wasting no time, Wyatt quickly crept back up the bank then took another look through the scope. The two alligators still lay motionless on the sunny shore. Each one looked about ten feet long. If he missed, the sound of his gunshot would immediately drive them both toward the water, so Wyatt decided to try to take the nearer one first. He might be quick enough to get off a second shot, but he doubted it.

Seeing the pine tree that he had searched for earlier, Wyatt stealthily worked his way closer. He stepped behind it then propped his gun up against its trunk. Reaching down, he quickly removed his leather belt.

After quietly picking up the gun, he looped the leather belt around the gun barrel, and then around one of the lower tree branches before buckling it. Twirling the gun in a circle, he tightened the belt until it steadied the gun barrel on top of the branch, but not so unforgivingly that he couldn't adjust his aim for a second shot. He pressed the stock against his shoulder and again looked through the scope. Moments later his right index finger gently curved against the trigger, then his thumb silently disengaged the safety.

He gauged the distance to his target, and the wind direction and speed. The northeasterly breeze seemed brisk and steady. After situating the crosshairs just above the head of the nearest alligator and a bit to the right to compensate for distance and wind, Wyatt took a deep breath. When his aim was as perfect as he could make it, he squeezed the trigger.

With a loud report, the rifle jumped in his hands. Without taking his eye from the scope, Wyatt immediately retracted the bolt and shoved another round home. Just as Ram had taught him to do, Wyatt resisted the temptation to see whether he had hit his first target and immediately searched for the other one. The second alligator was scurrying toward the water. Trying to gauge the animal's speed as best he could, Wyatt let go with another round.

With one eye still looking through the scope, Wyatt exhaled and surveyed his handiwork. The near alligator had been killed by Wyatt's first round. Quickly moving the gun to the left, he searched for the other one. It, too, had been stopped. As he lowered the gun he wished that Ram had been here, for trying to convince the old man of this would be nearly impossible.

After ejecting the second spent shell casing and ramming a fresh round home, Wyatt freed the gun from his leather belt and again propped it against the tree trunk. With the belt returned to his waist, he walked back to his mare. After untying her, he climbed up into the saddle and got her moving again. Given the keen ability to sense life and death that all horses seem to possess, this time the mare obeyed Wyatt's bidding.

The two alligators appeared to be dead. He slid the rifle back into its scabbard, turned the big mare northward, and spurred her into a light gallop.

It seemed that Big John would be getting those new boots after all.

❧

WYATT'S CABIN SAT on the northern edge of the lake. It was decidedly humble when compared with the big house, but in some ways Wyatt liked the cabin better. He and Krista had hired a Boca architect to design it for them. Following the architect's plans, Wyatt and a group of ranch hands had built it themselves.

On reaching the cabin, Wyatt slid off his saddle and led the mare toward a small split-rail corral that stood nearby. He unsaddled the horse then walked her into the corral and removed her bridle. Glad to be free of her burdens, the horse rubbed her face against Wyatt's shoulder then wandered off to test her new confines. Wyatt picked up the saddlebags and rifle and headed for the cabin.

About one hundred feet from the edge of the lake, the cabin stood on ten-foot-high stilts to guard it from predators. A grassy expanse lay between the cabin and the sandy lakeshore. With the help of some Flying B hands, Wyatt had built a wooden dock that extended thirty feet out over the lake. An aluminum fishing boat with a gas outboard motor lay on the shore, protected from the elements by a canvas tarp. A ramshackle barrel float with a wooden deck was anchored about seventy feet from shore, bobbing lightly on the waves.

After unlocking the door and putting the key back in its hiding place, he went inside. Wyatt quickly went from room to room, opening the screened windows so that the breeze could flow through. He finally returned to the master bedroom, facing the lake, opened his saddlebags, and removed the sandwiches and bottled water that he had brought along.

There was no electricity here, and that was the way Wyatt liked it. At first he had considered installing a generator and wiring the place, but decided against it. Creating electricity was a noisy affair, and Wyatt valued the peace and quiet too much to violate them with a rattling generator. In place of a refrigerator there were cupboards full of canned food, and an ancient gas grill stood outside. Light came from propane lamps hanging in each room, and water was supplied by a nearby well.

Walking back into the kitchen, he put the sandwiches and water down on the counter. In one corner of the kitchen lay several feed bags. He hoisted one over his shoulder and went back down the front steps. After feeding and watering his mare, he returned to the cabin.

Wyatt often swam in the lake, and as the sun started to set over the distant skyline he decided that tonight would be no exception, alligators be damned. He eagerly stripped off his clothes and stepped into a pair of worn leather sandals. Grabbing a towel and a bar of soap, he walked naked to the lake.

The water felt cool and refreshing. Rather than dry himself with the towel, he decided to lie on the dock and let the fading Florida sunshine do the job. On realizing that he was falling asleep, he finally stood and walked back to the cabin.

He dressed again and lit the cabin lights. After walking out onto the porch to sit in one of several rocking chairs, he ravenously devoured the food, then walked into the kitchen and returned with a bottle of Jack Daniel's and a highball glass. Before sitting down, he switched on a battery-powered CD player. As the soothing sounds of piano music drifted across the porch, he poured himself some of the bourbon.

Wyatt loved it here, and so had Krista. This had been their place to get away from everything; to laugh, and to drink, and to swim naked in the cool lake. Here they had made love with abandon, and were completely unencumbered by the affairs of the ranch. Wyatt and Krista had come here often, so much so that the always irreverent Ram referred to the simple cabin as Krista and Wyatt's "love shack."

Wyatt found Ram's comment embarrassing, but Krista had taken the sting out of it by laughing along with him. Her psychological training had provided her with ways of creating proper boundaries for herself, especially where Ram was concerned. Because Ram most respected those who stood up to him, Krista's sly ability to hold him at bay had caused the old man to love her all the more. And then Wyatt thought of Gabrielle Powers.

Ram was right, Wyatt realized while taking another sip of bourbon. He had come searching for more than alligators. He was in fact looking for some peace of mind about his decision to allow the Powers boy into the New Beginnings Program. He also couldn't escape the growing feeling that there had perhaps been another motive for his decision—one that brought a sharp pang of guilt.

Gabrielle had impressed him. He hadn't felt that way about a woman for five years, and the sensation was jarring. It was more than the respectful way she had asked for his permission, or even that she had bravely forced him to again confront his life's greatest tragedy. There had been real honesty in the compassion she had shown him, something that only they shared because of their common sense of loss. And she had been right about another thing, Wyatt realized. He did have much to remain thankful for, despite his reluctance to admit it.

What is her son like? he wondered. He would find out soon enough. He had little doubt that the boy needed professional help, but that alone was no proof that Trevor would benefit from the program. Many of the teens did, but some of the more hardheaded ones did not. That was just the way of things.

As the darkness outside the cabin finally became total, Wyatt finished his bourbon. Next Monday the program would start in earnest. What would it be like to see Gabrielle and her son wandering around the ranch three afternoons a week?

Perhaps it didn't matter, because the program was limited to twelve weeks and Gabrielle and Trevor would be gone, whatever the outcome. As in Krista's day, the program's effectiveness would then be evaluated, and a decision made as to whether to offer it again.

Wyatt never intended for the therapy program to be offered free of charge indefinitely. If this first twelve-week session was successful, he would decide whether to start charging for it, or abandon it for good. His real intention had been to honor Krista's memory. Either way it went, he knew that were she here, she would understand.

Still, a sense of guilt haunted him. Was he right to allow the son of the drunk who had killed his family to participate in his late wife's cherished dream? Had Jacobson been right when he said that this was what Krista would have wanted? Wyatt didn't know and the longer he sat thinking, the more conflicted he became.

Enough of this, he thought.

Shrugging off his concerns, he stood and stretched. If he rose before dawn, he could arrive home in time to attend the last church service of the morning. Leaving the bottle behind, he walked through the cabin and extinguished the lamps. Wyatt checked his watch again then wound an old alarm clock sitting on the crude bedstead and set it to ring at five A.M. Finally he extinguished the last lamp and took off his clothes.

Eager for sleep, he slipped naked into the master bed that he and Krista had once shared. For a time he lay there peacefully, wishing that her warm, seductive body was beside him in the Florida moonlight. As he listened to the various night creatures, Wyatt turned over and stretched his muscles across the welcome coolness of the sheets.

He was asleep in minutes.

EIGHT

TREVOR WAS IN a particularly sullen mood as Gabby navigated her weather-beaten Honda through the upscale streets of Boca Raton. It was Sunday morning, and she and her son were on their way to church. As she passed sidewalk cafes, palm trees, and trendy boutiques, Gabby realized that she would have to hurry to make the ten o'clock service at St. Andrew's.

Although living in Boca taxed the limits of her income, Gabby loved this stylish and beautiful city. She smiled to herself as she remembered something that Reverend Jacobson had mentioned in one of his sermons. In biblical times, prosperous cities were known as the lands of milk and honey, he said. But today, many upscale places like Boca Raton had become the lands of plastic surgery and stock options. Sadly, he had added, many modern-day people couldn't tell the difference between the two, nor did they care.

Because Trevor hated going to church, his last-minute acquiescence had come with a price. He would remain in his usual clothes or he wouldn't go, he had said. Although Gabby liked to believe that she ruled the roost in her small family, in truth there was little she could do to force her son into the car. And so she had reluctantly agreed to Trevor's demands, while also praying that his appearance wouldn't draw too much disapproval from the well-to-do congregation.

Gabby knew that today's worship service would not convert Trevor to an avid churchgoer, nor was that her goal. She had another reason for wanting Trevor to accompany her. If Wyatt Blaine was there, Gabby would introduce him to her son. But most of all, she would make sure that Trevor thanked Wyatt privately for allowing him to enroll in the New Beginnings Program.

She had waited to tell Trevor her motives until after they were well on their way. It had been a sneaky thing to do, but these days it seemed that sneakiness had become a necessary part of her life. She would be greatly relieved when Trevor started the program, and all this subterfuge was finished. Manipulating people wasn't like her.

As Trevor listened to his mother's confession, his face flushed with anger. He surprised her by not saying a word, his only reaction one of scowling and slumping farther down in his seat. The brooding ghost of James Dean overcame him again as his pinched expression negated every trace of the fragile goodwill that had existed earlier. Gabby skillfully changed the subject, but Trevor's only response was to defiantly turn up the collar of his red Windbreaker.

That's just as well, Gabby thought, as she turned into the St. Andrew's parking lot. *Let his dead alter ego take over for a while. If we're going to be in church, I'd rather he be quiet than have to endure another angry outburst.*

As they entered St. Andrew's, the organist was already playing and the congregation members were on their feet, preparing to sing the first hymn. After greeting the ushers, Gabby guided Trevor toward the left side of the sanctuary where she found vacancies in the fourth row. On her immediate left stood two wealthy dowagers who were dripping with diamonds and wearing large, floppy hats.

The imperious women took little notice of Gabby, but regarded her oddly clothed son with blatant disapproval. Soon they were whispering to each other in that condescending way that some elderly women do so well. Trying to ignore them, Gabby took up a hymnal and found the first selection listed in the program. As the congregation sang, she turned to search out Wyatt.

Doing her best to be discreet, she looked past the women and toward where Wyatt always sat. She found him in his usual row singing among the other parishioners. He was dressed in a tan suit, a crisp white shirt, and a green-and-beige regimental tie. She couldn't know whether he had seen her and Trevor come in, but that didn't matter. If Wyatt held true to his habit, Gabby knew when he would leave.

As the service progressed, Trevor fidgeted, slumped, and scowled even more. Gabby didn't care, provided he proved to be polite toward Wyatt—an outcome that was far from certain. Although she had coached Trevor on what she wanted him to say, she remained nervous about how things would go. But first she had to be sure that Wyatt didn't drive off before she and Trevor caught up with him.

Thirty minutes later, Reverend Jacobson finished his sermon. It had had something to do with respecting other religions, but Gabby had been so busy eyeing Wyatt from time to time that she remembered little of it. Then she double-checked her program. She was right—the blessings were next.

His voice tired and hoarse, Reverend Jacobson left the pulpit and walked before the gleaming white altar. He raised his hands in a gesture of welcome.

"Will anyone wishing to celebrate a birthday, an anniversary, or other special day please come forward for the blessings?" he asked.

As people started rising from their seats, Gabby turned and again gazed past the pair of old Boca dragons sitting on her left. By now, they had become even more disapproving of this strangely searching woman and her even odder son. Sure enough, Gabby watched Wyatt rise from his seat and start heading toward the rear of the church.

Gabby nudged Trevor with one elbow. "Come on!" she said. "We're leaving!" As they hurried out, the two old ladies shot more disapproving glances at them.

"Well, I never!" one announced.

"Nor I!" the other answered harshly. "The nerve of these young people today!"

Ignoring them, Gabby quickly ushered Trevor away. Gabby hustled Trevor outside to see that Wyatt had already crossed the parking lot. She quickened her pace, but already his tie was undone, and he was unlocking the door of his Jaguar. She didn't want to shout at him, but there seemed to be little choice.

"Wyatt!" she called out. "Wyatt, wait!"

Wyatt turned in search of the person who had called out his name. When his eyes met Gabby's, he stiffened.

Oh, God, she suddenly realized. *Have I just made a terrible mistake? What if he thinks that I'm bushwhacking him again?*

But the die was cast, and so she bravely led Trevor onward. Wyatt remained still as Gabby and Trevor walked up to him.

"Hello, Gabrielle," he said politely. "I saw you come into church." He turned and looked at Trevor. "This must be Trevor, right?"

Gabby suddenly felt even more flustered. The last thing she had wanted was to seem like some desperate widow, but there was no going back now.

"Please call me Gabby," she said. "And forgive me for calling out to you that way! I wanted you to meet my son."

"That's okay," Wyatt answered. "It's been quite a while since a pretty woman chased after me."

Trevor scowled. "Doubt it . . . ," he muttered.

"I'm sorry?" Wyatt asked.

Gabby nearly died from embarrassment. Coming up behind Trevor, she instinctively grasped the tops of his shoulders, as if she could somehow squeeze only the right phrases out of him and keep all the unwanted ones inside.

"Don't mind him," she said. "You know teenagers! Anyway, Trevor has something that he wants to tell you."

Wyatt's guilt over his decision about Trevor took hold again, but he managed to give the boy a smile. "Okay," he said.

To Gabby's relief, Trevor decided to obey his mother's wishes. He held out his right hand. "It's a pleasure to meet you, Mr. Blaine," he said. "And I want to thank you for allowing me to join your horse-therapy program."

Bless you, Trevor, Gabby thought. *Even if it did sound rehearsed.*

"It's my pleasure," Wyatt answered. "And call me Wyatt."

Trevor shook hands like a man and looked Wyatt straight in the eye, almost as if he was challenging him for some reason. *Ram is going to like this kid,* Wyatt thought. *They're cut from the same cloth.*

Wyatt wasn't sure of what to do or say next, and Gabby's appearance wasn't helping. Because he had been so upset during their first meeting, he hadn't paid much attention to her looks. Wyatt had long been a fan of old films, and as Gabby stood before him, he realized that she looked very much like Lauren Bacall in her younger days. Her innocent gaze somehow engulfed him from head to toe all at once, causing him to suddenly feel uneasy.

Jacobson was right, Wyatt decided. Gabby was a looker, and then some. *But what to do now?*

After Gabrielle's heartfelt rush to greet him, simply saying good-bye and driving away would seem too brusque. He always went to brunch after church—it had been a tradition with him since Krista and Danny's deaths, and he had had every intention of going there when Gabrielle called out to him.

Still wondering what to do, he took a closer look at the Powers boy. The kid seemed normal enough, despite his fifties vintage look. And besides, Wyatt reasoned, he would have to get to know these people sooner or later. Perhaps now, in the relatively quiet confines of a restaurant, might be better than trying to do it during the always harried first day of New Beginnings.

What the hell . . . , he finally decided.

"I was headed to brunch," he said. "Would you and Trevor like to tag along? It's my treat, of course. I know a place that's very good."

Although Wyatt surprised Gabby, she was far from disappointed. She wanted to accept, but she couldn't know how much longer Trevor's false courtesy might last. Deciding to risk it, she nodded.

"We'd like that very much," she answered. "Perhaps you could tell us more about New Beginnings while we eat."

Trevor's face quickly grimaced with distaste. "Jesus, do we *have* to?" he exclaimed. But when Gabby shot him a sharp look that said she meant business, he soon sighed with resignation. "Sorry, Mr. Blaine," he said quietly. "Brunch would be okay, I guess."

"That's all right, Trevor," Wyatt answered graciously. "I know it's probably not your kind of thing, but the food's really good."

Wyatt returned his gaze to Gabby. "It would be best if you followed me in your car," he said. "We'll go to Chez Paul. I always see Sunday brunch as a personal reward for sitting through Jacobson's long-winded sermons! It's just around the corner, at Mizner Park."

"That's fine," Gabby said. "We'll see you there."

Soon Gabby was following Wyatt's Jaguar through downtown Boca. When Wyatt stopped before the parking valet at Mizner

Park, Gabby pulled in behind him. She felt decidedly out of place as she parked her dented Honda in the valet line among the many glittering luxury cars, but being Wyatt's guest gave her a welcome sense of belonging.

The three of them walked across the central plaza and toward Chez Paul, where a long line of people wound through the foyer and spilled outside onto the stone patio. The wait to get inside looked like it would take forever.

"All the snowbirds are still here," Gabby said. "Maybe we should try another place."

For the first time, Gabby saw Wyatt genuinely smile. The real thing was rather conspiratorial looking, and she liked it.

"That's okay," he said. "Leave everything to me. Like I said, it's my Sunday tradition."

With Trevor and Gabby in tow, Wyatt wended his way into the restaurant. When Wyatt approached the hostess, she eagerly kissed him on one cheek. She had an exotic look about her and, as Gabby was about to discover, she and Wyatt knew each other well.

"*Daahling!*" she shouted above the din. Her accent was decidedly French, and Gabby found it attractive.

"I was starting to wonder whether you were coming!" the hostess said. "I nearly gave your table away!"

"Better late than never, Claudette," Wyatt said. "We're three today."

Claudette gave Gabby and Trevor a rather surprised look that quickly became one of genuine friendliness. "So I see," she answered. "You can go straight in, handsome. Your usual table is waiting. I'll send Jean-Claude right over."

"Thanks," Wyatt said.

Wyatt led Gabby and Trevor through the crowded dining room. Every table was full, save for theirs. It seemed a welcome oasis in a sea of flashing tableware, well-to-do people, and tinkling glass, because Gabby could almost feel the nasty looks coming from those patrons still waiting to be seated.

Their table was one of the best in the place, and it was set with sparkling silverware, leaded crystal, and a perfect white tablecloth. A little chrome stand in the table's center held an engraved card bearing the single word: *Reserved.* After the three of them sat down, Wyatt discreetly scooped up the card and placed it facedown on the table.

Gabby gave Wyatt a curious look. "How'd you mange this?" she asked. "Not that I'm complaining, mind you! I've never eaten here, but I know for a fact that this place doesn't take reservations."

"I know the owner," Wyatt answered as he placed his napkin on his lap. "Blaine and Blaine did some legal work for him last year. I got the idea of getting a table in here anytime I wanted in return for a break on our fee. The owner was only too glad to agree. Claudette is his wife."

Gabby smiled. "And just how many more such 'arrangements' in Boca does Blaine and Blaine enjoy?"

Wyatt's infectious smile surfaced again. "A few."

Their waiter arrived, and he greeted Wyatt warmly. Wyatt introduced Gabby and Trevor then ordered three brunches from the buffet. After asking Gabby about her drink preference, Wyatt ordered two Bloody Marys plus two coffees, and a diet soda for Trevor. Trevor was so hungry that his stomach growled noticeably. Gabby blushed; Wyatt smiled. Gabby turned to look at the buffet line and saw that it had grown long.

"Go ahead," Gabby said to her son. No one needed to tell Trevor twice. He hurried over to the buffet and got in line.

Soon the drinks came, and Gabby and Wyatt sipped their Bloody Marys for a time in silence. After glancing back at Trevor, Wyatt put down his cocktail then gave Gabby a knowing look.

"Let me guess," he said. "James Dean, right? Red Windbreaker and all."

Gabby nodded. "Straight out of *Rebel Without a Cause*. And kudos on your powers of observation. Most people don't connect Trevor's appearance with the actor. Instead they think that my son is just some throwback greaser-in-training."

Wyatt couldn't help but laugh. "Well, I don't mind his look. All he's missing is a cute girlfriend in a poodle skirt and a vintage Porsche! And speaking of clothes, did you buy him a Western hat and a pair of boots? It might sound silly to you, but he really will need them."

Gabby took another sip of her Bloody Mary. It was a bit spicy, just the way she liked it.

"It was a struggle," she answered. "The only way I got him to agree was to convince him that James Dean sometimes wore Western clothes. That was his principal's idea."

Wyatt nodded. "I know Roy," he said. "He's a smart man."

"And just why do the kids need boots and hats?" Gabby asked. "I don't know anything about horses, but it seems to me that a person could ride while wearing almost any getup, right?"

Wyatt shook his head. "The hat will protect his head and face from the sun, and keep the sweat out of his eyes. The heels on the boots will help keep his feet planted in the stirrups. And make sure that the boots are his only footwear while he's at the ranch. Trust me, that's how you'll want it."

"Why?" Gabby asked again. She feared she was starting to sound like a pest, but she was becoming genuinely interested.

"Because part of Trevor's equestrian training will be mucking out stalls," Wyatt answered, "and you don't want him dirtying every pair of shoes he owns! It's part of the overall therapy process. Nothing takes the starch out of a hard-nosed teenager like an hour or two of shoveling that stuff. I did plenty of it when I was his age. And like Trevor, I had my share of undeserved swagger."

Gabby smiled. She had difficulty envisioning the well-dressed lawyer sitting across from her as ever having had to shovel out horse stalls. She also began wondering what Wyatt would look like in Western-style clothes. He seemed the type of man who could wear whatever he wanted to and get away with it. Then she thought about Trevor again. After everything her son had put her through, she had to admit that the image of her own little James Dean shoveling horse manure possessed a certain appeal.

She was just getting to know Wyatt, and before coming here today she had silently vowed not to mention the fatal car crash that had so tragically entangled their lives. Even so, there was something she thought Wyatt deserved to know, something she had neglected to tell him during their meeting with Reverend Jacobson. The longer she sat across the table from him, the greater her need to admit it became.

Her omission had haunted her ever since Wyatt agreed to

accept Trevor into the New Beginnings Program. As the past week had gone by, she worried more and more that had Wyatt known, he might have refused her request. Even now, she didn't know whether her silence had been accidental or intentional.

Worse, she feared that if she told him, he might decide he had been doubly tricked and angrily rescind his offer. But if there was one virtue Gabby Powers steadfastly refused to compromise, it was her honesty. And if she was going to risk telling Wyatt, it needed to be done before Trevor returned to the table. As she tried to prepare herself for his response, Gabby took a deep breath.

"There's something I need to say before Trevor comes back," she said. "It's important to me that you hear it. I should have told you about it that day in Reverend Jacobson's office, but I was so happy that you gave us your permission, I could hardly think of anything else. I can only hope that you will take it in the spirit in which it is given."

Wyatt took a final pull on his Bloody Mary then called the waiter over and ordered another one. Gabby declined. Wyatt gave her a stern look.

"It's about the car crash, isn't it?" he asked.

"How did you know?"

"You've got the same somber look on your face that you had back in Jacobson's office," Wyatt answered. Then he stared down at his drink for a time.

"That crash is the eight-hundred-pound gorilla in the room," he finally added. "I suppose that it always will be. But you've come this far, so you might as well get all your cards on the table for good."

Hoping that she was about to do the right thing, Gabby nodded.

"Trevor believes it was Krista who caused the crash, rather than his father," she said. "I've tried and tried to tell him the truth, but he won't have any of it. He even refuses to read the newspaper clippings or the police report. Jason was everything to him, and in his eyes, his father could do no wrong. Roy believes that's why he imitates James Dean—he's looking for a male role model who died young in a tragic car crash, just like his father. Without Jason in his life, he's searching for an identity. But it goes even deeper than that, Wyatt. In Trevor's warped view of things, he not only holds Krista responsible for Jason's death but your entire family as well."

Wyatt sat back in his chair, thinking. "I'm sorry to hear that."

"I'm simply at my wits' end with him, and before you agreed to enroll him in your program, I was getting desperate," Gabby added. "Your kindness was the only thing that kept him from being expelled six days ago! I can only hope that after hearing this, you'll still allow him to participate. There's a lot of good in him, Wyatt, I just know it. But he needs this program right now. I might as well also tell you that I'm scared to death of horses, and I almost didn't agree to this."

Wyatt's face became emotionless, impossible to read. Gabby held her breath as she waited for his answer.

"First you surprise me in Jacobson's office, and now you tell me all this?" he asked. "It's a lot to absorb."

"Then perhaps it was best that it came in bits and pieces," Gabby offered.

To Gabby's surprise, Wyatt's tone hadn't sounded angry. Even so, she sensed that what little warmth was growing between them had suddenly chilled.

"Do you really believe that being around my family is what Trevor needs right now?" Wyatt asked. "How on earth is that going to help him?"

"I think that your program is *exactly* what he needs," Gabby said. "If he spends time on the ranch and sees that the Blaines are normal, maybe he'll accept reality. I'm no psychologist, Wyatt. But if there's a chance that it might work, Trevor needs to try it."

As Gabby held her breath, Wyatt sat in stony silence. He took another long slug of his drink. When he set the glass back down, it landed hard.

"Is there anything else you haven't told me?" Wyatt asked. "Because if there is—"

"No, I swear it."

"Then my answer remains the same," he said. "I still believe that I made the right decision, because this is about Trevor, not you and me. But if I find out that you're hiding anything else—"

"Oh, Wyatt, thank you!" Gabby interjected. "I promise that you won't be sorry!"

Forgetting herself for a moment, she touched his hand. Unsure of how to respond, Wyatt simply let it happen. The two scarred souls who were so inescapably linked by their mutual sense of loss sat quietly for a time, looking into each other's eyes and not knowing what to say. Just then Gabby saw Trevor coming back, and she pulled her hand away.

Trevor returned to the table with a plateful of pancakes,

bacon, and sausage, all of it drowning in maple syrup. Like most boys his age, he was a food destroyer of the highest order. Oblivious to the meaningful conversation he had just quelled, he started gobbling down his brunch.

Wyatt looked across the table at Gabby. "I think he has the right idea," he said. "Shall we?"

Gabby nodded. "I'm starved."

After making their way through the buffet line, Gabby and Wyatt returned to the table. Everyone ate in silence for a time then Wyatt politely asked Gabby about herself. She gave him a quick thumbnail sketch, and he reciprocated. Although Trevor's quiet moodiness had returned, Wyatt considered the boy's presence a blessing. So long as he was there, there would be no more talk of the car crash, or of why he needed the therapy program. Wyatt used the opportunity to talk a bit about his father.

Gabby smiled. "Ram sounds like quite a character."

Wyatt swallowed another bite of his eggs Benedict before answering. "You have no idea! You'll meet him tomorrow. He's heard about you and Trevor, and he's eager to meet you. And when it comes to interesting characters, Big John and Aunt Lou aren't far behind. You'll like them, too. They live in the big house with me and Ram."

"The 'big house'?" Gabby asked. "You make it sound like a prison."

Wyatt smiled. "I don't mean to. It's just that it's, well, big. There are more than fifty rooms."

"Are you serious?" Gabby asked.

Wyatt nodded.

"Who takes care of it all?"

"The ranch hands do the landscaping, painting, and so on," Wyatt answered. "Aunt Lou does all the cooking and oversees a few maids who clean and do the laundry and such."

"Someone else to do all the housework," Gabby said wistfully. "A girl can only dream."

"Is it hard to ride a horse?" Trevor asked.

"It's like anything else," Wyatt answered. "Some people learn quickly, and others struggle. The trick is to become one with the animal, and to let him do all the work."

"What kind of horses do you raise on the ranch?" Gabby asked.

"American quarter horses," Wyatt answered. "They're Ram's favorites. They're very fast and highly adaptable to all sorts of tasks. Sometimes for fun we barrel-race them."

Again the three of them ate quietly. After devouring a second plateful of food, Trevor had finally reached his limit. The look on his face told Gabby that he had more than fulfilled his promise to her, and he wanted to get away from the adults for a while.

"Can I go outside?" he asked. "I want to look at some of the shops."

Gabby nodded. "Sure, but aren't you forgetting something?"

Trevor stood from his chair and looked at Wyatt. "Thank you for brunch . . . Wyatt," he said.

"You're welcome," Wyatt answered. "I'll see you tomorrow. And don't forget to wear your boots and hat."

Trevor's pinched expression returned for a moment, then he rummaged up another unconvincing smile. "I won't," he answered. Without further ado, he made his way to the door and out onto the plaza.

Wyatt took another sip of coffee. "He certainly *seems* normal enough," he offered.

Gabby snorted out a short laugh. "He wasn't too bad. But you haven't seen the real Trevor."

With Wyatt and Gabby alone once more, the awkward silence returned.

"I want to thank you again," she said. "If there's any way I can make it up to you . . ."

Wyatt shook his head. "Let's just hope that Trevor benefits from the program. It might be harder for him because of how he feels about my family, so we'll just have to wait and see. I'm no great judge of kids, but you're right about one thing."

"What's that?" she asked.

"I see a lot of good in him, too," Wyatt answered.

It was suddenly hard for Gabby to fight back tears, but she managed. After collecting her purse and clearing her throat, she stood. Wyatt stood with her.

"I'd best be going," she said, "before my young hoodlum knocks over one of the stores."

"Call me if he does," Wyatt answered. "You'll need a good lawyer."

Gabby smiled. "Until tomorrow, then."

"Until tomorrow," he answered.

Wyatt remained standing as he watched Gabby leave the restaurant. Her stride was unconsciously seductive, causing several men to turn their heads as she went by. Only then did Wyatt sit back down at the table. To his surprise, for the first time since starting to come here for Sunday brunch some five years ago, he felt completely alone in a sea of people.

After ordering another coffee, he signed the check. For some reason, he didn't feel like leaving. Perhaps he simply didn't want to risk bumping into Gabby and Trevor again, because he might find it awkward. Whatever the cause, he stayed for a while and nursed his coffee in silence.

As the time passed, Gabby remained in Wyatt's thoughts. She had courage, that one. She could easily have hidden Trevor's feelings about Wyatt's family. Instead she had chosen to be honest, regardless of the possible consequences. And there was something else that Wyatt admired about her. Unlike some women Wyatt had met, she hadn't appeared interested in his wealth. For now, at least, it seemed that she valued a man's self-worth more than his net worth.

But there was much more to Gabby Powers than her courage and her honesty. Only moments ago, he'd told Gabby that this was all about Trevor. But with each passing day, he feared that it had more to do with Gabby than he was willing to admit.

For better or for worse, she had unexpectedly entered his life. She was the only woman in the last five years he had felt truly interested in, but with whom he couldn't allow himself to become entangled. After finishing his coffee, Wyatt rubbed his face with his hands.

"Christ," he muttered to himself. "Of all the women in all the world . . ."

NINE

"THE SONOGRAM CONFIRMS a colt, Mr. Ram," Big John announced happily. "It's gonna be a boy."

As if in answer to Big John's statement, the pregnant gray mare named Sadie whinnied then shook her mane and halter. After resting his forearms on top of the open-stall Dutch door, Ram again looked toward the prized broodmare.

Sadie was one of the Flying B's finest. She had been bred several times before, and each time she had "taken" and delivered without incident. Serviced ten months ago by one of the Flying B's best studs, Sadie would give birth soon. The resulting foal would be very valuable to the ranch.

Even so, the impending newborn was less important to Ram than his mother. For Ram, the mare formally registered as Sadie of the Flying B, was more than just another of the ranch's many quarter horses. Sadie had the perfect lines, refined head, and broad chest that were such highly prized characteristics among her breed. Sadie was Ram's favorite, and he would be desolate if he lost her. As she snuffled and swished her longish gray tail, he smiled. Opening the stall door, he walked in.

"Are you sure?" he asked Big John.

Big John nodded. "No doubt about it." From within his worn overalls he fished out a copy of the sonogram and handed it over.

"How soon, you figure?" Ram asked.

"She's getting heavy," Big John answered. "Seven more weeks, I'd say. Maybe eight."

After examining the sonogram, Ram walked up to Sadie and stroked her head. He squatted down and looked at her underside. Big John was right. Like all the ranch's pregnant mares, Sadie had recently been trucked to a Boca veterinary hospital where precautionary sonograms had been taken.

"Is there anything else we can do for her?" Ram asked.

"After she gives birth, start her on a wet bran mash," a female voice called out from the other side of the stall door. "Use two-thirds regular grain and a third wheat bran. It'll keep her from getting colicky."

Ram and Big John turned to see a woman standing in the corridor. She opened the stall door and walked in.

"How long have you been standing there?" Ram asked.

"Long enough to hear you old men blathering to each other," she answered.

Mercedes Lawson was one of Ram's ablest ranch hands. Although she had never been formally trained, some said that she knew as much about caring for horses as Big John. Ram had often suggested that she attend college and then vet school, but she always argued that Big John was a far better teacher than any "mealymouthed professor." The more that Mercedes learned about horses, the more Ram decided that she was right.

Like Big John and Aunt Lou, Mercedes had started working at the Flying B while she was young. When she'd answered an employment ad that Ram had placed in the Boca paper, she was eighteen years old and fresh out of the Florida foster-care system. Some said that experience had left her with a chip on her shoulder that she carried to this day.

More out of pity than any notion that she might actually succeed, Ram offered her a job. When Big John informed Ram that she was secretly sleeping in the hayloft at night because she had nowhere else to go, Ram allowed her to stay in one of the four guest cottages near the barn. That had been seventeen years ago, and what had started as a temporary lodging arrangement had eventually become permanent. By this time, Ram judged her lodging to be part of her pay, and, as with Aunt Lou and Big John, he considered her a family member in everything but name.

Mercy, as she was called, soon became a good ranch hand, hungering for more knowledge and responsibility. She shadowed Big John day and night, soaking up every bit of wisdom she could. The rest of her impressive education came from Big John's vet manuals that she read during her spare time, and often the lights in her cottage burned into the wee hours of the morning. Most of the ranch hands thought it was crazy for an attractive woman to spend her nights that way, but every one of them respected her knowledge. Ram liked Mercy immensely, but she could be difficult to manage. As he watched her approach, he smiled.

The quintessential tomboy, Mercy was on the short side, with an attractive figure and medium length, dirty blond hair that was perpetually woven into two braids. Her eyes were light blue, her lips pouting and full. A smattering of freckles had survived her youth, their wayward scattering always turning a bit darker during summertime. On the rare occasions when Mercy chose to wear a dress and do something more creative with her hair, the transformation could be spectacular.

As usual she was wearing snug jeans, a wide leather belt with a silver buckle, and a denim work shirt. Her scuffed boots were made of black lizard hide. She had rolled up her shirtsleeves, and an old Stetson dangled down her back from a leather string lying across her throat. Soiled work gloves covered her hands. She looked dirty and tired, like she had just finished some disagreeable chore. Walking nearer, she pulled off her gloves and stuffed them into the back pockets of her jeans.

Ram looked at her curiously. "Where the hell have you been? I haven't seen hide nor hair of you all day."

"I just got back with some of the boys," she answered. "It was my turn to help ride fence."

"I've told you a thousand times you don't have to do that," Ram said. "It's tough enough work for a man, let alone a woman."

Mercy laughed. "But I want to do it! The day that I can't hold my own around here will be the day that I leave."

Ram shot a quick glance at Big John. Big John had no easy answer, so he simply grinned. Ram sighed and shook his head.

Sometimes Mercy was about as easy to handle as a coiled-up Florida rattlesnake.

"She's right about the bran mash, boss," Big John said.

"Anything else?" Ram asked.

"We should also start her on a probiotic, to make sure that she provides enough milk for the new foal," Big John answered. "And we'll give her some daily exercise in a corral of her own. Aside from that, it's nature's job. When Sadie's time comes, she'll let us know."

Ram turned toward Mercy. "Are you staying or going?" he asked.

"Going," she said. "I gotta wash all this Florida off me."

Ram nodded. "Walk with me. I want to talk to you about something."

Mercy accompanied him out of the barn and into the late-afternoon sunshine. She didn't know where they were going, nor did she particularly care. But her interest was finally piqued when Ram escorted her to the Blaine family cemetery.

When Ram opened the gate, its hinges sounded a familiar creaking. After beckoning Mercy to enter the cemetery with him, he led her to a stone bench where they sat down.

"Why did you bring me here?" Mercy asked.

"I like this place," Ram said. "It's peaceful, and no one else will hear what I have to say."

Mercy gave Ram a curious look. "What's on your mind?" she asked.

Ram pointed toward two gravestones. They were neatly tended and surrounded with colorful flower beds. The stone markers belonged to Krista and Danny, something Mercy knew as well as Ram.

"You loved them, didn't you?" Ram asked.

"Course I did," Mercy answered. "Why in hell would you ask me such a thing?"

"Because I need a favor from you, and it's one that you will probably find hard to grant," Ram answered.

"What is it?" Mercy asked.

Ram turned and looked Mercy straight in the eye. "Wyatt's program starts tomorrow," he said, "and this place will be full of brooding teenagers and anxious parents. You know what that's like, from when Krista ran the show. But Krista is gone, and the program is Wyatt's baby now."

"I already know all that," Mercy answered.

"Yeah," Ram answered, "but you don't know about one of the teens and his mother. I don't want your famous sense of righteous indignation to upset Wyatt's apple cart. I want this boy and his mother to be treated the same as all the others. It was Wyatt's decision to allow him into the program, and we're all going to respect his wishes."

"What in God's name are you talking about?" Mercy demanded. "Why would I treat one of the kids differently? You're not making much sense." Mercy smiled and elbowed him in the ribs. "You're not having another of your senior moments, are you?"

Ram smiled back. Mercy was one of the few people in the world who could joke about his illness and get away with it.

"No," he answered. "Just now I have total clarity."

"Okay," Mercy said. "So who's this special boy I'll be teaching?"

"His name is Trevor Powers," Ram answered. "It seems that he's something of a hard case. He has a unique history with the Blaine family that will only make things more difficult. And by that I mean difficult for *all* of us, not just for him and his mother."

Something about the boy's name tugged at Mercy's memory, but she couldn't place it so she let it go. "So what's the problem?"

"I'll put it in a nutshell for you," Ram answered. "Trevor's father was Jason Powers, the drunk driver who killed Krista and Danny."

Mercy was thunderstruck. She remained uncharacteristically quiet for a time, trying to absorb Ram's jarring revelation.

"Why in Christ's name would Wyatt agree to that?" she finally asked. "Having that boy and his mother at the ranch will be nothing but trouble."

"It wasn't Wyatt's idea, I assure you," Ram answered. "He got roped into it by our preacher, James Jacobson. But you wouldn't know who he is, what with you being a heathen and all."

Mercy had to agree with Ram on that one. She was far from the churchgoing type, and everyone at the ranch knew it. She much preferred a poker table and cigar smoke to a church pew and incense any day.

"So why single me out to tell me this?" she asked.

"I want you to treat the Powers woman and her boy with respect," Ram said. "And as for why you might not, well, I think you know. You're in love with Wyatt, aren't you?" As if a great weight had been lifted from the old man's shoulders, he sighed.

"There, I finally said it," he breathed. "It took four years, but I finally got it out. I might be old and my brain riddled with Alzheimer's, but I still don't miss much. You've been in love with

Wyatt for a long time. I know you, Mercy, nearly as well as you know yourself. You're one of the most overly protective creatures on the planet, especially where Wyatt is concerned. I tell you these things because you mustn't get your back up when the Powerses arrive. Things'll be hard enough around here without you pecking away at Gabrielle and her boy because of Jason's mistake. And we both know that you're not above it."

Like Mercy, Ram could be agonizingly blunt. Although she was accustomed to his directness, his words affected her greatly. Ram was right. She did love Wyatt, but until this moment she believed that only she and Wyatt knew.

Four years ago Mercy had foolishly blurted out her feelings to Wyatt, on the night of the annual Flying B ball. To make matters worse, she had had far too much to drink and made a pass at him. The only silver lining was that by then all the guests had gone home, leaving her and Wyatt very much alone when she poured out her heart to him.

Wyatt had been kind, but firm. He did not feel the same, he told her. After drunkenly stumbling back to her cottage, she'd cried until dawn—not only because of Wyatt's answer but also because she had made such a damned fool of herself.

They hadn't spoken of it since. To Mercy's great relief, Wyatt's brotherly attitude toward her remained unchanged. But Mercy had been devastated by Wyatt's answer. Even now, she tried to repress her feelings whenever Wyatt was near, but she doubted that she was very convincing.

She brushed away a tear, something few people aside from Wyatt had ever seen her do. Ram produced a handkerchief for her. Mercy sighed and dabbed at her eyes.

"You were right about telling me here," she said. "I wouldn't want any of the other hands to see me like this."

"You're human, just like everybody else," Ram said. "Even though you don't like to think so."

Mercy's gaze became searching. "Did Wyatt tell you?"

Ram shook his head. "He's too much of a gentleman for that. Besides, you know Wyatt. The man explains his feelings about as much as a fish."

"So how did you guess?" she asked.

Before answering, Ram plucked a blade of grass and chewed it thoughtfully. "You could call it fatherly intuition, I suppose. You both probably thought that you could hide it, but not from me."

"Is Wyatt aware that you know?"

Ram shook his head. "Nope. And it's gonna stay that way. If you tell him, I'll have you shoveling manure twenty-four-seven."

Mercy sighed and returned Ram's handkerchief. "So I've been found out . . ."

Ram crossed his legs. "Yep. This means a lot to me, Mercy. I want Wyatt's program to go smoothly. Even after all this time he seems to have no real life outside the ranch, and I worry that his revival of Krista's program might only make him retreat inward even more. But he's a grown man, and he wants to do this thing. So can I rely on you to behave yourself? All of that shoveling aside, that is?"

Mercy tried to smile. "I'll try. But if that woman or her son crosses me, or if they disrespect you or Wyatt in any way, then all bets are off. Even with you."

Ram hoped that he had gotten his point across, but he couldn't be sure. Mercy was the most stubborn person he had ever known. He would just have to wait and see how all this shook out. But one thing was certain. Things were about to get damned interesting around here.

Ram stood and looked around. The sun was starting to set, and it was almost time for his nightly porch visit. After a moment, he looked down at Mercy.

"Would you like to have dinner in the big house tonight with me and the family?" he asked. "It's fried-chicken Sunday."

Mercy shook her head. "After everything you've told me, I think I'll go home and lick my wounds. I could use a drink, and tomorrow is going to be a long day."

Ram placed one hand on Mercy's shoulder. She was shaking a bit, and her tears had come again. *Better to leave her alone,* he thought. Before walking away, he again lent her his handkerchief.

This time, Mercy took it without looking at him.

TEN

"DISH IT UP, GIRL!" Celia Ward exclaimed. "I didn't come all the way over here just to drink your bad coffee! So what's Wyatt Blaine *really* like? Inquiring minds want to know!"

Before answering, Gabby watched her freshly poured creamer create burgeoning clouds in her coffee. She knew that Celia was only kidding about her coffee-brewing skills, but the inquisitive redhead was right about one thing. She had not come to Gabby's town house simply to share a good cup of java.

In truth she wasn't sure how much she wanted to tell Celia. Part of Gabby ached to tell her everything, if for no other reason than to confide in a close female friend. But another part of her psyche wanted to keep the memories of this morning all to herself. She wanted to lock them away in her heart, where no one could find them and set them free. What she didn't know was why. It was confusing, and she couldn't recall ever feeling this way.

She took her first sip of the strong coffee then sat back in her chair. In the end she decided that if she couldn't share her feelings with Celia, she couldn't share them with anyone.

Gabby sighed and looked into Celia's eyes. "I wanted Trevor to personally thank Wyatt for his generosity," she answered. "God, Celia, I nearly died of embarrassment when we had to run across the parking lot to catch him. And I never expected him to invite us to brunch. He knows the owners of Chez Paul, and he can get a table there anytime he wants one."

Celia took another sip of Gabby's coffee. It was hot and good. As she put down her cup, the look in her eyes said that Gabby wasn't going to get off the hook that easily.

"You told me all *that* over the phone," she snapped. "I want all the details, and I want them now."

Despite her reluctance, Gabby laughed. It seemed like forever since she had laughed so freely. For the first time in ages she sensed that her world was starting to brighten, and the welcome change in her was not lost on the ever watchful Celia.

"Come on!" Celia pressed. "There *must* be more to it than that. Just look at you. You're positively glowing."

Before Celia arrived, Gabby had handed Trevor some money and given him permission to ride his bike over to Boca Towne Mall. She wanted to speak freely with Celia. Glad that the two of them were alone, Gabby gave Celia a contented look.

At forty-five, Celia remained an attractive woman. She loved coffee and practically lived on the stuff, the caffeine boost always heightening her well-known sense of urgency. Her snoopy personality was famous among the Jefferson High School staff. She was not a malicious gossip, but she loved being on the "inside of things," as she put it.

"It isn't what people *say* about you that matters," she often warned. "It's what they *whisper*." And Celia's whisperings carried more weight than most.

She, too, was unmarried, and that commonality had drawn the two women closer. Because her ex-husband was a successful Boca estate planner, the divorce judge had seen fit to award Celia enough funds to meet her obligations for some time to come. Still, with two children in college, she carried a heavy financial burden. She had been working as Roy Marshall's assistant for nearly twelve years. The job granted her good medical and retirement benefits that would be difficult to equal elsewhere, so when her divorce became final she had decided to stay on.

"What about *him*?" Celia pressed. "I've seen Wyatt only once. It was just after his wife and son died. He came into Marshall's office to formally remove Danny from the school rolls. I'm ashamed to say it, but even during those dark days he was very striking. Ah, the strong, silent type! They set my heart to fluttering every time. Sometimes a woman gets to wondering where all the real men have gone, and then—bam! You unexpectedly see one, and you realize that they might not be extinct after all."

Gabby laughed again. "I know what you mean! But he seems impossibly difficult to get to know. Call me a sucker for lost causes, but there's something about that man that keeps revisiting me. It's confusing . . ."

"No, it isn't," Celia countered.

"What do you mean?"

"You're smitten with him," Celia answered.

"I am not!" Gabby exclaimed.

"Are, too!" Celia answered, laughing.

"Stop acting like the girls in my tenth-grade history class!" Gabby retorted. "I know my feelings!"

"Do you?"

"Yes! No! Oh, hell, I don't know . . ."

"Well, there's always the practical side of things to consider," Celia said cryptically.

Deciding to let Gabby ponder that last comment, Celia stood and poured another cup of coffee. She then rummaged unabashedly through Gabby's cabinets until she found an unopened bag of cookies, which she promptly ripped open.

Gabby scowled at her. "What are you talking about?"

"The *other* side of Wyatt Blaine," Celia answered as she arranged some pecan sandies on a plate. "You know—the *money* side. You can't honestly tell me that you haven't thought about it."

"No, I haven't."

"Then maybe you should."

"It isn't like that," Gabby protested.

Celia returned to the table. She took a discerning bite from a sandie, followed by another sip of coffee.

"You meet a rich, attractive man you're obviously drawn to, and you have the gall to sit there and tell me that his money never occurred to you?" she asked. "Did you suddenly become a saint or something? I'm afraid that you're going to have to explain that one, girlfriend. Last time I checked, you and Trevor weren't living on easy street."

"I'm not after him for his money," Gabby protested.

Celia smiled. "Okay, then why *are* you after him? Personally speaking, I can think of one reason that has nothing to do with his wallet."

"That's not what I mean," Gabby insisted. "I'm not *after* him at all."

"Are you sure?" Celia asked.

"It's not like that," Gabby said. "Yes, he's wealthy. And I know that it might sound weird, but his money doesn't matter to me."

Celia snorted out a short laugh. "Sure."

"It's true," Gabby said. "Wyatt isn't showy, and he doesn't talk about money. He's not trying to impress anyone. As far as I can tell, his one true love seems to be the ranch."

Celia drummed her fingertips on the tabletop. "Hmmm . . . he sounds like Sir Galahad in cowboy clothes."

"Not really," Gabby said. "Wyatt isn't trying to save anyone."

"What about the troubled teens in his New Beginnings Program? He's trying to save *them*, isn't he?"

"Perhaps in his own way, I suppose . . . ," Gabby answered.

With that the two women sat in silence for a while, enjoying their coffee. The easy quiet reminded Gabby of something her mother had once told her. *If you can remain comfortable in another's company without feeling the need to speak, you've found a good friend indeed.*

Soon Celia had another thought. "I wonder what the ranch is like," she mused.

Gabby shook her head. "I have no idea. I've never visited a horse ranch, so I don't know what to expect. All I know is that the mansion has more than fifty rooms."

Celia nearly choked on her coffee. *"Fifty rooms? Jesus . . ."*

Soon her sly look returned. "Maybe I can give you a leg up on that," she said.

"What do you mean?"

Celia stood and crooked an index finger at Gabby. "Follow me," she said.

Without further ado, she led Gabby into the living room. She sat down at the writing table that held Gabby's personal computer.

"May I?" Celia asked.

Finally understanding, Gabby smiled. "Use 'Flying B Ranch,'" she suggested.

"And I'll add 'Florida,'" Celia replied, "just to make sure."

Celia typed in the words then hit Go. Soon a list appeared. She clicked on the entry designated as the "Flying B Official Site." What the two women saw was impressive.

Celia beamed. "And there you have it. Your own private tour of the Flying B."

Celia stood so that Gabby could sit down before the screen.

Gabby was impressed. The Web site had been professionally and meticulously crafted. The Flying B had an elegant, Old South look that she immediately found alluring.

"It's amazing . . . ," she breathed.

Celia smiled. "Did you expect anything less? At least now you won't wander around the place with your jaw hanging open, like the mere peasant you are."

Gabby laughed and poked Celia in the ribs. "Shut *up*!" she shouted.

Celia looked at her watch. "I should go so that you can pursue your new voyeuristic tendencies in private. Come and walk me out. There's something I want to tell you before I leave."

Gabby followed Celia to the door. When Celia turned to face her, the mischievous look in Celia's eyes was gone.

"What is it?" Gabby asked.

Celia took Gabby's hands in hers. "Now listen to me, Gabbs," she said earnestly. "I've been around the barn more times than you, no pun intended! Maybe you really are this naive, and you don't realize it. Or maybe you do know it, but you don't want to admit it. Either way, you care about that man."

Gabby didn't know what to say so she remained quiet, waiting for Celia's other shoe to drop.

"What I'm trying to say is that you must be careful," Celia said. "Wyatt Blaine isn't like other men you've known. From what you tell me, this one's charming *without* premeditation. That kind of man can get a girl into far more trouble than any classic womanizer who ever lived. But a smart girl like you already knows these things."

"Then what is it?" Gabby asked.

"Just because you put Jason behind you, you can't assume that Wyatt has done the same with Krista. You've been holding on to your love for a long time, Gabbs. When you finally release it, be sure that you give it to the right man."

Celia smiled and gave Gabby a peck on the cheek. "Time for me to go," she said. "I hope that I haven't said too much."

Gabby smiled. "Never," she said.

"Good," Celia answered. "I'll see you at school tomorrow. And until then, remember: it's not what people say about you that matters—"

"It's what they *whisper*," Gabby replied.

"That's my girl," Celia answered.

ELEVEN

O N RISING FROM bed and walking to the balcony, Wyatt heard a horse whinny, and the unmistakable smells of fresh grain and loose hay rose to tease his nostrils. Like usual, the familiar old banty rooster that had for so long owed his existence to Ram's protection was haughtily marching to and fro as if he owned the place. The rooster suddenly flapped his wings and let out a brash cry, as if to inform everyone that it was high time to awaken and start work. It was Monday morning, and the first day of Krista's revived New Beginnings Program.

That old rooster and Ram are kindred spirits, Wyatt decided sleepily. *They each like to push people around while crowing about it at the same time. Maybe that's why Ram won't let Aunt Lou ring the old bird's neck and put him into a pot.*

After shaving and showering, Wyatt donned a fresh pair of

jeans and a worn black work shirt. Then he pulled on his boots and grabbed his battered black Stetson. As he made his way toward the foyer, the welcoming smells of Aunt Lou's cooking became stronger.

Like Ram's "fried-chicken Sundays," daily breakfast was a tradition at the Flying B. Ram insisted that breakfast be served strictly between 7:00 A.M. and 8:00 A.M. each morning. At 8:00 A.M. sharp, whatever remained of the food was cleared away by Aunt Lou and fed to hungry ranch hands. If you snooze, you lose, Ram was fond of saying. The same was also true for dinner, which was at 7:00 P.M. Everyone was on his or her own for lunch. When he was younger, Wyatt had chafed against the rigidity of this tradition. But now that he had grown older, he had come to actually enjoy it.

Breakfast was always served buffet style in the formal dining room. That suited Aunt Lou just fine, because she could arrange the food on the sideboard and let everyone help himself. Most days, Ram, Wyatt, Aunt Lou, and Big John breakfasted together. Although Mercy had an open invitation to breakfast and dinner, she usually ate in her cottage while poring over vet manuals.

Wyatt entered the dining room and looked around. This room had been one of his late mother's favorites, and she had taken particular care in its decoration. Since the day of her death, Ram had insisted that it remain unchanged.

The room was long and finished in dark hardwoods. Befitting the Blaine family heritage, paintings of old English hunting scenes hung on the walls. Several open pairs of French doors lined the entire west side, allowing the morning sunshine to come streaming in, and a cooling breeze to stir the lace curtains. At the near end of the room, a huge portrait of Phoebe Blaine hung above the mahogany sideboard on which breakfast was always served.

During his youth, Wyatt had often wondered why Ram insisted that everyone gather here each morning and evening. As the years passed, Wyatt gained a greater appreciation for not only the dining room's loveliness but also for what it meant to his father. He now understood that because his mother had lavished so much love and attention on this room, Ram gathered his "family" here in honor of her memory.

"It's high time you got here," Ram said as he sat shielded behind his morning newspaper. "Hurry up and eat something. I heard your stomach complaining from as far away as the staircase. Hurt the dogs' sensitive ears, it did!"

Wyatt snorted out a short laugh. "Fine, Dad, and you?"

Aunt Lou also laughed. Big John was seated between his wife and Ram at the near end of the table. Although Ram and Lou had finished their breakfasts, Big John still ate hungrily. So few people sitting at a mahogany dining table that could accommodate twenty-two always looked a bit strange, but Wyatt was accustomed to it. Butch and Sundance lounged at their master's feet on the polished hardwood floor. When Butch saw Wyatt, he thumped his tail happily.

Wyatt gave the Beauregards a smile. "Hey," he said.

"Hey back to you," Aunt Lou answered. The red-and-white-checkered dress that she seemed to continually wear was covered in the front by a white apron. An onyx crucifix hung from a silver chain around her neck, its revered symbolism lost somewhere between her ample breasts. Still eating, Big John nodded, smiling.

Among his many other opinions, Ram was notorious for his hatred of what he called "fake food." His list of transgressors was long and included such supposedly horrid items as margarine, skim milk, and artificially colored egg whites, to name but a few. Moreover, he considered such blasphemies as tofu, soy, and any meal labeled "vegetarian," to be culinary heresy. He fervently claimed that all such culinary abominations tasted largely like wallpaper paste and couldn't possibly be good for anyone, so he forbade Aunt Lou to stock them. Because Lou shared the same view, Ram's orders were enthusiastically obeyed.

Wyatt sat at the table, a plate filled with bacon and scrambled eggs in one hand, and a cup of steaming coffee in the other. Butch thumped his tail again then quickly sat up, eagerly hoping for a handout.

"How's your breakfast?" Ram asked, his face still ensconced behind the Boca newspaper.

"Good, as always," Wyatt answered.

"Well, it isn't Bloody Marys and eggs Benedict from Chez Paul, but it'll have to do," Ram answered slyly.

Wyatt stopped his forkful of eggs halfway between his plate and his mouth. *Jesus,* he thought. *How does he find out about these things?* For several moments Wyatt considered taking his plate out onto the pool patio, but finally decided to face the music. *Might as well get this over with . . .*

Ram smiled and lowered his newspaper. Its folds were clean and crisp because Aunt Lou ironed each one before giving it to him. Franklin-style reading glasses lay perched near the end of his longish nose. After folding the paper and removing his glasses, he lit his first cigarette of the day then drew a crystal ashtray nearer.

"It seems that bumping into the Powers woman has become something of a habit with you," Ram said. "Why do you suppose that is?"

"So you heard about yesterday morning," Wyatt said.

"Yep."

Wyatt took another sip of coffee. "How'd you manage that?"

"You're forgetting something," Ram answered. "I know *everybody* in that town."

"Except for Gabby and Trevor, it would seem," Wyatt countered. "Well, don't worry. You'll get to meet them this afternoon."

"Who's Gabby Powers?" Big John asked.

Wyatt paused again. Word about Gabby's and Trevor's connection to the Blaines would get out soon enough, he realized. *What the hell,* he thought. *I might as well come clean now, rather than later. But I'll leave it up to the instigator.*

"You can tell them," Wyatt said to Ram.

Ram gave his son a questioning look. "You sure?"

"Why not?" Wyatt asked. "That's why you brought it up, right?"

"I guess it is," Ram answered.

For the next few minutes, Ram explained the situation to Big John and Aunt Lou. When Ram finished, he sat back in his chair and stubbed out his cigarette.

Lou placed one hand on Wyatt's. "You're doing a good thing, Mr. Wyatt," she said softly. "I can only imagine how hard this will be for you. Two weeks ago I told you that Krista would be proud of you. Now I think that goes double. She would gladly have welcomed Gabby and Trevor to the Flying B, I just know it."

Wyatt tried to summon a smile. "Thanks, Aunt Lou. I hope you're right."

"She is this time," Big John teased. "Lord knows that my old girl ain't right very often, but she's got this one pegged."

"Hush, fool!" Aunt Lou exclaimed.

"What time do the two psychologists arrive?" Ram asked Wyatt.

Glad for the chance to talk about something else, Wyatt perked up a little. "They're due at three. The parents and the teens are due by four."

Wyatt turned to look at Aunt Lou. "Are you sure you'll have everything ready?" he asked.

"You betcha," she answered. "Soon after they arrive, I'll have a nice spread all laid out by the pool."

Suddenly Lou's expression turned protective, and she glared at Big John. "You'd best warn all your stinky ranch hands to stay away from my food!" she warned. "It's for the guests! If any of your manure managers come near my cooking, I'll swat them with a broom!" Big John just laughed.

A sudden concern struck Wyatt. "Will the three house girls be enough help?" he asked Lou. He had been so preoccupied with everything else that he had forgotten to ask her until now.

"Don't worry your head none," Aunt Lou answered. "We've been through this before, you know. Just like when Krista ran the show, we'll get it all done. It won't be fancy, but it'll be good."

Wyatt hoped so, and he trusted Lou. But this was the first time that the New Beginnings Program would be conducted without Krista's guidance, and he could imagine lots that might go wrong—especially with Gabby and Trevor suddenly added to the mix.

"I've got something to show you, Mr. Wyatt," Big John announced proudly.

Wyatt pushed away his plate. "What is it?" he asked.

B.J. shoved his chair back. Knowing full well that it would rile Lou's ire up, he raised both feet and brazenly set them on top of the table. Ram and Wyatt laughed. Angry beyond words, Lou fumed in silence.

"So what do you think?" B.J. asked.

Wyatt stared at B.J.'s new boots, made from the skin of one of the alligators he had shot. They were immaculate and had yet to see any barn time. The boots were beautiful things, expertly crafted and dyed light gray. Wyatt smiled appreciatively.

"Nice," he said. "Who did the work?"

"An old-time shoe and boot maker friend of mine in Boca," B.J. answered. "I saved his dog's life once. The mutt was hardly worth the effort, but one good turn deserves another. The dog's dead now. And by the look of him, I don't think the boot maker's gonna last long either!"

Wyatt laughed. "What about the other skin? Do you still have it?"

"Course," B.J. answered. "I wouldn't get rid of something that valuable. Why? You got a use for it?"

Wyatt thought for a moment. "Maybe. I'll let you know."

Ram again looked at Wyatt. "Who are you using as equestrian instructors this time?" he asked.

"Mercy and Jim Mason," Wyatt answered.

"Good choices," Ram said. "Where did you find the psychologists?"

"I was able to rehire the same ones from when Krista ran things," Wyatt answered. "When they heard that I was reinstating the program, they were happy to participate again."

Just then the grandfather clock on the other side of the dining room chimed eight times. It always announced when breakfast was officially over, and Ram liked that it did the task for him. As if on cue, the dogs stood and stretched.

With that, Wyatt and B.J. left the house to go about their work. Ram strode to the sideboard and poured another cup of coffee. When Aunt Lou rose from the table, she gave him a stern look.

"Breakfast is over, old man," she said. "Your famous grandfather clock just said so. Breakin' your own rules, are you?"

Ram chuckled. "They're mine to break, aren't they?"

Aunt Lou paused for a moment before starting to clear away the breakfast things. When she again looked at Ram, her expression had softened.

"Will Mr. Wyatt be okay today?" she asked.

Ram sighed. "Hard to say, Lou. But I sure am interested in meeting this woman who's got him so unsettled. I haven't seen him like this since he met Krista."

TWELVE

O F ALL THE ROOMS in the big house, Ram's study was his favorite. Like the dining room, it had remained unchanged since Phoebe's death. The antiquated study always comforted Ram, no matter his troubles. After opening the mahogany door, he carried his coffee and newspaper inside.

The study was large and decorated with custom-built furniture that Ram's father had commissioned long ago. The walls and floor were made of mahogany. An oriental rug lay on the floor, its highly patterned design the room's only exotic touch. The twin desk lamps and matching wall sconces were authentic Tiffany, and had also been purchased by Ram's father.

An oversize desk sat on the far side of the room, facing the door. The wall behind the desk held a sliding glass door that led out onto one of the ranch's many emerald lawns. The sliding door was hinged with matching mahogany plantation shutters that were usually closed, giving the room a secluded feel.

Ram's study was his own special province, and everyone who lived and worked at the Flying B knew it. Only Aunt Lou was allowed to enter the study at will, to clean it and place the daily mail on the desk. Aside from her, no one entered or exited without Ram's blessing.

He could still recall the times he'd summoned Wyatt and Morgan here, usually because of some youthful transgression. After they'd graduated from law school, they'd started attending the Blaine corporate meetings that were regularly held here. It was in this room that the family always charted their next business move, be it for Blaine & Blaine or the Flying B.

Although there were many elegant offices at the family law firm in Boca, Ram preferred to conduct his business meetings here, in the comfort and privacy of his study. He felt unassailable behind his great desk, and he wasn't about to change his habits this late in his life. It was in this room that he did his clearest thinking and accomplished his most important work.

And so he came to his study every morning about this time to sip his coffee, to finish reading his newspaper, and to look over the mail. But those reasons were only part of it. Ram also came here each day to perform a secret bit of work that had become of vast importance to him.

The tasks he was about to do were intensely personal, so much so that he kept the paperwork associated with them well hidden. Only Aunt Lou knew where it could be found. But even she did not know its purpose, and Ram had secretly forbidden her to read it. Ram had issued her only one standing order about it.

In the event of my death or dementia, he told her, *you will deliver the documents to my boys. When they read them they will understand, and they may do with them as they wish.*

When the idea first came to him, Ram was reluctant to put it into action for fear that he was admitting defeat. But he soon realized that these daily rituals helped him to secure a small measure of personal control over his life, however fleeting and useless it would ultimately become. Sometimes these tasks ended with the dark realization that he was continuing to fail. But even such disappointments had their place in the grand scheme of things, so he did his best each day to accept the good with the bad.

After putting his coffee and newspaper on his desk, Ram walked to the great bookcase that lined the far wall. Twenty feet long and ten feet high, its shelves were heavily burdened with law texts and other volumes, some of them very old. The higher shelves were reachable only via a wheeled library ladder.

Ram rolled the ladder across the floor and toward the area of the bookcase he needed to access. Hiding his secret documents in plain sight made him feel very clever, and he often chuckled to himself as he retrieved them. After replacing them he always moved the ladder to a different spot, thereby putting the finishing touch on his subterfuge. On climbing the ladder, he grasped two items lying deeply sandwiched between a pair of old law books and pulled them free. With what he needed in hand, he climbed down and returned to his desk.

After placing the books on his desk, he sat down. Several old photos of him jumping horses were arranged there, near one elbow. Ram had once been an award-winning horse jumper, and he still treasured those memories. But dealing with the present was what concerned him now, and it was the great irony of his life that it could best be done by remembering his past. The moment he'd learned of his shattering diagnosis, a stark conclusion had visited him. A man cannot know where he is going, Ram realized, without first remembering where he has been.

There was no personal computer on Ram's desk, for he mistrusted them. He knew that they were essential devices in this day and age, but they were meant for other people. For him, computers were little more than electronic blackboards on which people painstakingly stored valuable information, every bit of which could be lost in the twinkle of an eye. Paper and ink, he had long reasoned, never failed. Moreover, he vastly preferred the sound of a high-quality fountain pen scratching across a page to the artificial tapping of cheap plastic keys.

Despite what many believed, Ram was not a skinflint. He was in fact willing to spend exorbitant sums, but only on items of world-class quality. This philosophy was evidenced by such possessions as his vintage wristwatch, his fountain pen, his prized collection of handmade shotguns, and his still pristine Packard convertible. Ram Blaine was not cheap by any means, but he ardently demanded quality in return for his money. More important, he stubbornly expected such investments to perform as advertised, and to last. As Ram settled into his chair, he was suddenly reminded of something his father had once told him.

"Now hear this, Ram, my boy," Jacob had said. "There is only one sure way to double your money—legally, that is."

"How?" Ram asked.

"That's simple," Jacob answered, flashing his larcenous smile. "Just fold it twice then put it back into your pocket." *Maybe my old man had a point,* Ram thought, as he took another sip of coffee.

Returning to the present, he opened the first of his two secret books. The smaller one was a monthly calendar he had special-ordered from an upscale stationery shop in Boca. It was bound in leather, and its cover carried an embossed gold imprint of the winged letter B. Turning to the month just past, he found the date for yesterday, February 28.

Ram's system was simple. In the space allowed for each day he wrote one of two letters. For every preceding day that he believed he could completely recall, in its designated space he wrote the letter *G,* for "Good." Each day that he could not recall in its totality was given the letter *B,* for "Bad." True to Ram's nature, there was nothing in between. In the space designated for yesterday, February 28, he wrote *G.*

He then counted the letters recorded for February. There were twenty-five labeled *G,* and only three marked with the dreaded letter *B.* Nodding appreciatively, Ram sat back in his chair. February had been much like the several months preceding it. After recording the tally at the bottom of the page, he closed the calendar and set it aside.

Keeping track of his days this way gave Ram a sense of how quickly his mind was deteriorating. He realized that his method was crude, and only as reliable as the diseased brain that had created it. But its imperfections didn't worry him. As best he knew, he had not suffered a month during which his bad days outnum-

bered his good ones, and for that he was thankful. His medication was helping, but it bothered his sleep and he longed to be
without it.

The second book was larger. It, too, was a leather-bound journal purchased from the same store. Like the calendar, its cover was
embossed with the flying *B*. After thumbing to the blank page
that held yesterday's date he paused for a moment, again doing
his best to recall yesterday in its entirety. He then started to write,
his finely crafted fountain pen weaving a broad trail of black ink
across the page. Thirty minutes later he had filled one page and
half of the next with his jagged, unmistakable penmanship.

Ram had but one regret about keeping a journal; he wished
he had started doing so much earlier. He couldn't change that, but
nothing could stop him from trying to record every day since his
terrible diagnosis. He would continue to do so until his dementia
precluded it, or he died. At first he was apprehensive about keeping a record of his remaining days. But as time went on, he came
to treasure both journal and calendar.

This other secret task was not born of a vaunted sense of ego,
nor in the belief that people would one day find his writings to be
fascinating reading. Rather, he lamented the lost ability to recall
any day of his life that he wished. Because his mind was going,
his sudden need to do so had become a priority. This regret was
especially true about his time with Phoebe.

*If only all my short-lived days with her had been put down on
paper,* he thought, *so that I could relive them at my choosing. How
wonderful it would be to "see" her face again, to "hear" her laughter,
to "feel" her presence . . .*

Ram closed the journal and removed his spectacles. After placing the two precious documents back in their hiding places, he moved the bookcase ladder to a different spot then returned to his desk. It was unusual for him to fully open the plantation shutters, but he did so. He had some thinking to do, and he wanted to look out across the Flying B as he did it.

Today would be important, Ram knew. He firmly believed that the revived New Beginnings Program would succeed. He also believed that before the program's twelve weeks were finished, more than one difficulty would come Wyatt's way. But Wyatt was committed to its success, and Ram knew that Wyatt would see it through.

Aside from his illness, Ram had few concerns in his present life. He had started the family law firm and successfully guided the Flying B through another generation. He had raised two honest and capable sons to carry on the Blaine legacy. Two grandchildren thrived; the future of the Blaine clan seemed bright. Even so, one unresolved issue haunted Ram night and day.

Wyatt, the son who had always been his favorite, was clearly suffering. Before his mind was totally gone, Ram desperately wanted to see Wyatt happy again. Ram knew the signs of Wyatt's torment well, for he had experienced much the same heart-wrenching trauma after the death of his beloved Phoebe from cancer, some thirty years ago.

Ram had dealt with his pain by burying himself in his work, both at the law firm and at the ranch. And like Wyatt, he had loved his wife so much that the very idea of becoming involved with another woman seemed treasonous. But recently, Ram had come to understand that he had been wrong, that remaining alone was not what Phoebe would have wanted. It was too late for him, and it broke his heart to know that Wyatt was committing the same grievous mistake. Worse, there was nothing Ram could do about it.

Ram had no such concerns about Morgan. Morgan's marriage was as solid as a rock, his law career was highly successful, and he was happy with his life. But Wyatt was different. Wyatt had always been uneasy about working at the family law firm. He felt obligated to work there, and he was a good lawyer. But Wyatt was a rancher trapped in a lawyer's clothes, perhaps even more so than Ram had been.

Ram's two boys had always been vastly different. From the day of Wyatt's birth, Ram had resisted his natural inclination to favor him over Morgan. But as time went on, Ram came to realize that denying his feelings was pointless, although he tried never to show them. Wyatt was the more physical one; he was the roust-about, and the one who always seemed to get into trouble. He was the more gifted student, but at the same time he didn't mind getting his hands dirty. And rather unlike Morgan, Wyatt was a man's man, through and through. But then Danny and Krista died, and everything had changed.

Ram desperately wanted to help Wyatt, but he didn't know how. The best that he could do was to hope that Wyatt might one day find another woman with whom to share his future. If and when that happened, Ram believed that Wyatt's soul would return to life.

Ram was about to leave his study when an idea occurred to

him. He opened a desk drawer and removed a blank sheet of Flying B stationery. After thinking for a time, he again uncapped his fountain pen and started to write. Some time later, he finished. He folded the stationery and placed it in an envelope. He then sealed the envelope with red wax and addressed its front side. The job done, Ram nodded.

Later that night he showed Aunt Lou where the letter would be hidden, and issued to her a final set of secret instructions.

THIRTEEN

A FTER LEAVING HIS study, Ram went about a few chores. At noon he returned to the big house to supposedly get some lunch, but his real motive was to spy on the furious activity taking place in the kitchen.

Given all that she had to do, Aunt Lou's tolerance for trespassers was even lower than usual. She soon became so fed up with Ram's snooping that she whacked him across the shoulder with a dirty spoon, banishing him from "her" kitchen. Ram laughed then went to sit on the front porch with his dogs to await the arrival of the visitors.

Wyatt had wisely left the menu planning to Aunt Lou. It was not his intention to feed everyone each time they visited the ranch, and he knew that they did not expect it. Wyatt decided to keep with Krista's tradition of providing food on the first day. Besides, doing so was a good ice breaker.

Lou had proposed her menu to Wyatt ten days ago, and he had eagerly approved of her choices. There would be Cajun chicken, boiled sweet corn and salt potatoes, and assorted beverages. The food would be served poolside, and the gathering would be a paper-plate affair. Feeding so many people would be a formidable task, but Lou insisted that she and her three house girls were up to the challenge. Anyway, she had said, managing this little shindig was simple when compared with the annual Flying B ball. The first day of the New Beginnings Program was always the most difficult for everyone, but after a few sessions, things settled into a familiar pattern. For Wyatt, this day would be especially long.

As Ram sat on the porch in his favorite rocker, his anticipation grew. He was eager to meet Gabrielle Powers. He knew that she had attended Danny and Krista's funerals, but he couldn't remember her. So curious was he that two hours earlier he had secretly phoned Reverend Jacobson and extracted a detailed description of Gabrielle and Trevor. Jacobson was only too happy to participate in Ram's little conspiracy, right down to telling him the make of her car and describing Trevor's ever present red Windbreaker.

Because Wyatt kept his personal life so hidden, Ram doubted that his son would make a point of introducing Gabrielle and Trevor to him. And so Ram decided to personally welcome them the moment they stepped onto the porch. He knew that it would get under Wyatt's skin, which made his mischievous decision even more delicious. He let go a wide smile. *This should prove interesting,* he thought.

A little after three o'clock, the two psychologists arrived in one car. Ram knew them from when Krista had run the program, and he greeted them warmly. Wyatt then ushered them into the library so they could iron out some last-minute details. Just as Ram settled back into his rocker, the first of the visitors started arriving.

Ram watched eagerly as automobiles both humble and proud crawled their way up the private drive. Soon Mercy appeared to show the drivers where to park on one of the side lawns. As Ram watched, a feeling of uneasiness crept up his spine.

Mercy was a wonderful woman, and Ram cared for her deeply. But he feared that her mercurial temper might erupt at any time, despite the warning he had issued to her. Because he had upset her, he also guessed that she had crawled into a booze bottle last night and awakened this morning with a terrific hangover. Going on benders was often her way of dealing with difficult situations, and Ram always worried for her when she did it. *Let's just hope that she behaves herself,* he thought.

Soon Ram saw a battered green Honda sedan drive up the path. He watched closely as it parked among the other cars. A woman and her son exited the car then spoke to Mercy. When Ram saw the boy's red Windbreaker, he knew.

For a few tense moments he watched Gabrielle and Mercy talk. Then the mother and son started for the big house. Ram let go a sigh of relief. If Mercy had learned Gabrielle's identity, she hadn't created a fuss about it.

Ram saw that Gabrielle was tall, with a shapely figure and long, dark hair. The boy was broad shouldered for his age, and the collar of his red Windbreaker was defiantly turned up, just as Jacobson had predicted. The look on the boy's face announced to the entire world that he was not happy to be here. He marched clumsily in his stiff new boots, and the fresh Stetson sat awk-wardly on his head.

As Big John politely ushered the visitors up the walk and through the mansion's entryway, Ram sat in silence. Sporting his Cheshire cat smile, he calmly watched the visitors file by. When Gabrielle and Trevor neared, Ram stood. They took little notice of him until he sauntered directly into their path. Ram smiled and tipped his hat.

"Gabrielle Powers?" he asked.

She regarded Ram with uncertainty. "Yes," she answered. "And you are . . ."

"Ramsey Blaine, ma'am. I'm Wyatt's father, and I'm pleased to meet you." Then he turned and looked at Trevor. "You must be Trevor," he said. Ram extended his hand to the boy.

At first, Trevor scowled. Only after Gabby unnecessarily cleared her throat did he try to smile. His mother had cautioned him to be polite to everyone at the ranch. He would obey her, but that didn't mean he had to like it. As his smile slipped away, he reached out to take Ram's hand.

"Pleased to meet you, Mr. Blaine," he said quietly.

Trevor's answer had been polite enough. But his handshake was overly firm, like he was telling Ram that he wasn't going to be pushed around. Ram responded in kind for a few seconds then released his grip, allowing their first skirmish to end in a draw. *Jacobson was right,* he thought. *This is one tough kid.*

Ram turned his attention to Gabby. "Might I have a moment alone with you?" he asked. When Gabby gave him an unsure look, he smiled. "It won't take long. Trevor can go on ahead."

"It's okay," Gabby said to Trevor. "I'll be there in a moment."

Before Trevor left, Ram reached out and took the Stetson from Trevor's head. "Men don't wear hats inside the house, son," he said. He handed the Stetson to Trevor. "Flying B rules."

If Ram's gesture had angered Trevor, the boy was wise enough not to show it. Hat in hand, he simply nodded then joined the others entering the house. As Trevor walked away, Ram pursed his lips in thought. *He also doesn't like rules . . .*

After Trevor disappeared, Gabby looked back at Ram. "Please call me Gabby," she said.

Ram gave Gabby another smile. "Will do," he said. "And you may call me Ram. Please come this way."

Ram escorted Gabby toward a white wicker table and four chairs that sat near one end of the great porch. The dogs followed, slumping lazily beside Ram's chair like the pair of ever present gorgons they were.

Gabby smiled. "Butch and Sundance, I presume?" she asked.

Ram smiled back. "Yep. Did Wyatt tell you about them?"

Gabby shook her head. "No," she answered. "Reverend Jacobson did."

Ram smiled and lit a cigarette. "I want you to know that the way you and Jacobson bushwhacked Wyatt never bothered me," he said. "You did what you had to to help your son. Besides, sometimes Wyatt needs a push in the right direction—especially where his feelings are concerned."

Ram looked up to see one of the housemaids approaching. Betsy was tall, about twenty-five, and was dressed in a black-and-white maid's outfit. Smiling, she placed two glasses filled with iced tea on the table.

Ram gave her a quizzical look. "Where'd this come from, Betsy?" he asked.

"Aunt Lou sent it to y'all," Betsy answered, in a heavy southern drawl. *Georgia,* Gabby guessed.

"How'd she know that Gabby and I were out here?" Ram asked.

"Same way she knows everything, I guess," Betsy answered. "That's just Aunt Lou."

"You're right," he said to Betsy. "Please go back and thank her for us. I'm sure that she must need you in the kitchen."

Gabby smiled as Betsy returned to the house. "Wyatt told me a little about Aunt Lou," she admitted. "She sounds like quite a woman."

Ram sipped his tea. "That's putting it mildly! She's an institution around here, and you'll meet her soon enough." He held his glass a bit higher then shook it, rattling the ice cubes. "This tea was her little way of telling me that she knew we were out here."

Looking over the top of his glass, Ram gave Gabby an unobtrusive once-over. Jacobson had said that she was attractive, but his description hadn't done her justice. Gabby was wearing jeans that were worn, but serviceable. The sleeves of her red-and-white-checkered shirt were rolled up above her elbows; its tails were tied in a bow at her slim waist. Ram guessed that she had chosen her new cowboy boots at the same time she'd purchased Trevor's. She didn't look like a Flying B ranch hand, but Ram found her attempt to fit in endearing. As he put down his glass, he smiled.

"I suppose you're wondering why I pulled you aside," he said.

"Well, yes," she answered, "besides our needing to meet, of course."

"Some things must be said," Ram offered. "Better now than later."

Gabby looked down at her hands. "Trevor and I don't want to create a disturbance here, or make things difficult for anyone. If Wyatt has changed his mind—"

"It's nothing like that," Ram interjected. "I'm sorry if I scared you. Wyatt and I have talked this out—as much as he ever talks about anything—and I wholeheartedly agree with his decision. Besides, if he changes his mind, I'll have him skinned."

Gabby laughed, her first time in Ram's presence. She was discovering that Ram was everything Wyatt had said he was. She finally started to relax a bit.

"So what's on your mind?" she asked.

"Two things," Ram answered. "First off, you and Trevor are welcome here, despite the tragedy that links us. I've explained the situation to the ranch hands and the house staff, and they all understand. You and Trevor will be treated graciously during your visits, or there'll be hell to pay."

"Thank you for that," Gabby said. "I guessed that Wyatt was starting to accept us, but I must admit that I was concerned about how everyone else might react. In fact, Wyatt has a name for what happened between our families."

Ram raised his eyebrows. "He does?"

Gabby nodded. "He calls it 'the eight-hundred-pound gorilla in the room.'"

Ram smiled. "I suppose he's right. But don't worry about that. This is a very big house. Hopefully, no one will notice a gorilla hanging around."

Gabby smiled again. She was starting to like this old man. "And what was the other thing you wanted to tell me?" she asked.

As Ram leaned forward, the look in his eyes softened. "There's something I must tell you about myself."

"What is it?" she asked.

"Two years ago I was diagnosed with Alzheimer's," he said. "You don't have to worry about spilling the beans—everyone at the Flying B knows. But if I should totally ignore you one day or say something hurtful, please understand that I didn't mean it. Luckily, my good days still outnumber my bad ones."

Ram gave Gabby a conspiratorial wink. "When I'm sharp, I'm sharp," he added. "But when I'm not, I don't know a goddamned thing and I behave outrageously. In fact, some people claim that they can't tell the difference!"

Gabby didn't know what to say. She felt sad for him, and she wanted to express her sympathy. But from what little she knew of Ram, she doubted that he wanted it. She liked the way he poked fun at his malady rather than explaining it with a big dose of self-pity. Ram clearly regarded his Alzheimer's as an adversary rather than a conqueror, and his Alzheimer's was in for a fight.

"I see," she said. "Wyatt didn't tell me."

Ram took another sip of tea. "He never tells people about it. Hell, most times it's hard getting him to talk at all. But he's a good man, Gabby. Eventually you'll come to see that." Ram heard boot heels striking the porch floor, and he turned to look. "And speaking of the strong, silent type . . ."

Gabby turned to see Wyatt approaching. He was still dressed in his jeans, wrinkled black work shirt, and worn black boots. His gait was smooth and sure, his strong arms and calloused hands swinging along easily at his sides.

This was the first time Gabby had seen Wyatt in ranch clothes, and he seemed to be in his element. Here at the Flying B there was a rugged, untamed look about him that she liked. Wyatt could be a bit of a chameleon, she decided. His casual appearance also told Gabby that although this was the first day of New Beginnings, his intention was to work rather than to impress. As he neared the table, he gave Gabby a nod.

"Hello there," he said. "Trevor told me you had been shanghaied by this old geezer. By the way, your son seems about as happy to be here as a cat in a rocking-chair factory. But that's normal. Most of the teens feel the same way right now."

"Hello, Wyatt," Gabby said. "I must say that this place is amazing. I'm starting to see why you love it so much."

Wyatt tilted his head in Ram's direction. "He hasn't been harassing you, has he?"

"No more than I would allow," Gabby answered. "I think he's rather charming."

Ram laughed. "Good girl! Keep that up and you'll do well around here!"

Wyatt looked at Gabby. "I hate to break up this little tea party, but it's time to get the introductory meeting started. You're the only parent who isn't inside."

Gabby stood. "It was a pleasure to meet you," she said to Ram.

"And you," Ram answered.

As Wyatt escorted Gabby down the length of the porch, he looked over his shoulder and shot a caustic glance at his father for kidnapping Gabby that way. Not to be outdone, Ram pointed at Gabby's backside then raised his bushy eyebrows up and down lasciviously.

After Wyatt and Gabby entered the big house, Ram saw Morgan's Mercedes approaching. He nearly set the dogs loose on it before reluctantly stopping himself. With all the guests here, this was not the time.

After Morgan parked near the main barn, Ram waved him over. Having come straight from the office, Morgan was still dressed for work. When he reached Ram, he stripped off his suit coat and tie then meticulously folded them on the wicker table. He looked longingly at Ram's iced tea.

"Is there more of that?" he asked.

"I'm sure there are buckets of it in the kitchen," Ram answered. "But Lou and her girls are frantic, so I suggest that you fetch it for yourself."

Morgan jerked one thumb back over his shoulder. "How's it going in there?" he asked.

"Dunno," Ram answered.

"Aren't you going to go inside and listen?"

"Eventually," Ram answered. "But first, you and I need to talk. There's something I want to explain before you go and help your brother, and believe me, it's something you need to know. Everybody else around here has heard about it. Now it's your turn."

Morgan frowned. "What the hell are you talking about?"

"Does the name Gabrielle Powers mean anything to you?" Ram asked.

"No," Morgan answered. "Should it?"

Ram leaned closer. "How about Jason Powers?"

Morgan's expression darkened. "Of course I know *that* name. What of it?"

As Ram explained the situation, Morgan became angry and thought that Wyatt had lost his mind. But as Ram kept talking, Morgan calmed down. Only after Morgan had agreed to the same terms that Ram had imposed on Mercy did Ram relent.

With their new agreement sealed, the old man and his eldest son finally entered the house.

FOURTEEN

GABBY SMILED AT Trevor as they sat together on the swimming pool patio. All the parents, teens, and staff were also there, getting to know one another and enjoying Aunt Lou's marvelous cooking. Gabby could sense that the other parents were as eager as she for the program to officially start.

Despite the pleasant scene, Gabby wasn't entirely comfortable. Like Ram had promised, the ranch hands and the program staff were treating her and Trevor with respect. But nothing could quell the rather prickly sense of curiosity that some of the parents showed.

Earlier, Gabby had seen a woman pointing her and Trevor out to two other parents. A bit later, she noticed a small group of parents looking her way surreptitiously and speaking in hushed tones. Similar occurrences had followed, causing Gabby to feel isolated. Sadly, she guessed that Trevor sensed it, too.

Gabby understood why she and Trevor were the objects of attention. She couldn't blame the others for being inquisitive, and their interest did not seem malicious. Despite hers and Trevor's personal discomfort, this first day of Wyatt's program had passed smoothly and the night would soon draw to a close. The next time everyone gathered here, the real business of horse therapy could start.

The welcome meeting had ended about two hours ago. After everyone had been ushered into the big house, Wyatt introduced Morgan, Mercy, Ram, Lou and John, and the psychologists and equestrian coaches to the group as a whole. Wyatt made everyone feel at ease, and he handled the subsequent session and answer session well.

The teens would be divided into two groups, he explained. While one was taking group counseling in the house, the other would be involved with the equestrian part of the program. When their one-hour sessions were finished, they would trade places. The basic idea was for the teens to take the practical life lessons they learned working with the horses and apply them to their counseling.

After the meeting, Wyatt escorted everyone on a walking tour of the ranch. The Flying B was far more impressive than Gabby had expected, despite viewing it on her computer yesterday. And to her surprise, the ranch had awed even her ever skeptical son.

Although this was her first visit to the Flying B, Gabby understood why Wyatt loved it so. The ranch was far more than just a beautiful place to raise horses. There was a real sense of tradition here, and the longer Gabby remained, the more she sensed it. Only when she passed by the melancholy little cemetery near the main barn did she become saddened. Her mind returning to the present, Gabby took another sip of beer and gazed around the lovely scene.

Night had fallen about an hour ago; the air was warm and still. Bright stars twinkled in the cloudless Florida sky. The kidney-shaped swimming pool and the flagstone patio that surrounded it rivaled those Gabby had seen at some hotels. Umbrella tables, chairs, and loungers were plentiful, and the pool was illuminated at either end by an underwater light. Flaming tiki torches stood here and there on the surrounding lawn, adding a welcoming glow to the night. Jazz floated out of the mansion, drifting across the patio.

At the far end of the patio stood a huge slate-and-mortar barbecue pit that was a good twenty feet long if it was an inch. It seemed that the Blaines didn't believe in grilling food with propane, and everything was being painstakingly prepared over glowing charcoal. As Gabby watched Aunt Lou, she couldn't help but admire the Cajun woman's work ethic.

Ram and Wyatt had been right, Gabby decided. Lou was indeed a dynamo. She seemed to be everywhere at once, keeping the three house girls nearly frantic as she barked out orders and oversaw the entire show. It was also clear that Big John enjoyed teasing Aunt Lou every chance he got.

Wyatt, Ram, Morgan, and the New Beginnings staff were dutifully milling among the guests and making small talk. From time to time, Gabby sought out Wyatt. He was always at ease, in a lanky, cowboy sort of way. Each time their eyes met, he nodded pleasantly.

ஜ

WHEN WYATT AGAIN looked Gabby's way, he couldn't help but feel sorry for her and Trevor. The two of them sat alone at a table, and Wyatt knew that it wasn't by choice. Trevor was morose, his James Dean persona in full evidence as he slumped in his chair. The collar of his red Windbreaker remained defiantly turned up, like some personal badge of rebellion.

And who can blame him? Wyatt thought. *He lost the father he so loved, and he never wanted to join New Beginnings. Right about now, Trevor probably wishes that he had been expelled after all.*

Trevor and Gabby needed someone to take them aside and make them feel accepted. Wyatt supposed that Gabby could shake off the attitudes of the other guests. But most of the teens seemed sullen, especially Trevor. If Wyatt could somehow make the boy feel special, it might help. It would probably put Gabby more at ease, too.

But how to do it? Wyatt wondered as he chatted up a wealthy couple from Boca. Then it came to him, and he smiled. Politely excusing himself, he left his guests and sauntered over to the beverage table.

Wyatt walked the length of the table until he came to where the coffee was being served. After grabbing two sugar cubes and stuffing them into a front pocket of his jeans, he headed for Gabby and Trevor's table. As he went, he saw that Aunt Lou was about to get there first.

❧

"GABRIELLE POWERS?" a female voice asked.

Gabby turned to see Aunt Lou standing beside her. Lou's apron was splattered with Cajun sauce, and she was perspiring heavily from working the huge barbecue pit.

Gabby stood and smiled. "Aunt Lou?" she asked.

Lou smiled back. "That's me!" she answered. "I'm mighty pleased to meet you. Is this your boy? My, but ain't he a handsome thing!"

For once, Trevor responded politely without being prodded. After wiping his fingers, he stood and eagerly shook Aunt Lou's hand.

"Pleased to meet you, too," he said enthusiastically. "I love your chicken!"

Lou laughed. "It's an old recipe that my great-grandmother passed on to me, God rest her soul. The piece of paper that she wrote it on has long turned to dust, so I make it from memory. It's an old N'Orleans recipe. That's where Big John and I hail from."

Lou pointed an index finger at one temple. "But don't you worry none, Trevor," she said. "The recipe's right in here, safe and sound. Maybe I'll teach it to your mother one day so she can fix it at home."

After making some more small talk with Gabby and Trevor, Aunt Lou gently pulled Gabby aside.

"Are you and Trevor doing okay?" she asked. "I'm sorely busy tonight, but I ain't blind. I've seen the looks that some of the other parents are sendin' your way. Damned rude, if you ask me. Much as I'd like to, I can't do anything about them. But if any of the ranch staff acts like that, you just let me know. I'll read 'em the riot act, but good."

Gabby smiled. "Thank you for that. It's only natural, I suppose. I'm hoping that as time goes by, it'll stop."

"All right, then," Lou said. "But if you have any concerns, you bring 'em to me."

"You're the second person to tell me that," Gabby said.

"And just who was the first one?" Lou asked. "That old buzzard Mr. Ram, I suppose? I heard that he kidnapped you, the second you set foot on the porch. Waylaying people like that is a favorite trick of his. That, and making sure that Butch and Sundance keep Wyatt's 'scratchy Jag' all messed up."

"'Scratchy Jag'?" Gabby asked.

"Yep," Lou answered. "But that's another story. Remind me to tell you about it sometime."

"By the way, Ram saw through your iced tea gesture," Gabby said. She smiled and leaned a bit closer. "I think he's got you figured out."

Aunt Lou threw back her head and laughed. "That's the problem with that man! He thinks he's got *everybody* figured out. Trust me, child, he don't."

"Are you talking about me again, Aunt Lou?" another voice asked.

They turned to see Wyatt approaching. "No, Mr. Wyatt," Aunt Lou answered. "Like usual, I was cussin' out that rascal father of yours."

"Do you mind if I borrow Gabby and Trevor for a while?" Wyatt asked.

"You go right ahead," Aunt Lou answered. "Besides, I need to get back to my chickens! These guests of yours are eating up a storm."

Wyatt looked at the mother and son. "You two are coming with me," he said with a smile.

"Where are you taking us?" Gabby asked.

"There's someone I want you to meet," Wyatt answered.

"You'll like her. But be forewarned—her condition is delicate."

Gabby and Trevor gave each other curious looks as Wyatt led them around the side of the big house and across the front yard. As might be expected, more than one pair of inquisitive eyes followed them.

On entering the well-lit barn, Wyatt turned a corner then led Gabby and Trevor down a section of a concrete corridor he had not shown the group during his tour. When they reached another row of stalls, Wyatt stopped before one of them. Gabby and Trevor looked over the top of the Dutch door.

"I'd like you to meet Sadie," Wyatt said. "She's formally registered as Sadie of the Flying B, but to us, she's just Sadie. She's pregnant, by the way. Sadie is the best quarter horse broodmare in Florida, perhaps in the entire country. I know that the therapy program doesn't officially start until Wednesday, but I thought that Trevor might like a head start on his education."

Everyone looked with admiration at the gray mare. She was a beautiful creature, her mane and tail a shade lighter than her coat, her strong chest and shoulder muscles bulging just beneath her skin. Although Gabby understood little about horses, she could see that Sadie was pregnant. Gabby also noticed that Sadie's stall was larger than the others, and there was more straw on the floor.

"Would you like to go in and see her?" Wyatt asked.

Gabby recoiled a little. For her, standing on one side of the sturdy door was one thing, but actually going into the stall was quite another.

"Uh, well, like I told you at brunch, horses scare me to death," Gabby answered.

"I know," Wyatt said. "But it'll be okay. Sadie's good with strangers."

Wyatt slid the bolt on the lower door, and the three of them walked inside. Wyatt walked up to Sadie and took hold of her bridle.

"Come on, girl," he said softly. "You've got visitors."

When Wyatt led Sadie closer, Gabby tentatively rubbed her head. Sadie's huge dark eyes were far apart, and seemed like deep, endless pools. His own eyes wide with admiration, Trevor simply stood there, staring. He had never seen so impressive an animal, and unlike his mother, he showed no fear at all.

"When is she due?" Gabby asked.

"Three more weeks," Wyatt answered, "perhaps four."

"Can I touch her?" Trevor asked Wyatt.

"Sure," Wyatt answered. "You might as well get used to it. Come Wednesday, you'll be handling horses a lot."

Trevor ran his hand along Sadie's slightly curved back. When she whinnied and swished her tail, Trevor smiled. For the first time in Wyatt's presence, Trevor's grin was truly genuine. Save for the red Windbreaker, James Dean had temporarily vanished.

Trevor glanced at Wyatt. "Can I help take care of her on the days I'm here?" he asked suddenly.

Wyatt was taken aback by Trevor's unexpected request. Moreover, he was unsure how to respond because Sadie needed special care that Trevor didn't know how to give. He was impressed by Trevor's obvious concern for the horse, and he wanted to encourage it. But if he agreed, he would have to limit Trevor's involvement to simple tasks.

Because this was Gabby's decision, Wyatt looked to her for guidance before answering. For a moment he thought he saw some shininess in her eyes. Then Gabby cleared her throat and gave Wyatt a nearly imperceptible nod. He nodded back.

"I think we can arrange something," Wyatt answered. "Perhaps you could clean her stall and brush her coat. Until you know more about horses, we'll have to limit it to that. But there's something else to consider."

"What?" Trevor asked.

"You'll still have to take care of the horse assigned to you during your therapy," Wyatt said. "After all, we can't forget why you're here. But if your mother agrees, I think we can work something out. Chances are, this will also mean that you two will be the last visitors to leave the ranch each day."

Trevor looked at Gabby with begging eyes. "Can I?" he asked.

Gabby nodded. "If it's all right with Wyatt, it's all right with me. But remember something. You're the one who asked for this extra responsibility. That means you can't shirk it later if you get tired of it. Wyatt will be relying on you to hold up your end, so make sure that you do."

"I will," Trevor promised.

Gabby nodded. "Then I guess Sadie is now partly your responsibility."

For the first time since his father's death, Trevor truly beamed with delight. "Thank you!" he said. "And thank you, too, Wyatt!"

Wyatt smiled. "Since that's settled, we might as well get this relationship started," he said.

He produced the two sugar cubes he had taken earlier and handed them to Trevor. "Those are for Sadie," he said. "You'll find that horses love sugar. Give her a sugar cube from time to time, and she'll be your friend forever."

"Really?" Trevor asked.

"Yep," Wyatt answered. "But first, let me show you a trick that no one else at the Flying B knows about. Until now, it had always been my and Sadie's little secret. First hold the sugar cubes in one hand."

Trevor did as he was told. "Okay," he said.

"Now I want you to lick the palm of your free hand," Wyatt said. "Get it good and wet."

"Why?" Trevor asked.

Wyatt smiled. "You'll see."

Trevor felt a bit foolish, but he did as Wyatt asked.

"Rub one of the sugar cubes hard against your wet palm," Wyatt said. "Do it until your hand is good and sticky."

As Trevor again obeyed, Gabby gave Wyatt a questioning look. Wyatt winked at her.

"Now you can feed Sadie the sugar cubes," Wyatt said to Trevor. "Fully open your dry hand, and place your thumb tight alongside it. Then make sure that your palm is as flat as it can be, and set the cubes on it."

Trevor did as he was told and held his hand out. After gently taking the cubes between her lips, Sadie munched them contentedly with her long, uniform teeth, then whinnied again.

"Now hold your sticky palm up to her muzzle," Wyatt said. "Don't worry—she'll understand. Sadie and I have been doing this for a long time."

"What part of her is her muzzle?" Trevor asked.

Remembering how little Trevor knew about horses, Wyatt smiled. "The muzzle is her mouth."

As Trevor followed Wyatt's instructions, Sadie eagerly licked his palm. When Sadie finished, Trevor briskly rubbed his palm against the leg of his jeans.

Wyatt laughed. "It tickles, doesn't it?" he asked.

"It does!" Trevor exclaimed. "Can I do it again?"

Wyatt shook his head. "Horses love sugar, but it's not good to give them too much. And now you must promise me something."

"What?" Trevor asked.

"You must never show Sadie's trick to anyone else," Wyatt answered.

"I won't," Trevor said solemnly.

Trevor rubbed Sadie's face again. No sooner did he stop than she affectionately nudged him, nearly toppling him. Trevor laughed.

"See?" Wyatt asked. "She likes you already."

Gabby looked at her watch. She would have loved to stay, but tomorrow was another school day. "Time to go, young man," she said.

Trevor's sadness returned. "All right," he said.

"Don't worry," Wyatt said cheerfully. "She'll be here waiting for you when you come back on Wednesday. Next time, I'll show you where I keep my secret stash of sugar cubes."

After Wyatt opened the stall door and the three of them walked out, Gabby leaned closer to him. "Can you think of a reason to send Trevor back to the big house ahead of us?" she whispered. "I'd like a word with you alone."

Wyatt shut the stall door, thinking. "Did Trevor like Aunt Lou's chicken?" he whispered back.

Gabby nodded. "Was there anyone who didn't?"

Wyatt smiled and looked for Trevor. The boy had wandered across the concrete alleyway. He was looking closely at an old weather-beaten saddle, lying on some hay bales.

"Hey, Trevor!" Wyatt shouted. "Go and tell Aunt Lou that I want her to wrap up some Cajun chicken halves for you and your mom to take home! Would you like that?"

"Yes!" Trevor answered.

"Then get going before they're all gone!" Wyatt said.

"Great!" Trevor exclaimed. In no time flat, he had run from the barn and was well on his way back to the big house.

As Wyatt and Gabby left the barn and started walking across the dewy grass, Wyatt turned to look at her. "So what's on your mind?" he asked.

When Gabby stopped walking, Wyatt paused alongside her. As she looked into Wyatt's face, the moonlight highlighted his prominent cheekbones and strong jaw, causing him to look like some heroic statue that had been chiseled from solid granite. She suddenly thought that he was the handsomest man she had ever seen as he stood before her in that relaxed way of his. Then she caught herself and forced her mind back to the moment.

"What you just did with Trevor," she said. "It was wonderful. I haven't seen him that happy since his father died."

Wyatt smiled. "Thanks. Horses and young people are good for each other. Trevor has a long way to go, but tonight was a start.

Perhaps we might turn your young James Dean into a proper cowboy after all."

"Tell me," Gabby said. "That business about Sadie licking Trevor's palm—is it really a secret?"

"It is," Wyatt answered, "and I was happy to share it with him. Every boy needs to feel special in some way, and having a secret helps. I remember one time when Danny was eight years old. He and I—"

Wyatt suddenly quieted. "Sorry," he said. "I didn't mean for that to come out."

"That's okay," Gabby answered.

Wyatt managed a little smile. "It seems that our eight-hundred-pound gorilla has shown up again. I must find a way of dealing with him. I'm pretty good at shooting alligators. Maybe I could just shoot him, too."

Gabby smiled thankfully. This time, it had been Wyatt who had put them more at ease. Even so, they each knew that becoming truly comfortable with each other might never be possible.

As Wyatt stood looking at her, he suddenly realized that this was the first time they had been truly alone. It felt good, like something that had long been missing had suddenly returned, and was breathing new life into his soul.

Reverend Jacobson had been wrong. Gabby wasn't just a looker. She was truly beautiful. But she was more than that. She was honest, caring, and strong. And as Wyatt continued to look into her eyes, he realized something else. He had become attracted to this woman.

But he also knew that he shouldn't be. Despite how much he

felt drawn to her, his wounds were still too deep, too overpowering, and, above all, too much like her own. Almost as quickly as his attraction had surfaced, his armor returned to again guard him from her, and keep him from violating Krista's memory. It was a protective reaction so instinctive and forceful, he doubted it would ever leave him. Trying to overcome the conflict roiling in his heart, he closed his eyes for several moments.

Gabby noticed the change in him. "Are you all right?" she asked.

Wyatt nodded. "Sorry," he answered. "Just a bit tired, I guess."

Jesus, he thought. *I can't afford to feel this way. It just wouldn't work . . . there are too many old hurts to overcome . . . Krista's memory is still too precious to me . . .*

Wyatt looked at his Rolex. It was nearly 10 P.M. "We'd best get back," he said. "You must be eager to get home."

For Gabby, nothing could have been further from the truth. She wished she could stand there looking into his face all night, as the moonlight shone down and the silky dew gathered around them. But she couldn't, and she knew it.

"You're right," she answered. "Everyone must be wondering what has become of us."

They remained quiet as they walked back to the pool area. It was a pleasant kind of stillness that Wyatt found comfortable and forgiving. When they reached the pool, they saw that the visitors were leaving. Trevor was sitting beside Ram, happily feeding left-over chicken bits to Butch and Sundance. Aunt Lou had wrapped several chicken halves in aluminum foil for Trevor to take home. As Wyatt left Gabby's side to bid farewell to the departing guests, Gabby walked up to Trevor.

"Did you ask Mr. Blaine if you could feed the dogs?" she asked.

"He didn't need to," Ram answered. "It was my idea. And for Christ's sake, don't call me Mr. Blaine."

Gabby laughed.

"What's so funny?" Ram asked.

"Seems like the apple didn't fall far from the tree," she answered.

"I hereby lay sole legal claim to that complaint," Ram said. "Hell, Wyatt's still a pup. He doesn't know the meaning of the word 'old'!"

After a time Wyatt returned, holding a glass of Chardonnay in one hand. Gabby walked up to him and looked into his eyes.

"It's late, and we should be going," she said. "Thank you for everything." She turned and looked back at Ram. "And thank you, too, Ram."

Ram smiled. "That's better," he said.

"Good night," Wyatt said to Gabby and Trevor. "We'll see you on Wednesday."

Trevor grabbed his precious chicken halves and he and Gabby headed for their car. As they went, Ram gave Wyatt a sly look.

"Pull up a chair and sit a spell before you turn in," he said. "You look beat."

Wyatt grabbed a pool chair and placed it alongside his father's. He stretched his legs before him, crossing one boot over the other. This first day of New Beginnings had tired him right down to his bones.

Ram looked at Wyatt's wine and scowled. "Let me taste that," he said.

"What for?" Wyatt asked. "You hate wine."

"Can't an old man change his mind once in a while?" Ram asked. "You'd best let me do so now, while I still have a mind left."

Wyatt sighed and handed over his glass. Rather than taste it, Ram chuckled and poured the Chardonnay straight into the grass. The delicate glass went straight down after it.

"Okay," Wyatt said. "I'll bite. Do you think I've had too much to drink?"

"Nope," Ram answered. "But if I've taught you anything, I've taught you this: if you're going to drink, do it right! No god-damned frog water! It's nothing more than old grape juice! I told your mother the same thing the day she announced she wanted to install a wine cellar! Besides, the French don't like us! If we're smart, next time we won't bail 'em out of their troubles!"

Wyatt sighed. He was too tired to argue, but Ram obviously wasn't. *Where does he get all that energy?* Wyatt wondered.

Ram walked to the beverage table then returned with a bottle of Jack Daniel's and two glasses. He poured some into each glass then handed one to Wyatt before sitting down again.

Wyatt relaxed into his chair and looked around. All the visitors had finally left; Aunt Lou and the three house girls were finishing up their cleaning. Butch and Sundance, their bellies full of chicken, lounged beside Ram's chair. Sundance snored lazily.

Wyatt took a sip of the bourbon and smiled. *The old man is right,* he thought. *This is better.*

"Did Morg leave?" Wyatt asked.

"Yep," Ram answered. "Like the nitpicker that he is, he took all the forms the parents signed home with him. He'll probably start filing them in his sleep."

"Could be," Wyatt said.

Ram sighed and shifted his weight in his chair. "I saw you skedaddle away with Gabby and Trevor. You raised some eyebrows, I assure you. Where'd you go?"

"I introduced them to Sadie," Wyatt said. "They looked like they needed a break from all the slings and arrows."

Ram nodded. "Yeah, I noticed that, too. It was to be expected, I guess. Did it help?"

Wyatt nodded. "Trevor finally perked up. I'm sure that you could tell."

"And his mother?" Ram asked.

"It helped Gabby, too," Wyatt answered simply.

Ram raised his bushy eyebrows. "Hmmm . . . so it's *Gabby*, now, is it? My, my . . ."

Wyatt took another sip of bourbon. "Jesus, would you lay off for once?"

Ram chuckled softly. "Okay, son. But just for the record, I happen to think she's one hell of a woman. A man could get lost in those eyes."

Wyatt said nothing while the tiki torches gently flickered, the smell of Aunt Lou's chicken lingering in the warm night air. As his father's words echoed in his mind, Wyatt closed his eyes and laid his head back against his chair.

FIFTEEN

I'M OUT," WYATT said. After tossing his cards on the table, he took another sip of beer.

"Me, too," Jim Mason answered.

Morgan was still in the game. Mercy was aggravating him, and he wanted to force her hand. "Call," he said while tossing another ten dollars' worth of chips into the pot. Big John also folded. Of the six players, only Morgan and Mercy were still in.

Mercy turned over her hole card. She held two pairs, aces and eights. It was the "dead man's hand," so called because it was exactly what Wild Bill Hickok was holding when he was murdered while playing poker in Deadwood, Colorado. Mercy looked into Morgan's best poker face.

"Dead man's hand," she said. "That's hard to beat, Morg. Let's see 'em."

Morgan scowled and revealed his hole card. He hadn't made his flush and had been trying to bluff her.

Rather than chide Morgan again, Mercy decided that it was Wyatt's turn. "You coward," she said to him. "Couldn't take it, huh? It's about time I started getting even."

Wyatt again sipped his beer. "I didn't have the cards. Knowing when to get out is just as important as knowing when to push it."

"Well, this time I pushed it pretty good!" Mercy exclaimed. Her tone was needlessly haughty, like she didn't care who she might offend.

Mercy gleefully raked in the chips. There had been about one hundred dollars in that pot. Wyatt was glad to see her win it, but he guessed that she was still in the hole. These were friendly games, but with moderate-to-high stakes. If the night went long, Mercy could lose more than she could afford. She was a good player, and she was known for clever bluffing. But her drinking sometimes made her reckless, causing her to bet foolishly.

Mercy was usually good natured during the games, even when she lost. But tonight her mood was unexpectedly combative. Since the moment the game started, she had consistently downed one gin and tonic after another. After a time she brazenly decided that she no longer needed the mixer, so she brought the gin to the table and started drinking straight from the bottle. The more she drank, the more her temperament and judgment deteriorated. It was as if she had some ax to grind and was determined to take it out on everyone.

Even so, Mercy was happy with her newly won pot. She giggled, then made a great show of clumsily stacking her chips with fingers that behaved like they had minds of their own.

Morgan looked at Wyatt and raised his eyebrows. Clearly, Mercy was getting on everyone's nerves. Wyatt could break up the game and send everyone home, but he still felt like playing. When he looked at Morgan, he only shrugged his shoulders.

It was nearly eleven P.M. The poker game had been in progress for more than four hours, but no one was ready to cash out. At the Flying B, a three-hour game was considered brief. Often they lasted five hours or more. It was not unheard of for the players to try to best one another until dawn.

Poker games were a long-standing tradition at the ranch, and they were always held the first Tuesday night of each month. Ram had started the tradition some forty-odd years before, when Blaine & Blaine was still a fledgling law firm. Back then he shrewdly used the games to expand his growing network of friends and business contacts, and he was also sly enough to know when purposely losing was to his advantage. Although on his good days Ram could still play with the best of them, recently he was content just to watch sometimes. True to his ornery nature, he had no qualms about openly criticizing someone's play. It also amused and pleased Ram to know that today's poker games were still being held on the same old mahogany table as in days gone by.

Wyatt loved poker because he considered it to be the only form of gambling that truly tested one player against another. He enjoyed Florida casino gambling from time to time, but never took it seriously because the odds were stacked against the player and the longer someone persisted, the greater the chance of losing.

Even if a player won, over time he would surely give it all back, and probably more. But with poker, everything was each one's own fault. The odds against each player were the same, making the game largely a matter of skill and nerve. Each person seated at this old table had plenty of both.

Like tonight, with the usual players being Wyatt, Morgan, Mercy, Big John, Jim Mason, and Kyle Jacobs. Jim and Kyle were ranch hands of long standing. Along with Mercy and Big John, Jim was one of the hands Wyatt had chosen as an equestrian coach for New Beginnings. He was a tall, quiet bachelor in his midfifties who had worked at the ranch for some thirty or so years. Kyle was a married Boca native in his midthirties.

The game was always the same—five-card stud, with four cards faceup and one hole card. Because it was Wyatt's turn to deal, he gathered up the cards then gave them two quick, waterfall-style shuffles.

After everyone anted up, Wyatt declared that deuces were wild. He then dealt one card facedown to each player and another one faceup. He glanced around the table to see that his show card, the queen of diamonds, was highest. That made him the first bettor. From this point forward, every card would be dealt faceup.

"Check," he said.

Morgan sat on Wyatt's left. "Five bucks," he said, tossing in a chip.

Mercy swallowed another belt of gin then clumsily threw a five-dollar chip onto the pile. Everyone else went in.

Wyatt dealt each player another card. This time Mercy held the high hand, with a pair of nines showing. She grinned stupidly

as she fumbled with her holdings. After painstakingly segregat-
ing four blue chips, she tossed them into the pot.

"Twenty . . . bucks," she said.

Everyone again stayed in. All the hole cards must be good,
Wyatt realized. If this kept up, the pot would become a big one.
He then dealt another round of cards.

Mercy got another nine, giving her triple nines and again
making hers the high hand. She tossed four red chips onto the
pile. "Forty bucks," she said thickly.

"I'm out," Big John said.

"Me, too," replied Jim.

Jim and Big John tossed away their cards.

"I'll stay," Kyle answered as he matched the bet. His show
cards were a five, six, and a seven of differing suits, probably
meaning that he was hoping for a straight.

Wyatt was showing the king, queen, and jack of diamonds.
They looked pretty, but like Kyle's cards, still didn't amount to
much. As he sat thinking, Mercy gave him a nasty look. Her eyes
were heavy; she started wavering back and forth in her chair.

"Stay in, you coward," she said thickly. "It doesn't matter if
you lose. You're a Blaine, after all. And everybody knows that the
Blaines have more money than God."

The game room went as silent as a tomb. Never had any
of these men heard Mercy say anything remotely critical of the
Blaine family, much less of Wyatt. For several tense moments no
one spoke. Morgan shot Wyatt another meaningful glance. Wyatt
quickly nodded back then looked across the table at Mercy. His
expression was unforgiving.

"You're drunk," he said softly, "so I'm going to let that comment slide. But don't push me again. I'm not in the mood. However this hand goes, it'll be the last one of the night."

Undaunted by Wyatt's warning, Mercy dismissively waved one hand in the air. "Yeah, yeah, cowboy. You in or out?"

Wyatt answered her by tossing forty dollars' worth of chips onto the pile. Then he dealt more cards to Mercy, Kyle, and himself.

Kyle's card was a jack, and of no help. "I'm out," he said. That left only Wyatt and Mercy.

Mercy looked stupidly at Wyatt's king, queen, and jack of diamonds. Wyatt was on his way toward a royal flush. But even in her drunken stupor, Mercy knew that the odds of Wyatt pulling off a royal flush were very poor. Mercy's three nines were still the high hand. Confident that she was about to win, she gave Wyatt an evil-looking smile.

"It's just you and me now," she said. She drunkenly counted out some chips and tossed them onto the pile. "One hundred bucks says you'll turn tail and run."

Wyatt answered Mercy's bet then dealt her final card. To everyone's amazement, Mercy got the last nine. That gave her four of a kind, a nearly unbeatable hand. Wyatt sat back in his chair, thinking.

What they say must be true, he decided. *God really does protect drunks and little children. And just now, Mercy is both.*

Wyatt dealt his final card. As it fell to the table, Big John whistled and Kyle said something that should never be repeated in church.

Wyatt now had the king, queen, jack, and ten of diamonds.

He was only one card away from a royal flush. Even so, the odds against fulfilling it remained nearly impossible. Still certain that Wyatt was beaten, Mercy gave him another nasty smile.

"You can't have the nine of diamonds," she said proudly, "because I've got it. That means the only way you can win is if you've got the ace. It isn't showing, but the odds against you having it are just too long, even for the famous Wyatt Blaine."

Reaching out, Mercy shoved all her remaining chips into the center of the table.

"All in," she said. "Top that, rich boy."

Wyatt was becoming incensed. Trying to remember that the gin was doing Mercy's talking for her, he regarded her calmly. He looked at his hole card and then into her eyes again. To everyone's surprise, he, too, pushed in all his chips.

"All in," he said.

Mercy turned over her hole card. It was the jack of clubs and no help to her. But that didn't change the fact that she held four of a kind.

Wyatt nodded. "You're right, Mercy," he said. "I don't have the ace."

Cackling with delight, Mercy reached unsteadily toward the huge pile of chips. For a moment, Wyatt thought she might fall out of her chair.

"Don't you want to see my hole card?" he asked.

Mercy snorted out a laugh. "What for? You already told me that you don't have the ace."

"I don't have *that* ace," Wyatt said. He then turned over his hole card.

It was the two of clubs—one of the wild cards that Wyatt had called at the start of the hand. It served as the ace of diamonds that he had needed. He had his royal flush, and it beat Mercy's four nines.

"Holy Christ," Morgan said.

"You can say that again," Kyle breathed.

Mercy was stupefied. Her drunken mind had forgotten that deuces were wild, and that Wyatt might be holding one.

"Son of a bitch . . . ," she breathed.

Because she had gone all in and lost, she was flat broke. She tried to stand, but no sooner did she come to her feet than her eyes fluttered closed and she collapsed. Morgan reached out and caught her in his arms.

"Jesus!" Morgan said. "She's so plastered she can't even stand up!"

Wyatt stood and gestured to Morgan. "Give her to me," he said. "I'll take her home."

Glad to be rid of her, Morgan did as his brother asked. She hung limply in Wyatt's grasp, her arms, legs, and blond pigtails all dangling lifelessly toward the floor. Wyatt looked over at Big John, who was serving as cashier.

"How much was her buy in?" Wyatt asked.

Big John consulted his notepad. "Four hundred," he said.

"This game is over," Wyatt said. "Cash everybody out. But before you do, get four hundred bucks from the till and stuff it into my pocket. Take it from my share."

"Will do, boss," Big John said.

After Big John did as Wyatt had asked, Wyatt started carrying Mercy toward the game-room door. "Everyone get some sleep," Wyatt shouted over his shoulder. "We have another big day tomorrow."

After Wyatt left the room, Morgan cashed out. He saw that Big John's face was long with worry. "What the hell was eating her?" Morgan asked. "I've never seen her like that! I know that she likes her booze, but Jesus . . ."

Big John rubbed his chin. "I don't rightly know. Whatever her demons are, they're doozies. But if anyone can find out, it's Mr. Wyatt."

"I hope you're right . . . ," Morgan answered.

&

FIVE MINUTES LATER, Wyatt arrived at Mercy's cottage. The place was dark and quiet. He gently lowered Mercy onto a porch chair then searched for the spare key.

To his relief, it still lay on top of the door sill. He opened the door and turned on the lights. After again taking Mercy in his arms, he carried her into the cottage. Before putting Mercy in the bedroom, Wyatt took a moment to look around. He hadn't been here in some time, but the place hadn't changed.

The cottage was small and attractively furnished. There was a living room, a kitchen, two bedrooms, and a den. Little reminders of Mercy lay all about—an open veterinary textbook here, a cowboy hat there, a cup of unfinished coffee sitting on an end table. Like Mercy herself, the place was a portrait in organized clutter.

Wyatt carried Mercy into the master bedroom and laid her on the bed. When her head hit the pillow, she let out a little groan and curled up in the fetal position. She looked childlike lying there, with her blond braids falling onto her shoulders. Wyatt considered putting her under a mercilessly cold shower, clothes and all, then decided to just let her sleep it off. He sighed and shook his head.

Come sunrise, I wouldn't want to be her, he thought. *No hangover remedy in the world is going to cure the result of this bender.*

Then he remembered her money. Reaching into his jeans, he retrieved the four hundred dollars. She didn't deserve it, but he wanted her to have it. As he placed it on top of the nightstand he spied a photo there, encased in a pewter frame. He picked it up and looked at it.

It was a shot of him and Mercy, taken inside the main barn. Because Krista had often prowled the ranch with her camera, Wyatt guessed that she had taken it. Wyatt and Mercy looked happy, but he couldn't remember when this photo had been taken. Deciding to leave the little mystery unsolved, he placed the photo back on the nightstand and headed for the door.

"Wyatt . . . ?" Mercy called out.

Wyatt walked back and sat down on the bed.

"What happened?" she asked thickly.

"You passed out from too much gin," he answered. "And you're still drunk. Rather than take you home, maybe I should have laid you down in the family cemetery because, come sunrise, you'll wish that you were dead."

She groaned and rubbed her face with her hands. "You're right," she said as she tried to focus on his face. "Either you're circling the ceiling . . . or . . . I'm loaded."

It was an effort, but she managed to rise up onto her elbows.

Her eyes closed tightly for several moments before opening again.

"The poker game . . . ," she said. "Did I make an ass of myself?"

Wyatt shook his head. "No," he answered. "You made a *perfect* ass of yourself. You said some pretty awful things, but I'm doing my best to forget them. I can't speak for the others."

Mercy's eyes filled with tears then she turned over and buried her face in her pillow. Wyatt waited quietly, hoping that her crying would soon stop. He wanted to leave, but first he needed to know that she would be all right.

Mercy finally quieted. When she again looked into his face, her expression was searching. She placed one palm against his cheek.

"Why did you do it?" she asked softly.

Wyatt took her hand from his cheek. "What are you talking about?" he asked.

"Why did you allow that Powers woman into our lives?" Mercy demanded. "Don't you know how much pain she'll cause to you and to me? She'll hurt us, Wyatt, I just know it. She'll take away what we have!"

Wyatt closed his eyes. *So this is what caused her to go off the deep end tonight. What a fool I've been not to see it.*

Wyatt looked sternly into Mercy's eyes. He wanted to make her understand. But if he was going to get through to her, he would have to be harsh. He took her by her shoulders and pulled her nearer.

"Listen to me," he said. "There is no 'us.' There never was. You're a wonderful girl, and any man would be proud to be with you. But I don't love you, Mercy, and I never have. You're like a sister to me, but that's as far as it goes. After what happened between us four years ago, I thought you understood that. If you didn't, you certainly should have."

Given the absent look in her eyes, he doubted that he was getting through to her. *Perhaps she wants "us" so badly that she simply refuses to listen.*

"You're falling in love with her, aren't you?" Mercy asked. The look on her face had suddenly become angry.

"What are you talking about?" Wyatt demanded.

"You heard me!" she shouted. "I was there, in the barn, when you took her and her son in to see Sadie! Then later, outside, I saw how you looked into her eyes!"

"You were there?" Wyatt demanded. "You spied on us?"

Mercy nodded stupidly. "Call it whatever you want! I might be drunk now, but I wasn't last night when I saw the two of you mooning over each other! You might as well have screwed her right there in the grass!"

Mercy's harsh outburst confused Wyatt. As he searched his feelings, he honestly didn't know whether he was angry because Mercy was being so brazen, or because she was right. Tired of trying to reason with a drunk, he let go of her and she slumped against the bed.

"I'm done arguing with you, Mercy," he said. "And I never want to talk about this again. There's nothing between us and there never has been. I've done all that I can to convince you of it. If you can't accept it, then I don't care anymore. You haven't totally burned your bridges with me, but you've come damned close."

Wyatt stood and looked down at her angrily. "Despite your condition, I expect you to be at work tomorrow. And one more thing—make sure that Trevor isn't among the teens you will be teaching. Steer clear of Gabby, too. I don't need any more problems than I already have."

Wyatt turned and walked to the door. As he went, Mercy started sobbing again.

When Wyatt turned out the light, she reached one hand toward him. As he stood there looking at her, the Florida moonlight streamed through the bedroom windows and highlighted his face. Just like Gabby Powers the night before, Mercy wanted everything to remain just as it was so that she could look at him all night.

"I love you . . . ," she whispered.

"It doesn't matter," Wyatt answered coldly. Then he shut the door and was gone.

SIXTEEN

T REVOR ANXIOUSLY LOOKED up from his reading. The wall clock in the Jefferson High School library said eleven twenty A.M. Only forty minutes remained before the start of his next class, and he wanted to use his time wisely. He had chosen this study-hall period to research American quarter horses.

Trevor was immensely glad that Wednesday had come. Although he wasn't looking forward to the group-therapy sessions, he was very eager to start the equestrian training. After meeting Sadie, he wanted to absorb as much about her breed as he could. He was stunned by how much there was to learn.

Trevor paused in his reading for a moment, remembering his first day at the ranch. His newfound excitement came as a welcome surprise to him. He had fully expected to hate the Flying B, and everyone and everything associated with it. But now he couldn't wait to get back.

All the way home, he had been an absolute chatterbox. Gabby had listened politely as Trevor went on and on about Sadie and how much he looked forward to caring for her. Trevor had done a marvelous job of overstating his importance, and Gabby had wisely agreed with him.

Trevor's exhilaration continued unabated after he and his mother arrived home. Although it was already late, he stayed up for another two hours, munching Aunt Lou's cold chicken and researching American quarter horses on the Internet. Only after Gabby insisted did he finally give in and go to bed.

Just prior to slipping between the sheets, he carefully placed his boots under his bed and hung his Stetson on one of the bedposts. Before sleep finally found him, he remained awake for hours, thinking of Sadie and the Flying B. The following morning Trevor had surprised Gabby even further when he insisted on wearing his new boots to school. Not wanting to waste another minute, Trevor eagerly turned his mind back to his reading.

Suddenly his schoolbooks went flying off the library table, and at first he didn't know what was happening. He looked down to see his books lying on the floor, still bound together by his father's old leather belt. As he bent down to pick them up, another pair of hands grasped them first.

Trevor looked up to see Tim Richardson, the boy Trevor had scuffled with not long ago, greedily clutching his books. John Hanson and Bill Memphis stood alongside Tim. The three were nearly inseparable. Roaming the school together lent the trio a boldness they might not have possessed individually, and they used it to their full advantage. Trevor wasn't the first boy they had harassed, nor would he be the last.

Trevor glared hotly at Tim. Like Trevor, Tim was large for his age. His nose remained somewhat bruised from Trevor's punch. As the three boys stood ominously before him, Trevor tried to control himself. His books could be replaced, but seeing his father's cherished belt in Tim's hands made him furious. When Trevor reached for it, Tim backed up. Teasing Trevor further, Tim started swinging the books to and fro by the leather belt.

"Give those to me!" Trevor shouted. "They're mine!"

Tim shook his head nastily. "They're mine now, you dumb bastard," he said. He pointed at Trevor's boots and laughed. "Look!" he said to Hanson and Memphis. "The horse retard is wearing cowboy boots! Isn't that sweet! Are those the same boots that you wear when you shovel horse crap? We hear that all the horse retards have to wear them!"

Trevor clenched his fists and took another step forward. But Tim was equally quick, and he backed up again.

"What did you just call me?" Trevor demanded.

"You're one of the horse retards!" Richardson answered. "That's what everyone is calling the losers in that stupid program! Horse retards!"

Trevor again reached out one hand. "Give me my books!" he ordered.

Tim made a great show of examining the leather belt. "Is this a *cowboy* belt?" he asked nastily. "It doesn't look lame enough to be a cowboy belt! I hear that it was your old man's belt. He wasn't stupid enough to be a cowboy, but I guess that his son is. Isn't that right, horse retard?"

"Give it to me!" Trevor shouted. "Or I'll paste you again!"

Tim smiled and shook his head. "This time you're outnumbered." As the words left Richardson's mouth, Hanson and Memphis stepped closer.

By now, other students had gathered around. Trevor took no notice of them. His eyes still locked on Richardson, he again reached out his hand.

"Give me my books," he repeated, "or you'll regret it."

"So this belt belonged to your father," Richardson mused. "I hear that he was dead drunk most of the time." Richardson suddenly grasped the irony, and he laughed.

"Get it, horse retard?" he said. "*Dead* drunk! That's funny, don't you think?"

That was the final straw. With no regard for the consequences, Trevor lunged at Tim. Just as he did, a booming voice called out from across the room.

"What's going on over there?" the head librarian shouted.

Trevor turned to see Mr. Sanford approaching. He was relieved, but disappointed. He wanted his father's belt returned, and it seemed that he would get it. But he would also be deprived of taking another whack at Tim Richardson, and he had wanted to.

Sanford was a tall, burly man in his early thirties. He was the school wrestling coach and head librarian, and known for not taking any guff from unruly students. As Sanford neared, Tim smiled innocently.

"I said, *what's going on here?*" Sanford demanded.

"Nothing, sir," Tim said. "Powers dropped his books, and I picked them up for him." He happily returned Trevor's books and belt.

Just then the period bell rang. Sanford gave Tim and his friends a harsh look.

"This is over," he said. "Get lost."

Tim sneered at Trevor. "Another time," he said.

"You bet," Trevor answered.

After Tim and his friends were gone, Sanford looked at Trevor. "Are you okay?" he asked.

"It wasn't my fault!" Trevor protested. "Those jerks started it! All I was trying to do was get my stuff back!"

Sanford nodded. "I believe you. Those three are real trouble. It's a good thing this didn't happen outside. You'd have probably gotten your lights punched out."

"Not without a fight," Trevor countered. Suddenly regretting his comment, he gave Sanford a contrite look. "Are you going to report this?" he asked.

Sanford shook his head. "No," he answered. "But I'd love to, if for no other reason than to put those three on notice. I'm a friend of your mother, and I know how badly she wants you to stay in the New Beginnings Program. So as far as I'm concerned, nothing happened here."

"Thank you," Trevor answered.

Now that the moment had passed, Trevor suddenly realized how close he had come to being expelled and perhaps never seeing Sadie again. All the other times he had gotten into trouble, he hadn't cared about the consequences. To his great surprise, a wave of relief ran through him.

Sanford gave Trevor a quick smile. "Now scram," he said, "before you're late for your next class."

❧

"WHOA THERE, HOSS!" Ram said. "If you keep that up, you'll dig all the way to China! You got an ax to grind or something?"

Trevor lowered the pitchfork and wiped his brow. His blood was still boiling from today's run-in with Tim Richardson. Desperate to work off his frustration, for the last twenty minutes he had been flinging soiled straw into a nearby wheelbarrow as if his life depended on it. Because of the heat, he had removed his red Windbreaker and laid it on top of the stall door.

Panting heavily, Trevor lowered the pitchfork tips to the stall floor and leaned down onto its handle. Under Big John's watchful eye, Trevor had done his best to learn how to brush down Sadie. He had done a poor job of it, but it had been a start. Before Trevor started cleaning her stall, Big John had led Sadie from the barn and into an outdoor paddock.

Like he had seen Big John do earlier in the day, Trevor took a handkerchief from his jeans and wiped the sweat from the inner band of his Stetson. With the hat back on his head, he finally turned and looked at Ram.

"You been there long?" he asked.

Ram smiled and leaned his forearms down on top of the Dutch door of Sadie's stall.

"Long enough to know that you won't last at that rate," he

answered. "A fella has to pace himself around here. This work isn't for sissies."

Trevor laughed derisively. "Oh yeah? That's not what they're saying at school."

Ram scowled. "What are you talking about?"

"Never mind," Trevor said. "It's my problem, not yours."

Again reminded of his close call with Tim Richardson, he returned to his labors. He certainly wasn't adept at handling a pitchfork yet, but that didn't slow him down. As he hurried, sometimes more of the soiled straw went back onto the floor than into the wheelbarrow.

Ram could sense something was amiss. Two nights ago, after visiting the barn with Wyatt and Gabby, Trevor's mood had been joyful. But today he was clearly troubled.

Despite the short time he had known Trevor, Ram had come to like him. It had been a long time since Wyatt and Morgan had been boys, and having young people swarming over the ranch helped make Ram feel vibrant again. Moreover, Trevor possessed the same brooding attitude that Wyatt had once had, and those dusty memories tugged at the old man's heart. Ram could see that Trevor was hurting, and, like Wyatt, he wanted to help.

"That's good enough," Ram said. "This is a barn, not a surgical ward."

Trevor shook his head. "I'm not done," he answered as he sloppily slung yet more soiled straw toward the old wheelbarrow, some of it hitting the wall instead. The stall was already satisfactory, but that didn't seem to matter.

"I own this ranch, young man," Ram said, "and I give the

orders around here. Now put down that pitchfork. Wheel the bar-
row out into the aisle and then bring in some fresh straw, just like
Big John taught you to do."

Trevor shrugged his shoulders. After wheeling out the bar-
row, he lugged four fresh straw bales into the stall. He soon realized that he had no way to cut the bale strings. When he had done
this job for the horse that had been assigned to him, Big John had
cut the strings.

Ram smiled and fished around in his Levi's. After producing
a pearl-handled pocketknife, he handed it to Trevor.

"Flying B rule number two," he said. "Always carry a knife.
Wyatt and Morgan have knives just like that one, and they
wouldn't be caught dead without them."

"What's Flying B rule number one?" Trevor asked.

"I already told you," Ram answered. "I give the orders around
here."

Trevor looked at the knife. It was old, but still beautiful.
When he unfolded the blade, he saw the letters *RB* engraved on
it. After cutting the bale strings, he folded the knife and offered
it to Ram.

Ram shook his head. "It's yours now."

Trevor's jaw fell. "I can't accept this! It looks like you've had it
for a long time."

Ram winked at him. "That doesn't matter. I don't do this
kind of work anymore, but you're going to be doing a lot of it. It
belongs in your pocket now."

Trevor beamed. "Thank you," he said.

"You're welcome," Ram answered. "Now finish your work.
Sadie and her unborn foal are counting on you."

Trevor pocketed the knife, then scattered fresh straw all around in Sadie's stall. When he finished he grabbed up the pitchfork and his Windbreaker, shutting the door behind him. Ram took the pitchfork from him and leaned it against the wall.

"Come with me," Ram said.

When they reached the end of the aisle, Ram motioned for Trevor to sit in one of several weathered Adirondack chairs near the barn's western exit. Trevor was more than happy to oblige. He was tired and hungry, but in no hurry to go home. Ram sat down beside him and stretched out his legs.

Trevor took a moment to look around the barn. Although he was still new to the ranch, he already loved this huge old building. Its unique smells, sights, and sounds provided a comforting feeling that he found nowhere else. And of perhaps even greater importance, it was becoming a sanctuary where he could be around horses and escape his troubles for a while. Then the memory of Tim Richardson seeped in again, and he scowled.

Ram casually crossed one booted foot over the other. "So tell me," he said, "how was your first real day of New Beginnings?"

Trevor looked down at his boots. "Okay, I guess."

"It's time you learned Flying B rule number three," Ram said. "Men always look into each other's eyes when they talk."

Trevor sat up and looked squarely at Ram. *That's better,* Ram thought. Ram crossed his arms over his chest.

"How'd your first group-therapy session go?" Ram asked.

Trevor shook his head. "It was weird! We were supposed to talk about our feelings, but I'd rather shovel horse manure! The girls talked a lot more than us boys. They seemed to want to, for some reason. Jesus . . ."

Ram laughed heartily. "You'd best get used to that! It's the way of the world, my boy!"

Just then Jim Mason walked by, carrying an old saddle and bridle. When Jim tipped his hat, Ram replied by doing the same. When Trevor did not, Jim stopped and waited. Guessing that he should respond, Trevor did his best to imitate Ram's gesture. At last Jim smiled and went on his way.

"Let me guess," Trevor said. "That was Flying B rule number four."

"Number six, actually," Ram answered.

"How many rules are there?" Trevor asked.

"Can't say," Ram answered. "Nobody ever wrote 'em down. Besides, don't forget that we're also a family of lawyers. If the Flying B rules were written down, I couldn't change them whenever I wanted. After all, if it wasn't for lawyers, the world wouldn't need any."

Silence passed between the old man and the boy for a time, as horses occasionally whinnied and the Florida sun started to dip below the western horizon. It was nearly time for Ram's nightly appointment with Butch, Sundance, and Jack Daniel's.

Ram gave Trevor a knowing look. "So what's eating you?" the old man asked.

"What makes you so sure that anything's eating me?" Trevor asked.

"I've raised two boys, and I can tell when something's wrong. So fess up. Maybe I can help."

With great reluctance, Trevor told Ram about his dustup with Tim Richardson. Ram nodded thoughtfully.

"Horse retards?" he said. "That's a new one."

"Tell me about it," Trevor said.

"There's no boy in the world who hasn't been bullied at one time or another," Ram said. "The question is not whether it will happen to you, but how you deal with it."

"But I don't *know* how," Trevor answered. "Except for fighting, that is. I'm pretty good at that. I don't have anybody to talk to about stuff like this. No *man,* at least. I sure as hell can't talk to my mother about it. She'll just tell me to take it and do nothing—especially with Principal Marshall gunning for me."

"Yeah," Ram said. "It's been tough on you since the death of your father. Would you like some advice?"

Trevor's expression turned needy. "Yes," he said quietly.

"Then I'll tell you the same thing I told Wyatt and Morgan when they were being bullied," Ram said. "It helped them, and it will help you."

"What is it?" Trevor asked.

"It's simple," Ram answered. "Never wrestle in the mud with a pig."

"Huh?"

"Imagine this Richardson kid as a muddy, ornery pig," Ram said. "From the way you describe him, that shouldn't be too hard, right?"

Trevor laughed. "Right!" he said.

"There are two reasons you should avoid wrestling in the mud with the 'Richardson pig.' Can you imagine what they are?"

Trevor scowled. "Not really."

"The first reason," Ram said, "is that you'll both get dirty."

"That's true, I guess," Trevor said. "And the second reason?"

"It makes the Richardson pig happy," Ram answered.

Trevor didn't fully understand Ram's meaning, but he nodded anyway. "Are you saying that I should *never* fight?" he asked.

Ram shook his head. "No! But I'm not surprised that you're confused. In this day and age, some boys are taught to never fight. That's the worst advice in the world. If you're attacked, you must defend yourself. It's the honorable thing to do. But starting fights isn't."

"So what about the Richardson pig?" Trevor asked.

"When the time comes, remember what I told you," Ram answered. "Most likely, you'll understand it then. But never believe the fairy tale that hitting a bully will always make him give up and leave you alone. That's pure crap. Truth is, he might get right back up and beat the hell out of you. So avoid him if you can. But if you must fight, fight to win. Even if he wins, at least you tried to give as good as you got."

Trevor remained quiet for a time, trying to digest the old man's words. "Understanding this is going to take a while," he admitted.

"That's okay," Ram said. "Wyatt and Morgan didn't get it right away either. But they eventually did, and so will you. Don't worry about it. Just remember it when the time comes."

To Ram's surprise, Trevor tipped his hat to him. This time, he did a more proper job of it. "Thank you," he said. "For everything."

"You're welcome."

Just then they heard voices, and they turned to see Gabby and

Wyatt approaching. Night was falling, causing the sky to change from Florida turquoise to deep indigo. Here and there, twinkling stars started puncturing heaven's canopy. As Gabby and Wyatt entered the barn, they smiled.

"We were wondering where you were," Wyatt said to Trevor. "Did my old man kidnap you?"

"Yeah," Trevor said. "But that's okay. I learned something today."

"Time to go, young man," Gabby said. "Tomorrow's another school day."

Everyone heard the clip-clop of horse hooves, and they turned to look. Big John was leading Sadie back to her freshly cleaned stall.

"Can I take her?" Trevor asked.

"Sure thing," Big John said.

He handed Sadie's bridle lead to Trevor. After stroking Sadie's head, Trevor walked her into her stall and closed the door behind him. "Good night, girl," he said. Sadie poked her gray head out over the stall door and whinnied.

Ram gave Wyatt a sly look that Wyatt didn't fully understand. "What's Aunt Lou cooking for dinner?" Ram asked.

"Pot roast and blueberry pie," Wyatt answered skeptically. "But my guess is you already knew that."

"And have all the other teens and parents left the ranch?" Ram asked.

"Yes," Wyatt said. "But I suspect you knew that, too. Because Trevor has taken on this extra work with Sadie, he and Gabby will probably always be the last ones to leave." Wyatt raised an eyebrow. Ram was up to something, but he couldn't figure out what it was.

Ram gave Gabby a smile. "Why don't you and Trevor stay for dinner?" he asked. "Everybody else is gone, so nobody will know but us fellow conspirators. After all, you have to eat."

Gabby was unsure. "Uh . . . well . . . we really shouldn't," she said. "We wouldn't want to impose."

"Impose, hell," Ram answered. "What's the matter? Don't you like Lou's food? If not, then you can march right up to the big house and tell her yourself. I'll buy tickets to that!"

Searching for reassurance, Gabby again looked at Wyatt. "Of course you should stay," Wyatt said. "Believe me, Aunt Lou always makes enough."

"Well, I guess that we could," Gabby said.

Ram clapped his hands together. "Then it's settled! Let's go!"

As Wyatt and Gabby walked out of the barn, Ram held Trevor back. "Let's give them a little breathing room, shall we?" Ram asked.

Trevor wrinkled his brow. "Why? I'm hungry!"

"Oh, I have my reasons," Ram answered. A few moments later, he started escorting Trevor out of the barn.

"Now then," Ram said to him. "About that knife I gave you. It has a long and storied past . . ."

As Ram and Trevor walked across the grass, night fell in earnest.

SEVENTEEN

"GET UP, MR. WYATT!" Aunt Lou shouted. "It's Mr. Ram! This time he's really gone crazy! He's gonna kill himself for sure!"

Wasting no time, Aunt Lou grasped the single sheet covering Wyatt's naked body then pulled it off him and onto the floor. Wyatt snarled something unintelligible and instinctively reached for the sheet, but Aunt Lou had been quicker. When Wyatt finally realized that she was glowering down at him, he covered his groin with both hands.

"Jesus Christ, Lou!" he protested sleepily. "What's going on?"

Lou threw a pair of jeans and boots at him. "Get dressed!" she shouted. "And stop wasting time covering yourself! I raised you, for God's sake!"

Wyatt jumped from his bed to quickly pull on the jeans and

boots. When he ran to fetch a shirt, Lou threw up her hands.

"There's no time for that!" she bellowed. "Come on!" Quick as a wink, she bolted from the room.

Wyatt was amazed by how fast the big woman could move. He chased her down the staircase, through the foyer, and onto the front porch. Lou immediately hurried Wyatt across the dew-laden west lawn and toward the white-rail paddocks. When she finally stopped, she raised an arm and pointed.

"*That's* what I'm talking about!" she panted.

As Wyatt looked across the lawn, his jaw dropped. "Son of a bitch . . . ," he breathed.

Dawn was fast approaching. The Flying B was quiet save for a lone horse and rider, galloping across the dewy west lawn. The horse was a black stallion named King, and Ram sat on top of him. King's shoes had unearthed hundreds of dark gouges in the wet grass, ruining much of it. Ram had equipped King with an English-style saddle and bridle, and he held a leather riding crop in one hand. Wyatt watched in horror as Ram slapped King's haunches with the crop and galloped him straight toward an empty white-railed paddock.

Jesus! Wyatt thought. *He's going to try to jump it!*

Wyatt immediately ran toward the paddock. But Ram saw Wyatt coming, and the old man spurred King on faster. Realizing that he couldn't reach them in time, Wyatt skidded to a stop, nearly tumbling to the grass. To his horror, he could only watch helplessly as Ram drove the stallion forward.

Please, God, Wyatt thought. *Let them get over it in one piece!*

Much to Wyatt's relief, King carried Ram safely over the top rail and down into the paddock confines. King's shoulders and muzzle were frothy, and the stallion appeared exhausted. There was no telling how many times King had already jumped, but one thing was certain—if Ram ordered King over again, they might not make it.

"Dad!" Wyatt shouted. "Dad, stop! Don't go again!"

Instead of heeding his son, Ram released a piercing rebel yell. He then spurred King into yet another gallop, steering the horse straight toward the far side of the paddock.

Running as fast as he could, Wyatt tried to gauge where King would land—assuming the horse cleared the rails. If King didn't make it over, the result could be disastrous. As King and Ram launched themselves into the air, Wyatt watched with dread.

This time the exhausted horse's front hooves struck the top rail, knocking it to the ground. Mercifully, the blow did little to hinder King's momentum. Barreling through the air, the horse landed shakily on the other side of the paddock rails.

Wyatt held his breath yet again as King skidded on all fours across the wet grass. The stallion and rider finally came to a stop. Wasting no time, Wyatt ran and grabbed King's bridle. Butch and Sundance suddenly appeared and started barking madly, adding to the confusion.

Just then King reared up, and it was all Wyatt could do to keep the stallion from bolting off again. Finally the nervous horse calmed down. In the growing light of day, Wyatt saw that Ram's face was twisted with anger. Ram angrily raised his riding crop.

"What the hell do you think you're doing?" he shouted at

Wyatt. "I own this place, and no goddamned ranch hand is going to tell me what to do! Now unhand my horse!"

"Dad!" Wyatt answered. "It's me—Wyatt!"

Ram looked at his son with unseeing eyes. For several moments he just sat on top of King as if trying to decide who Wyatt was. Then his expression softened. He lowered his crop.

"Now climb down, Dad," Wyatt said. "King needs attention."

Ram finally did as Wyatt asked. Taking no chances, Wyatt relieved Ram of his crop. Ram rubbed his face with his hands and blankly looked around. For several more minutes he stood there quietly, his confused expression unchanging. Dawn had arrived and from somewhere near the main barn, Ram's old banty rooster crowed.

"Jesus," Ram finally breathed. "How the hell did I get *here*?" He looked around again then stared into Wyatt's eyes. "And what in Christ's name happened to the lawn?"

"Never mind that," Wyatt said. "I'll explain it all to you later. Right now, we need to get you into the house. And King's forelegs must be tended to."

Ram's face screwed up. "What's wrong with King's legs? And where in hell is your shirt? You look like you were raised by wolves!"

"Not now, Dad!" Wyatt said. "I want you and Aunt Lou to go back into the house."

Ram dismounted and stared incredulously at King's forelegs. Both were cut and bleeding where they'd struck the top rail of the paddock. The wounds weren't serious, but they needed care or they could turn septic. As Ram examined King, Wyatt used the opportunity to take Aunt Lou aside.

"Were you the first one to see him out here?" he asked.

"Must be," she answered. "I was gettin' up, just like I do every day about this time, when I heard whoopin' and hollerin' coming from the paddocks. I looked out my bedroom window and I saw your father out here, having a grand old time for himself. John was already about his chores, so I came and fetched you first."

Wyatt nodded. "Take him back to the big house," he said. "I'll be along after I see to King."

Just then another thought occurred to Wyatt. "After you get Ram situated, find his prescription bottle and bring it to me," he said quietly to Lou. "But don't let him know that you're doing it."

Lou scowled. "What you got in mind?"

"I've got a hunch about something," Wyatt said. "Now please take him and get going."

Wyatt and Lou heard voices, and they turned to see Mercy and Big John running toward them. Mercy was still buttoning her shirt.

"What the hell's going on?" Big John shouted.

Wyatt took Big John and Mercy aside. "Ram had another spell," he said quietly. "He was jumping King back and forth over the paddock rails. The last time, they nearly didn't make it."

Big John whistled. "In the dark and on slick grass? Christ, it's a wonder that Ram and King aren't all busted up, or worse."

Wyatt looked at Mercy then back at Big John. "King's forelegs are bleeding," he said. "The wounds don't look bad, but they need attention."

"Sure thing, boss," Big John said.

Mercy walked over to King and took his reins. After examining King's wounds, she looked at Ram. He seemed to recognize her.

"Jesus Christ, Mercy!" Ram exclaimed. "What's everybody so goddamned worried about? Can't a man go for a dawn ride anymore? Back in my day I did this every morning, come rain or shine! Who the hell made you people the boss of me?"

Wyatt walked back to where Ram was standing. "Come along, Dad," he said. "It won't be long before breakfast."

"Good!" Ram exclaimed. "For some reason, I'm starving!"

And save for you, we all know why, Wyatt thought.

While Wyatt and Lou escorted Ram back to the big house, Mercy and Big John led King away. From somewhere near the main barn, Ram's old rooster let go another arrogant cry that seemed to forgive his master's foolishness and welcome him home.

⁂

"YOU'VE BEEN FOUND OUT, old man," Wyatt said.

When Ram didn't answer, Wyatt sighed and leaned back in his chair. He knew that this talk would be difficult, but it was needed. His suspicions had been proved right, and he couldn't allow Ram to keep on fooling everyone—including himself.

It was nearly eight A.M. Despite the fracas Ram had caused, Aunt Lou had managed to lay breakfast out on time. Everyone had finished eating and was dawdling over coffee.

Ensconced behind his freshly ironed newspaper, Ram acted for all the world as if his recent misadventure had never happened. Ram sat on Wyatt's left; Big John was on his right. Lou and Mercy sat across from them. Their bellies already full of bacon and sausages, Butch and Sundance sat at Ram's feet, diligently waiting for more.

As Wyatt gave Mercy a deadpan glance, her only response was

to sheepishly look down at the remains of her half-eaten breakfast. Wyatt had told no one of their argument in her cottage, nor had he and Mercy spoken of it since. That suited Wyatt, because he was still angry with her. But in his heart he knew that he would eventually forgive her. After all was said and done, her only indiscretion was to love him, and the gin had done most of the talking. Despite his anger, Wyatt had asked Mercy to join everyone at breakfast. Wyatt was about to confront his father, and he would need all his allies around him.

"I know what you're up to," Wyatt said to Ram.

When Ram still didn't answer, Wyatt stood and pulled down Ram's crisp newspaper. As Ram removed his glasses, he scowled.

"What the hell did you do that for?" he demanded. "It's bad enough that you interrupted my morning ride. Can't a man enjoy his paper in peace anymore? I can still read, despite what you might think."

"You didn't answer me," Wyatt said.

"I didn't hear you," Ram protested.

Wyatt smirked. "You might be forgetful, but you're not deaf. So I'll put it another way. We're on to you."

"What are you talking about?" Ram asked. His lawyerly attitude had surfaced, telling everyone that he was ready for a fight.

Wyatt reached into a shirt pocket and produced Ram's Alzheimer's medication. He placed the Aricept bottle on the tabletop for everyone to see.

"That's your medication," Wyatt said. "Let's call it exhibit A."

"So what if it is?" Ram asked. "Do you think I can't recognize my own medicine anymore?"

Wyatt picked up the bottle and rattled the pills. "This bottle is full, but the date on the label says that it was issued four weeks ago. You've gone a full month without your meds and maybe longer. You should've flushed the pills down the toilet so that it looks like you're taking them. You're trying to do without them, aren't you?"

Ram looked away. "I must have forgotten to take them."

"Every morning for an entire month?" Wyatt asked. "I doubt it. Are you purposely trying to get by with less?"

"Asked and answered, Counselor," Ram said.

Wyatt sighed. "Permission to treat the witness as hostile?"

Ram only grunted and hunched his shoulders.

"Please, Dad," Wyatt said. "We need to know. It's in everyone's best interests that you take your meds."

Ram looked angrily around the table. "What is this, some goddamned intervention? If so, I don't need it!"

"King's scraped forelegs and the wrecked paddock say otherwise," Wyatt answered. "We'll call them exhibits B and C."

While Ram considered his options, the only sound was the comforting ticktock of the old grandfather clock. "Opposing counsel is badgering the witness," he finally said.

"Let's stop the courtroom banter, shall we?" Wyatt asked. "Please tell us, Dad. Are you purposely avoiding your meds?"

Ram folded his arms across his chest. "The stuff kills my appetite."

"That's horse crap!" Aunt Lou interjected. "You gobble down your artery-clogging food as good as you ever did!"

Ram shot Lou a gruff look. "Okay . . . so I still eat the same. But the Aricept keeps me awake at night, and that's the truth. An old buzzard like me needs his rest."

"So instead of telling anyone, you just stopped taking it?" Wyatt protested. "Jesus, Dad, what if everybody thought that way?"

A microsmile passed across Ram's lips. "Then I'd be a damned fool to think any other way, wouldn't I?" he asked.

Wyatt sighed and leaned back in his chair. Sometimes there was just no point in arguing with Ram. On his clear days he was as sharp as a tack, and could make even his ass-backward logic sound reasonable. But this issue was too important to ignore.

"There's more at stake here than your beauty sleep," Wyatt said. "Suppose King had gone down on that wet grass? You could have killed yourself, and King might have been injured, too. If he had broken a leg, we'd have had to put him down. Not to mention perhaps burying you, and I'm in no hurry to do that. But another stunt like this might change my mind."

Wyatt leaned closer. "I'm not sure what *your* old hide is worth these days," he added sternly. "But King is extremely valuable, not to mention the possible loss of his stud fees. And you know damned well that our insurance doesn't cover horses that are injured because of our negligence. Even Blaine and Blaine couldn't get us reimbursed for a stunt like that."

After another period of tense silence, Ram sighed. "I know all those things *now,* son," he finally admitted. "But I didn't know them *then*. I didn't know anything, except that I wanted to keep jumping King."

"I understand that, Dad," Wyatt said quietly. "That's why things have to change."

Part of Wyatt's heart felt sad for his father. But when dealing with Ram, sentiment could easily turn the tables on you. *Time for some tough love,* Wyatt thought.

"Here's what's going to happen," Wyatt said. "If you can't sleep, we'll ask your neurologist to prescribe something else for you. So that you don't 'forget' anymore, Aunt Lou will bring your new medication to breakfast each morning and we'll all watch you take it."

Ram sighed again. He had been outfoxed, a rare occurrence. Even if he protested, Wyatt would ensure that he took his medicine every day. Despite his defeat, he had to admire the way that Wyatt had outmaneuvered him. Sometimes he forgot what a good lawyer his younger son was.

"All right," he said. "The verdict is in. But I reserve my right to appeal the sentence. You know what the doctor said. The meds won't keep me from forgetting—they only slow down the process."

Wyatt smiled. "That's okay, Dad," he answered. "But you don't have to like your medicine. You just have to take it."

Wyatt removed one pill from the bottle and held it out. Ram grudgingly swallowed it with some lukewarm coffee.

"Thank you," Wyatt said.

"We all thank you," Mercy added.

"That's right," Big John added with a grin. "Besides, there's always plenty of barbed-wire fence that needs fixing. We don't need to be repairing paddocks, too."

"Very funny," Ram said. "Now then, if it's okay with all my jailers, I'm going to take my newspaper and coffee and retreat to my study. And I think I'll take Butch and Sundance with me this time. They seem to be the only ones around here who aren't trying to run my life."

Ram collected his glasses and newspaper then went to the sideboard and poured a fresh cup of coffee. With the ever faithful dogs in tow, he trudged off toward his study. When Ram was out of sight, Wyatt looked at Aunt Lou and nodded gratefully.

As he went, Ram shook his head. His experiment had failed. He had in fact been purposely ignoring his medication. Yes, it interfered with his sleep. But more important, he saw it as much a crutch as a help, and Ram had always loathed the idea of not functioning on his own.

Instead, this latest adventure of his had nearly killed him, and had injured one of the Flying B's most valuable horses. Worse, Wyatt had found out, and there could be no going back now. He took a deep breath and shook his head.

Times are changing, he thought. *Even for me . . .*

EIGHTEEN

T REVOR WAS BORED to death. *I hate these sessions,* he thought. He stole a quick glance at the grandfather clock. *Ten more minutes, and then I get to ride again. But it'll seem more like ten hours . . .*

Four full weeks of New Beginnings had passed. Seven other teens and the group's psychotherapist sat with Trevor at one end of the massive dining room table. Eight more enrollees and their therapist were holding their own session down the hall in the big-house library, while the rest of the teens took their equestrian training.

Leaning back in his chair, Trevor crossed one boot over the top of the other. He then turned and looked at Sally Hendricks, who always sat beside him during these sessions. They hadn't known each other before joining New Beginnings. During the first day's orientation at the ranch, they learned that they attended the same school, and that Sally took one of Gabby's history classes. From that knowledge, a friendship had sprung up between them.

Sally was a tall girl, Trevor's age, with long, dark hair, and a bright mind. Like Trevor, Sally had been slipping academically. The further her grades fell, the more distant she became from her family and her usual circle of friends. Of even greater worry to her parents was that Sally had started wearing Goth-style clothing and makeup, and had become part of that odd clique.

But since entering the New Beginnings program, she seemed somewhat happier and more outgoing. Her grades had improved a bit, and she spent less time with the Goth kids. Although she hadn't totally abandoned that culture, she now wore less of the getup that went along with it.

When Sally glanced back at Trevor, he crossed his eyes and abruptly stuck out his tongue. Sally giggled and unintentionally interrupted Jasmine Andrews, the black teen who was speaking.

Jasmine always had definite opinions and no problem expressing them. Horses were a lot like boys, Jasmine was insisting. It was impossible to manage a horse, she said, and managing boys was no easier. After smirking at Trevor, she added that maybe it was because boys were as dumb as horses.

Knowing full well who the troublemaker was, the psychotherapist cast her gaze Trevor's way. Always the professional, she made sure that her expression was judgment free. Nonetheless, it spoke volumes.

Her name was Clarissa James, and all of the teens were required to call her "Dr. James." Trevor obliged, but whenever she crossed his mind the name "sourpuss" popped up so vividly that he had to make a concentrated effort not to actually blurt it out. As Dr. James laced her fingers together on the table, she fixed her stare solely on him.

"Was there something you wanted to share with the group, Trevor?" she asked.

Trevor stared down at the shiny tabletop. Sally giggled again, this time at Trevor's expense.

"Uh . . . not really," Trevor answered.

He stole another glance at the grandfather clock. Eight minutes left. He could endure anything for eight minutes, he decided, including the laserlike stare of Dr. James.

"Well, perhaps you could share your viewpoint on what Jasmine was just saying," Dr. James suggested.

"What was that?" Trevor asked.

"About how it's so hard to control a horse, silly," Jasmine chimed in. "Don't you ever listen?"

"Oh yeah, that," Trevor answered. "You're wrong—it's not that hard."

"Well . . . ?" Dr. James asked.

Trevor thought for a moment before again looking across the table at Jasmine. "It's your fault, not the horse's," he said with authority.

"Would you care to explain that?" Dr. James asked.

"I've seen the way you ride," Trevor said to Jasmine. "You're terrible at it. When your horse doesn't do what you want, you just sit there and yell at him. That's not how it works. Do you think that he's going to answer you back or something? Jesus . . ."

Several of the teens laughed, but Dr. James was not amused. She certainly didn't condone Trevor's bad language. But so long as Trevor didn't use it too harshly against someone else, she had decided to tolerate it because the overall therapy process was far more important to Trevor than trying to correct a single bad habit.

"Those last comments of yours were interesting, Trevor," Dr. James said. "Would you like to explain them further? Perhaps you could apply that same reasoning to how we interact with people. Besides, what's so strange about talking to animals? We do it all the time with our pets, right? Jasmine is no different."

"But people talk," Trevor answered. "We can tell them what we want."

"Of course," Dr. James answered back. "But what if all the talking in the world doesn't convince someone of your needs? Or what if the other person is deaf? What would you do then?"

Trevor thought for a moment. "Then I'd have to *show* him what I wanted," he answered. "But I'd be patient."

Dr. James resisted an impulse to literally beam at Trevor. "Very good," she said. "Just like you do when you're learning to ride a horse, right? You move the reins left or right to give the horse direction, or you pull them back to make him stop. And it's all done without the spoken word. It might be a cliché, but sometimes actions truly are louder than words."

Trevor looked at Jasmine. "See?" he asked. "Horses are more like people than you think."

Just then the grandfather clock chimed, ending the session. Soon the teens were heading for the main barn by way of the dining room's French doors. After grabbing their hats from the table, Trevor and Sally also started to go.

"Trevor?" Dr. James called out. "Please wait. I need to speak with you."

Trevor groaned. He wanted nothing more than to start the day's equestrian training. But for some unknown reason he would now have to stay behind with "sourpuss." After trudging back to the table, he morosely reclaimed his seat.

To Trevor's surprise, Dr. James remained quiet. Soon the other therapist and two of his teens entered the room, causing Trevor to become even more curious. To his dismay, the other kids seemed as confused as he.

The other therapist's name was Jim Weston. A bald-headed man with a thick mustache, he was often kidded about how much he resembled Dr. Phil. Trevor didn't know him well, but he seemed nice enough. The two teens were Sean Baker and Tina Brooke. Trevor knew Tina slightly. She was a freckle-faced blonde, and one of the prettiest girls in New Beginnings. Sean was a tall, lanky kid with dark hair.

Clarissa smiled at Jim. "These two?" she asked.

Jim smiled back at her. "Yes," he said.

Clarissa nodded, then she motioned toward Trevor. "I have just this one," she said cryptically. Then she smiled and shook her head. "He's ready, but heaven help us!"

Trevor was about to ask what was going on when he heard footsteps coming down the hallway. Soon Wyatt and Ram walked in and sat at the table. For some mysterious reason, they seemed particularly pleased to see him sitting there with the two others.

Trevor looked pleadingly at Ram for answers, but the old man only winked.

"Is this all of them?" Wyatt asked Clarissa.

Clarissa nodded. "At first I wasn't sure about Trevor, but lately he's made some excellent progress."

"What's going on?" Trevor asked Wyatt.

"You three have been chosen to begin a higher level of equestrian training," Wyatt answered. "Barrel racing, to be exact. It's a Flying B tradition. At this stage in the program, the therapists and equestrian coaches are asked to select some teens who have progressed far enough in both areas to take up the challenge. A few more have also been chosen from the alternate group. Everyone's parents have given their permission. You'll be training in the larger ring, while all the other teens continue their more traditional riding lessons in the other one."

Wyatt looked at each teen in turn. "So what do you think?" he asked. "Are you interested? Or would you prefer to stay behind with the others and stick with walking, trotting, and cantering?"

Overcome with joy, Trevor leaped from his chair. During his time at the ranch he had learned what barrel racing was, and he had seen Mercy perform the maneuvers a few times. He had watched with awe as she charged her horse into the ring, around the barrels, and then thundered out again, all in about fifteen seconds or so. But never in his wildest dreams did he think that he'd get the chance to learn. He positively beamed at Wyatt.

"You bet your ass I would!" he shouted, causing Dr. James to sigh and resignedly shake her head.

Wyatt looked at Sean and Tina. "And you two?" he asked.

After they both heartily agreed, Ram leaned across the table and raised his bushy eyebrows up and down. "Then we might as well get this party started," he said. "Let's go."

As Dr. James watched them leave through the French doors, Jim turned and looked at her. "Did the Blaines pressure you to include Trevor in this?" he asked. "I know how fond they've become of that kid."

Clarissa shook her head. "They know it would have been unethical. And besides, the amazing truth is that Trevor's ready. That last exchange between him and Jasmine cinched it for me. Must be that his riding instructor thinks he's ready, too."

She again looked out toward the barn. Ram, Wyatt, and the three teens were at last walking inside. Then she laughed and shook her head.

"He's a caution, that one," she said, half to herself. "But he's also a charmer."

Jim smiled. "Yeah," he said. "And so was James Dean."

NINETEEN

WHILE TREVOR TOOK his first barrel-racing lesson, Gabby glanced around the busy game room. Most of the other parents were also there, waiting for their teens to finish so they could take them home.

At first Gabby wasn't sure about allowing Trevor to participate in the racing instruction. But Wyatt had assured her that it would be all right, and so she had agreed. Despite Wyatt's promise, she decided not to go and watch because she knew it would be too stressful for her. Just the same, she hoped that Trevor would do well.

In for a penny, in for a pound, she thought.

Gabby relaxed in her chair and took a moment to look around the room. She knew most of the other parents by now. She couldn't go so far as to say that the ice had truly been broken.

But it was at least melting a bit, and she hoped that with time she would be able to count the other parents as friends. Deciding to stretch her legs, she left the game room and headed toward the foyer, the crossroads of the great house.

Gabby had been hugely impressed by this mansion the moment she first saw it, and she was dying to see more of it. She would do some innocent exploring, she decided. She was of course already familiar with the great foyer, the dining room, the kitchen, and the game room. But there remained several hallways leading off from the foyer that she had yet to investigate. Wondering what she might find, she chose one and started on her way.

She soon passed a sitting room, its ornate French doors lying open as if inviting her to come inside. The dark hardwood floor was immaculate, and partly covered with tasteful oriental rugs. The exquisite furniture had certainly been crafted during an earlier, more elegant era. Like in the formal dining room, here, too, hung a lovely oil portrait of Phoebe Blaine.

She passed several more rooms, each of which also boasted French doors. There was a library, a music room, and a room whose walls displayed equestrian antiques and old photos that had presumably been saved from the ranch's earlier days. After savoring the bygone atmosphere for several moments, she continued her journey.

Soon another door loomed on her left, this one made from solid oak. The door was slightly ajar, but not enough for her to see inside. A brass key protruded from the keyhole.

Her curiosity mounting, Gabby entered the room, leaving the door open. The door hinges squeaked slightly as she let herself in.

She had fully expected it to be much like the others. But to her surprise, she had been wrong.

This room was rather dark and somber. A large bay window was in the far wall. Each of the other three walls was nearly covered with black-and-white photographs, all of them encased in matching pewter frames of varying sizes. Her curiosity growing, Gabby ventured farther into the room.

A large desk and a swivel desk chair sat before the bay window. On the marble window ledge were several leather-covered photo albums. In the nearby right-hand corner there stood a coat rack that held an English-style riding hat, a pair of riding gloves, and a leather crop. As she looked longer, Gabby realized that everything was coated in a fine layer of dust.

Gabby quietly approached the desk. On it lay a collection of fountain pens in a wooden-and-glass case, an old PC, a desk pad, and several more framed, black-and-white photos. On the desktop pad was a five-year-old day planner, its pages opened to the anniversary of the terrible car crash that had entwined her and Trevor with the Blaines. Covered in a fine layer of dust, the time and date of Wyatt's tragic birthday party was noted there in red fountain-pen ink.

On reading the day planner, a possibility occurred to her. *Is this Wyatt's office?* she wondered. *But if it is, then why isn't it cleaner?*

She went to the window and picked up one of the photo albums. After blowing off the dust, she opened it to see pictures of Wyatt, Danny, Krista, Ram, and other people of the Flying B during earlier, happier days. Eager to see more, she started to turn the page. Just then she heard the door hinges creak again.

"What do you think you're doing?" a male voice asked.

Gabby knew immediately who it was. She slowly turned and gazed into Wyatt's eyes. His face held an odd expression. To her relief, she couldn't call it anger. Rather, it was an odd mixture of sadness and remembrance.

Wyatt purposefully crossed the room. Reaching out, he took the photo album from Gabby's hands.

"What do you want here?" he asked, so softly that she barely heard the words.

Unsure of how to answer, Gabby took a deep breath. "I'm sorry if I ventured somewhere that I shouldn't have," she offered. "I was out exploring, and the door was open. I never meant to intrude."

Wyatt slowly closed the album then carefully returned it to the exact place from which it had come. Without speaking, he turned and looked out the window. Unsure of what to say or do, Gabby simply stood there beside him, waiting. As the deafening silence continued, the dusty room and its treasured memorabilia seemed to start crowding in on her.

When her eyes again fell on the coat rack holding the riding things, this time she understood. The hat and gloves were too small to belong to a man, she now realized, and so they must have been Krista's. This room was her office, her private place whenever she and Wyatt visited the ranch.

Gabby sighed and closed her eyes. "Wyatt, I'm sorry," she said. "Until this very moment I didn't realize that this room had been Krista's."

"Yes," Wyatt answered quietly, his eyes still gazing out the window, his voice cracking with emotion. "And as you can see, she was a wonderful photographer. It was a great passion for her. But if you don't mind, I'd like to be alone just now."

"Of course," Gabby answered. She wanted to reach out and touch him before going, but decided not to. Saying nothing more, she crossed the room and shut the door.

∽

"WHOA, THERE, YOUNG LADY," Ram said. "Why the long face?"

Ram was sauntering down the hall, approaching Gabby as she made her way back to where she hoped the world would make sense again. Ram saw that Gabby was upset, and he purposely blocked her path. Taking her hands in his, he tried his best to smile at her.

"What's wrong?" he asked.

Gabby sighed. "I was walking around the house," she answered. "This place is so lovely—I just wanted to see more of it. But I went into a room that I shouldn't have, and Wyatt found me there."

Ram understood at once. "Come with me," he said. "We need to talk."

He escorted Gabby back to the foyer and then out onto the broad porch. The sun was just starting to set, and for the first time since coming to the ranch, she was truly glad to be out of the house. Ram led her to the same wicker table and chairs where they had first gotten to know each other.

After they sat down, Ram looked compassionately into Gabby's eyes. "It was Krista's study, wasn't it?" he asked.

Gabby nodded.

Ram sighed and shook his head. For several moments he gazed out across the grounds, collecting his thoughts.

"You know," he said, "Wyatt and Aunt Lou are always criticizing me about my office being off-limits to everyone. But that room you just came from is the *true* inner sanctum in this place. To the best of my knowledge, no one but you and Wyatt has set foot in there since the day of the crash. Right or wrong, that's how Wyatt wants it. I wouldn't go so far as to call it a shrine, but it's damned close. I've tried and tried to get him to pack up all of Krista's things and let some new life return to that room, but he won't hear of it. It's his personal time machine, I guess."

Gabby nodded. "To a lesser degree, I can understand his feelings. I have a box containing some of Jason's things in my bedroom at home, and truthfully, if I walked into the room and saw someone handling them, I'd be upset, too."

Ram again looked out across the ranch that he so loved. "You know," he said, "death's leftovers can be mixed blessings. The possessions that our loved ones leave behind can sometimes seem as alive as those who once owned them. Maybe that's because they're all that's left to us. But sometimes those same keepsakes can become too coveted."

Gabby nodded. "You're right. Although Wyatt and I were the only two people in the room, it felt pretty crowded."

"I know, dear," Ram said quietly. "Believe me, I know."

TWENTY

C ELIA WARD SIPPED her iced coffee then languorously crossed one leg over the other. She turned and gave Gabby an inquisitive look.

"So tell me," Celia said. "How are you and your cowboy getting along since your unbidden trek through the mansion?"

As she remembered accidentally violating Krista's study, Gabby sighed. "Let me guess. An inquiring mind wants to know."

From behind her sunglasses, Celia winked. "You bet!" she answered.

Before answering, Gabby looked across Celia's well-tended lawn and flower garden. Butterflies hovered among the colorful blossoms. A squadron of wild Dutch parrots yammered noisily at each other as they careened through the air, gone as quickly as they had come. Before the garden lay Celia's swimming pool, its turquoise water shimmering brightly beneath the hot Florida sun.

Gabby and Celia were wearing swimsuits and lying on loungers on Celia's back patio. As was often the case, the two women were sharing a well-deserved Sunday afternoon away from Jefferson High. Gabby very much wanted to go for a swim, but she knew that wouldn't happen until the ever curious Celia had gotten her answers.

Gabby sipped her iced tea then put it down alongside the remains of the crab salad she and Celia had shared for lunch. As she thought about Wyatt, she shook her head.

"I'm not sure how to answer you," she said. "Despite what happened, I'm more attracted to him every time I see him. Sometimes it hurts just to be near him. But I have no idea what he thinks about me. Ever since that unfortunate moment in Krista's study, he's been distant."

"I'm sorry, Gabby," Celia said. Looking for solace from a female friend, Gabby had told Celia about the incident the same day it had happened. "From what you tell me, it must have been a very difficult moment."

Another week had passed since that fateful afternoon, and the second month of the New Beginnings Program had begun. After eight more weeks, there would be little reason for Gabby and Trevor to visit the ranch. The grains of sand were slipping through the hourglass that she and Wyatt shared; and even faster now, it seemed, since that incident. To her dismay, she felt powerless to stop them.

As Gabby had told Celia, Wyatt remained standoffish. Gabby was not offended by it because she realized that had their roles been reversed, she would feel the same way. But she badly missed the fragile warmth that had once existed between them, and she desperately wanted it back.

During dinner that first night, Ram had brazenly suggested that Gabby and Trevor stay and eat with them after every session. But Gabby feared that doing so would be too much, and so she and Trevor usually shared dinner with the Blaines only on Monday nights.

Despite Wyatt's coolness toward her, she had come to love those precious times at the great table, the breeze rustling the silk curtains and Aunt Lou serving her wonderful food. Ram and Aunt Lou sometimes told stories from Wyatt's youth. They were the only times Gabby saw Wyatt blush, and she found it endearing.

"And Trevor?" Celia asked. "How's he doing with the New Beginnings Program?"

At last a topic had surfaced that Gabby could smile about. "I can already see a difference in him," she answered. "He hasn't totally abandoned James Dean, but it's a start. He's happier and more focused. He's learning to barrel race, but by his own admission his progress is slow. I haven't watched that because the thought of it makes me too nervous. Although Trevor doesn't like the group-therapy sessions, I think they're helping. Along with the horse assigned to him, he's taking care of a pregnant mare named Sadie. Because of that, Trevor and I are usually the last guests to leave the ranch. Sometimes we stay for dinner."

Gabby's comment about dinner flashed brightly on Celia's radar. "What was that last part?" she asked.

"You heard me," Gabby answered.

"Despite what happened between you and Wyatt?"

"Yes," Gabby answered. "Ram insists on it. He can be very persuasive, to say the least."

Celia yanked her sunglasses down and shot Gabby a sly look. "Well, thank heaven for dear old Ram!" she exclaimed. "But it's time to fess up, girlfriend," she said simply. "What's really going on with you and Wyatt?"

And there it is, Gabby thought. *The ultimate question.* She closed her eyes for a moment. "I'm not sure," she answered. "Despite what happened, I think I'm falling for him. And it's kinda scaring me."

This was the first time she had fully admitted it to anyone, including herself. Her confession was liberating, and also terrifying. As she examined her feelings, a quick shudder ran through her.

Celia smiled. "High time you admitted it. It's been written all over you."

Gabby reached out and took Celia's hands in hers. "What should I do?" she asked.

"You must tell him," Celia answered.

Gabby shook her head. "I can't," she protested. "He's not ready to hear it. Especially now, after that faux pas of mine. Plus, he still wears his wedding ring. More than anything else, that tells me he's not ready to let Krista go. And there's something more—something I haven't even told *you*."

Celia raised her eyebrows. "What is it?"

"He still leaves the church service every time Reverend Jacobson performs the blessings. Five years later and he's still grieving. Maybe he always will be."

Gabby again gazed out at the inviting pool. "Besides, it was you who warned me that just because I'm ready to move on doesn't necessarily mean that Wyatt is, too," she added softly. "I have to remember that."

"So you still go to church every Sunday?" Celia asked.

Gabby shook her head. "Not since that day Wyatt took me and Trevor to brunch. It would be too awkward, especially now. Maybe I never will."

"I can understand that," Celia said. "But if you're not attending church, how do you know that Wyatt still leaves early?"

"I called Reverend Jacobson and asked him," Gabby admitted.

"You *didn't*!"

"I did," Gabby answered. "He told me that if Wyatt ever stays for the entire service, or if by some miracle he comes forward to take the blessings, that he'd let me know. It seems that the good reverend has taken an interest in us."

Celia laughed and slapped one knee. "Gabbs," she said laughingly, "you've finally restored my faith in your feminine wiles!"

TWENTY-ONE

T HE FOLLOWING DAY was Monday, the start of the sixth week of New Beginnings. The sky was dark, threatening to make good on its promise of rain. Like usual on program days, Ram and Wyatt sat on the front porch in their rockers, waiting for everyone to arrive.

Thinking, Ram sat back and lit a cigarette. For some reason, he always cogitated best while smoking. He smiled as he wondered whether nicotine had anything to do with increased mental clarity.

Makes me wonder what all those fool doctors might have to say about it, he thought. *Next time I see mine, I'll have to ask him.*

Ram's mind soon turned to other matters. All the prior week he had wanted to talk to Wyatt about what had happened in Krista's study, but he was unsure about whether to do it. It was obvious that Wyatt's attitude toward Gabby had cooled, and Ram just as easily recognized that Gabby felt hurt by it. But anything having to do with Krista's study was always a touchy issue for Wyatt. If Ram brought it up, he would have to tread lightly. Then he thought about it some more, and he scowled.

Tread lightly, my ass, Ram thought. *If he gets mad, so be it.* Deciding to throw caution to the wind, he looked over at his son.

"I'd like to talk to you about something," Ram said.

Wyatt put his boots on the porch railing. "No need," he said. "I already know what you've got in mind. It's my business, not yours."

"Maybe," Ram answered. "But how could anything that's so clearly bothering a son of mine *not* be my business?"

Wyatt looked over at his dad. "You're going to get into this whether I want you to or not, aren't you?" Wyatt asked.

"Yep," Ram answered.

Wyatt sighed. "Then say your piece and get it over with," he said.

"You're being too hard on her," Ram said. "She didn't do anything wrong. And she sure as hell didn't know what was in that room, or what it means to you."

Wyatt uneasily shifted his weight in his chair. Ram was right on both counts, even though he didn't want to admit it. Gabby had upset his orderly world yet again. And because he didn't know how to deal with it, he felt uncomfortable around her.

"Is that all?" he asked his father. "Please tell me that this is the end of the lecture."

"No," Ram said, "it isn't. You've been so self-absorbed lately that you've totally missed something else of importance."

Wyatt scowled. "What the hell are you talking about?"

"I'm talking about Trevor," Ram replied. "Given the way you're treating Gabby, you're running the risk of making her so uncomfortable that she might stop bringing him to the ranch. Besides, I've grown to like that kid. I'd hate to see her yank him from the program just because of your attachment to a bunch of old mementos sealed up in some dusty room."

Ram dropped his spent cigarette to the porch floor and crushed it beneath one boot. "There, now I'm finally done. So if you want to be angry with me, go right ahead. But you're wrong on this one, son, and deep down, I think you know it."

As usual, Ram's bluntness carried the unmistakable ring of truth. Wyatt had also come to like Trevor. And like Ram had said, that part of it hadn't occurred to him. But it should have, he realized. If Gabby pulled Trevor from the program because of him, Wyatt knew he could never forgive himself.

But this was about far more than just Trevor. Deep down, he knew that he had been too hard on Gabby, and his behavior bothered him. Even so, her unconscious violation of Krista's study still weighed on his heart. He suddenly felt the need to go someplace where he could be truly alone, to sort though his feelings in private. And only one place would suffice.

Instead of waiting to greet Gabby and Trevor on the porch, Wyatt stood and walked into the house. After striding down one of the hallways, he stopped before the door to Krista's study.

Pulling his key ring from his jeans, he selected the one he needed and unlocked the door. After Gabby's intrusion, Wyatt had locked the door and kept the key. The door squeaked with familiarity when he opened it and walked inside.

As his eyes scanned the drab, dusty room, it seemed to yawn back at him. He walked to the window where he and Gabby had stood, and he gazed out at the darkening clouds. A flicker of lightning flashed on the far horizon, its brief appearance a sharp, silver zigzag against the battleship gray sky.

He then looked down at the windowsill. The photo album he had taken from Gabby's hands still lay there, exactly where he had placed it one week ago. In the fading light he saw his and Gabby's fingerprints commingled on top of the dusty album cover. Seeing them together like that suddenly tugged at his heart, and his path became clear.

Wyatt turned and walked back to the door. Leaving the room, he closed the door behind him and again reached for his key ring, thinking. This time he left the key in the keyhole, and the door ajar.

∞

HE FOUND GABBY in the foyer, chatting with some of the other parents. When he walked up to her, she did her best to smile.

"Do you have some time for me?" he asked.

"Sure," Gabby answered.

"Let's talk in the gazebo," Wyatt suggested.

"But it's about to rain, isn't it?"

A brief smile crossed Wyatt's lips, the first he had shown Gabby in a week. "Then we'd better hurry," he answered. As they walked away, several of the other parents watched with obvious curiosity, while others reacted by rather urgent whispering among themselves.

A white, ornate gazebo stood about fifty yards southwest of the big house. Ram had ordered its construction ten years ago, and its octagonal shape held a matching bench that ran all around its inside wall. As rain clouds continued to gather, Wyatt and Gabby scurried toward it.

"Whew!" Gabby said, catching her breath. She sat down on one of the eight short benches just as the rain started falling. "That was close."

Wyatt sat beside her. "Yes," he answered. "But we'll be okay here."

Gabby turned and looked at him. She couldn't know why he had brought her here, but that didn't keep her from hoping.

"What did you want to say to me?" she asked.

The rain came harder now, falling in dense, waving sheets. A short clap of thunder resounded across the sky.

"I want to apologize for the way I've treated you this past week," Wyatt said. "It was wrong of me, I know. Please forgive me. I was just trying to make sense of it all. You did nothing wrong. Even so, I reacted poorly."

Those were the words that Gabby had been longing to hear. Her heart relieved, she smiled.

"There was never any reason to forgive you," she answered. "What happened was my fault, not yours."

"Thank you," Wyatt said.

His conscience finally unburdened, Wyatt looked searchingly at Gabby, almost like he was seeing her for the first time. He sat beside her like that for several moments, luxuriating in her presence but saying nothing.

Gabby smiled at him again before looking out at the weather. It seemed to be abating a bit. In Florida, such brief but strong storms were a fact of life.

"Do you think we should go back," she asked, "or stay here for a while?" Although she had given him the choice, she knew which answer her heart preferred.

"Let's stay," Wyatt answered.

After a time, the rain finally stopped. Without talking further, Gabby and Wyatt watched as dappled sunshine gradually returned. They each knew that nothing more needed to be said just now, regardless of what the future might hold for them. It was Gabby who finally broke the silence.

"Let's go back," she offered. "Everyone must wonder what's become of us."

Wyatt nodded his approval. Soon they were walking unhurriedly back toward the big house, their boots becoming wet with fallen rain.

From his vantage point behind an upstairs window, Ram smiled as he watched them return.

TWENTY-TWO

D O YOU THINK we'll be shoveling manure again today?" Sally Hendricks asked. It was one week later and Monday morning at Jefferson High. Trevor and Sally were walking to their next class.

Trevor laughed. Unlike most teens in the New Beginnings Program, he didn't mind mucking out stalls. To his way of thinking, it beat sitting through the tedious group-therapy sessions. And besides, cleaning stalls meant being close to Sadie. Trevor knew that Sadie would foal soon, and he desperately wanted to be there when her time came.

"We'll probably clean stalls every time," he answered Sally. "But I like being at the ranch, don't you?"

Sally nodded enthusiastically. "Yeah, but I could live without all the shoveling."

Trevor remembered something Wyatt had told him at the start of the program. "It's all part of the process," he said, trying to make himself sound knowledgeable. "We gotta take the good with the bad."

"I know," Sally answered. "But when I get done, I stink!"

For Trevor, watching Sally change was a bit like looking into a mirror. He, too, was happier. Visiting the ranch had grounded him and given him more confidence. He also realized that life's annoyances didn't anger him quite so much, nor did he take himself so seriously anymore. On Mondays, Wednesdays, and Fridays, he was so eager to leave school and head for the Flying B that he could barely contain himself.

Trevor looked down at Sally's feet and smiled. She, too, had begun wearing her boots to school. They seemed strange companions to her black clothes and brazenly dark eye shadow. With Trevor in his James Dean Windbreaker and Sally in her Goth mode, they made for a decidedly odd couple.

On turning the next corner, Trevor stopped abruptly. Wondering why, Sally also stopped. Tim Richardson and his two buddies stood in the middle of the hall, laughing and holding court. For several moments Trevor stood stock-still, wondering what to do.

He didn't want to risk another fight, but because he was on probation he mustn't be late for class. He and Sally could turn back and take another route, but they probably wouldn't arrive in time. There seemed to be no choice but to walk straight past the dreaded trio and hope for the best. As they started moving again, Sally gave Trevor a worried look.

"You know what'll happen when they see you, right?" she

asked worriedly. "If you get into another fight, you'll get expelled."

Trevor set his jaw and kept going. "Yeah . . . ," he said.

"So why go this way?" Sally pleaded. "It's trouble!"

Trevor gave her a hard look. "Because I have to. I can't live like this forever."

As Sally accompanied Trevor down the hall, she swallowed hard.

Tim saw them coming, and he smiled nastily. He shouted at John and Bill, telling them to look alive. The trio quickly formed a line, blocking Trevor and Sally's way.

"Well, look at what we have here, boys!" Tim exclaimed. "Two manure-shoveling horse retards! And one of them is a Goth slob, to boot! So tell me, Powers, are you and the Goth slob sweet on each other? Don't knock her up! There's no telling what some bastard from the two of you would look like!"

Trevor tried to ignore Tim and lead Sally around the three boys, but the trio quickly blocked their way again. "Leave us alone," Trevor said quietly.

Tim stepped nearer. "Or what, horse retard? Are you gonna hit me again? Oh, that's right—you can't, or you'll get kicked out of school. Even your mother won't be able to save your ass again!"

A leer appeared on Tim's face, and he edged a bit closer. "By the way," he said quietly, "your old lady's the best-looking MILF I've ever seen. I wouldn't mind doing her myself."

Trevor's rage immediately boiled up. In an attempt to keep from hitting Tim, he tightened his right hand around his book strap and slipped his left hand into his trousers pocket. He had forgotten that he was carrying the knife Ram had given him. As he wrapped his fingers around it, its smooth handle reassured him. Trevor knew better than to pull his knife. But as he stood glaring at Tim, it suddenly reminded him of Ram, and of what Ram had told him that day in the barn.

Never fight in the mud with a pig, Trevor remembered. The words rang so clearly in his mind that it was as if Ram was standing right beside him.

There are two reasons, Trevor heard Ram say. *The first reason is that you'll both get dirty. The second is, it makes the Richardson pig happy . . .*

A smile suddenly spread across Trevor's face. "The Richardson pig . . . ," he said, half to himself.

Tim screwed up his face. "What did you say, horse retard?" he demanded.

Trevor took another good look at Tim. Like Ram had told him to do, he imagined Tim as a pig. And like Ram had predicted, it wasn't difficult to do.

Trevor suddenly laughed. It was a loud, insulting laugh, and it was directed straight at Tim. As Trevor laughed harder, other students started crowding around, wondering what was so funny. Trevor's unexpected laughter confused Tim, and he scowled.

"What's wrong with you, you crazy son of a bitch?" Tim shouted. "Let's get this over with, once and for all!"

Sally's face twisted in fear and she tugged on Trevor's sleeve. "Jesus, Trevor!" she whispered. "Stop laughing! Can't you see that you're only making him madder?"

"I . . . can't!" Trevor answered.

Trevor turned and looked at Sally. By now he was laughing

so hard he seemed to look through her, rather than at her. When he again confronted Tim his howling became even stronger, causing him to uncaringly drop his books and literally bend over in convulsions.

Sally didn't know why but she also started chuckling at Tim, which only fueled his rage and frustration. Soon her laughter grew louder, nearly rivaling Trevor's.

"The Richardson pig . . . ," Trevor muttered again, this time laughing so hard that he could barely get the words out. He took his free hand from his pocket then pointed his index finger straight at Tim's nose. "Never . . . wrestle in the mud . . ."

Sally had no idea what Trevor was talking about, but it didn't matter. Not only was she laughing hysterically, but it had spread to some of the other students in the quickly growing crowd.

"What the hell is wrong with you?" Tim demanded again.

Trevor was able to calm himself just long enough to get a few words out. "What the hell is wrong with *you*?" he shot back. He raised his arm again and pointed straight at Tim. "*You're* the one everybody's laughing at!"

Tim's face went red with anger; he looked like he was about to explode. As he took another step forward, he glanced around at the crowd. To everyone's surprise, Tim slowly lowered his fists. Totally stripped of his defenses, he simply stood there looking at Trevor, as if Trevor had suddenly gone mad.

"Jesus Christ!" Bill Memphis shouted at Tim. "Hit the bastard!"

Tim just shook his head. "No . . ."

"Do it, you pansy!" Bill demanded.

"Why bother?" Tim answered. Trying to save face, he made a throwaway gesture with one hand. "The horse retard isn't worth it. Besides, where's the fun in beating up a crazy person? Come on, let's go."

As Trevor and Sally watched the trio move away, their laughter finally quieted. Trevor collected his books, and he and Sally started moving again. Sally gave Trevor an incredulous look.

"What just happened back there?" she asked. "And what was that business about 'the Richardson pig'?"

Trevor smiled and shook his head. "I'll be damned . . ."

"Huh?" Sally asked.

"It's something that Ram taught me," Trevor answered.

"*Ram* taught you *that*?" Sally asked incredulously.

Trevor nodded. "I didn't get it at first, but I do now. I'll explain it to you sometime." Trevor and Sally walked to their next classes: biology for her, and English for him.

Tim Richardson and his gang never bothered either of them again.

TWENTY-THREE

LATER THAT DAY as Wyatt walked from the barn to the big house, he passed the several pairs of French doors lining the dining room's west side. Looking through the windows, he smiled.

Eight teens, including Trevor, were seated at one end of the dining table, engaged in their psychotherapy session. A black girl was shouting angrily and pointing an accusatory finger at Dr. James. Because the doors were closed, Wyatt found the girl's voice indecipherable. That was just as well, he realized. If the teens were to benefit from therapy, their privacy was paramount.

Dr. James turned and discreetly rolled her eyes at Wyatt as he went by, causing him to smile. *That isn't a job I'd want,* he thought.

On entering the house he made his way to the game room where most of the parents usually waited. The place was busy and, as he had hoped, Gabby was also there.

During the introductory meeting, Wyatt told the parents that they could avail themselves of refreshments in the game room bar. To make sure they didn't abuse the privilege, Betsy always oversaw things. Gabby sat at the bar's far end, nursing a glass of ginger ale and making small talk with three of the other parents. She was wearing jeans, a white shirt with its sleeves rolled up, and her cowboy boots.

Perfect for what I have in mind, Wyatt thought. As he approached Gabby, some of the others shot him surreptitious looks.

Wyatt laid his Stetson on the bar. "Hey there," he said. He tilted his head toward Gabby's glass. "Be careful with that stuff. You still have to drive Trevor home, you know."

"Hey there yourself," Gabby answered back with a smile. "Don't worry. I think I can handle it."

Wyatt laughed. "I have a surprise for you," he said softly.

Gabby regarded him skeptically. "Why are we whispering?"

"Because it's very hush-hush," Wyatt answered. "It's all arranged. You're coming with me."

"Where?"

"You'll see," he answered.

Gabby's eyes narrowed. "What if I don't want to?"

"You have no choice," he answered. "Now move it, Powers, or I'll have you shoveling manure instead."

As Gabby picked up her hat and began following Wyatt from the game room, several of the men watched with curiosity, while some of the wives put their heads closer together and murmured discreetly.

After leaving the house, Wyatt and Gabby headed across the

lawn. Although Gabby was intensely curious, she guessed that it would be pointless to ask. Besides, she relished every moment with Wyatt she could get.

Wyatt led her into an area of the barn that was unfamiliar to her. Because half of the teens were taking equestrian training in the two indoor rings, the barn was relatively quiet. When they entered an open-ended corridor, Gabby stopped dead in her tracks. She gripped Wyatt's arm and looked pleadingly into his eyes.

"Oh, no . . . ," she whispered.

"Oh *yes*!" he answered. "It's high time you got more involved, and you're not getting out of it!"

Big John stood before them. In his hands he held the reins of two saddled horses, a roan mare and a black gelding.

"Wyatt . . . ," Gabby protested. "I can't . . . I just can't! Oh, God!"

"Sure you can," he answered reassuringly. "You'll see." Taking Gabby's arm, he walked her toward the waiting horses.

As part of the registration process that first day, Wyatt had asked all the parents if they would be interested in going riding with him sometime over the course of the program. When Krista had been alive this had been her job, and he had decided to keep the tradition. The therapists believed that the rides would help the parents better understand what their kids were experiencing, and it was strongly encouraged.

Most of them had signed up, and about half had already gone with him. Gabby, however, was one of the few who had declined. Wyatt hoped that if Gabby went riding, she, too, might better understand what Trevor was experiencing here at the ranch. But in a tiny corner of his heart, he realized that he was doing it for selfish reasons as well.

Gabby stared wide-eyed at the two animals. "I didn't sign up for this!" she protested. "I already told you how I feel about horses. I love them, but they scare the hell out of me."

Wyatt smiled. "We've got young kids riding these very horses," he said. "Are you going to tell me that you can't?"

Gabby angrily freed her arm from Wyatt's grip. "Goddamnit!" she exclaimed. "I don't want to do this! Why do you think I should have to?"

Wyatt was rather surprised by her outburst. As if requesting advice, he looked at Big John. Deciding that this was no time to add his two cents, B.J. only shrugged his shoulders. Wyatt sighed, wondering how he could convince her.

"There's really nothing to worry about," he finally answered Gabby. "I'll be with you every step of the way, so to speak."

"Are you really going to make me do this?" Gabby asked.

Pushing his Stetson back toward the crown of his head, Wyatt sighed again. "Well, I'm not going to pick you up and throw you onto the saddle, if that's what you're worried about," he said. "But I do think you should better understand what Trevor is experiencing."

Gabby scowled. "Don't bring Trevor into this," she growled. "This is about you and me, and you know it."

Wyatt pursed his lips. "Okay," he said. "Sorry if you took that the wrong way. But please come, won't you?"

Remaining quiet for a time, she again took in his rugged

good looks, and the lanky, relaxed way he stood before her. As she did, for better or for worse, she felt her resolve slipping. *Maybe it would be okay,* she thought. *After all, most of the other parents are doing it . . .*

"All right," she finally said, "but just this once. You understand?"

Wyatt smiled. "Loud and clear," he said. "Now come closer and lift your left foot."

When Gabby did as Wyatt asked, he gently guided her foot into one stirrup. "Up you go," he said.

With Wyatt's help she clumsily mounted the black gelding. He was a beautiful thing, with a long mane and tail. His saddle and bridle were tan and scattered with silver studs. The horse danced a bit, causing Gabby to let go with a little shriek and grip the saddle pommel for dear life. As her gelding calmed, Gabby realized that the saddle was actually comfortable. Big John handed her the reins.

"What's his name?" Gabby asked.

"Caesar," Wyatt answered. "And the mare is named Cleopatra. Or Cleo, for short."

Gabby snorted out a little laugh. "Cute . . . ," she said.

After taking Cleo's reins from Big John, Wyatt swung up into the saddle. As he wheeled Cleo around, Gabby noticed that a rifle lay in Wyatt's saddle scabbard.

"It's simple, really," Wyatt said to Gabby. "When you want to turn him, pull the reins to the left or right. When you want him to go, gently nudge your heels into his sides. To stop, pull back on the reins. There's no need for perfect technique. Caesar's been doing this for a long time."

"But I haven't," Gabby answered meekly.

Wyatt laughed then looked down at Big John. "We'll be back in about half an hour," he said.

"Okay, boss," John answered. "See you then."

To help Gabby along, Wyatt grasped Caesar's bridle and guided both horses outside. Once they were free of the barn, Wyatt let go.

"Just do your best to keep Caesar alongside me," Wyatt said. "I always use him for the parents' rides, so he'll probably stay close anyway."

As Gabby adjusted to the motion of her horse, she found it surprisingly pleasant. She was struck by how powerful Caesar seemed, carrying her with ease as they traveled along. She had always felt sorry for horses whenever she saw them being forced to carry people on their backs. But today she realized that her weight on Caesar was a mere afterthought.

The farther they went, the more she understood why Trevor liked riding. Wyatt had at least been right about that part of all this, she realized. Keeping to a walk, Wyatt headed them onto the dirt road leading to his lake cabin. The ground was flat, the wind was calm, and the sun was high.

After a time, Gabby looked over at Wyatt. "This isn't so bad, I guess," she reluctantly admitted.

Wyatt smiled and tipped his hat at her. "Told you so," he answered.

As they rode they talked pleasantly about Trevor, the ranch, and New Beginnings. The farther they went, the more comfortable Gabby became. She was about to actually ask Wyatt if they could do this again sometime when he pulled Cleo to a stop.

"Just pull back on the reins," Wyatt said. "We'll rest them a bit before heading back."

To Gabby's relief, Caesar obediently stopped. He shook his mane and bridle for a moment before finally settling down.

Highly pleased with herself, Gabby beamed at Wyatt and he nodded back his approval. They stayed like that for a time, quietly enjoying the scenery. Insects hummed pleasantly and the wind freshened, cooling them a bit.

Suddenly Caesar lowered his muzzle to the ground and began an unbidden exploration for some tender grass, causing Gabby to stiffen. Then he snuffled and took a couple of unexpected steps to explore some more virgin territory. A terrified look came over Gabby's face.

"What do I do?" she asked urgently.

"It's okay," Wyatt said. "Just let him go. He won't travel far."

Gabby let Caesar wander a bit. True to Wyatt's word, he stayed nearby.

Gabby smiled. "You're right," she said. "I guess that's what comes of being around horses all your life."

Wyatt was about to answer her when he noticed something. The grass was moving near Caesar's lowered muzzle. Then he glimpsed a familiar pattern, and the breath caught in his lungs. Just as he reached for his gun, the telltale rattling began.

Gabby heard it, too. Frightened out of her wits, she looked helplessly at Wyatt. She was about to scream when the startled diamondback lashed out, jaws wide and deadly fangs glinting in the sun.

Wyatt's rifle roared twice and Caesar reared on his hind legs;

everything happened so quickly that it seemed simultaneous. Gabby fell backward from the horse and tumbled to the grass, hard, then was motionless where she lay. After whinnying fearfully, Caesar thundered away, reins and stirrups flapping wildly.

"Jesus, God, no . . . ," Wyatt breathed.

He was off Cleo and by Gabby's side in a flash. Reaching out, he gently turned her over. As she looked up at him, her eyes slowly refocused.

"Are you hurt?" Wyatt asked.

"Dunno . . . ," she whispered thickly.

"Let's see if you can stand," Wyatt said.

When he helped Gabby to her feet, she winced. For several long moments he held her in his arms, looking searchingly into her eyes. When he finally let her go, he felt a sense of loss touch his heart.

Gabby winced again. "My right wrist . . . ," she said.

"Anything else?" he asked.

Still dazed, Gabby shook her head. "I don't think so," she said softly. "Poor Caesar . . . shouldn't we go after him?"

Wyatt shook his head. "I don't know if Caesar was bitten—it all happened so fast. But you're more important than any goddamned horse. I've got to get you back."

Wyatt gingerly escorted Gabby to where Cleo stood. But to his surprise, when he tried to help her up onto the saddle, she used her good hand to brusquely push him away. Her terrified expression was gone, and had been replaced by what Wyatt could only describe as a look of deep betrayal.

"If you think that I'm ever going to ride one of your stupid horses again, you're dead wrong," she protested. "I knew this was a bad idea, but you just wouldn't listen. I'll *walk* back, if it's all the same to you."

Wyatt apologetically held up his hands. "But that's silly," he said, immediately regretting his words. "Uh, what I mean is . . . you should ride back, because of your wrist."

"So now I'm *silly,* am I?" Gabby shot back. "Well, my hand might hurt, but my feet are just fine, thank you very much."

At once she turned and started marching back along the trail, her good hand cradling her injured one. Wyatt just stood there in awkward disbelief, watching her go.

After she had gone about twenty paces, Gabby stopped. Then she let go with an exasperated sigh and turned around to glare at him again. The hugely contrite look on Wyatt's face didn't faze her in the slightest.

"Well, Jesus!" she shouted at him. "Are you coming, or not?"

Wyatt finally snapped out of his daze and jumped on Cleo. After making sure that the rattlesnake was dead, he spurred the mare into a quick trot and caught up with Gabby.

Ten minutes later, he felt so guilty about riding while she stubbornly trod homeward that he finally dismounted and walked alongside her.

TWENTY-FOUR

TWO DAYS LATER, Reverend Jacobson was once more about to deliver his weekly sermon to the congregation at St. Andrew's. Every pew was full, and today's collection would be a good one. After making the sign of the cross, he told the parishioners to sit. As they did, he said a silent prayer that his gravelly voice might prevail yet again.

"There once was a minister who occasionally shirked his holy duties," Jacobson began. "He usually accomplished this deceit by feigning sickness on Sunday mornings. Rather than conduct the church services, he left the responsibility to his assistant, and he went and played golf." Pausing for a moment, Jacobson watched his flock settle into the pews.

"One Sunday morning, God and St. Peter watched from heaven as the irresponsible minister played golf alone," Jacobson said. "After a while, God turned to St. Peter. God winked and said: 'Watch this.' When next the minister teed off, God ensured that he shot the first hole in one of his life. Then God saw to it that the same thing happened three more times in a row. As one might expect, the minister was beside himself with joy. God seemed pleased by what he had done, but St. Peter was clearly puzzled.

" 'That minister should be in church, attending to his flock!' St. Peter said. 'Instead, he's down there playing golf, and you granted him four straight holes in one!'

"God smiled at St. Peter. 'That's true,' God said. 'But who can he tell?' "

Some twenty minutes later, Jacobson finished his sermon. He looked to the pew in which Gabby Powers usually sat. Like the last eight Sundays in a row, she was absent. He then looked to the other side of the aisle in search of Wyatt Blaine. Wyatt was dressed in a dark suit and was seated in his usual place.

The reverend cleared his throat. "Would anyone interested in celebrating a birthday, an anniversary, or any other special day please come forward for the blessings?" he announced. Wondering for the thousandth time whether this would the day, Jacobson again looked at Wyatt.

Wyatt stood and walked to the back of the church. After handing some cash to one of the ushers, he left.

‰

AS JACOBSON WALKED to his office, he realized how truly tired he was. During the service he had performed two baptisms, and the ensuing coffee hour had run especially long. Fortified with caffeine and sugar cookies, a pair of elderly Boca widows had buttonholed him about St. Andrew's upcoming silent auction. He had chatted with them politely, but what he wanted most was to return to the quiet comfort of his office. As he neared the office door, he saw a familiar figure waiting for him.

Like that eventful Sunday nine weeks ago, Wyatt Blaine again sat on the reverend's wrought-iron bench. Jacobson noticed that Wyatt seemed weary.

"The prodigal son returns!" he said. "To what do I owe the honor?"

"I know how tiring Sundays are for you, but can you spare me some time?"

"Of course," the reverend answered. "Would you like some coffee? If I know Stella, there's a fresh pot waiting."

Jacobson unlocked the door, and the two men walked inside. Although Stella wasn't there, the smell of freshly brewed coffee filled the air. After pouring two steaming cupfuls, the men entered Jacobson's inner office.

"What's on your mind?" Jacobson asked as he sat down behind his desk.

Wyatt took a seat in one of the guest chairs. He then looked over at the other chair, remembering when Gabby had first asked him to help Trevor. Sometimes that day seemed like a lifetime ago; other times it felt like yesterday. For a few moments Wyatt looked down at his shoes and rolled his coffee cup between his palms. When he looked back up, his expression was searching. After explaining Gabby's riding accident to Jacobson, he was quiet again.

"Is she okay?" Jacobson asked.

Wyatt nodded. "A sprained wrist," he said. "But she's angry and avoiding my calls."

"Hard to believe," Jacobson said sarcastically.

"Yeah, I know that I screwed up," Wyatt answered. Silence reclaimed the room as Wyatt considered the greater reason for his coming here.

"I have a foolish question to ask you," he said. "I'm sure that you've heard it a thousand times before, but never from me."

Jacobson sipped his coffee. "There are no foolish questions regarding the eternal verities. Only foolish answers. What is it, my son?"

Wyatt took a deep breath. "Do you believe that our departed loved ones watch us from the afterlife?"

Jacobson raised an eyebrow. "You can use her name. This time we both know who you're talking about."

Wyatt nodded. "Okay. Do you think that Krista watches over me?"

Jacobson sighed. "I have indeed been asked that question before, and more times than you might imagine. Personally speaking, I don't know. Nor can these things be proved. But what *I* believe isn't important. All that matters is what *you* feel in your heart."

"I don't know either . . . ," Wyatt said.

"Then it doesn't matter."

"How could it not?" Wyatt asked.

"For the very reason that I just mentioned," Jacobson answered. "Because it can't be proved. Instead, cling to what you know for sure."

"And what is that?" Wyatt asked.

"That Krista loved you. And that no matter where she might be, or whether she watches over you, she would want you to be happy. Denying your future because you worry that Krista is watching you isn't an answer, Wyatt. It's an excuse."

Silence reigned again as Wyatt considered Jacobson's words.

"Now may I ask *you* a question?" Jacobson said.

Wyatt nodded.

"Did you and Krista ever discuss this subject?"

"No. We thought that there'd be lots of time for such things."

"Young couples always do," Jacobson answered. "During the early years, the future seems limitless. Had she given you her blessing to move on in the event of her death, your heart would be free to love again. Instead you're here with me, asking questions that have no answers."

"But it went unsaid between us," Wyatt replied. "And so I'm left to wonder."

"If you wonder about it for too long, you'll wonder your life away." Sighing, Jacobson placed his palms flat on the desk. "May I be blunt?"

Wyatt thought for a moment. "All right."

"You have to choose, Wyatt. Either choose the past or choose the future, but *choose.* You're living somewhere in between, and it's killing you. You've allowed your heart to become imprisoned by a ghostly memory. And if I may say so, you're acting much like you did right after Krista and Danny died."

"That's not fair," Wyatt said.

"I can't bestow fairness on your life. Only God can do that.

All I can offer you is what I believe to be the truth."

Wyatt rubbed his face with his hands. "It's not that simple, James."

Jacobson narrowed his eyes. "Go on . . ."

"I believe that I'm just as responsible for Danny's and Krista's deaths as Jason Powers."

"Why do you feel that way?" Jacobson asked.

"If my birthday party had never happened, they'd still be alive," Wyatt said. "The day's entire sequence of events would have been different, and they would never have taken that car ride. But there's more to it than that—something that I've never told anyone."

"Go on, my son."

"Danny and Krista went out to buy ice cream that day because I *asked* them to," Wyatt answered, his voice a barely audible whisper.

And there it is, Jacobson realized. *After five years, he finally reveals why he still grieves so badly.*

"But that's no proof that they'd still be among us. Or you either, for that matter."

"It's proof enough for me," Wyatt answered.

"Have you always felt this way?"

Wyatt nodded. "From the very moment Morgan told me they were dead."

"I don't mean to be harsh, Wyatt, but stop blaming yourself!" Jacobson said. "You didn't ask for that party! And above all, you didn't cause Jason Powers to crash into your wife and son! How can you feel this way? If nothing else, the lawyer in you should know better!"

"My head understands those things," Wyatt answered. "But my heart can't accept them."

"Like I said, if it's forgiveness you seek, you've come to the wrong place," Jacobson replied. "As your minister I can absolve you of sin, but I can't bestow forgiveness on you for something you didn't do. You must forgive *yourself*, rather than ask for it from others. But why tell me this now?"

Jacobson believed that Wyatt knew the answer, but Wyatt remained silent. As the seconds ticked by, the reverend decided that if Wyatt wouldn't say it, he would.

"That reason," Jacobson said softly, "is Gabrielle Powers."

Wyatt still didn't answer, but the look on his face spoke volumes.

"It's no coincidence that you tell me these things only after Gabby entered your life," Jacobson said. "I think that you've fallen in love with her, even though you won't admit it. And you fear that loving Gabby is wrong because it would somehow betray Krista. You believe that you need permission to be happy, and that you might find it in this office. But it's not here, Wyatt. It never has been, and it never will be. You must search out *forgiveness* rather than permission. And the only place you'll ever find the forgiveness that you need is in your own heart."

Wyatt stood and looked Jacobson in the eyes. "Thank you, James. I guess that I never really expected you to solve this for me. But I'm glad I finally told someone my secret, just the same. I may never find happiness again. Perhaps that will always be my lot in life, I don't know. But as badly as I want it, I still can't forgive myself for what happened."

Jacobson nodded. "You're a good man, Wyatt."

Wyatt shook Jacobson's hand then walked to the door. Before leaving, he turned and looked back. "I'm denying my own future, aren't I?"

"Yes," Jacobson answered. "And the future of the woman you're keeping yourself from."

"And because of my own stupidity, I may have just lost her, too," Wyatt said softly. "Good-bye, James."

"Good-bye, my son. And go with God." Jacobson sat in silence as Wyatt left the room and crossed the outer office.

TWENTY-FIVE

JESUS, CELIA!" GABBY said. "Every time I think about him, I get so mad I can't see straight! Why the hell did he make me do that?"

Two days had passed since Gabby's riding accident. Tomorrow would be Monday, and another week of New Beginnings would start. Gabby and Celia were eating an early supper at Legal Seafood in the Boca Towne Mall. They both liked the place, and if they wanted they could shop afterward. Before answering, Celia appreciatively slurped down another raw oyster.

"I know you're mad, Gabbs," she said. "And I can only imagine how much it scared you. But what happened wasn't Wyatt's fault. My guess is that he thought he was helping in some way."

Gabby scowled. True to her word, she had stubbornly marched the entire way back to the ranch. Still unaccustomed to her cowboy boots, by the time she arrived her feet were blistered and killing her. But she'd be damned if she'd admit that to Wyatt.

Her wrist hadn't been broken but it was badly sprained. The Blaine family doctor that Wyatt had rushed her off to see placed it in a soft cast, and said that she was to avoid using it for the next ten days. After Wyatt graciously paid the bill, he drove Gabby and Trevor home. Gabby's good-bye to him had been extremely brittle and equally terse.

Because Gabby's Honda was a stick shift, driving was nearly impossible—not to mention all the other things she shouldn't do. She felt helpless, and she hated it. Blessedly, Celia had offered to drive her and Trevor to and from school.

Gabby defiantly held up her cast. "It wasn't his fault, huh?" she asked. "Tell that to my swollen right hand! How'm I supposed to use the blackboard, for Chrissake?"

Gabby was truly angry with Wyatt, and she thought she had every right to be. He had apologized profusely, but it hadn't gentled her mood. Despite the confidences she had already shared with Celia, she wasn't even sure whether she wanted to see him again.

For the first time since leaving Jason, she felt truly betrayed. This new and unexpected wound had gone deep, and her fantasy had been shattered. Despite her anger, she had to admit that she'd always enjoyed visiting the ranch. Being there had grounded her and helped to make her feel that she was a part of something again, however temporary it might prove to be.

But Wyatt's actions had unexpectedly cut her emotions loose from all that. So much so that she could almost feel her heart floating away and becoming as errant and homeless as it had been before all of this had started. It was an uncomfortable and lonely feeling, to be sure. Even so, she didn't know whether she wanted her original feelings to ever return. Because of her anger, she was screening her calls and had so far avoided talking to him.

Gabby was having clam chowder, although eating it with her left hand was proving more difficult than she had imagined. As she fumbled with a package of crackers, she might as well have been trying to raid Fort Knox.

Celia laughed. "Give it here, you cripple," she said. She opened the crackers then unceremoniously dumped them into Gabby's chowder.

"So are you ever going to forgive him?" Celia asked.

Gabby shrugged her shoulders.

Celia smiled. "If you ask me, I think it's kind of romantic."

"*Romantic?*" Gabby asked. "Are you nuts?"

"Well, let's review," Celia answered. "A handsome cowboy kills the deadly snake, and then rescues the fair maiden who escapes the ordeal with little more than some bruised emotions. And then comes the really good part! Instead of riding home, you insist on walking and giving yourself blisters, to boot! You're right—that's showing *him* a thing or two!"

After smiling for a moment, Ceclia nodded. "Hell yeah, it's romantic! If you were in my shoes, you'd agree. And by the way, if you ever talk to Wyatt again, you can tell him that I'll go riding with him anytime!"

"None of it's funny, damnit."

"Actually, it kind of is," Celia answered. Pausing for a moment, she got the waitress's attention and ordered her third iced coffee. "Want to know what else I find funny?" she asked. "In return for squiring you and Trevor back and forth to school, you're buying dinner."

Gabby sighed again and clumsily ate some more chowder. Sometimes the urge to forgive Wyatt tried to sneak into her heart. After all, he hadn't known about the snake. But he hadn't respected her fear of horses, and that was what hurt most.

She had told Wyatt that she didn't want to go, but he hadn't listened. To her chagrin she had gone against her better instincts, just to spend time with him. She needed to be more levelheaded, she realized. She was all that Trevor had now, and she couldn't afford to behave recklessly. Worse, giving in to Wyatt had made her angry not only with him but also with herself. And given how upset she was, returning to the ranch was unthinkable. Gabby angrily finished her chardonnay then promptly ordered another.

"Drowning your sorrows?" Celia asked.

"I'd rather drown in wine than be bitten by a rattler," Gabby answered. Her fresh drink arrived, and she took a sip. "I need another favor from you, girlfriend," she said. "And it's a big one."

"Let me guess," Celia answered. "You also want me to drive Trevor back and forth to the ranch for you. And given how mad you are at Wyatt, I'd bet that you won't be joining us. You're right—it is asking a lot. But I'll do it."

"Just like that?"

"Just like that."

"It's that snoopy nature of yours, isn't it?" Gabby asked.

"Mostly I want to help you and Trevor," Celia answered. Then she let go with another of her crafty smiles. "But I must admit that I wouldn't mind seeing the place."

Gabby suddenly felt an unexpected pang of jealously because Celia would now be visiting the ranch in her place, and she found the revelation confusing. But her mind was made up, so she shoved her feelings aside.

"Thank you," she said.

"You're welcome," Celia answered. "But you're taking a big risk, Gabbs."

"How?"

"The longer you stay away, the harder it will be to go back if you want," Celia said. "I think your pride hurts more than your wrist, and you're letting it get the best of you. And there's something else to consider. Even if Wyatt cares for you, his feelings might change while you're gone. The old saying isn't always true, you know."

Gabby put down her glass. "Which one?" she asked.

"That absence makes the heart grow fonder," Celia answered.

Gabby sat back in her chair and sighed.

Maybe you're right, Celia, she thought. *But I'm no longer sure that I really care . . .*

TWENTY-SIX

THE NEXT MORNING broke bright and clear, revealing another lovely day in paradise. *At least the weather is cheerful,* Gabby thought as she did her best to guide her Honda through the streets of Boca Raton.

Changing gears hurt her injured hand and she knew that she shouldn't be driving, but she had resolved to do this thing. She was unsure whether today's short pilgrimage would provide any answers. But even if it didn't, there would be no harm in trying. She needed to go someplace where she could think undisturbed, and only one spot would do.

Because it was Monday and she should have been at school, she had had to divulge her scheme to Celia. After Celia and Trevor left the town house, Gabby had called Roy Marshall and fibbed that she had forgotten about a follow-up doctor's appointment for her hand. True, it had been the palest of white lies. But given how Roy had helped her during her time of need, even such a tiny falsehood had produced a guilty pang.

After parking her car she stood for a time and stared at the gold-colored cross rising from the roof of St. Andrew's, unaware that Wyatt had done the same thing after she and Reverend Jacobson first met with him. Then she sighed and headed for the church.

Gabby was familiar with the St. Andrew's weekday schedule. There was always a prayer service at nine A.M. and Holy Eucharist at noon. In between the two services, the church remained open so that people could meditate in the pews, and pray at the candle votive stand. Because it was after ten, the first service was over.

Gabby entered the sanctuary to find that she was alone. Walking up the center aisle, she made her way to the left side of the far wall and kneeled before the votive candle stand situated there.

After bowing her head she made the sign of the cross, then selected a long-stemmed match from a wooden holder sitting on the stand. Several of the candles were already alight, their combined glow casting ephemeral shadows against the back wall. After striking the match she lit a candle, and then placed the extinguished match in the waste receptacle. She closed her eyes again, clasped her hands before her, and bowed her head in prayer.

Before coming here she knew who she was going to pray for. It wasn't to be for her, or for Wyatt, or even for Trevor. As she implored God in the name of her late husband, memories both harsh and happy came flooding back.

She had loved Jason despite his many faults. Yes, he had been domineering and ultimately abusive. Even so, she hoped that his soul had found its just measure of peace. He had been Trevor's father, and nothing could ever change that. But she and Trevor had new lives now, lives that no longer included him. And it was those new lives that she must nurture and protect.

After putting a modest sum into the votive offering box, Gabby walked to her usual pew and sat down. The view from there was more familiar and comforting. In truth, she had come here for two reasons, and praying for Jason had been only the first of them. The second was to try to sort through her mixed feelings for Wyatt Blaine.

She looked back to where Wyatt always sat. She could easily imagine him rising from his pew, just as Reverend Jacobson began to conduct the blessings. Wyatt would then hand some cash to one of the ushers before heading off toward brunch, his tie already undone and the top down on his Jaguar convertible. As these sentimental memories tugged at her, Gabby's eyes started glistening. Turning forward to again face the altar, she tried to compose herself and look into her heart.

The only two men I have ever loved have both hurt me deeply, she thought. *Is it because I love too ardently? Do I give too much? Is that why I always become so vulnerable?*

If Wyatt can't respect my feelings now, what would he ultimately be like if our hearts were truly joined? Can I risk that? The same problem occurred with Jason, little things at first, but they eventually grew into problems of great importance, driving us apart.

Suddenly another concern seized her, causing her to wonder why she hadn't considered it sooner.

My God . . . does Wyatt see me and Trevor as replacements for Krista and Danny? she wondered. *Reverend Jacobson said that Krista had been a marvelous horsewoman. Was that why Wyatt pushed me so hard to go riding with him? Is he trying to fashion me in her image? And if he truly fell in love with me, how could I ever know that it was for the right reasons?*

I can't afford to blindly deny all these fears. And because that's the case, then neither can I afford to become more deeply involved. I couldn't bear having my love for him die the same slow death as it did with Jason. I just can't endure that again.

And so you must end your love for him before doing so becomes impossible, her heart of hearts told her. *You must let him go and never look back.*

As the stark realization took hold, she started trembling.

But there is more to consider. Trevor still needs the program. And so I must rely on Celia to take him to and from the ranch, because I can never go there again. Seeing Wyatt and knowing that we can never be together would be too painful, no matter the circumstances. It will be a huge burden for Celia, but New Beginnings won't last much longer. And when all of this is over, I will find some way to repay her many kindnesses.

Her mind finally made up, Gabby lowered the upholstered bench for her pew with trembling hands. She again went to her knees then placed her hands together on top of the pew before her. As she prayed for strength, she hoped with all her heart that she had made the right decision, no matter how painful.

She finally put the kneeler back into place and started walking out of the church. Partway out, she stopped and took a farewell look around the sanctuary that she so loved. Like the ranch, she would never return here. Loving Wyatt Blaine had cost her much, it seemed.

And so she would have to find another church. And perhaps, with luck, another man to love. But she doubted that any man would ever affect her as deeply as Wyatt. Before leaving, she couldn't help but look one last time at where he always sat, her heart deeply mourning what might have been.

As she drove out of the St. Andrew's parking lot, she finally exploded into tears.

TWENTY-SEVEN

THAT SAME AFTERNOON, Ram and Wyatt sat on the front porch of the big house, waiting for the teens and their parents. Without being told, Ram knew full well that Wyatt wanted to greet Gabby the moment she arrived. Likewise, Wyatt understood that his father's infamous curiosity was killing him, and nothing short of a natural disaster could keep the old man from seeing what would happen.

Looks like I'll be eating humble pie, Wyatt thought. *Truth is, I deserve it.*

Wyatt felt terrible about what had happened. When Gabby fell from Caesar, he had immediately feared that she was dead. A terrifying host of emotions had run through him, much like those he had felt on learning Krista's fate. It was a gut-wrenching kind of dread that he never wanted to suffer again, and it had shaken him to his very core.

It didn't take a wizard to realize that Gabby was angry. Given the chance, he would do his best to apologize again and set things straight, but he feared it wouldn't work. He also worried that Gabby might become unduly concerned about Trevor's safety and pull him from the program. If she did, he would be powerless to stop it.

Ram leaned back in his rocker. "Did they find Caesar?" he asked.

Wyatt nodded. "Yeah, but it took some doing. He's okay. Must have reared up just in time."

"Good," Ram said. "By the way, is Gabby still missing in action?"

Wyatt nodded.

"Bad sign . . . ," Ram said.

"I know," Wyatt answered.

Ram sighed. "Women are a lot like horses, Wyatt," he said. "It takes a long time to earn their trust, but only a moment to wreck it. And once it's wrecked, it's not easily mended. Your mother was like that, God rest her soul."

When the cars started arriving, Wyatt watched anxiously. Soon Gabby's battered Honda turned off the highway and started up the drive. He breathed a sigh of relief.

"Well, at least they've come back," Wyatt said. "Looks like it's time to face the music."

Ram pursed his lips. "Yep," he said.

"Any advice?" Wyatt asked.

"Yeah. With women, go slow and don't expect miracles."

They watched Trevor get out of the car. When Wyatt saw the unfamiliar driver, he stiffened.

"Uh-oh," Ram said softly. "That's a bad sign. You don't need a weatherman to know which way the wind blows on this deal."

"Maybe Gabby can't drive because of her hand," Wyatt said hopefully.

"Yeah, but I'd bet the ranch that isn't all of it."

When they reached the porch, Wyatt went to greet them. The redheaded woman regarded Wyatt politely.

"Mr. Blaine?" she asked.

"Please call me Wyatt," he said.

"My name's Celia Ward," she said. "I'm a friend of Gabby's, and I'll be bringing Trevor to the ranch for the remainder of the program."

Wyatt tried to hide his shock and disappointment, but it remained clear that Celia's words had hit him hard. He knew full well that Gabby was angry, but he hadn't expected such a final pronouncement.

"A pleasure to meet you," he said, trying to remain cheerful. He turned and looked at Trevor. "How's your mom?" he asked.

"She's okay, I guess," he said. "But her hand still hurts, and she's been kind of cranky."

Wyatt nodded. "You'd better get inside, Trevor. Your therapy session starts in ten minutes."

As Trevor entered the house, Ram left his chair and sauntered over. He tipped his hat at Celia.

"I'm Ram Blaine," he said. "Glad to meet you."

"Likewise," Celia answered. "Gabby's told me all about you."

"And you decided to come out here anyway?" Ram asked, giving her a wink.

Celia smiled. "I did," she answered.

"Could we talk a bit?" Wyatt asked her.

"Sure," Celia answered.

"Use my office," Ram said to Wyatt.

As Wyatt escorted Celia through the mansion, she looked around with awe. When they reached Ram's office, Wyatt motioned Celia toward one of the guest chairs, and he sat down behind Ram's desk.

Celia looked around admiringly. "Such a beautiful room," she said.

"Thanks," Wyatt answered. "So tell me, how do you know Gabby?"

"I'm Roy Marshall's assistant," Celia answered. "Gabby and I have become close—especially lately, what with all of Trevor's shenanigans. Until he started New Beginnings, he spent more time in Roy's office than he did in class."

"And how is Roy?" Wyatt asked. "It's been a while since I've seen him."

"Roy is Roy," she answered. "He never changes."

"True," Wyatt said.

"You and I met once before," Celia said, "but I'm not surprised that you don't remember."

"Really? When was that?"

"Shortly after Danny died," Celia said respectfully. "You visited the office to remove him from the rolls."

"Ah, yes."

Silence soon overtook the room as Wyatt considered his next question. No fool, Celia had a good idea what it would be about. As she waited, she better understood Gabby's attraction to him. *Damn, he's good looking,* she thought.

Wyatt cleared his throat. "And how is Gabby?" he finally asked.

"She'll be okay," Celia answered. "She was shaken up, but she's a tough cookie."

Wyatt nodded. "May I ask you a personal question?"

"You can ask . . . ," Celia said.

"She's still too upset to see me, isn't she?" he asked. "I realize that she probably can't drive, but she could have come along today anyway."

And there it is, Gabbs, Celia thought. *Just how do I answer that one?*

Celia sighed and slid her chair closer. "I don't want to tell any tales out of school," she said, "no pun intended. Gabby's my best friend and I won't violate her trust. But she's way past mere anger. I saw that this morning when she asked me to bring Trevor here for the duration of the program. She's truly upset—more so than I've ever seen her."

"Are things salvageable?" Wyatt asked.

"Maybe, but it would take one helluva gesture. I sure wouldn't count on her ever coming back."

"Thanks," Wyatt said. "I'm sorry if I put you on the spot. It's just that—"

"I know," Celia answered.

After thinking for a moment, Wyatt stood. "Seeing as you'll be spending some time here, would you like the grand tour?"

Relieved that their awkward talk was over, Celia smiled. "I'd love it," she said.

❧

HALF AN HOUR LATER, Wyatt returned to the porch. Ram was still staring out across the emerald lawns while Butch and Sundance prowled the grounds, diligently searching for something to chase. Wyatt sat down beside his father.

"Where's Celia?" Ram asked.

"I showed her around then left her in the game room with the others," Wyatt answered.

"So what's the verdict?" Ram asked.

Wyatt sighed. "Seems I'm guilty as charged."

"Thought so . . . ," Ram said. "Any chance for an appeal?"

"Maybe," Wyatt answered. "But it's going to take a great closing argument. I'm not sure I'm lawyer enough to do the job."

Ram nodded. "Well, one thing's for sure," he said. "Unlike before, this time the mountain won't be coming to Mohammed."

TWENTY-EIGHT

"H OW ARE THEY doing?" Ram asked Wyatt later that afternoon.

Wyatt looked over at his father. "Not too badly," he answered. "But they're still new at it. You know what they're like at this stage."

"Yep," Ram answered. "They all want to run before they can walk. And if I remember right, you were the same way."

Ram and Wyatt were standing in the larger Flying B riding ring. Six teens, including Trevor, sat in a line on their horses, waiting. Three blue, fifty-five-gallon plastic drums had been arranged on the ring floor in a precise clover-leaf pattern. Just then everyone heard a sharp rebel yell, and Mercy rode into the ring. As she did, Wyatt started his stopwatch.

Although Wyatt still had issues with Mercy, he had to admit

that she was the best barrel racer he had ever seen. With Krista's blessing, Mercy had always overseen this part of the equestrian training. After some soul searching, Wyatt had countermanded the harsh order he had given Mercy about staying clear of Trevor. Although Trevor had been selected for this training, he told her, she would still be running this show. He also said that if she knew what was best for her, she wouldn't treat Trevor any differently from the others.

Wyatt and Ram watched Mercy's horse charge headlong toward the first barrel. Approaching it properly was critical. The rider had to control the horse's speed perfectly as they entered the "pocket," the area in which the horse could make its fastest turn. Just as important, performing the first turn well was crucial to properly setting up the two more that would follow.

As her horse entered the pocket, Mercy's form was perfect. Sitting deeply in her saddle, she held onto the pommel to steady herself, her other hand using the reins to guide her horse quickly around the barrel. Mercy's inside leg was wrapped tightly against her horse's ribs, to provide her mount with a steady focal point for the turn.

Dirt flying from her hooves, the horse raced off toward the next barrel. After completing two more barrel turns, Mercy charged her back out the way she had come in, and Wyatt stopped his watch. From start to finish it had taken only sixteen seconds, a good time for any barrel racer.

Mercy walked her panting mount back into the ring then turned to face the group of waiting teens. After removing her hat and letting it hang down her back, she leaned down onto her saddle pommel.

"Because you're here for only a short time, you won't be making turns that fast," she cautioned them. "Just the same, like anything else, you've got to do it *right* before you can do it *fast*. Because you've all done this well at a walking pace, today we'll start trotting. Only after you've mastered this phase will you be allowed to gallop. And remember—we succeed only as a *group*. Nobody moves on to the galloping phase until everyone gets this part right. Also remember that, like you all, your horses are also being trained in barrel racing for the first time. That's another part of the process—learning something together. Now let's get at it. Trevor, you're first up."

Just as Mercy had taught him, Trevor trotted his mare out of the ring and into the yard outside. Then he trotted back in and made for the first barrel. At about ten feet away he slowed his horse to a stop and then backed her up a bit, to remind her of where the turn would begin. He then prompted her again and trotted her around the barrel.

When he had cleared the first barrel, he promptly started trotting her toward the second one. This stop-and-start procedure was to be the same at all three. But this time, after stopping his mare and then starting her again, Trevor's eagerness got the better of him. He spurred her on too fast and drove her too close to the second barrel, knocking it over.

Mercy was about to shout at him gleefully before remembering her promise to Wyatt. Instead, she bit her tongue and trotted her gelding over. Trevor was already off his mare, cursing to himself as he set the barrel upright.

"Do you know what you did wrong?" she asked.

"Yeah," Trevor answered angrily. "I hurried her."

"And how will you do it differently next time?" Mercy asked.

"Keep the speed the same as we enter each pocket," he answered. "But it's so hard! Keep the speed even, grab the saddle pommel, keep my inside leg tight, steer the horse . . . Jesus, how'd you get so good at this? I'll never get it!"

"With an attitude like that, you're right," Mercy answered. "Okay, you can get back in line."

After Trevor and Mercy had ridden back, Mercy looked at Tina. "You're next," she said. "Let's see what you've got."

Like Trevor, Tina trotted her horse outside and then wheeled him around. After taking a deep breath she trotted back inside then made straight for the first barrel. But unlike Trevor, she negotiated each of the barrels almost perfectly before leaving the ring. As she trotted back in, a huge smile spread across her face.

"Well done!" Mercy shouted, barely hiding her joy that a girl had just bested one of the boys. "Okay, John, now let's see how you go!"

As John started riding out of the ring, Ram turned to again look at Wyatt.

"Looks like James Dean's got some practicing to do," he said dryly. "That's all right. It builds character."

Wyatt smiled. "That's true," he answered. Then he sighed and shook his head.

But I wish that Gabby were here, just the same . . .

TWENTY-NINE

TWO DAYS LATER Gabby sat at her homeroom desk, taking roll for her next class. As usual, her blasé tenth-graders slumped, chewed gum, and cast vacant looks at her. It was mid-afternoon, her wrist ached, and she was tired. Celia would soon drive her and Trevor home, and then take Trevor back and forth to the Flying B. Gabby would later share some Chinese takeout with Trevor, take a hot bath, and hopefully get a decent night's sleep.

Ten minutes into her talk about the battle of Gettysburg, a man opened the door without knocking and brazenly entered the room. To Gabby's utter amazement, it was Wyatt.

He was casually dressed in a navy polo shirt, tan slacks, and brown tasseled loafers. Without saying a word he found an empty desk about halfway back, and he sat down. After looking him over, several of the girls huddled across one of the aisles and started whispering urgently.

Gabby glared angrily at Wyatt. She simply couldn't believe her eyes.

"Excuse me?" she asked loudly.

"Why?" Wyatt asked. "Have you done something wrong?"

Gabby stood from her desk and placed her hands on her hips. "That's not funny!" she answered.

Several of the huddling girls started giggling openly.

"Be quiet, you three!" Gabby ordered. She refocused her glare on Wyatt. "What are you doing here?" she demanded.

"I've come to plead my case," Wyatt said. "This seemed like the best place to do it."

Gabby's eyes narrowed. "How'd you get past security?"

"I'm friends with Principal Marshall, remember?" Wyatt asked in return.

"He knows you're here?" she demanded.

"That's right," Wyatt answered. He rummaged around in his pants pockets and produced a piece of green paper. "He even gave me a permission slip to visit your class. Wanna see it?"

More giggling arrived, louder this time. Gabby glared at the girls with deadly intent, and they quieted.

"No, I don't want to see it!" she said to Wyatt. "What did you mean by, 'plead my case'?"

Wyatt looked around the room. "What do your students know about the legal system?" he asked.

"Very little, I imagine," Gabby answered. "Why?"

"I've come to appeal my sentence," Wyatt said, "and I thought they could serve as the jury." He stood and looked around at the students. "You see, your teacher hurt her wrist because I insisted on taking her riding, and she fell off her horse. I think that I should be forgiven. All in favor raise your hands."

Gabby was about to protest when a slew of hands went into the air, most of them female. She scowled at Wyatt.

"Please meet me in the hall, Mr. Blaine," she said. "Right now."

Wyatt stood and cast another smile around the room. "She'll be right back," he said. "I think."

Laughter erupted again as he followed Gabby into the hallway. Gabby slammed the door so hard, Wyatt couldn't believe its glass panel hadn't shattered.

"What the hell is wrong with you?" she demanded. "This isn't the Flying B! You can't just barge in here and do whatever you want!"

"Never know until you try," Wyatt answered. "Besides, you've been avoiding my calls."

"There's a good reason for that."

Wyatt crossed his arms over his chest. "So are you always this excitable around men, or is it just me?" he asked.

"Yes—no—Christ, what has that got to do with anything?"

Wyatt's expression sobered. "You left me little choice, Gabby," he said. "I needed to confront you where you couldn't avoid me. I thought about going to your town house, but I figured that you'd shut the door in my face."

"At least you got something right," she answered.

Despite her outward anger, Gabby sensed her affection for him trying to overcome her heart again. "Why'd you make me go on that ride?" she demanded. She seemed so upset that Wyatt thought she might actually stamp her feet. "I told you I was afraid of horses!"

Tears started invading her eyes, and she angrily brushed them away. "Goddamnit, Wyatt, I'm not Krista! And Trevor isn't Danny! Can't you see that? All the horse riding in the world isn't going to change that! You didn't respect my feelings, and I'll never forget it! And I'll never come back to the ranch!"

Gabby saw Wyatt suddenly blanch. He remained quiet for a time, thinking about what she had just said. It was clear that her words had stunned him. For a moment she thought she saw his eyes well up.

"And I'm not Jason," he answered hoarsely, his voice a near whisper. "I have no need to control you, Gabby—that's not how I'm built. But you're right—I shouldn't have pushed you into it. And of course I understand that you and Trevor could never be substitutes for Krista and Danny, and that you would never want to be. Like I said, I'd hoped that if you went riding, then maybe you'd better understand what Trevor was experiencing. But I must admit that there was another reason . . ."

"What?" she asked.

"I wanted an excuse to be alone with you," he answered quietly.

For a millisecond, a little smile crossed her lips. "Then why in hell didn't you say so?" she asked.

"I don't know," Wyatt answered. "I know now that I should have. But if I hadn't intruded in this way today, you might never have known." After looking at his shoes for a moment, he took a deep breath.

"When you fell off Caesar, I feared you were dead," he said quietly. "So many terrible things ran through my head that I could scarcely breathe. The idea of losing you was unthinkable."

His heartfelt words surprised her. But she was still unsure, and Wyatt's revelation only confused her all the more.

"Thank you for that," she said quietly. "But I'm still not sure how to feel about the riding incident, or about you, or about ever going back to the ranch . . ."

After quickly looking up and down the empty hallway, Wyatt decided. He simply couldn't, wouldn't lose this woman. Taking Gabby abruptly into his arms, he instinctively pulled her close—so close that his cheek touched hers and she could feel the warmth of his breath. The suddenness of it was shocking, but she didn't fight it.

"I'm truly sorry, Gabby," he whispered. "I meant every word I just said, and I need to be forgiven. We men can be slow learners, I know. But I understand about respecting your feelings. It'll never happen again, I promise. Please . . . I want you to come back . . ."

As she became lost in his embrace, for a few precious moments she put her arms around him. When he released her, her eyes remained closed, as if she was lost in some personal reverie from which she had no wish to awaken. Soon her eyes fluttered open, and she looked at his face.

"So am I forgiven, or not?" he asked.

"Did you really mean what you just said?" Gabby asked.

Wyatt smiled a little. "Cross my heart," he replied.

She nodded quickly several times. "Then yes . . . ," she answered quietly.

"Good," Wyatt said. "I'll look forward to seeing you out at the ranch later today, along with Celia and Trevor."

After giving her a long, commanding look, he headed down the hall.

Still overcome by what had just happened, Gabby watched him go until he turned the corner. Then she leaned back against the wall and took a deep breath.

"Oh, my . . . ," she said quietly.

THIRTY

FROM HER PLACE behind the ring wall, Gabby anxiously
watched Trevor. Under Mercy's watchful gaze, he and the
five other teens chosen to learn barrel racing were sitting on their
mounts in the indoor ring, awaiting her orders.

Two more weeks had passed. Gabby's wrist had healed and
the cast had come off, meaning that she no longer needed Celia's
chauffer services. She had also fully forgiven Wyatt, despite his
rather embarrassing way of asking. Although neither of them had
mentioned it since, Gabby's memories of it remained as sharp as if
it had happened only moments ago. She smiled knowingly.

Unorthodox, yes, she thought. *But I have to admit that it worked.*

Because Gabby feared horses, she had at first harbored mis-
givings about letting Trevor learn to ride. And falling from Caesar had certainly done nothing to help her overcome her dread,

either for herself or for her son. Even so, the program was helping Trevor change for the better, and she was immensely thankful. But during the last week or so, another worry had surfaced.

What will happen when the New Beginnings program ends? she wondered. *Will he revert to the sullen, introverted young man he once was, or will the changes in him be permanent?*

During her last meeting with Dr. James, Gabby had asked that very question. Dr. James's answer had been honest, but far from reassuring. Sometimes the teens' improvements remain, she said; sometimes they do not. The only course of action was to wait and see.

Wait and see, Gabby thought. Then her thoughts turned to Wyatt, and she sighed.

That seems to be the case with so many things in my life . . .

Gabby looked down along the observation path. Although she had always avoided watching the barrel racing, she'd come because today Wyatt had made a special point of asking her. He stood about twenty feet away, chatting with some of the other parents. His black Stetson was pushed back onto the crown of his head. The sleeves of his wrinkled, white work shirt were rolled up to his elbows; his expressive hands rested casually on top of the wall. When Wyatt smiled, Gabby watched the crow's-feet deepen in his tanned face and a pang went through her heart.

If wishes were horses, she thought, *I could stay here with him forever.*

As she returned her gaze toward the teens, she saw that they had begun trotting their horses around the outer edge of the ring. They were warming up, she guessed correctly. She became so engrossed in watching her son that she didn't notice Wyatt approaching.

"A penny for your thoughts," he said.

Gabby turned to him and smiled. "Private stuff," she said simply.

"Fair enough," Wyatt answered.

They stood in silence for a time, watching the teens ride. Even when Wyatt didn't speak, Gabby felt his presence strongly. It was almost like she could hear his heartbeat and sense his masculine energy. *If only I could read his thoughts, too,* she wished.

"Trevor is getting better, isn't he?" she finally asked.

Wyatt again leaned his forearms on the ring wall. "Yes," he answered. "He's had his share of difficulties, but he's improved a lot."

Suddenly Gabby's worries about Trevor resurfaced, reminding her of the favor she wanted to ask of Wyatt. Deciding that now was as good a time as any, she turned and looked into his damnably blue eyes.

"There's something I want to ask of you," she said. "I know how much you've already done for me and Trevor, but it would mean a lot."

Wyatt smiled. "What is it?" he asked.

"After the program ends, could I bring Trevor out to the ranch once in a while?" she asked. "I'm worried that the changes I see in him might disappear after he leaves here. If he could ride one of the horses occasionally, it might mean all the difference. I'd be happy to pay you, and—"

"Pay me?" Wyatt interrupted. "Your money's no good here,

Gabby. Of course you and Trevor can visit, and as often as you want. It will be nice to see you again."

Gabby didn't know what to say. Like so much about Wyatt, his answer had been cryptic. Although he had agreed, she had been hoping to hear more regarding how he felt about her. But still it hadn't come. As she turned to again look at the teens, Wyatt's words echoed in her mind. *"It will be nice to see you again . . ."* he had said. And that was all.

She had gotten her answer, but it felt unsatisfying. Then she looked at his right hand and again saw his wedding ring. It seemed that the simple gold band was an insurmountable barrier for each of them. Gabby did her best to smile.

"Thank you, Wyatt," she said. "I really appreciate it. Trevor will be thrilled."

Just then Mercy barked out another order to the riding group. Soon the teens and their horses had formed a line along the far side of the ring. Mercy dismounted and started carefully situating the three blue barrels on the ring floor. Despite Wyatt's apparent confidence, Gabby's all too familiar sense of worry again crept up her spine.

"Will he be okay?" she asked Wyatt.

Without taking his eyes from the rink, Wyatt nodded. "If not, I wouldn't allow it. And I'm particularly glad that you're staying this time."

"Why?" she asked.

Wyatt smiled again. "Oh, I have my reasons," he said.

After making sure that the barrels were placed properly, Mercy looked at Wyatt and he nodded back. She then singled out

Trevor and spoke to him. It seemed that at Wyatt's suggestion, Trevor was to go first. Trevor unexpectedly looked at his mother and tipped his hat toward her, causing Gabby to realize how much like a grown man he suddenly seemed.

Trevor sat tall on Gypsy, the bay mare that had been assigned to him early in the program. He looked totally at home in the very boots and Stetson that he once swore he would never wear. Gabby had come to understand that the Flying B was a world away from the glitz and glamour of Boca Raton. She also knew that unlike most of the other teens, Trevor fit in this other world completely and without reservation. He sometimes seemed as much at home here as Ram and Wyatt. On a signal from Mercy, Trevor trotted Gypsy out the far exit.

After taking a deep breath, Trevor slapped the reins hard against Gypsy's rear quarters. Spurring her into a frantic gallop, he steered her back into the ring. Dirt flying crazily from her hooves, Gypsy thundered hard toward the first barrel. As Gabby watched her only child charge headlong across the ring floor, she held her breath.

To Gabby's amazement, Trevor was in total control of his horse. He stood confidently in his stirrups, letting Gypsy do all the work. His riding was so smooth and accomplished that his upper body hardly shifted on the thundering mare. While Gypsy's muscles moved smoothly beneath her shiny coat, Gabby caught an occasional microflash of the mare's shiny horseshoes, furiously throwing up dirt.

Trevor and Gypsy rounded the first barrel well, and then charged headlong toward the second one. Gabby watched in awe as they also navigated that barrel with apparent ease. Trevor again slapped his reins against Gypsy's haunches, and they headed pell-mell toward the last one.

Digging in her heels, Gypsy seemed to literally spin on her hooves as Trevor gripped his saddle pommel and guided her through the pocket, his inside leg hard against her ribs to provide a strong focal point for her during the last turn. Then they thundered across the floor and back out the exit again.

Wyatt looked at Gabby and smiled. "Told you so," he said quietly.

Gabby was speechless. She'd had no idea that her son could ride like that! From this day forward, she would never see Trevor in the same light as before. As Trevor and Gypsy reentered the arena, the parents clapped and cheered. Trevor rode Gypsy up to where Wyatt and Gabby stood waiting.

"That was wonderful!" Gabby exclaimed. "I had no idea that you were so good!"

Trevor beamed at her, and he again tipped his hat the way Ram had taught him. "Thank you, ma'am," he said simply.

"Trevor and Gypsy have one more surprise for you," Wyatt said. Without waiting for a reply from Gabby, Wyatt looked at Trevor and nodded.

Trevor produced a leather riding crop from beneath his saddle. As he spoke to Gypsy, he lightly tapped the crop against her right shoulder. Gypsy then lifted her right foreleg and bent it beneath her shoulder, causing her to lower on one side. As her other foreleg stood firm, she bowed her head before Wyatt and Gabby, her dark mane falling forward.

Gabby was so overwhelmed that again no words would come.

But it didn't matter, because no sooner had she reclaimed her voice than Trevor wheeled Gypsy around and trotted her back to the line of waiting teens.

"My God . . . ," Gabby whispered.

Then she realized something, and she looked at Wyatt. "You helped Trevor cook up that last bit for me, didn't you?" she asked.

Wyatt smiled. "Guilty as charged, yet again," he admitted.

Gabby simply didn't know what to say. The gesture had been so touching that she would never forget it. "Thank you, Wyatt," she said softly. "And thank you for taking such an interest in my son."

Wyatt's gaze turned thoughtful. "You're welcome. Trevor is an easy person to like. And if I may be so bold, so is his mother."

They stood there quietly for a time, looking into each other's eyes in much the same way they had that first evening of New Beginnings. Then they again turned and gazed across the arena. Mercy was sending the next teen out to begin her barrel ride.

Wyatt cleared his throat and looked down at his boots. "It's Monday," he said. "Will you and Trevor be staying for dinner?"

Gabby nodded. "I'd like that. Besides, Trevor will brag about this all night! He might as well have an audience!"

"Good," Wyatt answered. "Anyway, I have to get back. Will you walk with me?"

"Shouldn't we wait for the other parents?" Gabby asked.

As Wyatt grinned, the corners of his eyes wrinkled up again. "Why?" he asked. "By now they can find their own way back to the big house, don't you think?"

While Gabby and Wyatt sauntered out of the ring, Gabby smiled.

THIRTY-ONE

A ND THEN THERE was the time that Wyatt shot one of the ranch trucks!" Aunt Lou exclaimed. "So help me God, he really did! Can you imagine such a thing? He couldn't have been more than sixteen! I'll never forget it as long as I live!"

Gabby's jaw dropped. During their visits to the Flying B, she and Trevor had heard several stories from Wyatt's youth. Once he was caught as naked as a jaybird in the hayloft with some town girl. Then there was the day that he broke his right leg trying to barrel race one of the farm's fastest studs without proper instruction. But of all the tales about Wyatt, this was surely the most outrageous. Gabby couldn't help but look at him and laugh.

"You shot a truck?" she asked.

When Wyatt nodded, Gabby turned to look at Trevor. Trevor seemed as shocked as his mother.

"My God!" Gabby said to Wyatt. "Why on earth would you shoot a *truck*?"

From the other side of the table, Ram chuckled. "Maybe he thought it was an alligator. He's real good at shooting *them*. He's shot lots of gators, but he's only blasted the one truck that I know of. Nowadays whenever he visits the ranch garage, the Jeeps all cringe in terror."

While everyone laughed, Wyatt sighed and shook his head. "It isn't what you think," he said to Gabby. "At least . . . not for the most part."

Eager to exploit this occasion, Gabby gave Wyatt a sly look. "So tell me about it," she said. "This I have to hear!"

"Ram and I were out on a hunting trip, searching for gators," Wyatt said. "I was about sixteen, and we were using one of the ranch pickups. We parked it near the lake then sat in the pickup bed in lawn chairs, waiting like that for hours. A couple of gators finally showed themselves, and I shot one of them. It was the first time I had ever been hunting, and I was as nervous as hell. Well, right after I shot the gator I lowered my gun. In my excitement I accidentally squeezed off another round, right through the bed of the truck and into the ground! It just missed the gas tank! If it had hit it, Ram and I wouldn't be sitting here today. Come to think of it, that might have been the same day that Ram's hair turned white!"

Gabby shot Ram a skeptical look. "Are you pulling my leg?" she demanded.

Ram smiled broadly. "Appealing as that might be, young lady, the answer is no. It's all true. I even kept that piece of the truck bed to prove it. There's a nice, clean, thirty-thirty hole through it, and it hangs on my office wall. I'd be happy to show it to you sometime."

Laughing uncontrollably again, Gabby covered her face with her hands. Wyatt just shook his head.

"I told Wyatt that I didn't mind him shooting the truck," Ram added casually, as he fiddled with his coffee spoon. "But what I could never figure out was how on earth he was planning to skin it!"

Gabby was soon laughing so hard that tears ran down her cheeks. She tried to talk, but couldn't. The best she could do was to shake her head and wave her hands, silently begging Ram to stop.

The six of them were finishing their pork chop dinners and Aunt Lou had again begun telling stories about Wyatt. Gabby knew how much Lou loved Wyatt, but that didn't keep her from brazenly relating some of the more embarrassing episodes from his past. Sometimes Gabby felt that the stories suited him. Other times they seemed quite out of character for the rather quiet, reserved man she secretly loved. That was partly because of how he had been tempered by the loss of his wife and son, she realized.

It would have been wonderful to have known him then, she thought, *when his heart was light and free.* Then Wyatt smiled at her again as only he did, and she realized that knowing him in the here and now was all that truly mattered.

Gabby knew that she and Trevor should be going, but she was enjoying herself. Besides, if they missed dessert Trevor would complain about it all the way home. Today had been special. She had never seen Trevor ride like that, and she wanted to stay a bit longer and enjoy the moment. As Aunt Lou left the dining room to fetch dessert, Gabby sat back in her chair and looked around.

Night had fallen in earnest. Butch and Sundance—awake for once—lay at Ram's feet. As the old grandfather clock struck nine times, Gabby wished she could stop that clock and with it time itself, so that she might stay here forever. Too few of these precious nights remained, and she was determined to make the most of them.

Soon the kitchen doors opened and Aunt Lou returned carrying a gorgeous-looking apple pie. Trevor grinned widely. No matter how much dinner he ate, he always had room for Lou's desserts. Lou placed the pie on the table.

"It looks wonderful, Lou," Gabby said. "How I wish I could bake an apple pie like that!"

"Pish-tosh!" Lou said. "There's nothin' to baking a good pie, child. First off you gotta start with fresh apples, then—"

Everyone suddenly heard boot heels running down the hallway. Mercy came barreling into the dining room. She was out of breath, and there was an excited look on her face.

"Sadie's water just broke!" she shouted. "Her foal is coming!"

Without a word, Ram, Wyatt, Big John, and Mercy hurried toward the open French doors. As the others started running across the lawn, Wyatt stopped and stared back at Gabby and Trevor.

"Aren't you coming?" he exclaimed.

Trevor jumped to his feet. "You're goddamned right I am!" he shouted.

"Trevor Powers!" she shouted. "That will be quite enough of that language!"

When Trevor reached Wyatt, they both turned and stared at

Gabby with equal incredulity. *God,* Gabby thought. *They're like two peas in a pod*. She suddenly realized that this wasn't the time for chastising Trevor, and she hurriedly joined them.

Wyatt shot a quick look at Aunt Lou. "Aren't you coming?" he asked.

As if nothing special was happening, Lou calmly poured another cup of coffee.

"Nope," she said. "I've seen it a hundred times before. Big John's been bringin' foals into this world for nigh on forty years. But my prayers go with you, just the same."

❧

BY THE TIME WYATT, Gabby, and Trevor arrived, Big John and Mercy were already tending to Sadie. As the others huddled together on the far side of the stall door, no one spoke. Gabby knew nothing about birthing foals, but she realized that the scene playing out before her was important. Sadie was lying on one side in the clean straw that Trevor had laid down only hours before.

"Do mares always lie down to give birth?" she asked Wyatt.

"Usually," Wyatt answered.

As Gabby looked over at Trevor, she suddenly realized that he had never witnessed a birth of any kind. He was fixated on the scene, his expression a mixture of worry and fascination. *This is indeed a day of firsts,* Gabby thought.

Soon Sadie's contractions started. As everyone watched, over the course of the next twenty minutes Sadie's foal was born. When the new colt arrived, everyone cheered. He looked perfect, with a gray coat like his mother's. Brushing tears from her eyes, Gabby laughed. Aside from when she'd first held Trevor in the hospital, she had never seen anything so wonderful.

"My God, Wyatt," she said. "He's beautiful."

Wasting no time, Big John cut the umbilical cord and Mercy painted the umbilical stump with iodine. They then gave the colt a quick examination to ensure that he was breathing regularly and to rule out unseen abnormalities. Soon he sat up on his hocks and elbows. When he started mouthing, Gabby realized that his suckling reflex had arrived.

"How many days before he stands all the way up?" Gabby asked.

When everyone laughed, she didn't understand. She gave Trevor a curious look.

"What's so funny?" she asked her son.

"He'll be up within two hours," Trevor said, his eyes still locked on the foal. "And soon after that, he'll be nursing." Trevor turned and looked apologetically at Ram and Wyatt. "Never mind my mom," he added casually. "She's still a city slicker."

As Ram and Wyatt laughed again, Gabby remained stunned by all that Trevor seemed to know about horses. "Did you learn those things here at the ranch?" she asked.

Trevor nodded, then returned his full attention to the foal.

Twenty minutes later, the foal was on his feet and eagerly suckling from his mother. When he had his fill, Sadie started licking him all over. Moments later, Ram beckoned Wyatt into the corridor. When they returned, each wore a mischievous smile. Gabby was about to ask what was going on, but Ram stopped her with a timely wink.

Ram cleared his throat. "So what do you think we should name him, Wyatt?" he asked.

"Well, I've got an idea about that," Wyatt said. "Do you suppose that Trevor should name him? After all, he's been taking care of Sadie for some time now."

Trevor immediately spun around and looked Ram straight in the face. Although words failed him, his delighted expression said it all.

Ram took a deep breath while making a great show of rubbing his chin. "I don't know. It's a big responsibility. Foals like this don't come along every day."

After silently torturing Trevor for a few moments longer, Ram smiled. "I suppose that it would be okay. Assuming Trevor suggests something we can live with, that is."

Trevor was so happy that he literally jumped up and down. *"Yes!"* he shouted jubilantly.

Big John and Mercy left the foal to his mother's care then walked over to join the others. As Big John hung his thumbs in his overalls, he gave Trevor a questioning look.

"So, young man," he said. "What's his name going to be?"

Unbeknownst to everyone else, Trevor had already selected a name. Since the day he'd first met Sadie and learned that her foal would be male, he had thought long and hard about it. He had even done extra research in the school library to help him decide. It was to have been his secret name for the foal, the name that only he whispered to him when no one else could hear. And now to his great amazement he had been granted the wonderful and unexpected chance to *actually* name Sadie's colt. His mind made up, he turned around and took a deep breath.

"We'll call him Doc," Trevor said simply.

This time Ram's skepticism was genuine. *"Doc?"* he asked. "That's all? I don't mind it, I guess, but it seems a pretty simple name for such a magnificent foal as this. What do you think, Wyatt?"

Wyatt was also hesitant. "I don't know . . . are you sure about this, Trevor?"

Trevor nodded. "We'll call him Doc," he insisted. Then he smiled. "But not just any Doc."

"What are you talking about?" Ram asked.

"We'll call him Doc *Holliday,*" Trevor answered gleefully. "You already have Wyatt and Morgan. It just seems right, don't you think?"

For several moments, no one spoke. Then Ram laughed uproariously. Soon everyone followed suit.

"By God, the boy's on to something!" Ram said. He grabbed Trevor's shoulders and gave him a strong hug. "Doc Holliday it is! And well done, too!"

As Trevor smiled from ear to ear, Gabby was overcome again. "Good job," she said quietly. "But we should head back to the house now."

Trevor looked at Sadie. "You did just fine, girl," he said quietly. "I'm proud of you."

Soon everyone save for Big John and Mercy started walking back to the mansion. This had been a momentous day for Trevor. But before the night ended, he would hungrily gobble down two big slices of Aunt Lou's apple pie, complete with vanilla ice cream.

It would be the best he had ever tasted.

THIRTY-TWO

THREE WEEKS LATER, on a Saturday afternoon, Trevor sat alone in his bedroom doing homework. The New Beginnings Program would end soon, and he already knew that he would miss the ranch badly.

His stomach growled, reminding him that he had skipped lunch. His mother had gone to run errands, promising to return in time to make supper. She would try to re-create Aunt Lou's Cajun chicken, she had said. Then she had laughed, adding that she could make no promises about the results.

Trevor sighed and turned the page in his geometry book. To his dismay, yet another group of incomprehensible problems stared back at him, daring to be solved. Prior experience told him that they were exactly the sort of thing that might prompt a surprise quiz. But as he examined them, he didn't care.

Whether his restlessness came from hunger or from pure lack of interest, he didn't know. He only knew that he missed the Flying B, and that Monday couldn't come quickly enough. Bored to tears, he decided to switch to his English homework. He was behind on his reading of *Moby-Dick,* anyway.

When he reached for his books, his elbow struck them, causing them to slide off his desk and onto the floor. They were still bound tightly by his father's belt, and had landed alongside his trusty red Windbreaker and beloved cowboy boots.

He started to reach for the books, then he stopped and sat back in his chair. There was something odd about the belt, the Windbreaker, and the boots all lying together like that. He couldn't remember ever seeing them that way, and he found it jarring. The belt spoke of his late father, the Windbreaker reminded him of his anger, and his boots took him back to the Flying B. He stared at the disparate objects for a long time, realizing that they represented very different parts of his life. *But which of them means the most to me?* he wondered.

No easy answers came, and the longer he wondered, the more the mystery deepened. Although the sudden realization had been nearly twelve weeks in the making, not until this moment had he felt so torn between different worlds. Feeling sad and powerless, he left his bedroom to sit on the town house balcony.

Although he had always enjoyed the balcony, nowadays it felt cramped. The view was nice enough, but it didn't compare with the one from the front porch of the big house. As Trevor reclined on one of the lounge chairs, he looked out over the canal that lay before the town house complex. To his left lay the swimming pool, its cool water filled with fellow residents and their children. Trevor sighed, again wishing that he was out at the ranch. It always seemed cooler there, and less crowded.

Wyatt, Aunt Lou, Big John, Mercy, and Jim Mason had all taken root in his heart. But it was Ram who had given him his treasured pocketknife, taught him to face down Tim Richardson, and allowed him to name Sadie's colt. It had again been Ram who was the most patient with him, and taught him the manly rules of the ranch. Of them all, it was that old, bowlegged codger with the shock of white hair he cared for most.

He also knew that he had learned more than equestrianism. He had come to realize that the Blaines were good people, and not the monsters he had believed them to be. That last thought again caused him to remember his father's death. For a long time he had tried hard to bury that special hurt, but it continued to haunt him. He sat there on the balcony for some time, again feeling threatened by it.

After staring blankly out at Boca Raton for another half hour, he finally decided. Leaving the balcony behind, Trevor walked into his mother's bedroom. Because she wasn't home, he felt like an intruder. When he reached the far side of the room, he slid open the closet door with unnecessary stealth.

On the top shelf of the closet lay a cardboard box. Reaching up, he gently took it down and placed it on his mother's bed. Gabby had often mentioned the box and where it could be found, but until this moment he had never wanted to see it. His mother called it "the Jason box," and she said that it contained mementos of Trevor's late father.

For the last five years, Trevor had been torn about whether to look inside the Jason box. He knew it contained things of his father's he wanted to see, and that knowledge heightened his curiosity. But knowing that certain other items were also there had always stopped him. For some reason that he couldn't explain, he suddenly needed to examine them all. With trembling hands, he removed the lid from the box and looked inside. What he found brought back painful memories, and he wiped away a tear.

He saw a lock of his father's sandy hair, its strands tightly collected by a red ribbon. There were two gold wedding rings, also bound with ribbon. Next to them was a white gold wristwatch that Trevor vaguely remembered. The watch crystal was smashed, its bent hands permanently frozen at 3:21. He saw the flaking remnants of a withered red rose, some wedding pictures of his mother and father, and a small stack of letters and greeting cards addressed to his mother in her maiden name.

When Trevor removed these things from the box and looked at them, his hands trembled because he knew what would come next. He tentatively looked back into the box. To preserve the precious documents, his mother had secured them in plastic zip bags. After gently putting the first objects aside, he removed the press clippings and the police report, and started to read.

∽

GABBY HAD BEEN AWAY longer than planned, and night had fallen. As she juggled her bags with one hand and unlocked the front door with the other, she was surprised to see that save for a shaft of light coming from the hallway, the town house was bathed in darkness.

She quietly placed the packages on the kitchen table then tip-toed to the hallway corner. The door to her bedroom lay open; the lights were on inside. For several moments she was afraid that an intruder had entered the house. But her maternal instincts quickly overcame her fear, and she had to know if Trevor was all right.

"Trevor?" she called out.

"I'm in here," he answered softly.

Gabby walked down the hallway and into her bedroom. When she saw Trevor sitting cross-legged on the floor, surrounded by the contents of the Jason box, she drew in a sharp breath.

For several moments, mother and son simply stared at each other. Then Gabby crossed the room and sat down on the carpet alongside him. Before looking into Trevor's eyes again she picked up the two wedding rings, remembering. After a time she gently placed them back on the floor.

Gabby realized that Trevor had finally read the press clippings and the police report, because they had been removed from their zip bags and lay unfolded on the carpet. Traces of Trevor's splotchy tears could be seen here and there on them, and his eyes were red. Gabby gave her son a compassionate look.

"So you finally read them," she said softly. "That's good."

Trevor sniffed and rubbed his nose. "If it was so good, then why does it feel so bad?"

"Because the old adage is right. Sometimes the truth hurts."

Trevor's face darkened. "My father was a drunk, wasn't he? He was a drunk who went out and killed two innocent people. The accident was his fault, not Mrs. Blaine's."

"That's right," Gabby answered. "And yes, your father had a

drinking problem. But he never meant to kill Danny and Krista, any more than he planned for himself to die. He wasn't a bad man, Trevor. He loved us both very much, regardless of what you might think."

Trevor blinked back some fresh tears. "Why don't the Blaines hate us?" he asked. "Especially Wyatt . . . I can't believe that he let me into the New Beginnings Program."

Gabby tried to smile. "Wyatt realizes that we aren't to blame. But he wasn't the only hurdle. Do you remember that day in Principal Marshall's office? It was like you *wanted* to get kicked out of school."

"I know," Trevor said. "And I'm sorry. I just didn't know who I was supposed to be, or how I should act."

Gabby nodded. "You've been through a lot. But tell me—do you see things more clearly now?"

Trevor looked down at the yellowed papers and nodded.

"And do you still love your father?" she asked.

He nodded again. "Yes. Despite what he did."

"That's good," Gabby said, taking Trevor's hands into hers. They felt warm, their palms still damp with his tears.

"And the Blaines?" she asked. "How do you feel about them now?"

"I love them, too. Is that wrong?"

Gabby shook her head. "No. We owe them more than we could ever repay. And now that you've told me all this, I realize something else about you."

"What?" Trevor asked.

Gabby placed her hands on either side of her son's face and

lifted it to hers. "You've forgiven *everyone*. You've come full circle, and you've made me proud."

For the first time since the car crash, Trevor laid his head on Gabby's shoulder. Seated among the aging mementos of her previous life, she held her son close.

"But the day after tomorrow starts the last week of the program," Trevor said quietly. "What will I do without the ranch?"

It had suddenly become Gabby's turn to become emotional. While fighting back tears, she searched for the right words.

"Oh, we'll go back once in a while," she said, her voice nearly cracking as she thought about Wyatt. "I've already asked Wyatt, and it's fine with him. But we mustn't go too often, or we'll wear out our welcome. And don't forget—the Flying B annual ball comes soon."

"But it won't be the same," Trevor said. "I'll miss it all so much."

So will I, Trevor, Gabby thought. *And in a special way that you will never know.*

THIRTY-THREE

"M AY I BE of help?" the saleslady asked pleasantly.

"I hope so," Gabby answered.

The woman standing before Gabby was slim and middle aged, with long, auburn hair. As befit her profession, she was impeccably dressed and coifed. The gold-colored nametag pinned to her suit coat read: GWENDOLYN MARCH, FASHION CONSULTANT. None of these elegant touches surprised Gabby. After all, this was Neiman Marcus.

"Please call me Gwynne," the other woman said.

"And I'm Gabby."

Gabby wanted help choosing a gown. She always knew her own mind when it came to clothes, and she had good taste. But by her own admission, this purchase had to be just right. To help make sure, she had asked Celia to join her in the hunt. As expected, the snoopy redhead had been only too happy to tag along.

"Is this for a particular occasion?" Gwynne asked Gabby.

"You can say that again," Celia chortled.

"And what sort of function is it?" Gwynne asked.

"It's a ball," Gabby answered.

"And I assume that it's formal?" Gwynne asked.

"Yes."

Gabby removed the engraved invitation to the Flying B annual ball from her purse and gave it to Gwynne. The ball was six days away. Gwynne recognized the invitation immediately.

"Oh, you lucky thing!" Gwynne said. "Every woman in Boca would give her eyeteeth to be invited!"

"No kidding," Celia quipped.

"You're the third woman this week I've assisted for this occasion," Gwynne gushed. "And that's a good thing, because it'll help keep you from showing up in the same dress as someone else!"

"Always a plus," Celia said under her breath to Gabby, "especially when peasants go hobnobbing with the rich and famous."

"Sorry?" Gwynne asked.

"Never mind," Gabby said. "May I see some recommendations?"

"Of course," Gwynne answered. "I assume that you're an eight?"

"Yes."

Gwynne returned the precious invitation to Gabby. "I'll be right back."

While Gwynne went to collect some dresses, Celia wandered over to a rack of gowns that were marked down. Even the sign announcing the deep discounts somehow exuded an air of superiority. As Celia perused the prices, she groaned.

"Good God, Gabbs!" she exclaimed. "This isn't retail therapy—it's credit report suicide!"

Gabby sighed. "I'd rather not think about that part of it."

"And just what part of all this *are* you thinking about?" Celia asked as she selected a dress for closer examination. "It wouldn't have to do with a certain eligible rancher, would it?"

Gabby only smiled.

Celia returned the gown to the rack then walked back to Gabby. "Fish that invitation out of your purse again," she ordered. "I never did get a proper look at it."

Gabby handed the invitation to Celia. It was made of bone-colored paper, heavily engraved in emerald ink. The Flying B insignia adorned the outside. As Celia opened it and read the particulars, she shook her head.

"What's wrong?" Gabby asked.

"You say that Trevor also got one of these?" Celia asked.

Gabby nodded. "Each of the New Beginnings kids did."

Celia grudgingly returned the invitation to Gabby. "Then what they say must be true."

"What's that?" Gabby asked.

"That youth is wasted on the young," Celia answered. "Now I've seen the proof."

Gabby was about to laugh when Gwynne and two more salesladies returned, each of them carrying a gown. When Gwynne beckoned Gabby toward the dressing rooms, the others followed. As Gabby went off to try on one of the dresses, Celia plopped down in an upholstered guest chair.

"Would you like some coffee while you wait?" Gwynne asked.

For Celia, that was manna from heaven. "God, yes," she

answered. "Please make it iced coffee, if possible, with cream and sugar."

A few minutes later Gabby emerged, wearing what Celia could only describe as some sort of red, bunched-up monstrosity that collected too high on the shoulders. Gabby regarded herself in the triple mirror for a moment before turning and giving Celia a questioning look.

"Must I say it?" Celia asked.

"Yes," Gabby answered.

"You look like a circus horse," Celia said.

"You're right," Gabby said.

After taking another sip of coffee, Celia waved Gabby away. "Back to the drawing board, girlfriend," she said.

The next time Gabby emerged, she wore something even worse—black, shiny, and truly awful. Celia shook her head.

"This time you don't have to say it," Gabby said.

"That's good," Celia answered, "because it's hideous on so many levels that I wouldn't know where to begin."

Gabby disappeared again. When next she returned, Celia nodded happily.

"Now that's more like it!" she said.

Gabby knew that this was the gown. It was a dark blue strapless affair with a form-fitting bodice and a ruffled hem.

Gwynne walked closer and cast her expert gaze over Gabby's selection. She smiled broadly.

"This might be the one," she said. "Tell me—will you be dancing?"

The image of being held in Wyatt's arms made Gabby smile. "I certainly hope so," she said.

"Then please put your heels back on and let me see you walk," Gwynne requested.

Gabby slipped back into her shoes and walked across the floor and back. Gwynne and Celia both smiled.

"That's the one, Gabbs," Celia said.

"She's right," Gwynne said. "It moves with you beautifully. And we won't have to alter it. You'll need full-length gloves and matching heels, though. I can help with both."

Gabby again thought of Wyatt, and of what the coming ball might be like. For a few moments she turned and wheeled around happily, letting the hem of the gown flow about her. Then she stopped and looked in the mirror again.

Will he really ask me to dance with him? she wondered.

THIRTY-FOUR

I'M SO SORRY that all this has to end, Gabby thought. *These last twelve weeks have been like a wonderful dream, and I will always treasure them. But if my fairy tale must stop, it is certainly doing so with style.*

It was a perfect Saturday evening, the night of the Flying B annual ball. Gabby was sitting at an outdoor table, sipping champagne and making small talk with some of her tablemates. Always the conscientious hosts, Wyatt, Ram, and Morgan were dutifully wandering among the many fashionable guests.

Gabby had never seen the ranch this crowded. Also, the Flying B was so elegantly decorated that it looked for all the world like some grand, five-star hotel. Dressed in formal attire, more than three hundred guests milled about the grounds and wandered in the big house. An annual ball tradition, many of the women were carrying fans to help ward off the humidity. Had Gabby known, she would have brought one, too.

Gabby looked splendid in her new gown and matching stiletto heels. They had cost her a small fortune. Her elegant full-length gloves had also been an extravagance, but worth it. Gifts from her late grandmother, a string of white Akoya pearls, lay around her neck, and a matching bracelet adorned her left wrist. This was the first and only time she had worn anything other than Western-style clothing at the ranch, and the change was welcome.

Wherever Gabby looked she saw important people, including several judges, the mayor, and many business and community leaders. There was also a gaggle of wealthy old ladies wandering about, who probably made it their sole remaining purpose in life to attend exclusive functions such as this one. Gabby smiled as she imagined them trying to chat up the ever irascible Ram. Then she smiled even more broadly as she imagined Ram trying to escape from them.

Also scattered among the decidedly upscale group were all of the teens who had just graduated from the New Beginnings Program, their parents, the two psychotherapists, and all the ranch hands. The program had ended yesterday with a brief graduation ceremony, during which each boy and girl received a diploma and a silver lapel pin formed in the shape of the Flying B insignia. The girls wore colorful party dresses. The boys wore jackets and slacks, and each teen proudly sported his or her new pin. Trevor was here, but Gabby had lost track of him some time ago.

No need to worry, she realized. *He's no doubt in the main barn with Sadie and Doc.*

Decorating the ranch had taken a full week, every bit of it done under the stern gaze of Aunt Lou. Dozens of tables for ten with matching upholstered chairs dotted the manicured grounds. Each tabletop was graced with an embroidered white tablecloth, a crystal candelabra, and a huge bouquet of fresh orchids. Each piece of china, flatware, and leaded crystal was engraved with the Flying B insignia. Uniformed waiters and waitresses continually offered up silver trays laden with succulent appetizers. Champagne flowed, while elegant music wafted on the evening breeze.

White lights had been strung on the big house, on the eaves of the barns and guest cottages, and in each of the magnolia trees lining the long private road from the highway to the mansion. Inside the house, garlands of fresh red roses graced the banisters of the magnificent staircase and the second-story railings. Elegantly dressed men and women gathered around the foyer grand piano as a pianist played one request after another. By Ram's edict, it was a long-standing tradition that only candles should illuminate the big house during the annual ball. Tonight was no exception, and the subdued glow gave the entire mansion a decidedly Old South feel.

Near the swimming pool, a portable dance floor had been assembled where a nearby band of twenty professional musicians played everything from waltzes to rumbas. Their cares seemingly lost in the moment, dozens of men in tuxedos and women in beautiful gowns glided across the dance floor. Many of the women held their open fans behind their partners' backs as they danced, adding color and gaiety to the scene.

Gabby sipped her champagne, thinking. The cost of this

soiree was surely huge, but she understood its immense business value to the Blaines. Most of Boca Raton's movers and shakers were here. Before this night ended, new business ventures would be born and old ones reaffirmed.

Gabby again looked at her place card. Like the invitation she had received in the mail two weeks ago, it was elegantly engraved in emerald ink. When she first found her seat, she was delighted to learn that Wyatt's card lay directly to her left, Trevor's card to her right. On the other side of Trevor's card lay the cards for Sally Richardson and her parents.

Gabby wanted to believe that Wyatt was responsible for the seating arrangements, but she couldn't be sure. As her curiosity mounted, she remembered that little went on around here that Aunt Lou didn't know about. Rising from her chair, Gabby made her apologies to her tablemates then lifted the hem of her gown and headed for the big house.

The foyer was filled to overflowing with happy guests. The sounds of laughter, popping corks, and tinkling glasses eagerly filled the night. Expensive perfume and Cuban cigar smoke conspired to lend an exotic aroma to the air. The game room was especially busy, with men playing pool and cards. Four liveried bartenders stood behind the mahogany bar, busily mixing cocktails to order.

Gabby saw Mercy seated at the poker table, eagerly dealing five-card stud to five unsuspecting men. Mercy's pale green gown was lovely, and her dirty blond hair had been freed from its braids and arranged in an upswept style that nicely suited her face. The effect was striking, and quite unlike the Mercy Gabby knew.

Gabby smiled, wondering how much money Mercy would rake in tonight. She then wended her way among the guests and down the hallway to the kitchen.

Gabby had expected the kitchen to be busy, but what she saw surprised even her. Despite Lou's ability to produce mountains of food, she and the three house girls couldn't handle such a large function all by themselves, and so the annual ball was always a catered affair. But that didn't stop Lou from taste-testing every course, and constantly harassing the many waiters and waitresses as if they were Confederate plantation slaves. As Gabby entered the kitchen she weaved and dodged, trying to avoid the hordes of busy workers who were furiously laboring under Lou's command.

"Damnit all!" Aunt Lou shouted at one of the cooks. "Can't you move any faster with them appetizers? The people out there are hungry!"

The cook scowled before wisely obeying the big woman who was pointing a massive mixing spoon at him like some kind of deadly weapon. Purposely avoiding her dark eyes, he picked up his pace. Then Lou saw Gabby, and she smiled from ear to ear.

"Miss Gabby!" she shouted from the other side of the great kitchen. "Come over here, child!"

Gabby carefully wended her way across the kitchen. The place was so crowded that she could hardly get through.

"Whew!" she said when she finally reached Lou. "What a madhouse! So this is how it all gets done!"

Lou smiled, her broad face shining beneath the kitchen's fluorescent lights.

"Yep!" she said. "The first of these shindigs was held some

forty years ago, and I told Mr. Ram right there and then that if he wanted the rest of the house lit only by candlelight, so be it. But I was goddamned if I was going to try and operate this kitchen under nothin' but candle power!" She gave Gabby a wink. "We argued about it for nearly a week before he finally gave in. Men aren't that hard to handle, once a girl knows how!"

Gabby laughed then turned and again watched the organized chaos taking place before her. The kitchen was filled to overflowing with food in various stages of preparation. Some of it was being cooked on-site while the rest had been prepared at the caterers and trucked in. The formal dinner menu was crab cocktail, Caesar salad, steak and lobster with mushroom risotto, and baked Alaska. It all sounded delicious, and with Aunt Lou watching over things, Gabby knew that it would be.

Gabby discreetly beckoned Lou toward one corner of the kitchen. "Can I ask you something personal?" she asked.

"Course, child," Lou answered. "You're damn near family."

"Do you know who was responsible for the seating arrangements?" Gabby asked.

Before answering, Lou grimaced then again aimed her big spoon at yet another unsuspecting waiter. "You there!" she shouted. "Straighten up that tray you're carrying, or those stuffed mushrooms will go all over my floor! Good God, boy, ain't you never done this before?"

Lou finally turned back to Gabby. "What was that again?" she said.

"The seating arrangements," Gabby answered, this time blushing a bit. "Do you know who put Wyatt beside me?"

Lou nodded. "Mr. Morgan always does it. He knows best who should go with who cause of all the business deals and such."

Gabby's heart fell. "Are you sure that Wyatt didn't do it?"

Lou gave her a teasing smile. "Now just why would you care *who* did it? The result is still the same."

"Please don't toy with me, Lou," Gabby answered. "I think you know why I'm curious."

"Truth is, I saw Mr. Wyatt change those cards after they had been put down," Lou answered.

"You did?" Gabby asked eagerly.

"Yep," Lou answered. "Just before the guests were due to arrive. He did it on the lowdown, like some kind of sneak thief or somethin'. He didn't see me watchin' him, but that don't matter."

Gabby couldn't have been happier. "Thank you," she said.

Lou took Gabby's hands and looked into her eyes. To Gabby, the Cajun woman's big, brown irises seemed endless and comforting. "He fancies you," Lou said. "Hell, a child could see it. And I can tell that you feel the same way about him. But . . ."

"But what?" Gabby asked.

Shaking her head, Lou sighed. "I jes' don't want you gettin' your hopes up about him. He's not like other men. Ever since Miss Krista died, he can't . . ."

"I know, Lou," Gabby answered. "And I thank you for your concern. But for now, I'll take however much of Wyatt that he'll give me. And if it isn't all of him, then I guess that it's better to have loved and lost . . ."

"I hope that you're right, child," Lou answered. Her broad smile reappeared. "Now get out of my kitchen! Besides, a woman as beautiful as you should be out on that dance floor, breakin' hearts!"

"I couldn't agree more," another voice added.

Gabby turned to see Wyatt approaching. She immediately worried that he might have overheard her conversation with Lou. But if he had, his face didn't show it.

This was the first time Gabby had seen Wyatt in formal attire. Again she realized that he could wear anything from Armani to Levi's with equal aplomb. His black tuxedo was perfectly tailored, and his bow tie had been hand knotted. A simple white silk hand-kerchief peeked discreetly over the top of his breast pocket. His tuxedo shoes had been shined to perfection; he smelled faintly of fresh cologne.

"Good evening," Gabby said to him. "You look wonderful." She stole a quick glance at his left hand to see that his wedding ring remained in place.

Wyatt let go with a disparaging smile. "We men all look the same in these penguin suits," he answered. He took both her hands in his and turned her one way then the other. "But *you're* a real stunner! Wouldn't you agree, Aunt Lou?"

"I would indeed," Lou answered. "But I want you two out of here, and right now! I got work to do!"

Wyatt guided Gabby across the kitchen and out the open French doors. As they walked, Gabby decided to take a chance. She stopped, causing him to stop with her.

"May I tell you something?" she said.

Wyatt turned and looked in her eyes. His face had the same craggily handsome appearance as that other night in the moonlight, not so long ago. Gabby knew full well that after tonight she might not see Wyatt for some time. She could always greet him during Sunday worship at St. Andrew's, she supposed, but it wouldn't be the same. And because of that, she wanted this moment to last.

Wyatt noticed the wistful look in her eyes. "What is it?" he asked.

Gabby wanted to tell him what was burning in her heart, but at the last moment different words escaped her lips. "Will you dance with me?" she finally asked.

Wyatt smiled. "I'm not very fond of it, but since it's you asking, okay. I must warn you that I'm pretty terrible at it. Those pretty feet of yours could become crushed beyond all recognition."

Gabby smiled. "I'll risk it."

As Wyatt led Gabby toward the dance floor, guest after guest turned to watch them. It was no secret that Wyatt didn't like to dance. Since Krista's death he was always deluged with requests at the balls, most of which he politely declined. While he and Gabby took the dance floor, women started speaking to one another in hushed tones behind the protection of their fluttering evening fans. Their men seemed no less interested as they looked Gabby up and down with approval, and in some cases lecherous envy.

Just as Wyatt and Gabby reached the dance floor, the current tune ended. Wyatt gave Gabby a thoughtful look. "Excuse me for a moment," he said. "I'm going to request something special."

When Wyatt walked over to the band leader and spoke to him, it became apparent that they knew each other. The band leader glanced at Gabby then smiled at Wyatt and nodded. When

Wyatt returned to Gabby, the band leader raised his baton.

As Gabby was taken up in Wyatt's embrace for what she feared would be the last time, she immediately recognized the song that he had requested. It was perhaps her favorite of all, and she could only wonder how he had come to choose it. It was "As Time Goes By," from the movie *Casablanca*.

Gabby soon found that Wyatt had fibbed about his dancing skills. As he smoothly led her across the floor, she was reminded of the song lyrics. She knew them by heart and they seemed especially poignant tonight. Holding Wyatt closer, she gently placed her cheek against his. As she smelled his cologne, she closed her eyes.

But for her, time was the enemy. She suddenly felt like Cinderella at the prince's ball, and that the hands on the great clock were quickly nearing midnight. But she was no true Cinderella, and she would leave no glass slipper behind for Wyatt to discover and return to her. For her the fairy tale would not come true, and once she left this enchanted place behind, her life would reclaim its particular brand of loneliness. But for now she was in his arms, and the world was theirs.

As the lyrics echoed in her mind and she drifted across the floor, she again wondered how it was that Wyatt had chosen this song. *Casablanca* was about two lovers who came to realize that a life together could never be. Was that what Wyatt was trying to say? Was this his enigmatic way of telling her good-bye?

While the guests watched and the music played on, Gabby held Wyatt closer.

THIRTY-FIVE

W HAT THE HELL is so important, James?" Ram asked. "And why must we talk in private? You're keeping me from my guests!"

"I know," Reverend Jacobson answered. "But since when did you ever worry about decorum, you old reprobate? You can spare the time."

Ram closed his study door. After putting a freshly opened Jack Daniel's bottle and two glasses on his desk, he motioned the reverend toward one of the twin upholstered guest chairs.

Before sitting down, Ram closed the mahogany blinds, shutting out the festivities. He then opened the humidor on his desk and selected a hand-rolled Cuban cigar. After running it under his nose, he cut its tapered end and lit the other. The reformed smoker sitting across from him found the aroma tempting.

Ram quickly sensed the reverend's need. Smiling, he selected another cigar and offered it to his friend. "Want one?" he asked.

"More than you could ever know," Jacobson answered.

"Then have one, for Christ's sake. I'll never tell anybody. And neither will God."

Jacobson raised an eyebrow. "How do you know God won't tell?"

Ram blew some pungent cigar smoke toward the ceiling. "Doesn't matter, even if he does. No one would believe it. You see, when people talk to God, it's called prayer. But when God talks to people, it's called paranoia."

Jacobson sighed. "Oh, what the hell . . ."

Ram cut another cigar; the reverend lit it. Ram poured some bourbon for each of them and pushed one of the glasses toward Jacobson. The reverend puffed on his cigar approvingly then sipped his drink.

Ram's little experiment had worked. If Jacobson was willing to placate Ram by smoking again, his reason for corralling Ram must be an important one. Each man was a master manipulator and always had been. One manipulated in the service of the Lord, while the other did so to serve his family. *We each have our cross to bear,* Ram thought.

Leaning back in his chair, Ram crossed his feet on the desktop. For the first time tonight, Jacobson realized that Ram was wearing an old pair of scuffed cowboy boots with his tuxedo. Jacobson couldn't decide whether the effect was comic or sad.

Jacobson shook his head. "You're wearing *boots*?"

Ram nodded and took another sip of Jack. "My shindig, my

rules. Now what's so goddamned important? Has St. Andrew's run out of money, or something?"

"No," Jacobson said, thoughtfully rolling the glass between his palms. "I've come to tell you something, and to also ask a favor of you. I've struggled with whether to approach you for some time."

Ram's eyebrows lifted. "What is it?"

Jacobson set his glass on the desk before looking back into his old friend's eyes. "I want you to tell Wyatt your secret," he said softly.

Ram's face turned scarlet. "That's no longer your business, and you know it! I thank you for comforting Phoebe and me when we needed you, but that time has long passed. Leave it alone, James."

"I know how you feel, but I have my reasons," Jacobson said.

Ram glared hotly at the reverend. "That doesn't mean I want to hear them."

"You might not *want* to hear them, but you *need* to hear them," Jacobson answered. "You're confusing 'want' with 'need.' It's one of your trademarks."

"Why should I listen to you?" Ram demanded.

"Because something has come to light," Jacobson answered. "But if I tell you about it, our conversation must never leave this office."

Ram raised his eyebrows. "Whatever it is, it must be a doozie," he said. "I can practically see a devil on one of your shoulders and an angel on the other, each of them whispering into opposite ears. I'm glad that I don't have that problem. Must be confusing as hell."

Jacobson nodded. "For you, hell is just a theory. For me, it's an occupational hazard." He paused for a moment then took another sip of bourbon. "The reason I'm being so insistent is because it concerns Wyatt."

With a swiftness that belied his seventy-seven years, Ram lifted his feet from his desk and sat upright. "Tell me."

"Wyatt came to me in confidence not long ago, searching for answers," Jacobson said. "He wanted to know if I believed that our loved ones look down on us from the afterlife. I'm afraid that I was of little help to him on that score. But something unsettling came out of that conversation, and I thought you should know about it."

"What is it?" Ram asked.

"Wyatt feels personally responsible for Danny's and Krista's deaths," Jacobson answered. "He is as certain of it as anything in his life. He said that if it hadn't been his birthday, they'd both still be alive."

When Ram started to object, Jacobson raised a hand. "There's more," he said. "It seems that much of Wyatt's misplaced grief is rooted in the fact that Danny and Krista went on that fateful errand because he asked them to."

A stunned look overcame Ram's face. "I never knew that," he said quietly.

"Apparently, neither did anybody else," Jacobson answered. "I know it's crazy. But I also know how much you can appreciate Wyatt's feelings. After all, you—"

"You can stop right there," Ram said. "We both know what you're talking about, and we agreed to never mention it again. It was a terrible time in my life. I don't need it resurrected by you or anybody else."

"That's just it!" Jacobson protested. "You found a way to forgive yourself. But Wyatt can't, and it's slowly killing him. I think that if you tell him, it will help. Besides, it's time that *both* your boys knew about it. Keeping it from them is a lie."

Ram shook his head. "No, it isn't. Besides, I promised Phoebe that I wouldn't."

Jacobson leaned closer. "I believe that you lawyer types call it a lie of omission. And besides, Phoebe isn't here. If she were, she would agree with me."

Feeling tired, Jacobson sat back in his chair. Arguing with Ram was always exhausting. He still didn't know whether Ram would agree to confide in Wyatt, but one thing was certain. If Ram continued to refuse, the reverend had one last card up his sleeve. He didn't want to play it, because it would hurt the wonderful old man sitting across from him. But if he had to, he would.

From out of nowhere an unexpected image appeared in the reverend's mind. Being in this secluded office and asking a favor of Ram reminded him of the first scene from *The Godfather*. While well-wishers enjoyed an elegant party at the family patriarch's expense, an acquaintance dressed in formal attire was seated before him in his office, humbly requesting a highly difficult favor. In some ways, Ram was like the Godfather. They were both commanding, strong, and often men of few words. And each of them was a patriarch for whom the well-being of his family was paramount. As the wall clock ticked off the seconds, the reverend waited.

Ram finally shook his head. "I won't do it, James. I can't."

"You must," Jacobson said. "You've got a boy who's in trouble."

"Goddamn it!" Ram bellowed. "Don't you think I know that?"

Angrier with himself than with Jacobson, Ram stood and turned around. Out of frustration he opened the blinds and looked out on the party.

Jacobson sighed. It seemed that he must play his trump card, after all. "There's another reason you should tell him now," he said.

Ram sighed and lowered his head. "Time," he said softly.

"Yes," Jacobson answered. "The sad truth is that one day you will lose your mind. You won't be able to recognize yourself, much less Wyatt or Morgan. I'm sorry, but there it is. By then, you will have lost your chance forever. Wyatt can still learn something important from his father. Please give him the opportunity before it's too late."

As Ram stood there remembering, he closed his eyes. What Jacobson was talking about had occurred long ago. He and Phoebe had been young then, and another of their many hopes was unknowingly taking form. Like so many important occurrences in Ram's life, his memory of it started in this very office . . .

❧

THE AUTUMN DAY WAS unusually warm even for Florida, as had been the blazing summer that preceded it. The Blaine Law Firm, as it was then known, was but ten years in the making and growing quickly. Morgan was ten years old; Wyatt was six. Fall had officially arrived three weeks before, and the boys had returned to school. In about two more hours, they would be home.

Ram sighed as he focused his attention on the will that he was writing for a prominent Boca businessman. Because it was Friday, he had chosen to finish the work here at the ranch and then enjoy the weekend with his family.

Hearing laughter, he swiveled his chair and looked out the blinds toward the newly constructed swimming pool. Dressed in a one-piece bathing suit, Phoebe laid poolside on a lounge chair.

Their liver-and-white springer spaniel, Calamity, was begging for scraps from the poolside lunch that Aunt Lou had just served. Ram's lunch lay untouched on a nearby table. Laughing again, Phoebe tore a bit of meat from her hamburger and tossed it into the pool. Calamity eagerly obliged and jumped in after it.

Ram sat there for some time lovingly watching his wife. Despite giving him two boys, her body remained lean and graceful. Her face was lovely, her blue eyes were bright and inviting, and her reddish-brown hair shone in the afternoon sun. She was the only woman he had ever met who could call his bluff, and she knew it. Ram loved her more than life, and despite his increasingly gruff demeanor he could deny her little.

Deciding to eat, he opened the doors of his study and walked across the lawn. Calamity was the first to notice and bounded toward him joyfully. Ram cringed as she shook the pool water from her coat.

He approached Phoebe and kissed her on the forehead. "And how's my other pet?" he asked.

Phoebe smiled as she adjusted her white sunhat. "Who wouldn't be fine on a day like this? Have you finished that will, you overpriced shyster?"

Ram took a judicious bite from his hamburger then ran one hand through his dark hair. "Nope. I saw a pretty girl by the pool, so I thought I'd come and see if I could have my way with her."

"Fat chance, cowboy," she answered coyly. "Business before pleasure, remember? Somebody has to pay the bills, and because you're too chauvinistic to let me work, I guess that 'somebody' must be you."

Ram sat down on a pool chair. "I suppose you're right," he said, hungrily taking another bite. "You usually . . . are . . ."

"Stop talking with your mouth full!" Phoebe ordered teasingly. "Were you raised in a barn?"

Ram laughed and pointed toward the stables. "Pretty much."

Phoebe leaned back in her chair and looked out over the shimmering pool. Across the way stood the boys' playground. Ram had ordered its construction eight years before. It had a slide, a sandbox, and several adult-size swings. The boys no longer used it, and Ram intended on tearing it down. Phoebe then returned her gaze to the man she loved so much.

She grinned as she watched Ram finish his lunch. Grabbing a napkin, she wiped some errant ketchup from his mouth.

"Now get back to work," she said laughingly. "Like I said, somebody around here's got to pay the bills!"

After giving her another kiss, Ram returned to his office and refocused his attention on his work. Realizing that he needed to consult a law volume, he left his chair and walked toward the massive bookcase lining the far wall.

Just then he heard Calamity bark and Phoebe laugh. Smiling, he stopped and looked out the sliding glass door to see what was going on. Phoebe was swinging wildly on one of the old playground swings. Calamity was barking madly and running back and forth, trying to keep pace with her mistress's speedy rhythm.

Just then Phoebe's and Ram's world changed forever, as one of the swing chains let loose from the top rail, sending Phoebe flying. Screaming, she landed hard some thirty feet away and tumbled end over end. His heart in his throat, Ram tore from the office and ran to her. When he turned her over, she tried to smile.

"I guess I should have let you have your way with me after all . . . ," she said weakly.

Crazed with worry, Ram looked into her eyes. "Are you all right?" he demanded.

Phoebe slowly moved each limb to find that they all worked. "I guess so. Help me up."

But as Ram started bringing her to her feet, she gasped and her eyes went wide. Then she suddenly collapsed in his arms. She reached up with one hand to weakly grasp his sleeve.

"Oh, my God . . . ," she said, just before passing out.

Phoebe recovered, but the newly conceived child within her had died on the spot. Even she had not yet known she was pregnant. When the doctors told them, Ram and Phoebe were desolate. They had wanted another child, preferably a girl. But now, that was not to be. Worse, Phoebe would bear no more children. After spending two days in a Boca hospital, she returned home.

Aunt Lou and Big John knew of the tragedy, because they had come running immediately after Phoebe fainted. The other hands understood, too, but over time they all left for different work and were replaced. Because the ambulance arrived before Morgan and

Wyatt came home from school, the boys remained unaware. To protect them from worry during Phoebe's time away from the ranch, Ram told his sons that she had gone to visit her sister.

While Phoebe lay sedated in the hospital, that very night Ram used a sledgehammer to personally demolish the accursed swing set. Big John heard the noise and came out, offering to help. With tears streaming down his face, Ram angrily ordered him away. He alone would destroy the thing that had killed his unborn child, he said. After nodding sorrowfully, Big John trudged back to the house.

Immediately after, Ram's guilt over not dismantling the swing set sooner began crushing his spirit. He had suspected that it needed to come down, but because the boys no longer used it, and because of his constant busyness with the ranch and his law firm, he had put it off. Instead, he had allowed it to kill his unborn daughter, and injure his beloved Phoebe. When he confessed to Phoebe in the hospital, she forgave him on the spot. But the self-forgiveness that Ram needed would come much harder, and be years in the making.

When she returned home, Phoebe begged him never to tell Wyatt and Morgan. No good could come from recounting the tale, she said. It would only rekindle his grief, and instill unneeded pain in their boys. And so their sons were never told, and life went on . . .

❧

WHEN RAM TURNED AROUND to again face Jacobson, his eyes were moist. The reverend looked at his glass for a time, then back at his friend's face.

"Phoebe was never angry with you," he offered. "There was no need—you blamed yourself enough for two. Yes, you should have dismantled the damned thing sooner. But what's done is done. After all, you didn't know that it would give way. And who could have guessed that Phoebe would ever do that? Self-recrimination is death to one's soul, Ram. It made no more sense for you back then than it does for Wyatt now."

"I know," Ram answered.

"I also know how close you are to your boys," Jacobson said. "But this secret wall between you and them must come down, if for no other reason than Wyatt needs you right now. It's amazing how such destructive barriers can grow up between people who love each other. And oddly enough, sometimes they're easily ignored. You have to tell him, Ram. It's what Phoebe would want."

Ram wiped his eyes. "Wyatt is right."

"About what?" the reverend asked.

"You really do know how to hit below the belt."

"You should see the other tools in my godly skill set," Jacobson answered. "So will you tell him?"

Ram took a deep breath. "I'll try."

"Thank you," Jacobson answered. "It seems that I owe you. I'll leave my payment right here."

Jacobson crushed out his cigar, telling Ram that he understood its meaning. His work finished, he left the study and quietly closed the door. After staring blankly at the door for a time, Ram closed his eyes.

He had of course long understood Wyatt's grief over the loss of his wife and son. And illogical as it might be, he also suspected that Wyatt might somehow hold himself accountable for their deaths. But until tonight, Ram had never grasped the full depth of Wyatt's personal guilt. And like Jacobson had said, the dual walls of tragedy that had grown between him and Wyatt had kept each of them from telling the other his secret. *Like father, like son,* he thought.

Feeling emotionally spent, Ram sat down heavily in his chair. The other part of what Jacobson had said was also true. Ram had largely forgiven himself for that awful day. But could he impart that wisdom to Wyatt? Would he be able to find the right words to help his troubled son?

Ram reached out and poured another two fingers of bourbon. As he sipped it, his tears came again. Then he grasped the beloved old photo of Phoebe that sat on the desk.

"If only you were here, my darling," he said softly. "I could use your help just now . . ."

THIRTY-SIX

A S THE PARTY wound down, Gabby glanced at Trevor. He looked handsome in his new blazer and slacks. He was eagerly chatting with Sally, causing Gabby to more fully realize how close they had become. With her Goth appearance banished for the night, Sally looked positively transformed. She wore a tasteful red party dress, with matching heels.

It was going on one A.M., and the formal dinner had ended hours ago. Most of the guests had left for home, leaving a few diehards partying inside the big house or gliding about the dance floor. Gabby couldn't compare this ball to previous ones, but if the guests' merriment had counted for anything, tonight had been a roaring success. Wyatt had left the table about half an hour ago to mingle with his remaining guests. Gabby guessed that Ram and Morgan were doing the same.

Gabby stared down at the remnants of her baked Alaska. There remained much that she wanted to say to Wyatt, even though the night was ending. Her best chance had been while they danced, but the moment had carried her away. During dinner, decorum had demanded that their conversation remain superficial. And so she bided her time, hoping that he would return to her.

Gabby again looked around. She would miss this place, and she was grateful to Wyatt for allowing her and Trevor to revisit the ranch anytime they wanted. But the more she thought about it, the more she guessed that it wouldn't happen. She had come to realize that seeing Wyatt occasionally, only to have their relationship never deepen, would be far too painful for her. Trevor would be disappointed, meaning that she would have to find a good excuse for not returning. If her fairy tale was to end, it was appropriate that it do so on the night of the annual ball. She would never forget the Flying B, and it was truly a pleasure to have known—

"Is this chair taken, young lady?" a gravelly voice asked.

Gabby turned to see Ram standing alongside her. He looked comic in his tuxedo and cowboy boots. Drink in hand, Ram sat heavily in Wyatt's chair.

"Looks like the party's nearly over," he said. "That's good! I love the yearly ball, until I remember how much damn work it always is. Then I can't wait to see everybody go home. It's like beating your head against the wall, simply because it feels so good when it stops." The old man rubbed his chin. "Does that make me a bad host?"

Gabby smiled. "There isn't a host in the world who hasn't felt that way at the end of a long night. That doesn't make you bad. It only makes you human."

"Bless you," Ram said. "How do you always know the right thing to say?"

Ram watched Gabby's expression sadden. "I don't," she answered. Again looking into Ram's old eyes, she decided to speak her heart. "Especially where Wyatt is concerned," she added softly.

Ram sighed. "You care about him a lot, don't you?"

Gabby nodded. "More than I have a right to, it seems."

For the first time since knowing Gabby, Ram scowled harshly at her. "Don't you ever say that again! He's the problem, not you! He couldn't find a better woman if he looked for a thousand years!"

Gabby was taken aback by Ram's outburst. Realizing that he had startled her, Ram took her hands into his.

"I'm sorry, my dear," he said. "It's just that I learned something about Wyatt tonight and it upset me. It wasn't totally unexpected, but it disturbed me just the same. It reaffirmed the fact that I'm probably not the world's best father."

"Is something wrong?" Gabby asked.

Ram picked up his drink and took a long swallow. "Nothing that hasn't been hanging around for the last five years."

Gabby was about to ask Ram what he meant, then saw Wyatt approaching. He looked tired, but he managed to smile.

"It seems that you two have become inseparable," Wyatt said.

Gabby laughed. "He can bother me anytime. I think he's sweet."

"*Sweet?*" Wyatt asked. "I've heard him called many things, but never that."

"Then it's high time that somebody did," Ram countered.

Wyatt looked over at Trevor. "How are you doing, pal?"

"I don't want to go home, but I'm tired," Trevor said.

"Before you leave, I want to see you and your mother alone," Wyatt said. "Would you mind coming into the house?"

"Why?" Trevor asked.

"You'll see."

Ram winked and nudged Trevor's ribs. "Don't worry," Ram said. "I'll keep all the other young bucks away from Sally until you come back."

Her mind racing, Gabby followed behind Wyatt and Trevor. She desperately wanted to talk to Wyatt, but what she had to say wasn't meant for Trevor's ears. After they entered the house, Wyatt shepherded them among the few guests still mingling in the foyer, and then toward the huge curved staircase.

Gabby and Trevor had never been upstairs. To their delight, they found it nearly as impressive as the first floor. As their curiosity grew, Wyatt led them down one hall and then another. After stopping before a pair of double doors, he opened them and ushered Gabby and Trevor into an elegant bedroom.

"Let me guess," Gabby said. "This one's yours."

"Yes," Wyatt answered as he walked across the room and toward another set of ornate doors.

He opened them to reveal a huge walk-in closet. After disappearing into the closet for a moment, he returned with two packages. Each was wrapped with blue paper, and bound with red ribbon and a matching bow. Wyatt handed the larger package to Gabby and the other to Trevor. The mother and son looked at Wyatt with surprise.

"What are these?" Gabby asked.

"They're going-away presents," Wyatt answered.

As the reality set in, Gabby took a sharp breath. *Going-away presents,* she thought. *It's really going to happen . . . I really am going away.* She did her best to smile.

"You didn't have to do this . . . ," she said.

"I wanted to," Wyatt answered. "So are you two going to open your gifts, or do you need another engraved invitation?"

Gabby and Trevor unwrapped the packages. When they saw their contents, their eyes became wide. Gabby's gift was a stylish gray alligator purse with sterling silver accents. It was a beautiful thing that would easily retail for two thousand dollars in any of Boca's classier boutiques.

Trevor's gift was equally impressive. It was an alligator hip wallet with an attached silver chain and was also dyed light gray. Both the wallet and the purse were tastefully embossed with the Flying B insignia. Gabby and Trevor stared at Wyatt with amazement.

"My God, Wyatt, they're beautiful," Gabby whispered. "But we can't accept them. They must have cost a fortune!"

"Not really," Wyatt answered. "Do you remember my story about those two gators I shot? Well, let's just say that their contribution was larger than mine."

"Holy shit!" Trevor shouted gleefully. "These are really made from those dead gators?"

Gabby started to reprimand Trevor then stopped, deciding that she hadn't the heart for it.

Wyatt laughed. "That's right. Big John knows a local leathersmith who did the work. Alligator hide is tough. Your presents should last forever."

But this evening won't, Gabby thought. As she stood looking at Wyatt, she blinked back tears.

While Trevor eagerly placed his wallet into the hip pocket of his slacks, Wyatt showed him how to attach the other end of the silver chain to one of his belt loops. When Wyatt finished, Trevor was grinning from ear to ear.

"Thank you, Wyatt!" he said. "Nobody at school has anything as cool as this!"

"You're welcome," Wyatt answered.

"Trevor, would you mind going back to the table?" Gabby asked. "I'd like to talk to Wyatt for a moment."

"Okay," Trevor answered happily. "I'll see you down there."

After Trevor left the room, Gabby took a deep breath and looked at Wyatt's face. If she never saw him after tonight, she wanted to remember him as best she could. And so she simply stood there for a time, drinking him in.

She gazed at his slightly graying temples, and the endearing crow's-feet at the corners of his amazingly blue eyes. His strong, expressive hands hung loosely by his sides. True to form, he had discarded his bow tie some time ago, and the top two buttons of his tuxedo shirt were open. A telltale five o'clock shadow had formed on his face and she could still smell faint traces of his cologne, reminding her of when they had danced.

Almost unconsciously she turned and looked around his bedroom, her searching gaze finally landing on the four-poster bed. Wyatt and Krista had shared that bed, Gabby knew. As an image of their entwined bodies crystallized in her mind, Gabby's emotions turned ever more bittersweet. She was glad that Wyatt had shared such intimate moments with Krista, but she was also saddened that she would never experience that kind of bliss with the enigmatic man standing before her. *Krista must have understood him,* Gabby thought. *But perhaps I was never meant to.*

The wistful look in Gabby's eyes was not lost on Wyatt. He reached out and took her by her shoulders. "What's wrong?" he asked.

Gabby looked into his face. "Nothing . . ."

"What was it that you wanted to tell me?"

Gabby hesitated for a moment before again glancing at his left hand. Just as she suspected, his gold wedding band shone in the light of the room. *That ring will be with him so long as he remains bound to Krista's memory,* Gabby realized. *His heart isn't ready for me. Perhaps it never will be.*

Wyatt pulled her closer. As she became lost in his embrace, Gabby closed her eyes. "Tell me," he asked again, quietly this time.

Very well, Gabby decided. *Because when all is said and done, I cannot lose a love that I never had . . .*

Gabby opened her eyes. "Wyatt, I—"

"Wyatt, where the hell are you?" a familiar voice unexpectedly called out.

The spell suddenly broken, Wyatt and Gabby turned to see Morgan come barreling into the bedroom. On seeing Wyatt holding Gabby that way, an odd look came over Morgan's face. Guessing that he had just interrupted a special moment, he unnecessarily cleared his throat.

"Sorry to interrupt," Morgan said, "but I've been looking all over for you. Dad wants us downstairs, and pronto. The Winthrops are leaving."

Wyatt gently released Gabby's shoulders. For her, the loss of his touch seemed final, irrevocable. Wyatt turned back and looked into her eyes.

"I'm sorry," he said, "but I have to go. The Winthrops are Blaine and Blaine's biggest clients. Will I see you before you leave?"

Gabby suddenly realized that her heart simply couldn't endure this scene again. The moment had passed forever, it seemed. Even so, she somehow forced herself to smile.

"Of course," she said. It was the only time she had ever lied to him, and doing so stabbed at her heart as sharply as knowing he was leaving.

After Wyatt and Morgan left the room, she sat heavily on the bed. The sounds of the waning party drifted up into the room, but for Gabby the festivities were taking place a million miles away.

When she again looked at her new purse, this time she opened it. To her surprise, one of Wyatt's engraved business cards lay inside. With trembling fingers, she removed it to find a handwritten note on its backside. Although the words were few, they broke her heart:

So that you will remember me . . .
—Wyatt

THIRTY-SEVEN

B Y THE TIME all the guests had departed, Wyatt was exhausted. It was nearly three A.M. He was sick of being sociable, and he hungered for some quiet time before turning in.

To his surprise, Gabby had left without saying good-bye and he felt her absence sharply. After bidding good night to the Winthrops he had searched for her, only to learn that she and Trevor had already left. Walking Gabby and Trevor to their car had become a welcome habit for him, and he missed doing so tonight more than he might have guessed. Because Gabby had left so suddenly, her behavior left him wondering. But as he sat on the porch with the night's final glass of bourbon, he could find no ready answers.

The ball had ended about an hour ago. All the guests, caterers, and musicians had packed up and departed, making the Flying B strangely quiet in their aftermath. The lights adorning the big house and the outbuildings had been switched off, leaving only moonlight to illuminate the grounds. Now the only music came from the chirping crickets, their gentle chorus accompanying the rhythmic creaking of Wyatt's rocking chair.

Gabby and Wyatt had parted company many times before, but never without saying good-bye. Because the New Beginnings Program had ended, Wyatt wondered whether he would ever see her again and the uncertainty stabbed at his heart. Her stealthy departure seemed somehow treasonous to him, like she had rushed off to become entwined in the arms of another man. But because she wasn't his, no such treachery existed. Even so, he felt abandoned.

Wyatt looked across the grounds and toward the old cemetery, its headstones glinting palely in the moonlight. He thought of his mother, of Krista and Danny, and of all the other Blaines who had been laid to rest there. He liked to believe that each of them had somehow secured his or her own measure of happiness before dying. *But will I?* he wondered.

Wyatt's next sip of bourbon tasted bitter—a sure sign that he had reached his limit. Moments later, Ram approached and sat down in the rocker alongside Wyatt's. For some time the father and son said nothing, each of them glad that another annual ball had come and gone.

"Good party," Ram said.

Wyatt nodded. "I guess."

Ram turned and looked at his son. "Why so glum?"

"Just tired, I suppose."

"Yeah, but that's not the entire reason, is it?" Ram asked.

Wyatt shrugged his shoulders. "Did you see Gabby and Trevor leave?"

"Yep. Gabby seemed upset. She tried to hide it, but I knew different."

When Wyatt didn't respond, Ram made up his mind. *Jacobson was right,* he realized. *This moment is long overdue.*

"I know that it's late," Ram said, "but we need to talk. Although you won't like what I have to say, you're going to hear it anyway." Despite his desire to call it a night, Wyatt waited calmly.

"Do you remember the old playground that used to stand near the swimming pool?" Ram asked.

The question surprised Wyatt. "Sure," he answered. "Morgan and I always wondered why it was there one day and then gone the next. You and Mom never told us."

His eyes shiny with tears, Ram told Wyatt the story that he had kept hidden for so long, including his failure to dismantle the swing set. Soon Wyatt's eyes were also moist. He stared incredulously at his father.

"My God . . . ," he whispered.

"Your mother begged me not to tell you boys," Ram answered. "So I didn't. Because I felt responsible for what happened, she didn't want to make things worse, or to have my sons think ill of me."

Wyatt gazed toward the family cemetery. "Was it a boy or a girl?" he asked softly.

Ram shook his head. "Dunno. There wasn't enough of the child to warrant a burial, and we didn't have such fancy tests in those days. That's why there's no marker in the cemetery. Even your mother didn't know she was pregnant until after the accident."

Ram also turned to look at the cemetery. "Phoebe and I even had names picked out ahead of time, if she ever became pregnant again," he said wistfully. "Another son would have been called Virgil. A daughter would have been named Annie."

Wyatt smiled faintly. "Virgil Earp and Annie Oakley . . ."

Ram nodded. "My first choice for a daughter was Calamity, after Calamity Jane. I thought that it was a fine name for a girl, but your mother wouldn't hear of it."

"And so you named the dog Calamity," Wyatt said.

"Phoebe and I compromised."

"Why tell me this now?" Wyatt asked.

"Because I've come to realize that my story has as much to do with you and Gabby as it ever did with Phoebe and me."

Wyatt scowled. "How so?"

"Whether you know it or not, Gabby has become the best thing in your life," Ram answered. "I'm not trying to belittle how much you cared for Krista and Danny. But by letting Gabby go, you're rejecting a wonderful future. The difference between her and you is that she knows it. She also understands that your heart is still burdened, so she keeps her feelings about you to herself." Pausing for a moment, Ram lit his first cigarette of the new day.

"I know that a man has to make his own decisions," he said. "But you're still devoting your life to two people who are gone and are never coming back. Krista wouldn't want that. And if Danny had been old enough to understand, he wouldn't have wanted it either. Blaming yourself accomplishes nothing, save for ruining your life. Trust me, I know. I suffered the same guilt about your mother and our unborn child. Some days, I still do. But I expect you to do better."

"I don't know if I can," Wyatt said.

Ram took another drag on his cigarette, its far end brightening in the relative darkness. "Then let me say one last thing, son. After that, I'll never speak of this again. Hell, Wyatt, dying is easy. Any dumb bastard can die. But living—really *living* after suffering a great personal tragedy—that's the hard part. It takes a brave person to get on with living again. And last time I checked, I hadn't raised any cowards. So whatever your real feelings might be, stop trying to deny them by smothering them in guilt. Instead, search your heart for what you really want and set it free."

Ram looked down at his boots for a time. When his eyes returned to Wyatt's, they held a faraway look. "I don't want you to end up like me," he said simply. Saying nothing more, the old man stood and walked into the house.

Left alone again, Wyatt pondered his father's words. As he did, he returned his gaze to the cemetery. He soon imagined another family headstone nestled there among the others. Somehow he knew that his mother's unborn child had been a girl. The imagined headstone was smaller, and it bore the name Annie Blaine. He again thought about Krista and Danny, and Gabby and Trevor.

And then, like a suddenly bursting dam, the floodgates guarding his heart finally opened. His armor had at long last been shed and his repressed wants and needs truly broke through, causing fully fledged tears to run down his face. Holding up his trembling left hand, he saw his wedding ring. The simple gold band suddenly seemed foreign and unnecessary. Soon he was on his feet and walking toward the cemetery.

As Wyatt opened the gate, its old hinges creaked with familiarity. He walked across the well-tended earth until he found himself standing before Krista's grave. After removing his ring for the first time since his wedding day, he stared in silence at Krista's cold, lifeless headstone. When Wyatt spoke, his words arrived as softly and earnestly as his tears.

"I still dream of you, you know," he said. "And Danny, too. Maybe I always will. And those dreams are the only way I have of seeing you again. I loved you more than life. But you're gone, and I have to face that." His tears coming harder now, he took a deep breath then let it out slowly.

"But there's something else you need to know, Krista," he added softly. "Although in my own way I will never stop loving you, my heart has finally been freed. Not from your memory, but from the mistaken belief that I could never love another the way that I loved you. I was wrong, my darling, and I hope you can forgive me for what I must now do."

Wyatt went to his knees. The earth was soft and gave way easily to his touch. After burying the ring before Krista's headstone, he stood.

"Good-bye, my love," he whispered.

With tears still streaming down his face, he finally stood. He then looked up at the stars, as if he could watch his heartfelt words rising toward the heavens.

"Wyatt?" a voice called out in the darkness.

Wyatt turned to see Mercy standing just outside the cemetery fence. After walking back through the gate, he faced her. She, too, was still wearing formal attire.

Wyatt took a deep breath. "You heard?"

Mercy nodded. "I didn't mean to. I couldn't sleep, so I was taking a walk. All the excitement, I guess. I'm sorry."

Wyatt shook his head. "Don't be."

Mercy took a deep breath then she, too, looked up at the stars for a time. Before gazing back at Wyatt, she wiped away some tears.

"The heart wants what it wants, Wyatt," she said. "And as much as it pains me to say it, we've both come to realize that your heart wants Gabby."

When Wyatt started to speak, Mercy reached out and placed her fingertips against his lips. She shook her head.

"It's all right," she whispered. "I suppose I've known ever since that night Sadie's colt was born. I saw her and Trevor leave tonight, and she seemed upset. Go to her, Wyatt, before it's too late."

Wyatt stepped closer. Leaning forward, he gave Mercy a light kiss on one cheek.

"Thank you," he said, and then he was gone.

THIRTY-EIGHT

S EVEN HOURS LATER, Gabby lay awake in bed. Her sleep had been fitful, at best. She looked at her alarm clock to find that it was nearly ten A.M. As she thought of Wyatt, tears came again and she quickly brushed them away. Then she remembered that it was Sunday, and she groaned. She and Celia had made plans to eat breakfast together and then go shopping.

Some retail therapy might do me good, Gabby thought. *But not so much as some hot coffee and a brisk shower . . .*

Right on time, the doorbell rang with an insistency that only Celia could somehow muster. Gabby groaned again and covered her head with her pillow. Celia was her best friend, but it was too early to suffer her snooping.

She'll be frantic to find out about last night, Gabby realized. *That's too bad, because she'll surely be disappointed.*

There was no point in dallying, so Gabby threw off the covers.

After trudging to the closet, she grabbed a nightshirt at random and pulled it on over her head. Without looking, she stepped into the nearest pair of slippers. As she shuffled toward the front door she realized that she had slept in her makeup and that she must look terrible, but she didn't care. Then the doorbell rang again.

"Jesus, Celia!" she shouted. "Knock it off! I'm coming as fast as I can!"

Without peering through the security lens, she opened the door. She was fully prepared to give the snoopy redhead a good piece of her mind when her jaw dropped open.

Wyatt stood there, looking her up and down with mild curiosity. He was dressed in ranch clothes. After pursing his lips, he made a comic show of examining the number on her town house door.

"The Powers residence, I presume?" he asked.

Despite last night's party he seemed as fresh as a daisy, with a smile to match. He checked the door number again then looked back at Gabby.

"Strange," he said, shaking his head. "I was told that a beautiful woman lived here. Do you know where she might be?"

Gabby was mortified. She instinctively moved to close her robe before remembering that she was wearing only the flimsy nightshirt. When she tried to speak, no words came.

"Wyatt . . . ?" she finally uttered.

"In the flesh," he answered.

Wyatt held a bulging Dunkin' Donuts box in one hand, and a tray containing two paper coffee cups in the other. Only he and God knew how he had managed to ring the doorbell.

"May I come in?" he asked. "I brought caffeine and sugar, two of my favorite food groups."

"Uh, er, yes—yes, of course," Gabby said, still nervously clutching the front of her nightshirt. Wyatt sauntered in and looked around.

"Please don't take this the wrong way," Gabby said. "But what are you doing here?"

Wyatt set the coffee and doughnuts on the kitchen table. After Gabby shut the door, Wyatt looked into her eyes.

"I need to talk to you," he said, "and I didn't want do it over the phone. I hope that you can forgive my barging in this way. I got your address from Trevor's New Beginnings application."

Wyatt handed her a cup of coffee. "Drink that. It's not as potent as Aunt Lou's, but it's pretty good."

"Bless you," she answered.

Like him, she drank her coffee black. The paper cup warmed her hands, and the life-giving brew tasted good. She suddenly wondered what she must look like, so she stared across the kitchen and into a wall mirror. To her horror, it was even worse than she'd thought.

Her hair and makeup were a total mess. The nightshirt that she had chosen at random had been a gag gift from Celia. Across its front, huge letters read: A DAY WITHOUT SEX IS LIKE A DAY WITHOUT SUNSHINE. Then she looked down at her feet. Her slippers were hot pink, with bunny faces embroidered across the toes and pink bunny ears drooping down on either side. Gabby groaned inside.

Jesus, she thought. *Of all the mornings in all the world . . .*

Wyatt sensed her embarrassment and smiled. Then he pointed

to her nightshirt. The phrase printed there hung strangely askew, as it blanketed the twin peaks of her breasts.

"I couldn't agree more . . . ," he said.

Wyatt's wolfish comment wasn't lost on Gabby, and she blushed. "Could you give me a couple of minutes to pull myself together?" she asked.

Wyatt smiled. "Sure. I'll just sit here with my health food. By the way, is Trevor home?"

Unsure, Gabby glanced at the message board clinging to the refrigerator door. It read: *"Gone to the pool."* She pointed it out to Wyatt.

"Ah," he said.

Desperate to make herself more presentable, Gabby left the kitchen. Ten minutes later she returned wearing jeans, a gray sweatshirt, and white Keds. Her face was washed, her teeth were cleaned, and she had put her dark hair up in a scrunchie. The new and improved Gabby certainly didn't qualify as a *Vogue* cover model, but she would have to do. She again joined Wyatt at the table. Too nervous to eat a doughnut, she politely took another microsip of coffee.

Wyatt smiled at her approvingly. "Better," he said.

"What did you want to talk to me about?" she asked. Beneath the tabletop, one of her feet began to twitch.

Wyatt put down his coffee. "Are you angry with me?"

"God, no! Why would you think that?"

"Because you left the ball without saying good-bye. Ram and Mercy thought you were upset. Was your Honda about to turn into a pumpkin or something?"

Her mind racing, Gabby tried to devise an answer that wouldn't give too much away. "I was very tired, and so was Trevor. That's all it was. I was planning to call you today, to thank you again for your wonderful gifts."

Wyatt sat back in his chair. "Okay. I'll settle for that."

Gabby said nothing for a time as she tried to adjust to the fact that Wyatt had come to visit her. Only minutes ago she'd thought she would never see him again. And now here he was, calmly drinking coffee at her kitchen table. Although the doughnuts weren't glass slippers, it seemed that the prince had found her after all.

"Was there something else?" she asked.

Wyatt nodded. "I know that it's a spur-of-the-moment thing, but I'd like you and Trevor to come with me. One of the ranch Jeeps is parked outside. We're leaving for the day—assuming that you're interested."

"Where are we going?" Gabby asked.

"Back to the Flying B. I was hoping that Trevor could spend the day there while you and I ventured off on our own."

"Where?" Gabby asked again. Her foot was twitching even faster now.

"I want to show you my lake house," Wyatt said. "It'll be just you and me, for once. Aside from your ill-fated horse ride, we've never spent more than an hour in private."

Gabby's heart leaped at Wyatt's offer, but she needed to be sure of his motives. She gave him a sly smile. "Why, Mr. Blaine," she said. "Are you asking me out on a *date*?"

"Yes, Ms. Powers," he answered. "I do believe that I am."

THIRTY-NINE

WYATT SHIFTED GEARS again as he steered the four-wheel-drive Jeep across the Florida grasslands. Gabby sat beside him, happily watching the countryside roll by. She was wearing sneakers, shorts, and a checkered shirt. At Wyatt's suggestion she had also brought along a swimsuit, which lay inside her tote bag. Wyatt was still wearing his ranch clothes. Before leaving, Gabby had called Celia and begged off on their plans for the day. True to form, Celia made Gabby swear to call her later and tell her everything that happened.

Courtesy of Aunt Lou, a cooler full of food and beer rested in the back of the Jeep. Gabby smiled, as she thought about the lovable old Cajun woman who was such an integral part of the Flying B. Gabby had long suspected that Lou was in her corner, especially after confiding to her that Wyatt had secretly rearranged the table seating at last night's ball. When Gabby told Lou that Wyatt was taking her on a real date, Lou kissed her crucifix then gave Gabby a celebratory hug. For his part, Trevor was ecstatic about returning to the ranch so soon. To Gabby's relief, he also seemed pleased that she and Wyatt were going off by themselves.

The day was hot and clear, and according to Wyatt the drive would take about fifteen minutes. Sometimes he came by horseback, he said, especially if he was planning to stay the night. Gabby thought that the landscape was pretty, in a rugged sort of way. She was eager to see the lake, and the small house that was Wyatt's private retreat.

Reaching into the back of the Jeep, Gabby retrieved a water bottle. After offering Wyatt a sip, she also drank some. As the Jeep jostled beneath her, she took a moment to consider the unexpected changes she was noticing in Wyatt.

He hadn't suddenly become a different person, but he did seem far happier and that made him even more attractive. Wyatt's mood had always been pleasant enough, if often somber. Like everyone who understood him, Gabby knew why. But for the first time, Gabby sensed a sustained lightness about him that hadn't been there before.

Earlier in the day she had also noticed that his wedding band was missing, and she suspected that its absence had something to do with his changed mood. She very much wanted to ask him about it, but she decided not to pry. If he wanted her to know, he would tell her in his own good time. For now she had Wyatt all to herself, and that was enough.

A few minutes later, Wyatt unexpectedly stopped the Jeep.

Gabby couldn't guess why, because she could see nothing before them but more scrubby grassland. Deciding to tease him a bit, she looked at him and smiled.

"If you wanted to go parking, all you had to do was ask," she said. "But I can think of more comfortable vehicles in which to do it."

Wyatt laughed. Leaning forward, he rested his tanned forearms on top of the steering wheel. "I want to show you something," he said.

Gabby raised her eyebrows. "Like what? There's nothing out here but a lot of grass and tree clumps. It's endless."

"Exactly," Wyatt said.

"I still don't get it."

Wyatt pointed into the distance. "Look out at the horizon," he said. "Then follow it full circle until your eyes return to their starting point."

Gabby did as he asked, but she saw nothing new. "Okay," she said. "What's the big secret?"

"No secret," Wyatt said. "It's just that for as far as you can see, you're looking at Flying B land. One needs to actually come out here in order to grasp the full scope of the ranch."

Gabby was amazed. Although she knew that the Flying B was huge, until this moment her idea of the ranch had been limited to the big house and its immediate surroundings. Like the man sitting beside her, the Flying B was much more than she had first supposed.

"My God," she said. "I had no idea."

Wyatt smiled and shifted the Jeep back into gear. "I know,"

he answered. "Nobody really gets it until they come out here. I'm glad that you could see it. I'm also glad that after five long years, I have someone to share it with again."

Ten minutes later, they arrived. The little house on stilts was adorable, Gabby thought. The lake looked broad and clean, its sky blue water rippling lightly in the wind.

"It's wonderful," she said.

Wyatt smiled. "Ram and Morgan don't think so! Morgan says that it's like being in prison, with a chance of being eaten by alligators."

Gabby laughed. "It can't be as bad as all that. If you love it, then I'm sure that I'll love it, too."

Wyatt parked near the front steps, then he and Gabby unloaded the Jeep. After taking the cooler and Gabby's tote bag up into the house, Wyatt started opening the windows.

Gabby immediately understood why Wyatt loved this place; the sense of solitude was wonderful. She could easily envision Wyatt swimming, fishing, and sitting in one of the rocking chairs as he watched the sun set. While Wyatt continued opening up the house, Gabby stepped onto the porch.

The view from the porch was lovely, and when the wind was right she could hear the lake waves rushing the sandy shore. Pine trees stood nearby, their aromatic tops waving lightly in the wind and sometimes pleasantly brushing across the roof. She decided that she quite liked the house being up in the air this way. After admiring the view for a few moments more, she joined Wyatt in the kitchen.

Wyatt opened the cooler and removed two long-neck beers.

After opening them he handed one to Gabby, and they clinked bottles. Gabby took a welcome sip then peered into the cooler. As was her custom, Aunt Lou had provided them with more than they would ever eat.

"Could we go for a swim first?" Gabby asked.

Wyatt nodded. "I put your bag in the first bedroom."

Gabby immediately left the kitchen, happily waving her beer bottle overhead as she went. "Last one ready has to clean up after dinner!"

Ten minutes later they were walking across the sand and toward the water. Gabby wore a one-piece white suit; Wyatt had donned a pair of simple black trunks. This was the first time Gabby had seen Wyatt this way, and she was far from disappointed. His body was hard and lean from his many years of working on the ranch.

Gabby put one toe into the water. "It's nice."

Wyatt carefully looked up and down the shoreline.

"Is it okay?" she asked.

"Yes."

"Then I'll tell you what," she said. "Let's race to the float."

"Why?"

"Because I'll win, that's why. You don't stand a chance."

"Like hell."

"Then prove it!" she shouted. Without warning, she ran into the water and dove in headfirst.

Wyatt was a fair swimmer, but she beat him by a good fifteen seconds, giving her enough time to recline on the float and gloatingly watch him struggle aboard. His lungs heaving, Wyatt collapsed onto his back. Gabby laughed.

"Jesus!" Wyatt exclaimed, gasping for air. "You're . . . amazing! But you conned me! I had forgotten that you're the girls' swim coach!"

Just then the sun peeked out from behind a cloud to begin drying their bodies. As Wyatt raised his left hand to shadow his eyes, Gabby again noticed the white ring around his third finger. This time she reached out and touched it.

"Do you want to talk about it?" she asked.

Wyatt looked into her eyes. "It's mostly why I brought you here."

"I'm listening," she said.

Wyatt told Gabby about Phoebe's unborn child. He also recounted how he had finally made his peace with Krista and Danny, and buried his wedding ring at Krista's grave. When he finished, Gabby had tears in her eyes.

"I understand," she said gently.

Wyatt smiled slightly, but said nothing. Then Gabby saw his jaw muscles harden a bit, and his blue eyes narrowed. Reaching up, he grabbed a handful of her wet hair. Suddenly he could wait no longer. He pulled her head down to his to find that her kiss came willingly, eagerly.

That first, new kiss is always a wondrous thing. More than any that might follow, it is the one that seals all the promises, exposes the heart's true secrets, and makes all things possible. For Wyatt, kissing Gabby was all of those things and more.

When he released her, she opened her eyes. He had always thought that her eyes were beautiful, but they now held an especially seductive quality he had not seen before. She smiled gently and brushed the wet hair from his forehead.

"Let's swim back," she said quietly. Saying nothing more, she stood and dove from the float.

Their return swim was slow and languorous. As they walked out of the water, Gabby held Wyatt's hand. Soon they were standing before the living room fireplace, their still wet swimsuits quietly dripping water onto the floor. Gabby walked closer and put her arms around his neck.

Wyatt kissed her again, harder this time. As she pressed her body against his, he felt the heat rise between them. Gabby took Wyatt's hand, placing it against one of her breasts. A hungry look possessed her dark eyes.

"Are you sure?" he asked.

"Yes, Wyatt," she answered softly. "I'm sure. I want it all . . ."

With a single movement, Wyatt scooped her up into his arms.

As she placed her head against his chest, he carried her into his bedroom.

FORTY

A S IS THEIR WONT, the days became weeks, and the weeks became months. Today the afternoon sun was high, and Trevor was thrilled to be riding alongside Ram for the first time.

Ram had wanted to take Trevor riding across open ground for a long time. But given what he had in mind, he first needed to be sure that Trevor's riding skills were up to the task, and so he had waited these many days to do so. Doc had been successfully weaned from Sadie, and he was growing like a weed.

Ram was on Sadie, and despite his advanced age, he rode expertly. Trevor sat on Gypsy. As Trevor rode across the scruffy grass, he felt a unique thrill of discovery that he would long remember.

Ram had insisted that they eat lunch before leaving, and Lou had happily obliged. After they downed huge ham sandwiches, homemade potato salad, and big glasses of iced tea, Ram pronounced the two of them fit for travel. He had then told Trevor to go saddle up Sadie and Gypsy. Trevor was already familiar with Gypsy, and Sadie needed the exercise, Ram said.

After saddling the horses, Trevor led them from the barn. Ram stood waiting in the yard, his still sharp eyes watching as the young man in the red Windbreaker walked their mounts nearer. When Trevor handed Sadie's reins to Ram, the old man smiled.

"Are the saddles cinched tight?" Ram asked.

Trevor nodded.

"Good," Ram said. "There's just one more thing to do before we go."

"What's that?" Trevor asked.

"Go and fetch my rifle. It's in the barn office."

Trevor eagerly hurried off. Since first hearing that Wyatt had shot two alligators, he very much wanted to learn about guns. After carefully taking the rifle down from its place on the office wall, he brought it to Ram.

"Good boy," Ram said.

Trevor watched Ram load the lever-action rifle with ten cartridges. Ram slid the rifle into Wyatt's tooled leather scabbard then tied it to his saddle.

"Do you think that we'll see any gators?" Trevor asked eagerly.

Ram shook his head. "Doubt it. We won't be near any sizable body of water. But it always pays to have a gun, just the same."

That had been half an hour ago. As they walked their horses across the grassland, Ram started schooling Trevor in riding across open ground.

"This isn't like riding in the ring," Ram said. "There the dirt is soft and uniform. There are no rocks, brush, holes, or weird critters in the ring. But out here it's a whole different story. We got snakes, lizards, burrowing creatures, bugs, and God knows what all. Most important, the only safe drinking water is in our canteens."

Trevor steered Gypsy right, guiding her around a rotting log. "Can't the horses drink from a stream?"

"In a pinch," Ram answered. "But they shouldn't. There's no telling what's in the stream water out here. Far as I know, only the water table can be trusted. Besides, it's far better to take them home thirsty, rather than with parasites in their bellies. Mercy and Big John would have our hides!"

After another ten minutes or so, Ram smiled. "So tell me," he asked. "How do you feel about Wyatt and your mother being together?"

Trevor adjusted his Stetson brim against the bright Florida sunlight. As he considered his answer, he scowled.

"They're sure sweet on each other," he said. "But my mom can be embarrassing! Sometimes she gets so eager to see him that I want to puke!"

Ram laughed so hard that tears came. "True enough! But how do *you* feel about it?"

"I'm glad," Trevor answered. "I really am. Besides, you know how much I like being at the ranch."

Ram nodded. "Indeed I do, son," he said quietly. "Indeed I do."

❧

AFTER A TIME, Ram looked over at Trevor again. "I think that you're ready," he said.

"Ready for what?" Trevor asked.

"Ready for a *real* ride," Ram answered, his eyes twinkling mischievously. "We're going to gallop for a bit. I want you to follow directly in Sadie's tracks. I'll look back at you occasionally, to make sure that you're okay."

Trevor was thrilled. *"Really?"* he asked.

"Really!"

Before Trevor knew it, Ram had slapped his reins against Sadie's haunches and they were tearing away. Not to be outdone, Trevor spurred Gypsy into action. Soon the two riders were galloping wildly across the open ground.

For Trevor it was like being in heaven. Even while barrel racing he had never felt such exhilaration! Galloping across the indoor riding ring had been but a short-lived thrill compared to this. Out here there was a sense of freedom and abandon that he had never known, and he immediately became addicted to it.

On and on the two riders charged, as Ram expertly wended his way with Sadie among the brush clumps and trees. Trevor stood confidently in his stirrups as Gypsy charged beneath him, her hooves flinging clumps of earth into the air. While Sadie galloped on, Ram looked back to see Gypsy's chest muscles and front legs straining beneath her shiny coat, her wide nostrils flaring with every breath and her luxurious mane flying. And as he had suspected, he was relieved to find that Trevor's riding skills were nearly as good as his own.

Damn! Ram thought, looking forward again. *That city kid has come a long way!* Deciding to give the horses a rest, Ram finally reined Sadie into a walk. Trevor caught up with them, and he slowed Gypsy.

"Goddamn!" Trevor shouted. "That was great!"

Ram laughed. "It was, wasn't it? Few things in life can compare."

Ram slowed Sadie to a stop then slid down off his saddle. He motioned for Trevor to do the same. "Time to walk them out," he said. "We'll head back now."

Grasping their reins, the old man and the far younger one began leading their horses back the way they had come. As they traveled, they talked of many things. With each step and every spoken word, the bond between them deepened. Ram had come to love this strapping, fatherless boy, and they both knew it.

Just then Ram noticed something in the distance, and he stopped. Trevor also stopped, but he couldn't understand what had captured Ram's attention. A softer, more faraway look overcame Ram's face.

"Did I ever tell you that I was once a prizewinning horse jumper?" he asked Trevor, his eyes still gazing across the grass.

"No," Trevor answered.

"Well, I was. During those days we had a big mare named Lucy. That horse could jump damned near anything. Sadie is almost as good. I miss those days. I don't admit that often, cause it worries everybody when I do."

As Ram continued to stare, Trevor still couldn't understand what had intrigued him so much. "What are you looking at?" the boy asked.

Ram raised one arm. "Do you see that clump of brush about thirty yards away?"

"The crooked, dead one?" Trevor asked.

Ram shook his head. "No, son. I'm talking about the green one, lying to the right. It's shaped like a rectangle."

"Yeah, I see it now," Trevor answered.

"Do you know what that reminds me of?" Ram asked.

"No," Trevor answered.

"It reminds me of an indoor jump. It's damned near exactly the right size."

Without a word of warning, Ram stepped into one stirrup then swung up into his saddle. "You stay here," he ordered. "Under no circumstances are you to follow me."

"What are you doing?"

"What do you think?" Ram answered. "Sadie and I are going to jump it."

Ram leaned down and placed his mouth near one of Sadie's ears. "How about it, girl?" he whispered. "One last jump for old time's sake?"

As if she understood, Sadie let go with an energetic whinny and pawed the earth with one front hoof.

"Are you sure about this?" Trevor asked nervously. He wanted with all his heart to stop Ram, but he didn't know how. If he had learned anything at the Flying B, it was that no one told Ram what to do.

"You're damned right I am!" Ram said. "Wyatt isn't around to stop me, and as of this moment, you're sworn to secrecy!" He gave Trevor a mischievous wink. "And yes, I'm in my right mind this time, if that's what you're worried about!"

"I didn't say that!" Trevor protested. "I just think—"

Before Trevor could finish his sentence, Ram dug his heels

into Sadie's flanks and the big mare started charging across the ground, straight for the rectangular section of brush.

Trevor watched in awe. He had never seen *anyone* ride like that! Ram was standing in his stirrups, but this time his upper body leaned so far down that his head was nearly alongside Sadie's neck. The horse and rider made a magnificent team as Sadie thundered toward the brush patch. When Sadie left the ground, Trevor held his breath.

Sadie's jump was magnificent, her front hooves easily clearing the top of the brush. Then Ram and Sadie flew down onto the other side, and for a few precious seconds Trevor lost sight of them. Suddenly Sadie let go a with blood-curdling scream, the likes of which Trevor had never heard. He had been completely unaware that a horse could make such an awful sound. It was a terrible, plaintive wail that spoke of extreme anguish. Then came only mind-numbing silence.

With his heart in his throat, Trevor jumped on Gypsy and he galloped her toward the brush patch for all she was worth. A long, exposed tree branch lay on the ground near the far side of the patch. Sadie's left foreleg was caught firmly in a crook of the branch. She lay on her left side, desperately trying to wriggle free. But Ram was nowhere to be seen.

Nausea overcame Trevor as he looked more closely at Sadie's injured leg. Her foreleg was broken below the knee, and the sharply splintered bone protruded through the gaping wound. Blood seemed to be everywhere; more was coming by the moment. As Sadie thrashed and screamed, Trevor's stunned mind returned to Ram.

Trevor wheeled Gypsy around full circle in an attempt to find the old man. Finally he saw him, lying some twenty feet away and jammed up against another clump of scrub. Whipping Gypsy madly, Trevor rode to Ram then jumped down from his saddle. Ram lay on his back with his eyes closed, his outstretched right arm lying at an awkward angle. At first Trevor feared he was dead.

Trevor immediately ran back to Gypsy and retrieved his canteen. With shaking hands he poured water onto Ram's face, but the old man didn't come around. Not knowing what else to do, he slapped Ram hard across the face. Ram finally coughed and opened his eyes. Sadie suddenly screamed again, causing Trevor to shudder.

"Can you sit up?" Trevor asked.

Ram nodded. But as Trevor started helping him to his feet, Ram cried out in pain and slumped back to the ground. Trevor helped him into a sitting position.

"What is it?" Trevor asked.

"Right shoulder . . . ," Ram gasped. "Dislocated . . . it's an old thing . . . help me up again . . ."

This time Trevor grasped Ram's good shoulder, and together they got him to his feet. Ram's pain suddenly overwhelmed him again, nearly causing him to faint. Then he looked over at Sadie, and he knew.

"Oh, God, no . . . ," he breathed.

Ram looked into Trevor's eyes. "Get me over there . . . ," he said weakly.

"What about your shoulder?"

"Later . . . ," Ram said, in between desperate breaths. "Get me over there!"

Trevor helped Ram shuffle over to where Sadie lay. She was

still thrashing about, trying to free herself. Trevor realized that what he'd first thought was a single, wayward branch was in fact a series of exposed roots, their opposite ends still embedded in the ground. One of them imprisoned Sadie's injured leg as surely as any man-made hobble ever devised. Her dark eyes looked hysterical, and foam was starting to flow from her muzzle.

"We've got to help her!" Trevor pleaded. "I'll try to free her leg!"

"No!" Ram shouted, as best he could. "That's not . . . the answer . . ."

"What, then?" Trevor demanded.

Unable to watch Sadie suffer, Ram looked at the ground. His right arm hung strangely from his body, as if it didn't belong to him.

"You must do as I say," Ram ordered, gritting his teeth through his pain. His knees shook, and he was close to collapsing.

"What is it?" Trevor asked urgently.

When Ram again looked into Trevor's eyes, the boy saw only sadness. "Go and get the gun . . . ," Ram said weakly.

Trevor was horrified. His eyes filled with tears. "No! There must be some other way! I won't let you shoot her!"

Ram shook his head. His strength was fading, and he would soon become unconscious again. "I'm not going to shoot her, Trevor," he said. "You are."

Trevor nearly fainted. He looked around madly, hoping that all this was some kind of monstrous dream from which he could awaken.

"I won't do it!" he shouted. "I love her too much! You caused this! You do it!" Just then Sadie screamed again, louder this time.

"I can't hold the gun, Trevor," Ram said. "It has to be you.

Trust me, boy . . . it's the only way. It's all my fault, and I will have to live with that. But it has to be done, and you're the only one who can. It's the most humane thing . . . now go and get the goddamned gun!"

Trevor turned and again looked at Sadie. She had quieted a bit, but Trevor correctly guessed that it was more from blood loss than any relief from her pain. As if in a dream, he numbly walked to Sadie then carefully slid the rifle from its scabbard. Like she somehow knew, Sadie whinnied softly. Trevor waited there, only a few feet from the stricken horse.

"Good," Ram said. "Now do exactly as I say."

Still in a state of numb disbelief, Trevor nodded.

"Grip the underside of the gun stock with your left palm."

Trevor did as he was told.

"Good," Ram said. Once again he winced and temporarily closed his eyes against the pain. "Now grasp the lever . . . with your right hand," he finally said.

Trevor did so.

"Swing the lever forward, toward the barrel end of the gun and then back again. That will cock the gun. After that, keep your fingers well away from the trigger."

Again, Trevor did as he was told. The lever was harder to work than he expected, but moved smoothly.

"Without touching the trigger, place the rifle butt against your shoulder," Ram said.

Trevor felt the unforgiving end of the gun stock bite into his shoulder. *What am I doing?* his mind shouted. *Can this really be happening?*

"Now gently curve your right index finger around the front of the trigger, but don't squeeze it yet," Ram said. The old man was so pain stricken that he was about to pass out. *Just a little longer, girl,* Ram thought. *Just a little longer, and your pain will be gone.* "Now look down the barrel and aim it at Sadie's head."

Trevor did as Ram said. His entire body was shaking.

"Pull the trigger," Ram said.

Trevor seemed to collapse a little, but he righted himself.

"Do it!" Ram said with what strength he had left.

The rifle bucked so hard in Trevor's inexperienced hands that the recoil nearly knocked him to the ground. When the smoke cleared, Sadie lay dead.

Trevor threw the gun away then fell to his knees before the beloved horse. He cried and shook uncontrollably. When next he heard Ram's voice, he didn't know how much time had passed. Sweating profusely, he pulled off his red Windbreaker and angrily threw it to the ground.

"Come here, son," he heard Ram say. The old man's voice sounded wispy and faint, like it had been carried over the grassland winds from a million miles away. Trevor walked numbly toward him.

"Now take off your belt," Ram said.

"Wha—what?"

"Take off your belt."

Trevor did as he was told. It was his father's old belt, the one he used to carry his schoolbooks.

"Loop the buckle end around your wrist," Ram said weakly, "then tie the other end around mine."

Again, Trevor obeyed. He could now guess what was coming, and he searched for more inner strength.

"Now stand back and use the belt to slowly raise my bad arm," Ram said.

As Ram's arm lifted, the old man screamed. Trevor felt sick again, but he held it in.

"When I tell you . . . pull hard and sharp," Ram gasped. "I've . . . done this before. But you gotta get it right the first time. There isn't another try in me . . ."

Trevor steadied himself.

"Are you . . . ready?" Ram asked.

Any moment now Ram would keel over, and Trevor knew it. He nodded.

"Then do it, boy."

As Trevor yanked hard on the belt, he heard the sickening thump of Ram's shoulder sliding back into place. Ram screamed and fell to his knees. After a time his color returned somewhat, and he stood again. Trevor removed the belt from Ram's wrist.

"Can you ride?" Trevor asked.

Ram nodded. "If you can get me onto Gypsy, yes."

Trevor tossed the leather belt to the ground alongside his Windbreaker. He then helped Ram hobble over to where Gypsy stood waiting. Between the two of them they were able to get Ram on the horse. Trevor used the stirrup to climb up and sit behind Ram on Gypsy's haunches. He took the reins into his hands, holding them before the injured old man.

"If I go unconscious," Ram whispered, "lay me facedown across the saddle and give Gypsy her head. She knows the way home better than you."

Trevor nodded. After thinking for a moment, he wheeled Gypsy around to face Sadie.

"Good-bye, girl," he said softly, his tears coming again. "I'll take good care of Doc for you . . . I promise."

Trevor turned Gypsy around, and the horse began taking them home. Gypsy had taken only a few steps when Ram lifted his head.

"You forgot . . . your belt and Windbreaker," he said weakly.

Trevor pulled Gypsy to a stop then turned and looked behind him. After a few moments, he got the horse moving again.

"No, I didn't," he said.

FORTY-ONE

ANOTHER TWO WEEKS soon passed, and although life at the Flying B had largely returned to normal, everyone knew that the pain of Sadie's absence would never be forgotten. But her bloodline and spirit would be carried on in Doc, and for that they were all grateful. It was a lovely Friday evening. Wyatt and Gabby were enjoying a quiet dinner out, happy to be spending some time alone.

After smiling at Gabby, Wyatt looked at their waiter. "I'll have a dry vodka Gibson," he said. "Very cold, please."

"And for you, madam?" the waiter asked.

"Chardonnay," Gabby answered.

"And for dinner?"

"The lady will have the chicken Kiev," Wyatt answered. "I'd like the lobster thermidor, and we'll each have a Caesar salad."

"Very good, sir."

After gathering up the two menus, the uniformed waiter went off to place the orders.

Gabby looked across the elegant table at Wyatt. "I'm so sorry about Sadie," she said. "I still can't believe that she's gone."

Wyatt nodded. "Sadie will be sorely missed," he said. "Sadly, seeing horses die is part of running a ranch. After everything that has happened, I thought we could use a nice night out. Given how wonderful you look, this is the only restaurant in town that deserves you."

Gabby savored the compliment happily. She also couldn't help but admire how handsome Wyatt looked tonight. He was wearing a dark blue suit, a white shirt with French cuffs, and a light blue tie. Gabby wore the ubiquitous "little black dress" that all stylish women seem to own, along with her faithful Akoya pearls.

Jack's was an elegant place, and Wyatt had often entertained law clients here. The restaurant was beautifully decorated all year round, especially at Christmastime. As the happy sounds of light music and pleasant conversation filled the sumptuous room, Gabby smiled. Despite the tragedy with Sadie, never in her life had she been so happy.

Sadie's death had been the only dark spot during this otherwise halcyon time. On Ram and Trevor's return home, Big John had forcibly loaded Ram into his car and driven him straight to the hospital. Gabby and Wyatt had done their best to console Trevor while they waited for them to return, but they were unsuccessful.

For Trevor, the shock of losing Sadie was insurmountable. He'd sworn that he would never forgive Ram for his foolishness, and he meant it. Gabby and Wyatt had hoped that Trevor's anger would run its course, and that he might forgive Ram without being asked. But so far he remained furious, and Ram was hurt by it.

An X-ray of Ram's injured shoulder showed that nothing was broken. But because of Ram's advanced age, the attending doctor gave him a full examination before sending him home. Ram's arm was placed in a sling, and the doctor said that it should remain that way for the next two weeks. There was nothing else for it at Ram's age, the doctor said, but to rest the arm. True to form, Ram preferred his own brand of recovery. After swearing Big John to silence, he used his good arm to remove the sling and then promptly tossed it out the car window on the way home. Because it had grown so late, Gabby and Trevor slept over in guest rooms at the ranch.

The following day, Wyatt took four ranch hands out to where Sadie lay. After retrieving the rifle and tack they photographed the scene for insurance purposes, then buried the dead horse. Wyatt later called Morgan to tell him the sad news and to say that Morgan should file an insurance claim, even though they both guessed that it would be rejected.

Like Trevor, Wyatt had been absolutely enraged with Ram. Losing Sadie was terrible, but that wasn't what bothered him most. The thought of Ram jumping again sent chills down Wyatt's spine. Wyatt had no way to be sure of what Ram's state of mind had been when he jumped Sadie. But from what Trevor had told them, it seemed that the old man's obstinacy had purposely overruled his common sense, making the tragedy even more disturbing. When Wyatt visited the scene, he was amazed that Ram hadn't been killed.

By the time Ram and Big John returned from the hospital, Wyatt's mood had calmed. Ram's expression was so uncharacteristically contrite that Wyatt hadn't the heart to bawl him out. After apologizing to everyone, Ram gave his son a one-armed hug. Holding his father close, Wyatt sighed resignedly.

"There's no fool like an old fool," Ram said, "and I'm living proof. Never again, son, I promise."

"An old fool is right!" Trevor had shouted angrily. "What the Christ were you thinking, jumping her that way? Now she's gone, and she's never coming back! If anybody else had done this, you'd be mad as hell at them! But since it's you, I guess that we're all just supposed to forget it, right?"

Trevor fished around in his pockets and removed the pearl-handled knife that Ram had given him. He angrily pushed it at the old man.

"Here!" he shouted. "I don't want this anymore! It only reminds me of you!"

Gabby had quickly reprimanded Trevor, but it had no effect on him. Without protest, Ram slowly pocketed the knife. Feeling dejected and guilty, he took another of the pain pills prescribed by the emergency room doctor then went straight to bed. During the last two weeks his ornery nature had resurfaced, his arm had improved, and ranch life carried on. But the relationship between Ram and Trevor remained deeply strained, and it showed.

When their drinks arrived, Gabby and Wyatt sipped them appreciatively. All the tension that once existed between them was gone, and had been replaced with a welcome sense of happiness they had believed might never grace their lives again. They saw each other whenever and wherever they could. They had become a pair of infatuated lovers, and like such lovers, they didn't care what anyone thought about them.

Two Caesar salads were prepared tableside. Wyatt ordered another martini for himself and another chardonnay for Gabby.

"Wyatt," she said, "there are a couple of things I'd like to discuss."

Before Gabby could continue, Wyatt laughed.

Gabby gave him a curious look. "What's so funny?" she asked.

"I'm just glad that you didn't say: *'We need to talk,'*" he answered.

Gabby laughed in return. "I promise that I'll never lay that one on you!" she said.

"Good!" Wyatt replied. "So what was it that you wanted to say?"

"This coming Sunday is your birthday," Gabby said. "It's an important day for all of us. Could we discuss it?"

Wyatt nodded and sat back in his chair. "I must admit that the same thing has been on my mind," he said. "But I've been so happy that I didn't want to mention it. I guess I thought that it might break the spell or something."

Gabby had hoped he would feel that way. Even so, she had taken Aunt Lou into her confidence again before asking Wyatt about it. She had been wise to do so, for Lou told her something she hadn't known.

Ever since the car crash, Wyatt had steadfastly refused to celebrate his birthday. Instead, he had always gone to his lake house and spent the day alone. Gabby wisely decided that she wouldn't try to influence Wyatt to do otherwise. Besides, any kind of joyous celebration would be inappropriate for everyone concerned. But if Wyatt would agree to spend the day with her, she would gladly do whatever he wanted.

"Lou tells me that you always spend your birthdays by yourself," Gabby said. "I understand that, Wyatt, I really do. And if that's what you still want, it's fine with me. But I was hoping that we could pass the day together."

Then she smiled. "I haven't seen our eight-hundred-pound gorilla lurking around anymore," she added. "But spending your birthday together might be a good idea, just in case."

Wyatt thought for a moment then nodded. "You're right," he said. "And we'll include Trevor."

"Can we start the day with church?" Gabby asked. "I've missed it."

"Sure," he said. "Afterward we'll return to the scene of the crime, and eat brunch at Chez Paul."

"Thank you, Wyatt," Gabby said. "That sounds wonderful."

Suddenly a concern occurred to her. She had gotten out of the habit of going to church, and was happy to be going back. But the coming Sunday was more than just Wyatt's birthday. Not only would it be the sixth anniversary of the car crash, it would also be the first time she and Wyatt had ever attended the services as a couple. After some thought she decided not to speak of her worry, for when the time came, it would be Wyatt's decision and no one else's. *But how will he react?* she wondered.

"What was the other thing you wanted to say?" Wyatt asked.

"What . . . ?" Gabby asked, her mind still engrossed with her earlier concern.

"You said there were two things," Wyatt answered.

"Oh, yes," she answered. "It's about Trevor and Ram."

Wyatt nodded. "I know," he said. "It's bad. In a way, I can't blame Trevor for being furious. And because Ram feels so guilty, I don't think he knows how to go about remedying it. He's already apologized, but that doesn't seem to be enough for Trevor. They're a real pair, those two, and I'm not sure which one is more stubborn. Something about an unstoppable force meeting an immovable object."

"It's just that Trevor loved Sadie so much," Gabby said. "He'll get over it eventually, I suppose, but it would be so much better if he could forgive Ram now, face-to-face."

Wyatt gave Gabby a little smile. "You want me talk to Trevor, don't you?" he asked.

Gabby reached out and touched Wyatt's hand. "Would you?" she asked. "In this case, it would mean more coming from you than from me. You know Ram better than anyone, I think. And Trevor always respects what you have to say. It would mean a lot to me if you'd try."

"Okay," Wyatt answered. "I'll do my best."

Soon their dinners arrived. The food was excellent, and while they ate, they talked happily. Coffee and dessert followed. As the night progressed, Gabby felt even more wonderful. Wyatt had granted both of her requests, and she was on top of the world. Then Wyatt's expression sobered a bit and he looked into her eyes.

"I have something for you," he said.

"You do?" Gabby asked.

Wyatt reached into his suit jacket and removed a slim, rectangular box. He handed it to her.

She looked at him with surprise. "What is it?"

"After you've opened it, I'll explain."

"But you've already done so much."

Wyatt gave her another meaningful look. "Please, Gabby . . ."

Gabby opened the box. Inside was a black Montblanc fountain pen, trimmed with solid gold.

"I want you to have that," Wyatt said.

Gabby looked at Wyatt's gift with welcome surprise. "It's lovely," she said. "And I know how prized these are. I also know that they cost a small fortune. Are you sure about this?"

"Yes," Wyatt answered. "But there's more to say. That Montblanc belonged to Krista. I selected it from the fountain-pen collection in her study. You may remember them—they sit on her desk in a wooden-and-glass case. Ram got her hooked on them shortly after we were married. It was her favorite, and it's important to me that you accept it."

Gabby's eyes started to well up. Wyatt's gesture had truly touched her heart. But this wasn't really about her needing a pen, she realized.

Rather, it was about where the pen had come from, and to whom it had once belonged. Gabby also realized that no matter what Wyatt had chosen to give her from that room, its symbolism would have meant just as much. If there had been any doubts lingering in her heart about Wyatt's break with his past, they were surely gone now.

"Thank you, my darling," she said. "I'll treasure it always."

As Wyatt looked at Gabby, her lips parted slightly, unconsciously. Suddenly, her next words came. She had been holding them in for a long time, and she could wait no longer. When they arrived, they came straight from her heart.

"I love you," she said simply.

At long last, her most intimate feelings had been fully revealed to him. Now there were no more secrets, no more wondering. At first she couldn't believe she had said it, and she feared his reaction. Her eyes searched his tanned face.

"I love you, too," he answered.

When he reached across the table and touched her hand, her heart sang.

FORTY-TWO

THE FOLLOWING DAY was Saturday, and Gabby and Trevor were again visiting the ranch. Without being told, Wyatt had a good idea about where he might find Trevor. Leaving Gabby behind at the big house, he sauntered down to the main barn and strode the corridor until he reached Doc's stall. Sure enough, Trevor was there, painstakingly brushing down the fast-growing colt.

Rather than announce his presence, Wyatt stood there for a time quietly watching. Like a true horseman, Trevor spoke softly to the colt as he tended to him. Wyatt rested his forearms on top of the stall door, thinking about how far the boy had come.

"You're going to spoil that colt," he finally said. "But that's okay. I know how you feel about him."

Trevor stopped what he was doing and turned around. After thinking for a moment, he said, "Maybe that's a good thing, seeing as how Ram killed his mother."

"Interesting answer," Wyatt replied.

Trevor left Doc and walked nearer. "Do you want something?" he asked.

"Only a little of your time," Wyatt answered. "Please come with me."

Trevor left the stall and the two of them walked the length of the barn. Soon they reached the far entrance. Unwittingly, Wyatt beckoned Trevor toward the same weathered Adirondack chair where Ram had explained about never wrestling in the mud with a pig.

Wyatt took the chair beside Trevor's. For a time they didn't speak, each one content to absorb the pleasant atmosphere of the huge old barn.

"My mom asked you to talk to me, didn't she?" Trevor finally asked.

Wyatt nodded. "She knows," he answered.

"So this is about Ram."

"It's about *you* and Ram," Wyatt answered. "If you still want to be mad at Ram after our talk, then I guess that's that. But there's something your mother and I want you to do."

"What is it?"

"We're hoping that you will forgive him," Wyatt said.

Before answering, Trevor looked across the way toward the big house.

"Why should I?" he asked. "He killed Sadie. He didn't mean to, I guess, but she's just as dead and she's never coming back. But what really makes me mad is that he jumped her on purpose. He wasn't having one of his 'spells' or whatever you call them. He did it because he just plain wanted to, and he thought that he could get away with it."

"Maybe," Wyatt said. "But before you pass final judgment on him, there are some things that you need to understand."

"Like what?"

"For one thing, Ram rules the roost around here. You know what he always says: 'My ranch, my rules.'"

"Yeah, I know."

"Well, he isn't one to ask permission," Wyatt said. "And he shouldn't have to. But that doesn't mean that he's always right. Nobody is."

"So what are you saying?" Trevor asked.

"I'm saying that despite his Alzheimer's, he can still be as impetuous as ever—maybe even more so. In fact, if I were asked to sum up my father's personality in just three words, do you know what they would be?"

Intrigued, Trevor turned and looked into Wyatt's eyes. "No . . . ," he answered.

Wyatt smiled. "Ready . . . Shoot . . . Aim."

Trevor couldn't help but smile a little. "You got that one right," he said.

"And there's something else," Wyatt said. "Ram is seventy-seven years old, and as best I know, he's had this willful streak all his life. If you're expecting him to change, don't hold your breath. Trust me—hell will freeze over first. But there's another reason you should forgive him, Trevor."

Trevor gave Wyatt a quizzical look. "What is it?" he asked.

"Despite what Ram told you that day about 'being in his right mind,' we will never be sure of it. Given his condition, who's to say what his 'right mind' ever is?"

A look of genuine concern crossed Trevor's face. "What are you talking about?"

"Sooner or later, my father will lose his mind completely. There's nothing anyone can do about that. One day he won't know who we are. Or even who *he* is, for that matter. He won't recognize the ranch, or be able to take care of himself. And perhaps worst of all, whatever we say to him will be meaningless. For him, our words will be like dust on the wind."

Wyatt paused for a moment, gazing out across the lush grounds. When he again looked at Trevor, his face was tinged with sorrow.

"If you don't sort out your differences with him soon, you may lose the chance forever," Wyatt said quietly. "Trust me on this, Trevor, because I know. That's why I always try to treat him with kindness and respect. I can never know when his mind might finally vanish for good, and I don't want our last meaningful exchange to be one of anger."

Trevor looked genuinely affected. "I never thought about it that way," he said quietly.

"I know," Wyatt answered. "So let me say just one more thing, and then I'll leave you alone. If you can't do as your mother and I ask, then so be it. But if there's the slightest bit of forgiveness in your heart, then you must tell him. The last thing in the world that you want is to finally do so, only to realize that it is too late. As a matter of fact, it was Ram himself who taught me that, and not so long ago."

Saying nothing more, Wyatt stood and walked back toward the house.

FORTY-THREE

R AM NODDED WHILE adding up the marks he had made in his secret calendar. Last month's final tally was heartening, with only two bouts of forgetfulness. His new medication was helping, even though taking it still rankled with his ornery sense of independence.

It was Sunday morning and breakfast was finished. Wyatt had skipped eating so as to drive into Boca early to fetch Gabby and Trevor. True to form, Ram had retreated to his private office with a fresh cup of Lou's coffee and his crisply ironed newspaper. As was also his custom, he had closed the mahogany plantation shutters to ensure his privacy.

Fall was here at last. It was a wonderful time of year at the ranch, and Ram always looked forward to it. Cooler weather would soon prevail, and the holidays were just around the corner.

From out of nowhere, a memory tugged at his mind. He again consulted his secret calendar to be sure. Yes, there it was. Next Sunday would be Wyatt's forty-first birthday, and the sixth anniversary of Danny and Krista's tragic deaths.

On closing the calendar, Ram turned and opened the shutters. As he gazed out across the perfect lawns and toward the old graveyard that stood near the main barn, his thoughts turned to Gabby and Wyatt.

They seemed very happy, and Ram was immensely grateful to the fates for bringing them together. They suited each other well, he thought. Ram had liked Gabby from the moment he met her, that tension-filled first day of New Beginnings. He also clearly remembered how hesitant and worried Gabby had first been, but no more. And despite his strained relationship with Trevor, the program had been especially good for the boy in helping him to overcome his difficult past. But most important for Ram, Wyatt seemed positively transformed.

Ram smiled. Phoebe would have been glad for these things, too, he realized. From his office he could not clearly distinguish her gravestone among the others, but that didn't matter. If our departed loved ones truly did look down on us from the afterlife, Phoebe would surely be smiling.

A knock came on the door, causing Ram to turn in his chair. "Who is it?" he called out.

"Trevor."

"Come on in."

Trevor opened the office door and stepped into the room for the first time. After looking around, he closed the door then walked nearer. As usual when visiting the ranch, he was dressed in his Western-style clothes. Just as Ram had taught him that first day of New Beginnings, he respectfully held his Stetson in his hands.

Ram did his best to smile. "Wyatt got you here fast," he said.

"Yeah," Trevor answered. "He came out early. He's always in a hurry to see my mom. Is my coming to your office okay? Wyatt said that I could."

"Sure," Ram said.

Ram sensed that Trevor had something important to say, and that he was having trouble finding the words. He motioned for the young man to sit in one of the upholstered guest chairs. Trevor sat down and respectfully set his hat on the desk.

"Is something on your mind?" Ram asked.

Trevor nodded. "It's about Sadie. We never really talked about it. If it's okay, I'd like to tell you something."

"Go ahead, son," Ram said quietly.

Trevor looked down at his hands then back into Ram's eyes. "I'm sorry that I shouted at you that night. I was just so mad . . . It's too bad that we lost Sadie that way. But I wanted you to know that I'm not angry with you anymore. Maybe it was just fate, I don't know. But I'm sure of one thing."

"And what is that?" Ram asked.

"If it was her time to die, then I'm glad she was with you when it happened," Trevor said. "I was the one who put her out of her misery, but she knew that you were there. That's what mattered most."

Ram swallowed hard. "Thank you," he said softly.

"There's something else," Trevor said.

"Yes?" Ram asked.

"Despite what happened, I want to thank you for that day," Trevor said. "I'll never forget riding like that. It was the best thing I've ever done."

For the first time in weeks, Trevor smiled at Ram. "Anytime that you want to go again, just let me know," the young man added. "Without the jumping part, that is. After all, somebody's got to watch you. Might as well be me."

Ram stood from his chair. "Come here," he said.

Trevor walked behind the desk. To his surprise, Ram put his arms around him and held him close.

"I want to tell you something, too," Ram said. As he let Trevor go, he blinked back a tear.

"What is it?" Trevor asked.

"I want to apologize again for jumping Sadie like that," Ram said. "What happened was my fault, and I will carry it with me all the rest of my days. Nothing can be done about that. But hearing that you don't hold it against me means more than you could ever know."

Trevor pursed his lips. "I love you, old man," he said quietly. "Thank you for always being there for me."

"I love you, too," Ram answered. "Now go and do something more useful than talking to an old buzzard like me! Doc's stall must need mucking out, or something. If you want to eat Lou's dinner tonight, you'll have to earn it. That's Flying B rule number twelve."

Trevor raised an eyebrow. "You just made that one up, didn't you?"

"Yep," Ram answered.

"I know," Trevor said. "Your ranch, your rules."

Ram fished around in one pocket of his Levi's and removed the pearl-handled pocketknife. Then he winked knowingly at Trevor.

"I don't rightly remember how that knife got into my pocket, but I think it belongs to you," Ram said. He held it out, and the boy took it.

"Thank you," Trevor answered quietly. He picked up his Stetson and headed for the door.

"Wait a minute," Ram said.

When Trevor turned around, he saw a smile spread across the old man's face.

"Even *my* rules were meant to be broken sometimes," Ram said. "Just this once, you can wear your hat inside the house."

Trevor beamed back at Ram. After placing the Stetson on his head, he smiled and flicked its brim with his middle finger like he had been doing it all his life. He then quietly closed the door behind him.

After reclaiming his chair, Ram again looked out toward the family grave sites. Then his thoughts returned to Phoebe, and another smile crossed his lips.

Things are finally right again, my love.

FORTY-FOUR

THE FOLLOWING MORNING, Reverend Jacobson again sat waiting before the great stained-glass wall of St. Andrew's sanctuary. Gabby and Trevor were seated in their usual places, waiting for Wyatt to arrive. To Jacobson's delight, the church was full.

Today's service was proceeding well. The first hymn, the collect of the day, and the first selected Bible reading were finished. As Jacobson watched, one of the church acolytes walked to the pulpit and started reading Luke 18:1–8, the Bible passage that would precede his sermon.

The acolyte soon finished reading the selected Bible verse, and it became time for the sermon. Jacobson dutifully stood and walked to the pulpit. After adjusting the microphone to his liking, he looked out over his congregation.

"One day at a Catholic elementary school, a well-meaning nun hung a sign in the lunch line directly above the apples," Jacobson began in his ragged voice. "As one of the school's more adventurous students approached the sign, he read: TAKE ONLY ONE APPLE! GOD IS WATCHING! The young man did as ordered, taking only one apple. A little way down the line, he and his friends soon spied the cookies.

"As fast as he could, the young man began piling his tray high with cookies," Jacobson continued. "While he did, a friend standing beside him became worried. 'What if you get caught?' his friend asked. With a smile on his face, the first young man answered: 'Don't worry! Take all the cookies you want! Today God's watching the apples!' "

While the congregation laughed, Jacobson noted that Wyatt still hadn't arrived. Since Danny's and Krista's deaths, Wyatt hadn't missed a single service. Although Jacobson found Wyatt's absence unusual, he could delay his sermon no longer.

❧

WHILE SHE WAITED, GABBY became increasingly anxious. Before leaving the ranch last night, she and Wyatt had agreed to meet at the church. At first she hoped that Wyatt was simply running late, but that wasn't like him. *Where is he?* she wondered. *He promised he would be here . . . this day has so much meaning for the three of us . . .*

Moments later, she excused herself to the ladies' room and tried to reach Wyatt by cell phone. He didn't answer, causing her to wonder all the more. When she returned to her pew, she began worrying that Wyatt had lost the fortitude needed to take the blessings.

Of far worse consequence, perhaps his feelings about her had changed. The mere thought of losing him—especially after they had gone through so much to be together—would be more than her heart could bear. Had her happy time with Wyatt been a mere interlude? Perhaps her fairy tale was about to end after all . . .

Tears came, and Gabby brushed them away. Trevor pursed his lips and took her hands in his. Cupped in her son's warm palms, Gabby's hands suddenly felt wet and cold, like those of some lifeless marble statue that had been left standing out in the rain.

His sermon finished, Jacobson left the pulpit to go and stand before the glistening white altar. It was time for the confession and absolution. Jacobson raised his hands and closed his eyes.

"Most merciful God," everyone recited, "we confess that we have sinned against you in thought, word, and deed, by what we have done, and by what we have left undone. We have not loved you with our whole heart; we have not loved our neighbors as ourselves. We are truly sorry, and we humbly repent. For the sake of your Son, Jesus Christ, have mercy on us and forgive us, that we might delight in your will, and walk in your ways to the glory of your name. Amen."

Jacobson again scanned the congregation. In the same way that Wyatt's silences could be deafening, his mysterious absence was equally imposing. But Jacobson knew that he must now perform the blessings of birthdays and anniversaries, with or without Wyatt. He again raised his hands.

"Would those wishing to have a birthday, anniversary, or other special day blessed please come forward?" he asked.

As about two dozen parishioners stood from their pews and started approaching, Jacobson again gazed toward Gabby and Trevor.

જંબ

TREVOR LOOKED WORRIEDLY at his mother. "What should we do?" he whispered.

Gabby took a deep breath. "We will take the blessings, just like we planned," she said.

"What about Wyatt?" Trevor asked.

Gabby shook her head as she brushed away another tear. "I don't know. Either he couldn't come, or he has chosen not to come. Whatever happened, we will do this."

Gabby and Trevor rose from their pew and started up the aisle. When they reached the altar, they knelt in the growing line of parishioners. After all those wishing to come forward had done so, they bowed their heads. But just as Jacobson was about to start the ritual, a disturbance among the congregation caused Gabby and some of the other worshippers to turn around.

Two men had entered the church. They were walking up the center aisle and approaching the altar. The men's cheeks were flushed; their eyes were red and glistening with tears. They walked tiredly but with purpose, as if they had just suffered some great ordeal. As they neared, they searched out Gabby and looked straight into her eyes.

The two men were Ram and Morgan Blaine.

Gabby's heart skipped a beat as she realized that neither Ram nor Morgan was appropriately dressed. Ram was wearing rumpled ranch clothes; Morgan wore a simple polo shirt and jeans. Each of the men looked exhausted, and their faces were unshaven.

Gabby held her breath as Ram and Morgan approached the altar. Jacobson also looked at them with surprise. While the entire congregation watched, Ram whispered a few words into Jacobson's ear. His face an unreadable mask, Jacobson only nodded before laying a comforting hand atop Ram's shoulder. Ram and Morgan finally went to the end of the line of parishioners, where they silently kneeled and bowed their heads.

Frantic to know what was happening, Gabby nearly broke ranks to confront Ram. But the scene soon calmed, and Jacobson again raised his hands. Fearing the worst, Gabby simply couldn't hold back her tears any longer and cried silently.

Starting with Ram, Reverend Jacobson began the blessings by placing one hand on Ram's bowed head and reciting the necessary words. Then it was Morgan's turn, followed by the next parishioner in line. While Jacobson blessed one parishioner after another, Gabby trembled.

"Excuse me, miss," someone whispered to her. "Is this spot taken?"

Her eyes filled with tears, Gabby turned to see Wyatt standing behind her.

Gabby nearly cried out with joy. Wyatt looked as spent as Ram and Morgan; his eyes were also red. Beside herself with relief, Gabby nudged Trevor to one side, allowing Wyatt to kneel beside her. Gabby took Wyatt's hand and held it tightly, like she would never let go.

"What . . . is going on?" she whispered.

Wyatt gave her a comforting look as he wiped away some of her tears.

"I'm sorry if we scared you," he whispered. "Ram decided to tell Morgan about our mother's lost child, and we ended up talking all night. At the last moment, Ram and Morg decided to come and take the blessings with me. Because we were running late, they insisted on marching in ahead of me while I parked the car. Don't worry, my love. For the first time in many years, all is as it should be."

At long last, Gabby smiled. "Everyone in this church must be watching us," she whispered.

"Good," Wyatt answered with a smile of his own. "It's my birthday."

Jacobson soon approached Wyatt and Gabby, and the kneeling couple lowered their heads. Instead of blessing them individually, the reverend extended his hands and blessed them simultaneously, as a couple. While Wyatt's hand lay ensconced in hers, Gabby felt the reverend's gentle touch grace her head.

As the words of blessing washed down over her, she could scarcely contain her joy.

FORTY-FIVE

*M*ANKIND HAS OFTEN *enforced a savage dominance over the horse, and for that he should apologize. These magnificent beasts toiled mightily over the centuries to help us tame the wilds, plow and harvest our fields, and transport our possessions, even die in our wars; and sometimes under the cruelest of masters. I am proud to say that I never participated in their abject slavery. Even so, I humbly request forgiveness from every horse that has crossed my path, for they are truly God's noblest creatures."*

After closing his journal and returning it to its hiding place, Ram went back to his desk. He smiled, thinking about that passage and how much it meant to him.

Ram loved the old quote, and he had committed it to memory as a young man. On realizing that it had never been included in his journal, he had decided to finally write it down. Although he realized that he might soon forget it, knowing that it lay safe among those pages granted him a unique kind of comfort.

Such phrases might sound silly to some, he thought, *but not to me. One must be a horseman to understand . . .*

Ram turned to look through the sliding glass door of his office and across the Flying B's lawns. Pale moonlight and evening dew had conspired to lend the grass a silvery sheen. It was nearly midnight, but recent events had buoyed him so much that he wasn't ready for sleep.

At long last, the final wall separating him from his sons had been torn down. Jacobson had been right. Such walls can be invisible, and far stronger than one might imagine. Last night's talk with Wyatt and Morgan had been cathartic, but worth the pain. Morgan cried openly when he learned of his lost sibling. Although Wyatt already knew the story, he again became teary eyed. As the three of them talked all night, never before had Ram felt so close to his sons, or they to him.

Wyatt had never intended to be late for church and worry Gabby, but he had been touched by her concern. When Reverend Jacobson blessed them as a couple, Wyatt realized that Ram must have requested it. For the first time in his life, Wyatt actually appreciated his father's intrusive nature.

Following the service, everyone ate brunch at Chez Paul and then went to the ranch. The day had passed happily, ending with another of Aunt Lou's fried-chicken dinners. The feasting had run late, with Gabby and Trevor staying overnight in two of the big-house guest rooms.

Ram turned in his chair and gazed about his office. As was

his habit, one by one he examined the mementos he had lovingly gathered. There were the many family photographs, his treasured gun collection, and his old English paintings. The twin Tiffany desk lamps purchased long ago by his father glowed with multi-colored hues. And mounted against the far wall was surely the most unique prize of all—the piece of truck bed through which Wyatt had shot his infamous bullet hole.

Such keepsakes were truly comforting. But Ram knew that as his mind slowly slipped away, these treasures would become meaningless to him. And so he cherished this moment for a while longer, quietly reflecting on a life that could still be remembered with a modicum of authority.

Ram finally straightened his old legs and stood from his chair. As he turned to close the mahogany plantation shutters, he again looked out across the lawn. He would visit the barn before turning in, he decided. After opening the sliding door, he stepped out onto the dew-laden grass then closed the door behind him. Walking purposefully, he soon neared the old family cemetery.

He stopped for a moment, thinking. Like Wyatt, he was convinced that Phoebe's lost child had been a girl. He couldn't say how he knew, he just did. And now that Morgan and Wyatt had been told, he could at last commission a small headstone in her memory. As he looked at Phoebe's grave, he knew that she would have approved. He then lit a cigarette and walked to the barn.

When Ram switched on the lights, some of the horses stirred, causing him to smile. Deciding to check on Doc, he turned a corner and headed for the colt's stall. He found Doc asleep on the deep, yellow straw that Trevor had laid down only hours before. For a time he remembered Sadie, and how much he had loved her.

He walked on.

Mankind has often enforced a savage dominance over the horse, and for that he should apologize. These magnificent beasts toiled mightily over the centuries to help us tame the wilds, plow and harvest our fields, and transport our possessions, even die in our wars; and sometimes under the cruelest of masters. I am proud to say that I never participated in their abject slavery. Even so, I humbly request—

Just then an overpowering stillness blanketed his mind, and he could remember no more of the beloved quotation. He stopped walking, trying to remember, but the words wouldn't come. As he anxiously looked about himself, he suddenly felt like a stranger, inhabiting an even stranger land. He recognized nothing—not a single stall, nor any horse, nor the way out. He didn't know where he was or how he had gotten here. And as his bewilderment grew, a paralyzing fear took root in his soul.

He tried to remember his name, but it was no use. He looked at himself to find that he was dressed oddly, like some cowboy character. Sweat broke out along his brow as he struggled to understand the understandable. As the pieces of the puzzle stubbornly refused to fit together, his terror grew by leaps and bounds.

His old heart beat faster, and his breath came more hurriedly. He knew only one thing. The walls of this foreboding place were closing in on him, and he had to get out. He desperately searched for an exit, but could find none. His fear mounted; his heart raced like it was about to burst through his chest.

After tossing away the unwanted cigarette, he started to cry.

∝

SUDDENLY THE LIGHTS IN Gabby's bedroom switched on, causing her to stir. As someone pulled the bedcovers off her, she growled sleepily. She looked up to see Aunt Lou standing over her. Lou's face was pale and twisted with fear.

"Get up!" Lou screamed. "Get up and come downstairs!"

Then Lou charged from the room.

Gabby hurried out of bed and quickly threw on a bathrobe. Just as she was about to run from the room, she sensed an ominous presence. Almost in slow motion she turned and walked toward the bedroom balcony. When she opened the doors, what she saw defied description.

The main barn was ablaze.

The huge old structure was heavily engulfed in flames. Fire roared through ragged holes in the roof and burst violently out the windows. Even from the relative safety of the big house, Gabby could feel the searing heat, and smell the dense smoke that was quickly fogging the grounds. Horses screamed, timbers creaked, and glass shattered crazily. For several moments she stood frozen in time, wondering if the world she had so come to love was about to end. Then she suddenly thought of Trevor, and she bolted from the room.

"Trevor!" she screamed as she ran down the hallway.

On reaching his room, she barged through the door. To her horror, Trevor was gone. Insane with worry, she ran for the staircase. When she reached the foyer, she saw Wyatt. He was shirtless and urgently shouting into the phone. Lou stood near him, her entire body trembling. Then Gabby saw Trevor, and she cried out in joy. She ran to him and pulled him close.

His expression desperate, Wyatt slammed the phone down

and spun around. Rushing up to Lou, he grabbed her by the shoulders.

"Where's Big John?" he screamed.

"He's in the barn!" Lou shouted. "He's the one who woke me and said to get everybody else up! Then he said that he had to try and save as many of the horses as he could! I tried to stop him, but he wouldn't listen!"

"What about Mercy?" Wyatt screamed.

"She went in, too!" Lou shouted back.

Everyone raced onto the porch, to see that the barn had become a raging inferno. Wyatt guessed that the fire had progressed so far that anyone who went inside might never return. Nor would the fire department he had just summoned reach the Flying B in time. Then the sounds of screaming horses returned, and a small herd of the fear-crazed beasts suddenly charged to safety through what remained of the barn's front doors.

His face a pale mask, Wyatt suddenly glared at Aunt Lou.

"Where's Ram?" he screamed.

Lou threw up her hands. "I . . . I . . . don't know!" she shouted. "I tried to find him, but I couldn't! Then I came and got you!"

His mind racing, Wyatt turned and again looked at the barn. Suddenly, he knew. When his eyes met Gabby's, she froze.

"I have to . . . ," he said to her. At once he was racing across the grass.

As she watched Wyatt go, Gabby felt something inside her die.

☙

WHEN WYATT CHARGED into the barn, he could hardly believe his eyes. Everywhere he looked he saw hell on earth. The two-hundred-year-old structure, with all of its tinder-dry hay stored on the second floor, was being consumed at a rate he would never have dreamed possible.

The ceiling creaked, smoke roiled, and heat-infused windows burst all around him. Here and there flaming ceiling beams were caving in, literally shaking the ground when they landed. As the intense heat sank into his being, Wyatt suddenly remembered that he was shirtless, and he spat out a single epithet.

Just then another massive beam fell to the floor, narrowly missing him and exploding in a cacophony of flames, sparks, and thunderous noise. The force of it knocked him to the ground and blocked the way he had come. He dizzily came to his feet, realizing that he would now have to go the long way around in order to reach the stalls. But could he make it alive? And was it really worth it?

Yes! his oxygen-deprived mind shouted. *You've got to find Ram!*

Ram would most likely be trying to free the horses, Wyatt realized. Coughing and peering through the lung-choking smoke, he finally managed to reach where the stalls lined either side of the long, sky-lit corridor. But there was no sign of Mercy, Ram, or Big John.

Most of the horses had been freed, their stall doors hanging open amid all the chaos. But others remained imprisoned, banging their bodies and hooves insanely against the walls of their stalls. His lungs begging for oxygen, Wyatt did his best to start throwing open the rest of the doors.

Their minds crazed from the fire, many of the horses simply refused to go. Wyatt could have blindfolded them, but there was no time. More often than not he had to scream wildly at them, and strike their haunches to get them moving and out into the alleyway. It was taking too long, he knew, but he kept on trying.

By now he was burned in several places, his lungs were heaving, and sweat poured freely from his body. When he thought that all the horses had finally been freed, he quickly looked around. As he peered through the smoke, his jaw dropped in terror.

Great, burning holes were forming in the ceiling and allowing blazing hay to cascade down, dripping fire as it came and turning the corridor floor into one long path of roiling flame. Still searching wildly for his father, Wyatt did his best to peer through the gathering smoke.

"*Ram!*" he screamed. "*Father, are you here?*"

Maybe they all got out, he desperately hoped. *Maybe they went while they still could . . .*

But just as he decided that was the case, another realization seized him.

Doc . . . , he thought. *He's always kept in the birthing stall!*

After quickly finding a rag and dipping it into a half-filled water bucket, Wyatt tied it around his head so as to cover his nose and mouth. Doing his best to avoid the flaming debris, he ran down yet another corridor and started making his way toward where Sadie had delivered Doc. As he clawed his way nearer, he heard the singularly horrific screams of a young horse in terror. Doing his best to peer through the smoke, he finally reached the stall.

Doc was thrashing about madly in the deep hay, his legs,

head, and body bloodied from banging himself against the walls of his fiery prison. Just then a flaming board fell from the ceiling, setting the stall hay on fire. Doc screamed even louder now, as the flames started licking his hooves and lower legs. Throwing open the stall door, Wyatt charged inside.

Screaming wildly at the colt, Wyatt got behind him and slapped his haunches. Finally Doc bolted from the stall and started charging madly down the only corridor that remained clear. Wyatt had wanted to guide him out, but the strong young horse disappeared into the smoke almost before Wyatt realized it.

Go, Doc! Wyatt's oxygen-deprived brain shouted. *Run away and live!*

Wyatt frantically looked around. He had saved the horses, but at what cost? He still didn't know where Ram was, and because of his searching, he had probably sealed his own fate. Trying to peer through the ever deepening smoke, this time he could find no way out. Even the way that Doc had gone was blocked.

Just then he heard a menacing creaking from above. He looked up to see another beam loosening from the ceiling, this time coming straight for him. As it came crashing down, all he could do was to desperately try diving out of its way . . .

༒

FOR GABBY, LOU, AND Trevor, the passing seconds seemed like hours; the minutes seemed like days. Lou and Trevor stood alongside Gabby, each of them watching a disaster that was horribly unjust, and equally unstoppable. Trevor tried twice to bolt away and follow Wyatt into the barn. It was all Gabby and Lou could do to hold him back.

Moments later, Gabby saw two figures flee the inferno. But because of all the fire and smoke, she couldn't tell who they were. To Gabby's great horror, each of them carried a charred body. Then Gabby recognized the two corpses, and she started to faint.

As Trevor caught her in his arms, the last thing she heard was the wailing of fire trucks, charging up the Flying B's private drive.

FORTY-SIX

The Flying B Ranch
Three Years Later

AS AUNT LOU entered Ram's office, her joints felt stiffer than in days gone by. Nowadays she hurt in places that had never bothered her before, and her gait was more deliberate. Even so, she adamantly refused to slow down in the performance of her duties. To slow down was to die, she had always believed. And there had already been too much death at the Flying B. Besides, there was still much to do, especially today.

Like she had done each day for more than forty years, she began cleaning and dusting the office. When she had finished, she sighed, remembering. Today was April first, three years to the day that Ram had issued his secret instructions to her.

Walking to the library ladder, she rolled it toward a spot

nearer the door. After climbing up two steps, she separated a pair of old volumes and slid Ram's letter from between them.

As Lou stared at it for a time, her old eyes started tearing. Ram had issued some simple instructions to her, but he had never told her what the envelope contained. Lou turned it over and looked at its backside, remembering. The red wax seal was still intact. Like so many things of Ram's that carried the symbol of the Flying B, so, too, did that bit of wax.

With a heavy heart, Lou placed the envelope into a pocket of her apron and left the room.

∞

SITTING IN ONE OF the rocking chairs on the big-house porch, Gabby looked out toward the Blaine family cemetery. Three headstones had been added since she had first visited the ranch. Because of their relative newness, she could easily discern them from the older ones. Butch and Sundance lounged lazily nearby. Today was Sunday, and Morgan and his family would soon arrive for dinner.

Wyatt took another sip of bourbon then placed his booted feet on the porch rail. The last three years had been momentous ones, both for him and the ranch. The fire had totally destroyed the Flying B main barn and killed three purebred horses. It would have been far worse had he, Mercy, and Big John not freed so many of them. After some intense legal wrangling by Blaine & Blaine, the ranch's insurance company had grudgingly reimbursed Wyatt and Morgan for their losses. A new barn had been built, and additional horses had been purchased from various parts of the country and trucked to the ranch.

Ram's and Mercy's funerals were two of the largest ever seen in Boca Raton. It was Wyatt who had carried his father's lifeless body from the barn that night; Big John had carried Mercy. While finally finding a last-ditch way out of the inferno, Wyatt had seen Ram's charred body lying on the floor. But only after laying Ram down, on the grass outside, did he realize that his father was dead. He had wept over the body for hours, oblivious to the chaos, the flames, and the manic firemen who had worked so hard to keep the fire from spreading to the guest cottages and the big house.

Big John had found Mercy, partially pinned beneath a burning ceiling timber. As he carried her out of the barn he thought he heard her whisper "Wyatt." But to his great sadness, he never really grasped what she was trying to say.

The services were held at the ranch, with Reverend Jacobson presiding. Afterward, Ram and Mercy were laid to rest in the family cemetery. Because of the tragedy, Wyatt had made the difficult decision to put the New Beginnings Program to rest for good. And rather than return to the law firm, he now ran the ranch in Ram's stead.

Taking Gabby's hand, Wyatt also looked out at the cemetery. Alongside the new headstones now stood a smaller one that was inscribed ANNIE BLAINE. Ram had never told Wyatt about his decision to commission that stone. In the end he hadn't needed to, for Wyatt had unknowingly fulfilled Ram's dream on his own. Just then Aunt Lou stepped tentatively onto the porch.

"Mr. Wyatt?" she asked softly.

Wyatt and Gabby turned to look at her. It was clear that she was crying. As Lou wiped her tears, Wyatt stood and went to her.

"Lou . . . ?" he said. "What's wrong?"

Lou momentarily closed her old eyes. "I have something for you," she said quietly. "It's from Mr. Ram."

Confused, Wyatt stood up. "What are you talking about?" he asked.

"You surely remember Mr. Ram's secret journal and calendar?" she asked. "The same ones that I gave you right after the fire?"

"Of course," Wyatt answered. "What about them?"

Lou reached into her apron pocket and produced the envelope. "There was this, too. Mr. Ram showed it to me and told me to wait until today, three years later, to give it you. I don't know why he decided on three years, though. Maybe he thought that was all the time he had left."

Wyatt took the letter from her. It was dated today, and Wyatt's name was written across its front in Ram's unmistakable penmanship. "When did Father write this?" Wyatt asked.

"It was about the time that you started up the New Beginnings Program again," Lou answered.

Wyatt touched Lou's face. "Thank you for remembering," he said quietly.

Wondering what the letter held for him, he again looked at the mysterious envelope. "I'd like to be alone with Gabby now," he added. "When Morgan's family shows up, we'll join you and Big John for dinner."

Lou nodded gratefully then returned to her work.

Still surprised by Lou's revelation, Wyatt slowly reclaimed his chair. He sat there quietly for a time, wondering. Before opening the envelope, he looked over at Gabby. She gave him a comforting smile.

"Don't worry, my love," she said. "I know that it's unexpected. But I'm also sure that it's something to be treasured."

Wyatt reached into his jeans and produced the pearl-handled pocketknife his father had given him so many years ago. He then slit open the envelope and removed a yellowed sheet of Flying B stationery. Its tightly packed words were handwritten in Ram's familiar black fountain-pen ink:

Dear Son,

>*As I write this letter, we each have our troubles. Your heart is wounded, and I am losing the one thing that might allow me to help you heal—namely, my mind. Unlike the concerns I bear for you, I have no such worries about Morgan. Morgan is Morgan and he always will be. And so before all that I know and love becomes lost to me, I have decided to pen these words to you. As you read this, I am probably either in the throes of full dementia, or dead. To me, they are one and the same.*

>*If I have finally lost my mind, I know that you are caring for me. All that I ask in that regard is that you allow me to live out my days on the ranch rather than in some faceless institution that imprisons such madmen as I. If I am gone from this world, do not mourn me, for my life was full. I raised two sons of whom I am very proud, and I enjoyed the love of a fine woman for as long as God would let me keep her. No man can ask for more.*

>*I can only hope that one day you will find the full*

*measure of happiness that is your due. The lucky few find
it in their own way, and in their own time. But I fear that
time is slipping away from you faster than you realize. If
you find the right woman, grab her up and never let her go.
And always remember that despite how much you love the
ranch or the law firm, true happiness will never be found
there. You will find it only with her, and if she's the right
one, you can lose everything else and still remain whole. As
you sadly know, the opposite is untrue.*

*And so I will close now, to let you go and lead your life
as you see fit. Please remember these words, for they will
surely be the last you will ever hear from me. And above all,
my son, remember that I loved you.*

*As always,
Your father*

Wyatt's tears came freely, and he wiped his eyes. He handed
the letter to Gabby. As she read it, she also cried. Wyatt folded the
letter then replaced it in its envelope.

"He was a wonderful man," Gabby said softly.

"Yes, he was," Wyatt answered.

They heard a car horn blowing, and they turned to see Morgan's Mercedes coming up the drive. A familiar memory tugged
at Wyatt. As he savored it, he smiled.

"Sorry, Morg," Wyatt said softly. "But as you know, it's a tradition around here." Wyatt looked down at Butch and Sundance,
giving each dog a nudge. "Hey, boys! Morgan's here!"

At once the dogs leaped to their feet and bounded off the

porch. No sooner had Morgan parked his car than Butch and Sundance started clawing at its doors. When Morgan exited the car, he glared angrily toward the porch and shook his head.

Just then Wyatt and Gabby heard the telltale sounds of a galloping horse. Seconds later, Trevor and Doc appeared. Sitting tall in the saddle, Trevor rode Doc well. Before guiding Doc into the new barn, Trevor pulled the young stallion up short and tipped his Stetson to them. Wyatt smiled. The confident way Trevor sat that horse reminded him of his father.

Pausing in his thoughts, Wyatt reached over to gently touch Gabby's wedding ring and then his own. Unlike his first ring, this new one bonded him with Gabby rather than separating him from her. Then his thoughts again turned to his late father.

Dad, I still don't know whether our departed loved ones can look down on us from the afterlife. Even your old friend Reverend Jacobson couldn't answer that one. But if you can't see me, don't worry, because I'm okay.

Wyatt then touched Gabby's swelling abdomen, and thought about the inherent promise lying within her. At long last, Wyatt and Gabby had finally packed away Krista's things and turned her old study into a nursery. Like Ram had wanted, that room would soon house new life rather than dusty memories.

We all are, Wyatt thought.

As Wyatt again faced the setting sun, his next sip of bourbon went down easily.

AUTHOR'S NOTES AND ACKNOWLEDGMENTS

Equine therapy, or "horse therapy," as it is more commonly called, is a rapidly growing phenomenon. Such programs are being conducted at increasing numbers of horse ranches and stables, both in the United States and abroad. I want to give special thanks to the staff at Horse Sense of the Carolinas, located in Marshall, North Carolina, for their willingness to inform me about equine therapy.

My thanks and gratitude also go out to my ever patient agent, Marly Rusoff, and to Mary Logue, author and freelance editor extraordinaire.

I also wish to thank my wife, Joyce Newcomb, PhD, for her valuable guidance regarding psychotherapy and Alzheimer's disease. And, as always, for her never-ending support.

Keep reading for an excerpt from

Robert Barclay's

More Than Words Can Say.

Coming in January 2012

from William Morrow.

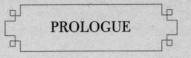
A s the young woman sat on the front porch of her cabin, her heart ached. Unable to sleep, she had left her bed and come here to gaze out over the moonlit lake she so loved. It had been her hope that the soothing waves might coax the sandman nearer, but so far, that had not been the case.

A black leather journal lay in her lap, its next empty page waiting to accept her troubled thoughts. To be sure, she had written other journal entries since coming here to spend the summer alone. But to her great dismay, each one had been more heart rending than the last. Worse yet, the one she was about to create would surpass even the sadness of its predecessors.

At last, she unscrewed the cap from her fountain pen, and she began to write:

Friday, August 7th, 1942; midnight:

This wonderful cabin is quite unused to seeing heartache. Instead, it has always been a place to which I could come and happily forget all about the world. But now a terrible war is raging; the same awful struggle in which so many other countries have been desperately fighting for years, but which finally engulfed the United States just eight months ago. So now, heartache and worry exist even here, instead of the happy and joyous feelings that had heretofore always filled these humble rooms. Even so, the war is but one factor in my grief, rather than the entire cause. Because most of my heartache, I must admit, is a product of my own making. . .

Before now, I had always loved being here. And for as long as I can remember, I had believed that I always would. But so much has happened to me during my brief summer stay that I can no longer be certain of those long held sentiments. Part of my anguish is because this terrible war has taken my loving husband far from me, so that he might finish his military training. And then he will go on to lead others like him in the killing of our enemies, leaving me alone and causing me to wonder if he will ever return . . .

Pausing for a moment, she put down her pen and then turned to gaze down the sandy, moonlit shoreline. A recently built cottage stood there in the darkness. Although no lights shined through its windows at this hour, she knew that he was there. She could almost feel his presence, beckoning her to go to him. As tears began filling her eyes, she again bent to her task . . .

As I look out at the lake, the intense quiet of this place only deepens the sense of guilt that has been growing in my heart since the day I first met him. I should go home, I know; back to Syracuse, where I would not be so easily tempted. And if I did return to my previous life, would it still hold the same meaning for me? Or, would the pain of being without him cause me to rush back? Sadly, I fear that it would be the latter . . .

I know that I should leave here and do my very best to forget him, but I cannot. Because so long as he remains, my heart won't let me. And so, I sit alone on my porch at midnight, watching the waves and wondering where the fates will eventually lead me. As I look at the sky, the clouds seem unusually bright this night, highlighted as they are by a magnificent full moon. Are all of the world's lovers like them, I wonder? Are we too just clouds of constantly changing nature, randomly colliding with one another in a turbulent sky?

On finishing her heart-rending entry, the distraught young woman closed the journal. And this time when she cried, her tears came without end . . .

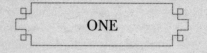

ONE

Early June, 1999
Syracuse, New York

"Congratulations," Allistaire Reynolds said. "Despite the tragic circumstances, of course."

Yet again, Chelsea Enright nodded incredulously. "Thank you," she answered. "I think . . ."

Allistaire leaned back in his chair. He was an attractive man in his early sixties, with a full head of gray hair and a matching, neatly trimmed moustache. The sleeves of his white dress shirt were rolled up, and a navy suit jacket hung informally from his chair back. A lifelong antique hound, he had tastefully decorated his law office with a selection of Americana that gave the room a homey, lived-in look.

"Your grandmother Brooke had me amend her will on the day that you were born," Allistaire explained. "Although she never said why, she wanted you to have the cottage rather than your mother. And for other reasons that she never divulged, after her car crash she never went back."

"I'm grateful to Gram, but I'm not sure about what to do with a cottage," Chelsea said. "I was aware that she owned it. But I've never seen it, and my inheriting it is a big surprise . . ."

Allistaire shrugged his shoulders. "I understand," he answered. "But before you pass judgment on a place that you've never even seen, let me explain a few things."

His lawyerly persona now surfacing in full, Allistaire leaned forward and laced his fingers atop the desk.

"As you probably know, your great grandfather James first owned the cottage," Allistaire said. "He was the one who had it built, back in the 1930's. Then, in 1943 while your grandmother was still in her in her mid twenties, she had her car accident. Because of the war and having to care for your grandmother, your great grandparents became too busy to get up there very often. When they died, your grandmother of course inherited the place, but she never returned there. Because of her handicap, she requested that this firm serve as her property manager. The first lawyer who handled it arranged for all of the cottage expenses to be sent here, where they were paid from Brooke's escrow account. That remains the case today."

Pausing for a moment, Allistaire took a sip of coffee and collected his thoughts for a few moments more.

"Anyway," he soon continued, "sometime around 1946 or 1947, your great grandparents thought it prudent to hire a young handyman to help look after the place. He's of French origin and quite ancient now, but believe it or not, he still does a pretty good job. Knows the property like the back of his hand. He oversees any needed repairs, keeps me updated, things like that. When the first attorney retired, your grandmother became my client, and I've taken care of all her affairs since then. Even though they never met, the caretaker served your grandmother steadfastly for all that time."

"Also," he added, "before her recent death, Brooke had the cottage's appliances and electrical service upgraded, along with the phone service. She realized that she wasn't getting any younger, and she wanted to know that when you inherited the place, it would be livable—or sellable, should you wish. She even had a dishwasher installed, but otherwise, nothing else about the property has changed. It must be an antique hunter's dream! Long story short, the place has been uninhabited for over sixty years, and now it's yours."

Allistaire gestured toward a thick file that lay atop his desk.

"Everything's in there," he said. "Repair bills, Brooke's will, tax receipts, deed, escrow account statements, your codicil—the works."

While staring blankly at the folder, Chelsea shook her head. "I still don't get it," she said. "That cottage should have gone to my mother."

Allistaire smiled again. "Perhaps," he answered. "But Brooke was a sharp old gal. She must have had some good reason for willing it to you, rather than to Lucy."

"But I'm not sure that I can afford to keep it," Chelsea answered. "The taxes, the maintenance . . ."

"Don't worry about all that," Allistaire answered. "There's enough escrow money—which, by the way, is now also under your control—to cover the expenses for a long time. And there are additional funds set aside in Brooke's will, should you need them. Plus, the property is completely unencumbered."

"So I can sell it, if I want?' Chelsea asked.

As Allistaire leaned back again, his chair hinges squeaked pleasantly. "Sure," he answered. "But you should at least go and look at it. Who knows? You might like it."

Chelsea doubted that, because she had never been the outdoors type. She didn't particularly like hiking or boating, the only place she had ever caught a fish was in her supermarket basket, and her most adventurous experience with wildlife had been raising Dolly, her beloved golden retriever.

While Chelsea considered his advice, Allistaire admired her. She was a tall, single, and attractive woman of thirty-three. Chelsea was a respected and tenured art teacher at a local Syracuse high school, and she loved her work. A confirmed bachelor, whenever Allistaire saw Chelsea, he sharply lamented their insurmountable age difference.

For his part, Allistaire Reynolds had long been a partner at Greyson & Stone, LLC., and he had handled the Enright family's affairs for decades. The Enrights were wealthy by Syracuse standards, and as is so often the case with people of substance, they had suffered their share of thorny legal issues.

"Okay," Chelsea said. "So I've inherited Gram's cottage. I know that it's somewhere up in the Adirondacks, but that's about all."

Allistaire opened the folder on his desk and took a weathered envelope from it, which he handed to Chelsea.

"Maybe that will help," he said. "Provided you had reached the age of thirty, your grandmother stipulated that immediately after her death, you should be given this letter in private. That's largely why I asked you to come here today. I wasn't made privy to what the letter says, but perhaps it will provide some answers about all this. It's been in this firm's possession for a long time."

As Chelsea stared at the yellowed envelope, she correctly surmised that it was a product of a different era. In her unmistakable penmanship, Brooke had addressed it with an old-fashioned fountain pen. Curiously, it read: "*To My New Granddaughter.*"

"I suggest that you read it now," Allistaire said. "And with your permission, I should probably read it too. There might be something in there that affects my duties in all this." Smiling, he produced a letter opener and handed it to her.

Her grief suddenly returning in full, Chelsea slit open

the yellowed envelope. Inside she found two sharply folded
sheets of her grandmother's personal stationary, and a small,
nickel-plated key. Like the envelope, the pages had been
written upon with a fountain pen:

My Dearest Child,

*Forgive me for how I address you in this missive,
but you were born just today, and your parents have yet
to christen you. Because you are reading this, I am at
last gone from this world. Due not mourn me unduly,
for my life was full—far more so, in fact, than you
ever knew.*

*By now, you realize that have inherited my prop-
erty on Lake Evergreen. You may trust in everything
that Allistaire tells you, but for reasons that will
eventually become clear, you must not allow him—or
anyone else—to read this letter. For now, all I can
tell you is that I have willed the cottage to you, rather
to your mother, because I am hoping that when you
grow older, your capacity for forgiveness will be the
greater one. Your mother knows that this was to happen, but she is unaware of the true reasons.*

*Because you are reading these words in the distant
future, I cannot possibly know what twists and turns
you life has taken, or in what manner you have chosen
to live it. Should you wish to sell the cottage, you have
my blessing. Nevertheless, you must not relinquish
ownership before you follow the instructions that I am
about to describe. Only then, my dear, should you decide whether to keep it, or to let it go. Please also know
that as the years go by, I will do my very best to be
there every step of the way; watching you, guiding you,
and mentoring you.*

Although it will be many years before you become a woman, I already sense that there will grow a strong bond between us—perhaps even greater than the one I already share with your mother. Regardless of what you may have heard, be assured that Lake Evergreen is a wonderful place. Because of personal reasons, I have not visited my cabin for many years, nor will I ever do so again. But that is all right, because it has now become yours. And, as you will soon learn, it was best that the cottage has lain undisturbed until this day, when you are at last old enough to understand.

Travel to Lake Evergreen soon, my dear granddaughter, and be sure to go there alone. When you arrive, go to the guest bedroom and move the bed aside. You will notice three certain floorboards, easily identifiable because their joints are scratched and worn. When you remove them, you will find an old tin box; its lock can be opened with the key you now possess. Inside the box are some additional things that I wish to bequeath to you. And like the cottage, only after much consideration should you decide what to do with them.

Whatever decision you choose to make, I'm sure it will be the right one. My soul has been bothered these many years, but I hope that placing this letter and my beloved cottage in your care will finally grant me a measure of peace. Lastly, my child, know that my thoughts and prayers go with you.

Your loving grandmother,
Brooke Bartlett

* * *

Stunned, Chelsea refolded the pages. Despite her over-powering grief, she knew one thing. She would trust in her grandmother's instructions and follow them to the letter. After collecting herself, she placed the letter and the mysterious key back into the envelope.